THE
TCHAIKOVSKY
FINALE

FUGUE & FABLE - BOOK III

To Jessica

And now... The Finale!

DARIN KENNEDY

Darin Kennedy

CURIOSITY QUILLS PRESS

A Division of **Whampa, LLC**
P.O. Box 2160
Reston, VA 20195
Tel/Fax: 800-998-2509
http://curiosityquills.com

© 2017 **Darin Kennedy**
http://darinkennedy.com

Cover Art by Brice Chaplet
http://www.nomastaprod.com

ISBN 978-1-94809-944-8 (ebook)
ISBN 978-1-94809-945-5 (paperback)

LIBRETTO

To Mom, my biggest fan.
Thank you for everything.

Music is indeed the most beautiful of all
Heaven's gifts to humanity wandering in the darkness.
Alone it calms, enlightens, and stills our souls.
It is not the straw to which the drowning man clings;
but a true friend, refuge, and comforter,
for whose sake life is worth living.

- Pyotr Ilyich Tchaikovsky, 1935 -

I

CYGNUS

I **cannot do this.**
Not the way she did.
I do not have the strength, the will, the fortitude.

But I must. This woman has given up everything for me, and I owe her no less.

She represents so many things to so many of us.

Mother. Daughter. Lover.

Storyteller. Warrior. Ballerina.

And finally, her bravest role of all.

Sacrificial lamb.

All different aspects of the same woman. Yet, despite the face she wore or the trappings covering her body, one thing always remained constant and true.

Hope.

No matter how many monsters my mind created to block her way, the faith she had that she could bring me through each and every torment never wavered.

That unfaltering belief led to her current state. Now, it's my turn to save her.

There's only one problem.

I don't have the first idea of how to start.

Mira Tejedor lies on the bed before me, her skin pale and breath shallow. A thin plastic tube rests taped to her arm, conveying clear fluid from a bag hanging above her head to an IV in the back of her hand. A second tube protrudes from her nose, currently disconnected. Mom says that one is how they're feeding her.

None of us talk about the third tube that snakes from beneath the sheets and leads to the container of yellow liquid hanging from the side of her bed.

Dr. Archer sits beside her, his hands shaking as he strokes her limp arm. Mom stands over them, her gaze flicking from Mira's still form to me and back again. If Mira were awake, I have no doubt she would sense the disapproval wafting off my mother like smoke off a smoldering fire. To be honest, I'm surprised Mom has even let the idea go this far, but if her distaste at this whole situation is the smoke, then guilt is the fire.

My brother Jason chose to stay home, his feelings about this whole idea more than evident as we left the house this morning.

My little sister, on the other hand, demanded to come. Seeing her weep over Mira's still form tore open another piece of my heart and did nothing but steel my resolve. Half an hour of pleading to be allowed to stay and help notwithstanding, Rachel finally agreed to go spend the day in town with Mira's mom. Didn't hurt that Mrs. Tejedor was already taking Isabella to see a Pixar double feature at the kid's museum. Though they've known each other less than a week, my sister and Mira's daughter have already become fast friends.

I suppose that's what happens when your first meeting consists of fighting your way out of a nightmare inflicted by one of your nearest and dearest.

Which, inexorably, brings me back to the task at hand.

When Dr. Archer took Mom, Jason, and me out for burgers and milkshakes yesterday, I already knew what he was going to ask.

As if I hadn't been considering the same thing for a week.

The lunch at Dairy Queen was the first time we ever met outside of his office or our house. Knowing what was no doubt coming, I was surprised Mom even agreed to the meeting.

Guilt, just like faith, can move mountains.

The scene plays out in my head for the hundredth time.

We arrive a few minutes late to find Dr. Archer already there. He waits for us to order, and then insists the whole thing is "his treat." Mom and I get to the table and dig in, famished as neither of us felt like eating breakfast.

Jason barely touches his food and instead stares sullenly across the table at Dr. Archer.

Not much is said at first, but once the conversation starts, Dr. Archer wastes no time getting right to the point.

"Mira needs your help, Anthony." In that moment, he seems smaller than I remember. Sadder. "She's gone beyond anything I or the doctors can do for her."

"We haven't even finished eating yet." Mom's fingernails dig into the faux wood tabletop. "Can't this wait?"

"There's no sense in dancing around the subject, Caroline."

Neither Dr. Archer nor Mom nor even Jason, surprisingly, says a word for a few seconds. I'm about to chime in when Mom breaks the silence.

"Fine, Thomas." She takes a big gulp of her soda. "Let's talk. But before you launch into a litany of whys and hows, I need to know. Are you about to ask of us what I think you are?"

Dr. Archer's head bobs in a subtle nod. "Mira's state is much like Anthony's nine months ago but worse. Catatonic and unresponsive, but otherwise stable. Her CT, MRI, blood work—they're all normal. Even the EEG seems to indicate she's merely in a deep sleep." In a rare show of emotion, Dr. Archer buries his face in his shaking hands. "It's like last year all over again."

"And so?" Color rises in Mom's cheeks the way it does when I'm about to get sent to my room. "Surely you don't expect me to be okay with—"

"It's all right, Mom." I set my milkshake down, maybe a bit too hard, and several heads at the next table jerk in my direction. "I know what he wants."

"We all know what he wants," Jason mumbles. "He wants his little mind-traipsing girlfriend back."

"Jason Faircloth." Mom's harsh whisper shuts my brother right up. He's lucky Mom's eyes aren't equipped with lasers or he'd be burnt to a crisp where he sits. "Show some respect."

I turn my attention back to Dr. Archer. His face bleeds a hopelessness that's foreign in the usually steady gaze of this man who has steered me through so many of my own obstacles. Our positions now reversed, I gain a new respect for everything he has done for me over the years.

None of which changes one simple fact.

What he's asking me to do, regardless of my belief it's the only thing that will save this woman that has pulled me kicking and screaming out of no less than three different nightmare worlds of my own making, is impossible.

He wants me to walk Mira's mind. To go and find her in the depths of her subconscious like she did me. To bring her out of the underworld and back into the light like Orpheus did Eurydice.

And we all know how that one turned out.

"Are you ready, Anthony?" Dr. Archer's question breaks me out of my reverie, the tension at the Dairy Queen yesterday paling next to the uncertainty that fills Mira's hospital room. My therapist for as long as I can remember, he does his best to maintain his customary facade of confidence, but the rings under his eyes and the slight tremor in his voice reveal a different truth.

Mom rests her hands on my shoulders. "You know I brought Anthony here today against my better judgment. I hope your plan is a little further along than what we discussed yesterday, or we're getting back in our car and going home."

"Hold on, Mom." I pull away and move to the foot of the bed. "This isn't Dr. Archer's fault. And anyway, we're here for Mira. Remember?"

"Of course, Anthony." She lets out a long sigh. "Of course."

I peer into Dr. Archer's faded eyes. "Tell me what it is you want me to do."

"For now? Listen." He straightens to his full height and clears his throat. "Over the last year, Mira and I have spoken many times about what exactly it is that happens between you two that allows things like the Exhibition or the world of *The Firebird* to exist."

It's no surprise Dr. Archer avoids any mention of *Petrushka*, the dreamscape setting where for all his intellect and accomplishments, he was reduced to the titular clown, or *The Rite of Spring*, where we all lost Mira to darkness.

"At first," he continues, "we thought Mira was leaving her own mind and wandering around in yours, but what has become clear is the truth may be far more complex."

"Mira told me as much." I shiver, remembering my many conversations with the woman who now lies comatose an arm's reach away. "She said our two minds were somehow merging to create something new and different. It was unlike anything she'd experienced before."

"And Thomas obviously wants to see if that common ground can be recreated." Mom fixes Dr. Archer with a look that could melt steel. "Isn't that right?"

"I love her, Caroline." Dr. Archer shifts his gaze out the window where a pair of cardinals, one red and one brown, flits from branch to branch, exploring the dying sycamore tree just beyond the glass. "But I can't reach her. Nothing the doctors or I can do is going to help her. You know that better than anyone."

"What I know is my son has suffered every day for a year dealing with the aftershocks of this phenomenon you're discussing. Now that he's finally free, you're asking him to step back into the lion's den."

"Don't you think I know that?" Dr. Archer whispers. "Do you have any idea how hard it is for me to ask such a thing?"

"We don't even know if it will work." My fists clench at my sides. "In case anyone has forgotten, Mira is the one who walked the Exhibition, thwarted Koschei and the Firebird, escaped the Russian fair, and danced *The Rite of Spring*." I trudge over to the window and stare out at the cloud-filled sky before turning back to face Dr. Archer. "I was nothing but a spectator."

"Oh, you were far more than that, Anthony." A spark flares to life in Dr. Archer's eyes. "Consciously or not, you once sent Tunny the Gnome to bring Mira back for you. On more than one occasion, you reached out to her from clear across town, even when she didn't want you to, and sucked her into this place you two weave between your minds. And then there's everything that went down last week." His gaze cuts away as if he's suddenly unable to stand the sight of me.

"I didn't mean to do any of those things." My entire body begins to shake. "You know that."

"Thomas..." Mom's voice takes on that edge that always raises the hair on my neck.

"My apologies, Caroline. Asking this is beyond difficult." Dr. Archer rises from the bed and stands over me, his eyes pleading. "You can *save* her, Anthony. You have to."

"Thomas!"

Dr. Archer's gaze shifts from me to Mom, the fire there extinguished as surely as if she'd thrown a bucket of water in his face.

"I'm sorry, Caroline. It's just that... Anthony is Mira's only hope." His head drops to his chest as if he's ashamed to look either of us in the eye. "You of all people should understand."

Before Mom can say a word, I raise a hand, silencing both the adults in the room.

"All that matters is that I understand." I keep my voice low, trying to keep a bad situation from getting worse. "And I want to help. I *need* to help. I just... don't know how."

The three of us stand in silent vigil over Mira's bed for seconds that seem to last days. As with yesterday's lunch, it's Mom who finally breaks the verbal stalemate.

"I have an idea, Anthony." She takes a deep breath and the crimson in her cheeks recedes a shade or two. "When Mira first started working with you last year, she'd always start the same way." Mom directs me around to the head of the bed and has me sit by Mira's shoulder. "She'd always make sure her body was protected and comfortable and then she'd make physical contact." She takes my hands and rests my fingertips on Mira's temples. "That's when the magic would happen."

"Magic," I mutter. "This is anything but a trick."

"Do you sense anything?" Dr. Archer asks. "Voices? Smells?" He pauses. "Music?"

"Give me a second." I allow my eyes to drift closed and take control of my breathing the way Dr. Archer himself taught me what seems like a century ago.

Meditation, he calls it. Mindfulness. Being in the moment. Things we discussed and worked on for years before any of this weirdness came along and I was just another kid with problems.

I focus on a single image. An image Dr. Archer taught me in one of our first sessions.

A placid lake at night, the full moon overhead reflected in the still water. A gentle breeze wafts through my hair, bringing jasmine and honey and moist earth to my senses. Crickets chirp in time to a rhythm only they can hear. The cool grass beneath my bare feet sends chills up my spine as I wait for something, anything, to happen.

But nothing ever does.

When I eventually open my eyes again, nothing has changed. Dr. Archer searches my face for even a glimmer of hope, and finding none, the desperation in his gaze becomes despair. Mom as well, her mouth hidden behind her clenched fist, stares at me with something akin to fear as if at any moment I might spontaneously combust.

"Anything?" she asks.

"Nothing."

"Are you sure?" Dr. Archer again tries to keep any trace of uncertainty from his voice, but I have little doubt his squinted eyes are holding back tears.

"I told you. The whole charging headlong into other people's thoughts at will is Mira's thing. With me, it just... happens."

Dr. Archer's shoulders fall like a balloon with the air let out. "Then this is it." He motions to the IV tubing going into her arm. "We keep her hydrated, continue her tube feeds, and wait till she wakes up."

"I'm sorry, Thomas." Mom's angry glare vanishes, replaced by compassion and shared sorrow. "I know how much you were counting on a breakthrough today." She leaves my side, goes around to the other side of the bed, and takes Dr. Archer's hand. "Maybe if Anthony's up for it," she shoots a glance in my direction, "we can try again in a couple of days."

Dr. Archer looks up at me, and I give him a quick nod, though in my heart, I don't know what the point of giving it another shot would be. Whatever abilities there may be knocking around inside my skull, I clearly don't know how to access them like Mira does.

And I may never learn.

"Mom, take me home please." I turn from the door, unable to look Dr. Archer in the eye.

"All right, Anthony." An obligatory goodbye, and she whisks me out of the room. The sterile hallway smells of cleaning spray and a funky odor I'd rather not identify.

Today was the first day I've been able to go and visit Mira, as she was just released from intensive care yesterday afternoon. Part of me is glad I came, but a bigger part wishes I'd stayed at home. Seeing her there on that bed, knowing if it weren't for me, she'd be fine...

Mom and I walk in silence to the car and other than asking me what I want for dinner, the ride across town is quiet as well. We're halfway home when Mom flips the radio from the pop station Rachel likes to her favorite easy listening channel. The Monkees song "Daydream Believer" is playing, but it isn't Davy Jones' vocals coming from the speakers.

"Who is that singing?" I ask.

"That's Anne Murray," she says, noting my confused look. "She redid this one a few years after the original. You like?"

"I suppose." Not the biggest fan of music with lyrics, I turn to the window and let out a yawn. Knowing we'd be visiting Mira today, I didn't sleep all that well last night and it's catching up to me.

I close my eyes and attempt to wedge the side of my head between the seat and the window. This section of road, however, is under construction, and the glass isn't exactly forgiving. I focus on the image from before, the image Dr. Archer taught me to help me relax, to reduce stress, to sleep.

Again, the dew-covered grass tickles my bare feet as I stare out across the mirror-like surface of the midnight lake. A full moon hangs in the sky like the only ornament on a jet-black Christmas tree lit with an infinite string of white lights. The rain-tinged air brings hints of loam and lilies. Soon, a gentle drizzle falls from the sky, and I turn my face skyward, letting the falling mist wash the fatigue from my mind.

Mentally refreshed, I return my attention to the placid lake. As with every visit to this corner of my mind, the water is preternaturally smooth, without so much as a ripple to mar its surface.

But this time, something is different. At first, I scarcely believe my eyes, but as I inch closer to the shoreline, there's no denying my senses.

I have a visitor in this, my most sacred of places.

At the center of the lake and oblivious to my presence, a lone white swan ennobled with a silver crown glides silently and gracefully across the water with the surety of one entirely at home.

II

ODETTE

The swan's crown twinkles in the light of the full moon as if a collection of stars from the evening sky above conspired to adorn the elegant bird's head. Dark eyes at the corners of an equally dark bill survey the peaceful lake with a tranquil curiosity, though the bird's speed as it crosses the lake leaves little doubt as to the ferocity of paddling below the surface.

Then, something new.

Music.

For all my love of strings, brass, woodwinds, and percussion, this lake has always been a place of silent reflection. Knowing the identity of my feathered visitor, however, leaves the tune hitting my ears anything but a surprise.

The melody is one I committed to memory a lifetime ago.

The composer? Pyotr Ilyich Tchaikovsky.

The piece? *Swan Lake.*

Knowing what I'm hearing and seeing, however, doesn't begin to explain what it means.

One lone thought, however, does filter through my imagination.

What if Dr. Archer's plan hasn't failed after all?

I trail the ivory swan from the lake's edge and wait for the graceful bird to come ashore. Together we travel what seems like a mile, though in this place of dreams, I'm fully aware only an instant may have passed. Regardless, as the open shore ends on the edge of a forest, the bird veers back in my direction and with a quiet call, steps from the water and onto dry land.

Like a ghost flitting between the trees, the white swan escapes my grasp several times. Still, I don't dare run in the near darkness. One misstep or fall and I might lose the swan forever.

Funny. This must have been how Mira felt as she stalked the Firebird.

And if this swan represents whom I hope it does, the comparison couldn't be more ironic.

I lose sight of the swan in the dense underbrush until my meandering path leads to a grassy clearing along the lakeshore. There, in the pale blue moonlight and several paces ahead of me, the swan preens its feathers and trembles in the chill of evening.

Or perhaps it isn't the cold.

From the line of trees at the edge of the clearing, a shadowy figure studies the swan with piercing yellow eyes. The spectral silhouette there one second and gone the next, I pray that whomever or whatever the shadow represents somehow managed to overlook my presence.

The wan glow of the moon intensifies around the snowy swan, the pale luminescence growing and growing until the bird disappears in a swirling mass of brilliance. Silver shafts of light pierce the darkness of the surrounding forest in every direction, and soon the clearing is lit up as if it were morning and the swan the rising sun. I close my eyes to block the dazzling glare and when I dare look again, the swan has disappeared.

Where the elegant bird rested at the center of the clearing now stands a familiar figure, her face the answer to a thousand prayers. Mira Tejedor, her body clothed in a white bodice and feathered tutu and her head topped in a gleaming silver tiara, stands *en pointe* as the moon beams down from above like a spotlight. Eyes open and staring skyward, she stands silently with only the moonlight glinting off her tears revealing the truth of her otherwise serene air.

"Mira?" My voice comes out ragged, like two rough logs rubbed together. "Is it you?"

Her head jerks in my direction, and she lets out a heart-stopping shriek.

The Halloween before he died, Dad let me stay up late and watch one of his black-and-white favorites. I've never been able to forget the way Elsa Lanchester moves in *The Bride of Frankenstein*. Mira looks on me now with those same terror-filled eyes.

But why?

For the first time in my countless trips to this lakeside place of peace, I'm curious as to how I must appear to others. A glance down reveals a body and attire both shocking and strangely familiar.

Once Mira wandered a place borne of both our minds to free me from a psychic prison of my own making. The Exhibition, first conceived by a Russian composer over a century ago, was both labyrinth and mystery. Mira made many friends along those parquet hallways—as well as more than a few enemies—all in one way or another aspects of me. Her first friend along that difficult path was a forest gnome whose flesh was fashioned from wood like a second-rate Pinocchio. As I run my hand down my chest and catch a splintered nail on one of the grimy leather coat's many buckles, I have little doubt as to the form I wear.

"Greetings." I step from the shadows of the forest edge into the pale moonlight of the lakeside clearing. "I am Tunny."

Terror flashes anew in Mira's eyes, but not even a glimmer of recognition. That's when everything becomes clear. There is no denying I face some aspect of Mira's consciousness, but just as I am not exactly Anthony Faircloth here, neither is she Mira Tejedor.

At least not yet.

The wide eyes that look upon my diminutive form with abject horror belong to neither Scheherazade the storyteller nor Ivanovna the warrior.

Nor even, ironically, the Ballerina.

"Odette, Swan Princess." I offer her a subtle bow, though as Tunny the gnome I can't get much closer to the ground than I already am. "I come desiring an audience."

I fear she's on the verge of running, but instead, the vision in white takes a step in my direction, extends a graceful hand, and beckons me to stand.

"For what reason do you seek an audience with a cursed princess, gnome?"

Now that's a good question. Absently, I scratch at my chin and multiple flakes of caked mud fall to the ground. No wonder the princess in white is giving me a wide berth.

"I may not seem like much, Princess of the Swans..." I allow the utterance of her other title to hang in the air. "But if nothing else, as you have no doubt already surmised from our brief conversation, I know many secrets."

"Secrets." She takes another precise step in my direction, and I am reminded that despite their beauty, a swan attack can be terrifying. "Do you know how to break the curse?" Another step. "Do you know how to free me from this damned lake and von Rothbart's evil?"

Von Rothbart, the evil sorcerer from *Swan Lake* responsible for Odette's predicament and, I suspect, the mysterious form that watched before from the shadows.

"Perhaps," I mutter. "Perhaps."

She rushes me, and any resemblance to the kind woman I know as Mira Tejedor disappears from her features. "Tell me, gnome. Tell me now, or I shall bring the dark one down upon you myself."

"Wait," I stammer. "I came only to talk." I dive inside a hollow stump and narrowly evade her grasping hands. "I wish you no ill."

"A likely story." With a single vault, she alights gracefully atop my hiding place. "You stalk me from the shadows and tempt me with promises of freedom and happiness."

"I can help you." I pop my head out of the stump. "You must believe me."

"I've trusted mysterious strangers in this wood before." She runs her hands down her feathered bodice and glares down at me, her eyes afire with anger. "See what my blind faith has gotten me?"

"Beautiful swan by day and even more beautiful princess by night." I climb from the stump, slip off my split leather hat, and knock at my wooden skull. "There are worse fates."

She steps down onto the mossy forest floor, her anger deflating. "You speak as one who is also cursed."

I shoot her a quick nod. "I may appear a hideous gnome, but beneath the grime and the wooden form lies the heart of a lad who wishes, much like you, simply to return to those he loves." I extend a hand in friendship. "If you will have me, I pledge my life to your service until this curse is broken."

"As if you can break my curse." This third voice, a deep baritone, echoes from the forest to our rear. The underlying melody of this place, quiet throughout my encounter with the Swan Princess, returns with a vengeance. French horn and rolling tympani followed by trumpet and violin assault my ears as a tune I know as well as I know my own breathing fills the air. "Odette is mine."

I peer up into the ancient tree above my head and find the piercing yellow eyes I noticed before now fastened on me.

A creature with the body of a man and the head of an owl sits perched in a low branch. Clothed in black and gray, the cloak thrown across his shoulders fashioned to resemble folded wings, von Rothbart glares down at us, every bit a bird of prey given human form. He steps from the branch and floats to the ground as gentle as a dark feather, the fabricated wings of his cloak spread wide enough to block out the sky. As the dark sorcerer lands before her, Odette bows her head and offers a simple curtsy before assuming a formal ballet pose.

"Master."

Shifting his avian head into a form slightly more human, von Rothbart smiles at the word before returning his attention to me. "You see, gnome? Young Odette knows her place in the scheme of things. A lesson you could stand to learn yourself, it would appear."

"Perhaps." I puff out my wooden chest, my attempt to look imposing no doubt futile. "Though it seems *you* should learn not to underestimate someone based on their size."

Von Rothbart throws his head back and laughs. "You think you represent even the slightest challenge, gnome?"

"I know your name, sorcerer. I know what you want, what you're capable of, and, most importantly, what this poor girl means to you." I cross my arms before my chest. "Can you say any of those things about me?"

Von Rothbart's eyes narrow at me before his gaze shoots to Odette. "What did the gnome tell you, girl? What secrets did he unveil?"

"Secrets?" Odette trembles as did the swan before. "No secrets, Master."

Except my name. Somewhere deep inside, Mira knows not to give this creature my name. My lips turn up in a hopeful smile.

"Very well." Von Rothbart steps back, frustrated. "Keep your pathetic confidences, girl. You know as well as I who holds your strings." His attention shifts back to me. "As for you, gnome, all I need to know about you is that wood burns." He stretches his spindly fingers in my direction, and above his palm, a ball of blue flame appears. "Leave this place and forget you ever laid eyes on the Swan Princess or your body will be the coals upon which I cook my dinner." The sphere of fire floating above his hand doubles in size. "Consider this a mercy."

I step forward and glare up into the man's owl eyes. "I won't leave her here with you."

At this, Odette shoots me a bashful smile, the simple show of gratitude provoking von Rothbart even further. He hurls the fireball at my feet, setting the grass aflame and forcing me to step away.

"Begone, gnome," von Rothbart whispers as he summons a second fireball. "Rest assured that next time, I'll aim for your head."

A searing pain radiates up my legs as my toes catch fire, the smell like burning tar. Though I rail against the thought of leaving Odette with her tormentor, I instinctively rush to the lake's edge and dive my stubby feet into the water. The fire extinguished, I spin around to face von Rothbart anew only to find him gone and Odette returned to her swan form. I step from the lake and creep toward the skittish swan, my hands raised before me.

"Don't run. Don't run. Don't—"

The swan catches movement from the corner of its eye and dashes for the water. I dive for the majestic bird as it rushes past, but I'm far too slow. Picking myself up from the grassy clearing, I peer out across the lake. There, just as when I first arrived, the crowned swan moves effortlessly across the placid water, the full moon still beaming down in all its glory. The music continues— tranquil, melodious, calming.

As if anything would calm me right now.

"Anthony?"

The word echoes down from the sky above as if the moon itself is calling out to me.

And in my mother's voice.

"Anthony?"

I awake to find my glasses crushed between my face and the passenger side window of Mom's car. I quickly wipe the drool from my chin and pull myself upright in the seat.

"Sorry, Mom." I straighten my glasses. "I must have dozed off."

"Are you okay?" She looks at me from the corner of her vision, concern etched in her features. "You were sleeping, and then you said... Mira's name."

"Turn the car around." I look out my window. "We have to go back."

"Back?" Mom stops at a red light and flicks a lost gaze in my direction. "But... Thomas' plan didn't work." She swallows. "Or did it?"

I shiver in the seat despite the summer heat. "I think it did, actually." Von Rothbart's yellow glare, even out here in the real world, still burns a hole deep into my soul. "Maybe a little too well."

Mom flips the turn signal and waits for traffic to let her in. "That's what I was afraid you were going to say." After she turns the car around and gets back on the road, she hits a couple buttons on her phone and puts it to her ear.

"Are you still with Mira?" she asks. "Good. Don't go anywhere. We're on our way back." Then, with a cold finality, "I'll explain when we get there. Or Anthony will." She glances in my direction. "To both of us."

As we arrive back at the hospital and navigate the labyrinthine parking deck, a collection of simple facts coalesces in my mind.

Along the Exhibition, all the people Mira encountered were in some way, like it or not, facets of my mind. Similarly, other than the remnant of Veronica Sayles left in my mind, all the characters of *The Firebird*, *Petrushka*, and *The Rite of Spring* ended up being pieces of me as well.

Each of the four places created by the melding of my mind and talents with Mira's has always had one thing in common: No matter the setting, Mira has always been a singular presence, while my mind has always been the one splintered into the setting and Mira's various friends and adversaries along the way.

Now, the roles are reversed. I stand, the lone wanderer of the world of dream formed from our blended consciousness, and she has become the object of the search.

I am Tunny the gnome and she the Swan Princess, Odette, from *Swan Lake*.

Which leaves several questions.

Who does von Rothbart represent and why does he hold Mira captive as Baba Yaga did me along the Exhibition?

Does the dark sorcerer represent some part of Mira that doesn't want her to awake?

Is von Rothbart, like almost every other character Mira has faced in her sojourns, simply another aspect of me, and somehow I'm up against myself in my quest to bring her home?

Or, worst of all, does he represent a third player in this horrible game?

Everything I've seen and understand screams Versailles is gone.

Veronica Sayles is finally, mercifully, dead out in the real world while Madame Versailles was slain on the battlefield of the mind, the Moor's blade ending her existence and freeing thirteen innocents from a hell, unfortunately, of my own making. Her scheme to take Mira's body thwarted, the teacher from *Tuileries* is nothing now but a memory.

Or is she?

If Versailles somehow lives on, then neither of Mira's sacrifices has amounted to anything, and I'm up against an entity that has cheated death twice.

More importantly, if Mira in her various roles as storyteller, warrior, ballerina, and sacrifice couldn't stop her, what possible chance do I have?

III

SIEGFRIED

Tell me." Dr. Archer paces the floor of the waiting room, his hands trembling with excitement. "What happened?" He kneels before me and grabs me by the shoulders. "What did you see? I need every detail."

I start at the beginning. The lake. The swan. Mira as Odette. My role as Tunny the gnome. Von Rothbart.

For Mom's sake, I leave out the part where the owl-headed sorcerer flash-fried my feet, but make a mental note to discuss that with Dr. Archer when we're alone.

"And that's it?" Dr. Archer asks. "Nothing more?"

"As best as I can remember." I glance over at Mom, who sits wringing her hands as she has nothing else to do. "We were almost back to the house when Mom woke me up and pulled me back from wherever I went."

"And you're sure this wasn't just a dream?"

My stomach clenches at the question. "How many times did you ask Mira that before you just believed what was happening?"

Dr. Archer releases my shoulders as if he's touched a live wire and returns to pacing. "Sorry. Just playing detective here."

"I thought that was my job." Detective Sterling, who has come around a few times in the last week, strides into the room, a small bouquet in his hand. "How's Mira?"

"No change." Dr. Archer eyes the flowers. "She's allergic to lilies, you know."

"I didn't, actually." Detective Sterling's lips draw down to a thin line as he tosses the flowers into a trash can by the door. "Wouldn't want to make Mira worse, now would we?"

Mom steps between them and shakes Detective Sterling's hand. "We did have a possible breakthrough, though it's a bit early to tell what it means."

Mom, Dr. Archer, and I all take turns filling the detective in on my recent waltz through *Swan Lake*. By the end, he's shaking his head in disbelief.

"Now Mira's the one with a dead Russian composer stuck in her head?" His eyes shoot from Dr. Archer to me, his shrewd gaze measuring me as if he was fitting me for a suit, or maybe a straitjacket. "Is that supposed to make any kind of sense?"

"Actually," Dr. Archer says, "it might." He goes to the whiteboard posted in the corner and grabs one of the dry-erase markers resting there. "Imagine this." He draws two interlocking circles, something like the Venn diagrams we learned about in math class last year. In one circle, he writes the letter A. In the other, M.

He points to the first. "This circle represents Anthony and his thoughts, both conscious and otherwise." His finger shifts to the other circle. "This one represents Mira and all she is." He then outlines the section where the two overlap. "This is the space the two share when they interact on the—bear with me here—*psychic* plane."

Detective Sterling and Mom share a long look, each appearing more befuddled than the other.

"Go on," Mom says.

Dr. Archer draws himself up straight. "Mira and I have discussed various theories on all that happened last year with Anthony and everything that's occurred since." His face darkens a shade. "Initially, she and I both believed her various visits to the Exhibition represented Mira leaving her mind and entering Anthony's."

Detective Sterling crosses his arms before him. "I'm guessing that's no longer the prevailing theory."

"Not precisely. Think of it more as a language." Dr. Archer motions around the room. "Out here in the real world, we communicate with words, facial expression, hand gestures."

"But there..." Detective Sterling's face screws up as if he's trying to solve a difficult math problem. "There, they talk with metaphor and story."

"Exactly." Dr. Archer points to the intersection of the two circles on the white board. "Like two waking dreamers that can somehow interact with each other. This common ground between Mira and Anthony originally took the form of the Exhibition, formed from their two minds and Anthony's command of the works of Mussorgsky and Rimsky-Korsakov. Left there to rot, the residual influence of Veronica Sayles repurposed the same space and drew from Anthony's mind the works of Igor Stravinsky to communicate her needs and desires."

"We know all this, Thomas." Mom stands and moves to my side, pulling me to her side like a mother hen protecting one of her chicks. "How does this explain what just happened to Anthony in the car?"

"Don't you see?" Dr. Archer's studies each of us before continuing. "If Veronica Sayles could use Anthony's encyclopedic knowledge of all things *Firebird* and *Petrushka* to build a trap for Mira, is it that far a cry to imagine Mira could do the same in her bid to escape that selfsame trap?"

"But with Tchaikovsky." Mom's voice threatens to crack. "So, we're right back where we started... except this time, Mira is the one who's stuck."

"Like I hadn't already figured that out." I trudge over to the water cooler in the corner and pour myself a cup of water. "Another nightmare world to explore, Dr. Archer?"

"With one difference, kid." Detective Sterling rubs at his brow as if a headache is coming on. "This time, everything is coming for you." He turns to Dr. Archer. "Unless I'm missing something, Doc, you're saying the kid's own mind is being turned against him, right?"

"If past experience is anything to go by." Dr. Archer watches me from the corner of his eye. "As you're well aware, none of Mira's trips to the dreamworld were a walk in the park."

"Still, we don't have much of a choice." Mom stands and brushes a tear from the corner of her eye. "Mira leaped into the breach with a lot less knowledge than we have, and now that all this has started, I have a nasty feeling ignoring it is going to accomplish nothing." She drops to one knee and pulls me around to face her. "Anthony, I want nothing more than to walk away and protect you from all of this, but we—you, me, and Rachel—owe Mira so much. Still, it's your decision to make." She looks up at Dr. Archer. "Isn't that right, Thomas?"

"Of course, Caroline." Dr. Archer pinches the bridge of his nose. "Do you want to think on it tonight, Anthony, and let me know in the morning?"

"No." My gaze flicks from Mom to Detective Sterling and then to Dr.

Archer. "I've already made up my mind." I take a deep breath. "No time like the present, right?"

"Are you sure you're up for another trip already?" He rests the back of his hand on my forehead. "These little sojourns always left Mira exhausted, especially at the beginning."

"I feel fine." I pull away from Mom and head for the door. "Guess I've been running this race long enough to build up some endurance." I glance back at Dr. Archer. "Coming?"

All the players are here, their previous roles from the various worlds in my mind swirling in my mind like a maelstrom of nightmares.

The skilled psychologist, his mind split between noble prince and awkward clown.

The police detective, reduced to jealous suitor and unrepentant murderer.

My own mother, the ancient witch who lives at the end of the hall.

And last, the woman who has saved me more times and in more ways than I will ever be able to understand or repay.

Storyteller. Warrior. Ballerina. Sacrifice.

Mira Tejedor, like it or not, I'm coming for you.

"So," Detective Sterling asks, "how do we begin?"

Dr. Archer looks my way. "That, I suppose, is up to Anthony."

"All right, son." Mom leans against the wall and motions in the direction of Mira's still form. "This is your show. What do we do now?"

I reflect on the strange connection Mira and I share. The endless permutations of how this scenario could turn out hit me like a tsunami.

Nowhere better to start, I suppose, than the beginning.

"The story of *Swan Lake* revolves around the love of Odette, the Swan Princess, and Prince Siegfried. On a moonlit hunt, he encounters Odette by the lake in swan form. He raises his crossbow to fell the majestic bird only to witness its magical transformation into the most beautiful girl he's ever seen. Siegfried instantly falls in love with the swan-turned-maiden and promises to marry her, as only a vow of eternal love can break the curse cast on her by the dark sorcerer, von Rothbart."

"The one with the owl's head." Detective Sterling shakes his head. "Even after everything I've seen over the last year, this all still sounds crazy."

"Regardless," Dr. Archer adds, "this insanity is now our reality." He turns to me. "I'm guessing you need a Siegfried?"

A quiet sigh escapes me. "My face in this new dreamworld has already been decided." I shake my head. "Unless I'm way off, no one is falling in love with Tunny the gnome."

"Wait." Detective Sterling stares at me, incredulous. "Are you two suggesting Anthony can take someone with him into the dreamworld?"

I glance over at Mira, the outward peace of her expression a boldfaced lie. "Until an hour ago, I didn't know I could go myself."

"We know one thing for certain." Dr. Archer sits on the bed by Mira and strokes her brow. "Others besides you and Mira can walk this realm you create between your two minds." He locks gazes with Mom. "Your voice, Caroline, was the first Mira heard in her many visits to the Exhibition." His eyes flick to Detective Sterling. "Our resident detective had major roles in both the Exhibition and the Russian fair." His head drops. "And me? I was taken, along with Isabella, Rachel, and the other girls, into the twin worlds of *The Firebird* and *Petrushka*, each of us left just as helpless as Mira."

"Which would suggest Dr. Archer has already walked the dreamworld, even if it wasn't of his own free will." Mom squeezes my shoulder. "From what you've told us, Anthony, Dr. Archer is already literally the Prince of the story. Isn't that right?"

"That's true." I catch a flash of disappointment in the detective's eyes. "Though if it weren't for the help of—"

"Looks like you won't be needing me, then." Detective Sterling heads for the door. "What you're talking about is so far out of my league, I'm afraid I'll just be in the way." He rests a hand on the handle. "If... I mean *when* Mira wakes up, I'd appreciate a call."

"Of course, Detective Sterling." Mom's brow furrows. "Thank you for dropping by."

Detective Sterling pulls the door shut behind him, leaving the four of us alone.

Dr. Archer motions for me to join him by the bed. "Any thoughts on how we reestablish your connection to Mira?"

"I have no idea. In case you haven't noticed, I'm making this up as I go along."

Mom moves around behind me and rests a protective hand on each shoulder. "We were halfway home when Anthony drifted off before. Does that help?"

"Of course." Dr. Archer studies me with a clinical gaze. "He had to relax his mind."

I bite my lip, doing my best to hide my nervousness. "I take it you have an idea?"

"Maybe." His gaze flicks to Mom and back to mine. "It's been some time since we tried hypnotism with you. It always used to help with your anxiety when nothing else would." He raises an eyebrow. "Would you be willing to let me try?"

"I suppose." An unconscious shiver works its way up my back. "Though you can probably guess that after everything that's happened in the last year, being put into a trance state scares the hell out of me."

"Don't worry, Anthony. Your mother will be right here the entire time, and if everything goes the way we hope it does, you won't be alone this time."

"What do you mean?" I ask.

"I plan to perform a bit of self-hypnosis while I'm working with you." Dr. Archer's eyes slide shut. "I'm hoping that somehow you can take me with you."

I take cold comfort in the words. If all goes well, I won't have to face von Rothbart alone. I've encountered Dr. Archer on the other side in the role of the noble Kalendar Prince and have little doubt such a force could help keep me safe. A part of me, however, still views him as Petrushka the clown.

It may not be fair of me to question the abilities of a man who's done so much for me over the years, but as both he and Mom tell me all the time, life isn't fair.

If my mind, which provides the libretto of this performance, doubts Dr. Archer, is he then just another lamb being led to the slaughter?

I push away my doubts and take Mira's hand in mine, holding out my other for Dr. Archer. "Shall we get started?"

He grasps my fingers with one hand and has Mom turn the lights down as he pulls a small flashlight from his pocket. "I had a suspicion I might need this today."

In a routine we've been through dozens of times over the years, Dr. Archer bobs the penlight back and forth before my eyes as he slides into his smoothest, most soothing voice. The words barely register, and it's no time before my eyelids grow heavy as if I haven't slept in days. Simultaneously, the rest of my body goes numb and weightless, as if it might float away.

Like a single cloud in an otherwise blue sky, I'm swept away, at the mercy of an invisible, inexorable wind.

And then, I'm back in the world of *Swan Lake*. The scene remains unchanged from my previous visit, though the form I wear couldn't be more different.

No longer Tunny the gnome, I stand nearly a foot taller than my normal fourteen-year-old self. Gone are the wooden skin, the split leather hat, the grime-covered clothing and boots. This new form is handsome and strong. A blue-and-white-checkered tunic covers my torso and my legs are clothed in white tights. I rush to the water knowing exactly what I am going to see before I arrive.

The face of my brother, Jason, stares back at me from the still water.

For my first trip, I assumed the role of Tunny. For my second, it would seem I am destined to be Modesto the troubadour.

I sit alone at the lake's edge just feet from where I faced off against von Rothbart for the fate of Mira/Odette's soul. Alone in the blue moonlight, neither the sorcerer nor the Swan Princess intrudes on my solitude, much less Prince Siegfried.

Still, I'm here. Dr. Archer's plan has worked, at least in part.

I sit in the dewy grass by the lake, alone and without a clue as how to summon Odette.

Unless...

Beneath my hand, a smooth, flat pebble presses into my palm, and before me, the mirror surface of the lake begs to be disturbed.

I wrap my fingers around the stone, stand, and fling the round hunk of rock sidearm like Dad taught me a lifetime ago. The stone skips seven times before sinking to a watery grave at the lake's center, leaving a sequence of ever-widening ripples across the lake—a trail that, if followed, would lead straight back to me.

At first nothing happens, and my simple plan seems an abject failure. Then, just at the limits of my vision, a shape materializes from the mist across the lake.

As graceful and snowy white as I remember, the crowned swan glides across the water in my direction. In no time at all, the elegant bird reaches the shore. Panic seizes my heart. Odette is one necessary ingredient, but without a Siegfried to find and woo her, she remains a helpless girl doomed to spend the rest of her days as a majestic swan and her nights trapped in a dark wood with her tormentor.

I move to the edge of the tree line and hide mere feet from the water just before the swan hits land. Preening itself in the pale moonlight at the water's edge, the majestic bird takes little notice of me... or the glint of moonlight off the crossbow bolt rising silently from behind a massive oak to my left.

I rush in the direction of the raised weapon, though the tree prevents me from seeing whose finger rests on the trigger.

As if there's any doubt.

"Siegfried," I shout. "Don't shoot."

Startled, the swan rushes for the water as the hunter comes around the tree and levels the crossbow instead at me.

As surprised as I was at the face looking back from the water's mirror surface before, it's nothing compared to my shock at the identity of the man who now has me in his sights.

Dressed in a black tunic with gold buttons and embroidery filling his broad chest and golden lace frill decorating his sleeves, the Prince Siegfried standing before me isn't a doppelganger for Dr. Archer, but Detective Sterling.

"Thank you, Benno," he whispers angrily. "You have spoiled my shot and therefore ruined my night."

IV

BENNO

Benno.

Prince Siegfried's best friend in older productions of *Swan Lake*, absent or replaced with a jester in more recent versions. Of all involved in this disaster, only I know that kind of detail.

Detective Sterling spoke true. I'm up against my own mind on this one.

As Sherlock Holmes would say, the game is afoot.

"My prince." I offer this Siegfried that wears Detective Sterling's face a respectful bow. "Pardon my interruption of your kill, but trust me. You do not want to slay such a unique creature as that swan."

"But you were the one who suggested this hunt." Siegfried's anger dissipates a bit, replaced with curiosity. "What makes yonder swan so special?"

"Come with me, my prince. If all goes as I suspect it will, you are about to witness a miracle." Keeping to the shadows, I direct him along the tree line to the apex of the clearing and locate a blind where we can survey the entire glade without being seen.

"So, Benno." His impatient gaze locks on the side of my head. "What is this miracle of which you speak?"

"I cannot say." I shoot him a nervous smile. "This wonder, my prince, is something you truly must see to believe."

He inhales to retort but instead holds his tongue and directs both his gaze and crossbow out across the moonlit clearing at the still lake. The placid water reflects the full moon, but other than the glowing orb at the lake's center, nothing else disturbs the mirrored surface.

That's when the music begins anew.

French horn and rolling tympani followed by strings and woodwinds summon not one, but many swans. Only one, however, wears a silver crown gleaming like a fallen star. One by one, the flock disappears behind the trees to our right, and as each vanishes from our sight, Siegfried becomes more impatient.

"What are we waiting for?" he asks. "This is truly the oddest of hunts."

"You have no idea." I point to a break in the copse of trees where the forest and water meet. "There. Do you see?"

A glimmer of light grows until it fills my vision. From within the nimbus of silver and white springs Odette. *En pointe*, she moves into the clearing as gracefully as a swan gliding across still water as the unseen orchestra shifts to a lone oboe. Her lithe arms and strong legs take her from one end of the glade to the other, each movement more fluid than the one before. As with our last encounter, the shining moon spotlights her every step. Though the woman before me is, in the real world, like a second mother to me, this moment brings a different emotion altogether.

To not fall in love with such a creature would be to have no soul.

One look into Siegfried's star-filled eyes lets me know he feels it too. Before I can stop him, he's on his feet and pushing the crossbow into my hands.

An odd hunt indeed.

Siegfried confronts Odette at the center of the clearing, his every step as graceful as hers, and she responds, as would any frightened bird, by fleeing to the water. Siegfried pursues her, cutting off her escape while maintaining enough distance to not appear a threat. One second, their game of cat and mouse seems destined never to end, and the next they dance together as if they've been rehearsing for decades.

Pirouetting around each other in perfect synchrony, they grow closer and closer, the ambient music and the connection between them building to a fever pitch. Their movements grow more and more intimate with each step till their dance and the beautiful melody guiding their feet reach a dramatic crescendo. Siegfried takes her hands in his, the love in his eyes as plain as if the word were emblazoned on his forehead.

Frightened once more by his nearness, Odette steps away, but only for a heartbeat.

Hand in hand they continue, his arm at her waist, hers at his shoulder, their eyes never leaving the other's.

Odette pirouettes before Siegfried's kneeling form, his every gesture magnifying her grace and beauty. The music swells as she runs to his side. He lifts her into the air, and together they spin once, twice, three times, before he returns her to the ground.

Odette runs from him, and at her invitation, he follows. No sooner does he reach her than she flees again, but this time, he simply begs for her to return. Kneeling, he awaits her, and she complies gladly, allowing his hands at her waist as she leans in for their first passionate kiss.

Their love as plain as the sun in a clear summer sky, and neither of them has spoken a word.

Their moment lasts just that, a moment, as the music shifts from alternating ardor and tranquility to discordant cacophony.

Von Rothbart descends from the sky on wings of night and alights near Odette and Siegfried. Torn from each other's arms by the sorcerer's dark magicks, Odette flees to one end of the clearing while Siegfried looks on helplessly. The spell of blissful silence cast over the glade broken, he rushes to my side.

"Benno," he gets out between panting breaths. "What is happening?"

I meet his confused gaze with one of cold certainty. "My apologies, my prince, but as my mother taught me from a very early age, love is never that easy."

Siegfried rushes toward Odette to begin their dance anew, but the addition of the malevolent third wheel steals the fire from the moment, the young lovers' unfettered infatuation now nothing but frustration and disappointment. His every approach blocked by von Rothbart's yellow owl's eyes, the handsome prince grows more desperate with each pass, and even more so when his gaze meets the dead stare in Odette's eyes.

"Release her, sorcerer." Siegfried and von Rothbart circle each other, the grace of their movements only underlining the violence implied in their every gesture. "The Swan Princess and I are betrothed, I to her and she to me."

"Ah, the folly of youth." Von Rothbart again shifts his face to a form somewhat closer to human only to sneer at Prince Siegfried. "To pledge something as important and fragile as your heart to a soul you've just met."

"I pity you." Siegfried darts one way and then another, trying unsuccessfully to get past von Rothbart. "A creature such as you would never understand something as wondrous and complex as true love."

"Pity yourself." Von Rothbart pulls his cloak tight about his body, his round eyes narrowing. "I too was young once, but years and pain have taught me many lessons." He spreads his woven wings wide in a show of power. "At least one of which you will carry from this place tonight."

Siegfried draws so close to the sorcerer I fear von Rothbart will rip open his throat with his cruelly hooked beak. "Let her go or I shall slay you where you stand."

"Slay me, Prince," von Rothbart whispers, "and the curse on yon maiden will remain in force forever." He motions to Odette, who still cowers in the corner. "By moonlight, you may dance with your love, but by day? A swan she shall be till the day she dies."

Siegfried pulls back as if struck. "She will never love you."

"Love is for poets, Your Highness." Von Rothbart's head tilts to one side. "It grows old. Fails." He snaps his beak shut an inch from Siegfried's face. "Dies."

Siegfried holds fast. "What a cold world you must live in, sorcerer."

"To the contrary." Von Rothbart raises an arm in the direction of the forest edge and the music shifts again. "As you will see momentarily, my nights are spent surrounded in warmth."

From the break in the trees where Odette emerged before comes a line of dancers, each in the same white bodice and feathered tutu that clothes this place's version of Mira Tejedor. Dancing in perfect synchrony with an upbeat melody I've had memorized since I was five, the ballerinas sort themselves into six columns of four and take command of the clearing. Each under von Rothbart's spell, not one responds when Siegfried searches their faces for the eyes of his love.

The music changes again, and another eight ballerinas in white sprint from the woods to join the initial twenty-four. They form two parallel lines, creating a path of beauty and grace and purity. Each dancer assumes the same position, one hand at their waist and the opposite arm curved above their head, emulating the graceful neck of a swan. Siegfried walks this gauntlet of white, his eyes shifting left and right, his body primed for an attack. The only blow that comes, however, is the reappearance of his new love.

Odette, striking in her immaculate white garb and sparkling crown, emerges again from the shadows at the forest edge and runs *en pointe* between the two lines of ballerinas only to assume the same position in the midst of her many sisters. The music shifts to woodwinds, oboe and piccolo accompanying Siegfried as he moves to free Odette from von Rothbart's control. A single touch, and she is free to dance again. Together, they exit the clearing to my right, leaving me alone to watch as the remaining thirty-two ballerinas begin to dance, no doubt at von Rothbart's pleasure.

Their every movement fluid and elegant, the ballerinas dance in perfect step with the music, though not a hint of joy invades any of their expressions. I almost leave my hiding place a dozen times, my heart breaking for each in turn, and a dozen times I remind myself of one simple fact.

This isn't my story.

Soon, Siegfried and Odette return. Violin and harp fill the air as their love manifest in dance continues. Closer and closer they grow, their movements in absolute synchrony as she falls into his arms again and again. The remaining ballerinas each pay silent homage to the lovers, but still no smile intrudes upon any of their countenances.

I can't help but think, however, as I wipe the tears from my face, that some small part of each of their hearts experiences a sliver of the love revealed in the soft moonlight.

Dance after dance. Siegfried and Odette. The ballerinas all together or in groups of four. Odette with her many sisters. The euphoric celebration of love seems to go on forever.

But I know exactly where all of this is leading, even if Prince Siegfried and his Swan Princess seem somehow blissfully unaware.

One second, Siegfried holds Odette aloft, their mythical love realized in a dramatic fanfare of brass, strings, and percussion. The next, the mournful oboe returns, and the lovers embrace one last time before being torn apart by forces unseen. Siegfried holds aloft a two-fingered salute, pledging his love for all to see even as the flock of swan maidens encircles the pair to protect them.

The seeming victory lasts but a moment. Von Rothbart reappears at the water's edge and with a simple wave of his hand, sends the thirty-two swan maidens into the surrounding forest, leaving only the owl-sorcerer, Siegfried, and Odette alone in the clearing.

The Swan Princess returns to her prince one last time and adopts a high arabesque pose before granting him one last kiss. Then, as surely as if pulled from Siegfried by a gale force wind, Odette returns to von Rothbart's side and resumes her swan form, the drama captured in violin, horn, and flute. The dark sorcerer smiles almost imperceptibly, not validating Siegfried with so much as a glance, and disappears into the forest as well.

Left alone in the clearing, Siegfried once again holds aloft his two-fingered salute, but as he takes a step in my direction, the entire world trembles as if in the throes of a massive earthquake. The last thing I see is the moon's pale face staring down upon the forlorn Prince Siegfried just before everything goes to black.

I awake on the hospital bed next to Mira's unconscious form. Dr. Archer shakes me by the shoulders, his panicked expression making it obvious I've missed something important. Mom stands off to one side, her hand over mouth and her eyes brimming with tears, a look I've seen far too many times in the last few weeks. I try to sit up and tell her I'm okay, only to discover such a statement would be a lie. My every muscle feels like melted butter and any attempt at speech comes out at best as a harsh whisper.

Like all the drug dealers on the cop shows say: the first one is free.

"Mira wasn't joking." I manage a pained smile. "This feels horrible."

Dr. Archer and Mom help me sit up. Once the dizziness has resolved to where I can stay upright under my own power, Mom grabs me a cup of water, which I take greedily and immediately choke as half the lukewarm liquid goes straight down my windpipe. Dr. Archer slaps me on the back a few times and helps me clear my throat.

Lesson learned, my next sip of water is just that.

Once my coughing spell ends and I can again breathe, I attempt to rise from the bed and shake the fatigue from my limbs, but my legs are having none of it. Mira told me how the aftermath of her various sojourns to the Exhibition felt, but to experience it, to feel as if you're a balloon with all the air let out, is another thing entirely. The fact that she went through this within minutes of our first meeting and didn't immediately get back in her car and drive away speaks volumes about her character.

Dr. Archer gives me a few minutes to gather myself before launching into the inevitable barrage of questions.

"What happened, Anthony?" He studies me with both the measured gaze of a trained psychologist and the desperation of a man on the brink of losing everything. "Where did you go? What did you see?"

"The lake." I take another sip of tepid water. "I was back at the lake."

"Did you see Mira this time?" Dr. Archer's hand trembles. "Was she... okay?"

"She was there." A succession of images spills through my mind. The crowned swan. Von Rothbart's round yellow eyes. Prince Siegfried wearing

Detective Sterling's features. "And she wasn't alone."

Dr. Archer's gaze drops. "I thought you'd be able to take me with you. I thought I'd be able to—"

"What the hell just happened to me?" Detective Sterling staggers into the room, his eyes locking on me. "Kid, was that you?"

Dr. Archer's already crestfallen expression falls another notch. "You took him?"

"I had just sat down in my car when I went under." Detective Sterling pours himself into a chair in the corner, his perplexed gaze never leaving my eyes. "Another minute and I'd have been out on the road and probably wrapped around a tree."

"Sorry." Unbidden tears well up at the corners of my eyes. "I don't know what I'm doing here."

Dr. Archer's eyes dart from Detective Sterling to me and back again. "You were both there?" He swallows. "With Mira?"

"You'd better sit down, Doc." Detective Sterling weakly slaps the seat next to his. "The whole thing was kind of like a dream, and it's already fading. The part I can remember, though?" He shoots a knowing glance in my direction. "It's going to blow your mind."

V

CHRISTMAS

The trip home from the hospital is all but silent. Mom pulls in at a Wendy's Drive-Thru and orders me a cheeseburger and fries, which I devour over the couple miles between there and home. Other than humming along with the quiet tones of Neil Diamond and other oldies from her younger years, she doesn't say another word.

Can't say I blame her. Walking the space between Mira's mind and my own may have left me exhausted, but Mom is the one who looks like she just missed a month of sleep.

We pull into the driveway and she barely remembers to shut off the car before climbing out and heading for the front door. As I step inside a few seconds later, she's already halfway down the hall leading to her bedroom.

"You're back." Jason, dressed for a run, all but bowls me over. The two words are the most he's said to me since yesterday at lunch.

"Yep." I peer down the darkened hallway to my right and catch Mom's quick tearful glance before she disappears into her room. "We're back."

"What the hell happened today?" The sound of a door clicking shut sends Jason's gaze shooting after mine. "Mom looked pretty fried." He gives me a frank up and down. "And you look like you were run over by a truck."

"You sure you want to know?" I slide past Jason and into the kitchen. "You didn't seem interested in having anything to do with any of this yesterday."

"Hold up." He follows so close I swear I can feel his breath on my neck. "I never said I didn't care. I just don't think risking your life again and again with all this psychic mumbo jumbo is a good idea."

"It's not mumbo jumbo." I flash him an angry glare. "And in case you've forgotten, we're doing all of this for Mira." I wash down the salt from the fries with a big gulp of OJ and set the glass on the counter, maybe a bit too hard. "You know, the woman who cleared you of a murder charge last year?"

Jason answers my glare with his own trademark glower. "Not funny, kid."

"Who's laughing?" I jump up and plant myself on the kitchen counter, leaving my legs dangling in front of the dishwasher. "If it weren't for Mira, I'd still be lying in a coma, you or Glenn Hartman would probably be in prison for Julianna's death, and Veronica Sayles would have gotten away with the whole thing."

"You think I don't know that?" He pounds the kitchen island. "You think a *day* goes by I don't think about last fall and what Mira did for all of us?"

I scrunch up my nose. "Then why are you so against me trying to help her?"

The anger in Jason's eyes softens. "You didn't have to watch your little brother spend a month in a near coma last year, in too much pain to wake up and face the world." He clears his throat. "Or watch your mother cry herself to sleep every night the whole time." At his sides, his fisted hands relax as his voice drops another few decibels. "You and Rachel? You're Mom's world. You screw up this thing and end up all gorked again, it will destroy her."

"Mira is lying comatose in a hospital bed right now, just like I was last year. None of what happened is my fault, but that doesn't change the fact that my mind is what put her there. How do you think that makes me feel?" I stalk over to Jason, and though he's got me beat by over a foot, I scowl up at him with as much fire as I can muster. "You've met Isabella. You want her to be without her mother?"

"Of course not." Jason musses my hair the way he always does when he's trying to smooth things over between us. "I just want you to be careful." A smile breaks through his stony features. "Hand-feeding you Jell-O pudding while you hang out in your bed all day for weeks may seem like fun to you, but for the rest of us, it's a pain in the ass."

"Got it." I answer his smile in kind. "You always brought butterscotch instead of chocolate anyway."

"All right." Jason grabs a sports drink from the fridge and we sit opposite each other at the kitchen island. "Let's hear it. What the hell is it this time?"

As best I can remember, I detail my two visits to *Swan Lake*. The crowned swan with the snowy feathers. Mira's role as Odette. Detective Sterling's as Siegfried. The mysterious von Rothbart. My dual embodiments, first as Tunny the gnome and second as Siegfried's best friend Benno.

"Hold on a minute." Jason rests his drink on the counter. "You're saying this Benno was me?"

"At least the version of you from the Exhibition." I shake my head and laugh. "With the exception of the ballet tights, Benno is basically a clone of Modesto the troubadour. This time, however, I'm the one in the driver's seat."

Jason glances across his shoulder in the direction of the bedrooms. "I'm guessing you still haven't told Mom everything."

My eyes follow his. "That I remember the Exhibition? *The Firebird*, *Petrushka*, *The Rite of Spring*?" My gaze drops to the granite countertop. "Absolutely not."

"And you still don't think you should?"

"I can't." A faint pain flares to life above my left eye. "She just walked into the house like a zombie from *The Walking Dead* after watching me take one quick lap through *Swan Lake*. What do you think happens when she finds out Mira didn't actually wipe her little boy's slate clean? That Versailles and Koschei and the Charlatan and even Baba Yaga still haunt my dreams every night?"

"You're going to have to tell her sometime, buddy." A quiet sigh escapes him. "You can keep her in the dark for a while, but our mother is a bloodhound. You know she'll figure it out. She always does."

"I just don't want to worry her." I slip off my glasses and rub at the bridge of my nose. "She already has more than enough to deal with."

Footsteps sound from the den. As if summoned, Mom appears in the kitchen doorway with her phone in her hand.

"Anthony, we're both exhausted, but Thomas just called." She rubs at her brow as if my growing headache is somehow contagious. "He wants to know if he can drop by this afternoon. Now that he's had time to put a few things together, he wants to talk to you again."

"Whew," Jason mutters. "That doesn't sound worrisome at all."

I shoot him an irate glare before shooting Mom my best smile. "Sure." My eyes suddenly heavy, I suck down the rest of my orange juice, step over to her side, and slide my arm around her waist for a quick hug. "But is it all right if I take a nap first?"

"Of course." Mom gives me a weary grin. "I'll ask him to come by around five." She waves me toward my bedroom and returns to the call, keeping her voice low.

I shoot Jason one last knowing glance and trudge down the hall. The trip seems to take an eternity, each step leaving me wearier than the one before. At the end of the strangely exhausting journey, I fall into bed without so much as taking off my shoes and am asleep before my head hits the pillow.

When I open my eyes again somewhere between a second and a year later, I find myself in yet another strange place, the faces surrounding me not the usual collection of hobbits, Jedi, and robots from my full wall of movie posters. Instead, I lie on a couch beneath a snowy window clothed with thick velvet drapes. A party is going on all around me, and everyone seems to be having a fine time. All Mom's age and wearing what must have been the height of fashion a century ago, each reveler flits silently from person to person to share in the joy of the event. Familiar orchestral music plays quietly in the background, though for once, I can't name the piece.

I pull myself up from the couch and discover that this isn't just any party, but a Christmas celebration. Between two grand windows stands a tree. Stretching to the top of the twelve-foot ceiling and decorated in metallic balls of red, gold, and silver as well as a white garland and crystal icicles, the tree is topped with an ornate star, shining as if it just fell from the sky.

A man and a woman in matching party dress join me by the couch. The man's face is unfamiliar to me. The woman's, on the other hand, is not.

Rosa Tejedor, or a much younger version of the woman I've come to know over the last few months, looks down on me with a mother's love. The man seems more put out than anything. Without a word, he points to a door across the room, making it clear I'm not supposed to be here. I raise a hand before my face, half-afraid he's going to strike me, but when no blow comes, I rise from the plush cushions of the couch and rush for the door. I step into the next room but leave a crack and peek back through just in time to witness the man turn to the tree. At his grand sweeping gesture, every branch from top to bottom comes alight with a warm white glow, bringing the Christmas tree to life. Beneath the decorated branches rest presents of every shape, size, and color, though I get the feeling the gifts are not for the many adults standing about the room.

This is Christmas. Where are the children?

No sooner does the question invade my thoughts than the answer comes in the form of a rush of footsteps from behind me. I dodge to one side as a dozen girls and boys in similar dress to the adults beyond the door rush past me to join their parents.

Taking what seems an obvious cue, I follow.

Soon, the party descends into chaos as each of the children opens the gift meant for them. Doll houses, play swords, toy locomotives; the children squeal with glee as they tear into their various presents and soon every corner of the room is filled with clusters of boys and girls comparing their loot.

When the fervor has died down a bit, I feel compelled to go to the tree myself. There, I find a long red and silver striped tube with the name written in silver ink.

Fritz.

My name, it would seem.

Inside, I find a toy gun, an old-timey rifle. No sooner is the weapon in my hand than I start to march around as if I'm one of the guards at the Tomb of the Unknown Soldier.

As if I'm a marionette in some grand puppet show.

I shudder at the thought.

On one of my many passes by the enormous Christmas tree, I note that one present beneath the sweeping branches remains undisturbed.

A large box wrapped in green with a large gold bow.

The name on the tag? Clara.

Wait.

Clara.

Fritz.

Christmas.

Suddenly, I know exactly where I am and, more importantly, why the melody filling the space seems so familiar.

The music rises. I spin in the direction of the other room where another familiar face greets me from the dark doorway to which I was previously banished.

Isabella.

No. Not Isabella, but her mother.

Though in this place she is closer to my age than her own, there is no mistaking the angelic features of Mira Tejedor.

With the poise of a young ballerina with experience beyond her years, this young version of Mira strides across the floor and greets her mother and a man who must be her father with the excited hugs of a child caught up in the excitement of Christmas Eve. Her parents apparently cast in the roles of Dr. and Mrs. Stahlbaum in this corner of the dreamworld she and I share, it's clear Mira's memories and imagination are providing the color in this place as mine once did the Exhibition.

As always, however, the world comes from me.

Dr. Archer could write a hundred papers on the two of us.

As if anyone would believe a word of it.

Overcome with excitement, the young Mira runs to the tree and grabs up the present wrapped in green and gold and shakes it, trying to determine what might hide inside.

Wait.

Green and gold.

Of course. Scheherazade's colors.

Mira, or, I suppose, Clara, tears into the brightly colored package and pulls out a miniature sleigh, much to her delight. She runs to her mother's side and nearly knocks this version of Rosa Tejedor over in jubilation.

The entire scene is picture perfect.

And if I recall my Tchaikovsky, this party is just getting started.

An orchestra hit marks the arrival of a mysterious man dressed in a dark cloak and a magician's coned hat. His face hidden behind a raised cape like Bela Lugosi in *Dracula*, the man creeps in Clara's direction. The girl, in turn, draws back in fear, hiding within the folds of her mother's formal gown and beneath her father's tails. The dark-clad stranger makes one full lap of the room, his piercing eyes terrifying each of the children who moments before had been basking in the joy of their gifts, and then returns to Clara.

As he lowers his cloak and reveals his face, both Clara and I let out an audible gasp.

The man's visage is one Mira should know well, but nowhere nearly as well as I do. She knows him as Mussorgsky, the Charlatan, Koschei the Deathless. His was one of the last faces she saw, the Sage that looked on dispassionately as she danced *The Rite of Spring* and sacrificed herself to free us all from Madame Versailles' evil machinations once and for all.

Here, in the opening act of Tchaikovsky's most famous ballet, however, he takes the role of Clara's godfather, Drosselmeyer.

Me? I call him Dad.

As the music shifts to one of Tchaikovsky's most famous marches, I fall into a double file line with the rest of the boys and we promenade around the room like half-size soldiers while all the girls huddle in one corner and Drosselmeyer holds Clara up to the tree so she can place an ornament.

On our first pass, a hand comes down on my shoulder and I spin around to find Drosselmeyer smiling down at me and pushing a stick horse and toy cutlass into my hand. Without missing a beat, I spin around and lead the formation of boys around the room as the grand march continues. The girls all leap to their feet, grasp their various toys, and line up in two parallel lines, providing a lovely thoroughfare for our underage squad of soldiers.

Soon, Drosselmeyer wraps a silk scarf around his head and leads a game of blind man's bluff. Then, as he nears the tree, he rips the blindfold from his face and rests the silk cloth across his clenched fist. With a magician's panache, he waves his other hand above the cloth once, twice, three times, and when he pulls the cloth away, a dove appears. The bird flies from his hand and disappears into the next room, all to the delight of everyone present. Clara in particular squeals in glee at her godfather's impressive legerdemain.

Next, the children all move to the periphery of the room while the adults gather in the center. Couples pair off and Drosselmeyer picks two well-dressed young ladies with whom to promenade as the intricate dance commences. Every step planned and performed with precision, it's like a trip back to a better, more formal time.

Once the dance is complete, Drosselmeyer takes center stage again and pulls a wand from inside his cloak, the move reminiscent of the Charlatan from *Petrushka* producing his magic flute from the folds of his magician's robes.

It's odd knowing that monster was me, at least in every way that counts.

At Drosselmeyer's direction, I and the other children take seats on the floor while Clara rushes to her mother's lap. A single wave of his wand and a puppet stage wrapped in ribbons of red, white, and blue rolls from a closet and to the center of the room. Soon, one puppet, then another, and finally a third appear atop the brightly decorated stage.

The tale that unfolds is one I know well.

A handsome prince meets a beautiful princess. They fall in love. They are attacked by the evil Mouse King. The prince defends his new love and slays the wicked monster. The prince and princess ride off into the sunset.

The only problem with this?

This realm that exists between my mind and Mira's doesn't seem to deal much in happily ever after.

As the puppet prince and Mouse King strike at each other with their tiny swords, the music reaches a fever pitch and every boy in the room flails their arms as if they were in fact the embattled hero. Unable to resist the pull of the music, even I strike out with an invisible sword. At my single thrust, the Mouse King falls, disappearing back beneath the stage. Terrified seconds before, Clara now beams as the prince and princess puppets are reunited.

The look is one I've seen on the real Mira's face far too little in the months we've known each other.

If this version of Mira knew what I knew, I don't think she'd be quite so enthusiastic.

The two puppets share one final kiss before they too disappear behind the stage. Drosselmeyer returns the brightly colored box to its dark hiding place in the corner closet with but a wave of his hand. I question whether Clara's godfather truly possesses power in this place or if this apparent magic is the work of puppeteers cleverly hidden inside the mysterious box.

Then I remember where I am.

And whose mind, as best as I understand it, makes the rules here.

The truth in this dreamworld, in some strange way, is whatever I decide.

Drosselmeyer gathers together all the boys and girls, and in a mad rush reminiscent of the children of the *Tuileries* garden, we all follow the dark magician in another full lap of the room, the mob eventually halting before the enormous tree. There, a line of adult revelers has gathered, each wearing the smile of someone who knows something you don't.

Another wave of Drosselmeyer's wand and the adults part like a curtain, revealing a sight that freezes my blood.

There, resting on the fine carpet before the Christmas tree, lie the three life-size puppets from *Petrushka*, though in this place, I suppose they'd be referred to as dolls.

Beneath his silk turban, which still sports the Firebird's feather, the Moor glares in my direction, his eyes burning with anger and contempt.

Between the two men, the Ballerina stares helplessly, her paralyzed gaze full of fear.

Behind a black mask, Petrushka's face is turned up in a fool's simple smile.

Though they represent the Toy Soldier, Colette the Columbine, and the Harlequin from Tchaikovsky's first ballet, their faces are unmistakable.

Detective Sterling.

Mira.

Dr. Archer.

Will this never end?

More importantly, which of the two Miras before me represents the woman I'm searching for?

The child enraptured by her godfather's magic show?

Or the Ballerina doll standing stock-still at the center of the room?

One by one, with similar flourishes to the ones the Charlatan used when controlling the puppets at the Russian Fair, Drosselmeyer animates each of the dolls.

He starts with the Harlequin. Though not as clumsy as the clown, Petrushka, nor as noble as Toma, the Kalendar Prince, elements of both are evident in the masked figure's leaping and cavorting as well as the ambling woodwinds and strings that guide his every step.

The Harlequin's dance done, Drosselmeyer turns his attention to Colette the Columbine who looks out with Mira's terrified eyes from behind all the pancake makeup and crimson lipstick. With each wave of Drosselmeyer's wand, she jumps, spins, and poses to a far more graceful tune than led the Harlequin. I pray if Mira is in fact a part of the creature before me, that she has no knowledge or understanding of what is happening to her.

To be forced yet again into the role of puppet seems a fate beyond cruel.

As if the role of "princess enchanted to spend her days as a swan and her nights as the slave of a half-owl sorcerer" is much of an improvement.

Her dance done, Drosselmeyer brings the Harlequin up from his position on the floor and forces him and Colette together for a waltz. Dancing in tandem, the Harlequin and the Columbine make magic, their moves fluid, refined, elegant. Still, in each of their faces, I find only sadness and longing. So close, they move as one, and yet a million miles apart in every way that matters. And through it all, Clara sits, entranced with the pair of magical dancing dolls, not knowing one of them represents a piece of her very own soul.

By far, the cruelest joke of all.

And I have a nasty feeling the universe is just getting started.

The dance ends with the pair separating to complete each of their performances alone. Colette goes to the center of the floor and spins *en pointe* like a tutu-clad cyclone while the Harlequin prances back and forth around her in a semblance of some strange mating ritual. Then, suddenly, each comes to a stop like a pair of toys reaching the end of their drawn string.

Not wasting a moment, Drosselmeyer rushes to the third doll's side. If the dances of the Harlequin and the Columbine were whimsical and light, the dance of the Moor is terrifying. As he did in *Petrushka*, the dark-skinned warrior adopts a box-like pose and with moves reminiscent of Boris Karloff's monster from *Frankenstein*, plods toward a collection of children huddled by the window to a boisterous melody of strings and brass. The children scream and scatter, and none louder or faster than Clara herself.

His dance strong and confident, the Moor quickly becomes a whirling dervish, rushing from one end of the room to the other, the music growing more and more bombastic with his every step. Half the children run to him as the other half flee, their squeals equal parts delight and terror.

More than any other facet of the dance, nothing chills me more than the cold stares the Moor shoots at Colette and the Harlequin with his every spin and leap. He circles them once, twice, three times, and with each pass, I fear for the Harlequin's life. I remember all too well the orchestral hit as the Moor struck down his clownish rival. Eventually, however, even the dark dynamo in green-and-blue silk comes to a halt, leaving all three dolls resting like their counterparts from *Petrushka*.

The spectacle over, three men from the party grab the dolls and, at Drosselmeyer's direction, drag them from the room.

I have a sinking feeling I haven't seen the last of any of them.

And now, the moment we've all been waiting for.

Clara rushes to her godfather's side, begging him for one more show, one more trick, one more bit of magic. At first, he plays dumb, his eyebrows high in surprise as if he has nothing else up his sleeve. But the subtle twinkle in his eye reveals a different truth.

He kisses Clara on the forehead before rushing to a table in the corner where an item covered in white cloth awaits. Pulling this mysterious object down from the shelf, he steps to the center of the room and rests the veiled secret on the carpeted floor. One child after another draws close, their curious fingers threatening to remove the cloth, but each advance is blocked by a stern glance and Drosselmeyer's wand.

Then, just when Clara and the others can't take another second of anticipation, the magician pulls away the cloth and reveals the doll for which this entire ballet is named.

VI

NUTCRACKER

At two feet tall and dressed impeccably in the white-and-gold uniform of a nineteenth-century German soldier, the Nutcracker stares in my direction, its wooden eyes reminiscent of a certain gnome I know all too well.

Less than eight hours have passed since I stood by von Rothbart's lake within Tunny's oaken form. Still, though I may walk around now as a real live boy, I remember all too well how it felt to be the Pinocchio of the other piece.

Which brings up the real question.

Who is trapped screaming inside the doll's inanimate form? Though a simple toy carved from wood, the story dictates that yet another prince rests at the Nutcracker's heart. Who could it be?

And after the Firebird's betrayal, can I even assume they're a friend?

The scene plays out the same as it has the hundred times I've watched various versions of the ballet. Though the remainder of the children couldn't be less interested in the hunk of wood carved into the form of a man—some even evince disgust at the doll's grotesque face—Clara stares at the doll in rapt wonder as if it's the most beautiful thing she's ever seen. She runs to Drosselmeyer and encircles his waist with an excited hug before kneeling in her fancy party dress to inspect her new toy.

Clara keeps her distance at first, as if she's afraid to touch the doll. Soon, however, the music takes her, and she rises to dance around her new toy in celebration, her every step drawing her ever closer to her destiny. Drosselmeyer, taking pity on the poor girl, scoops up the doll from the floor and holds it out to Clara. A moment later, the magician and Clara circle the room in an elegant dance, the doll held between them. Once, twice, three times, they skirt the periphery of the crowd, the three of them alone in their own little world.

On their final pass, Drosselmeyer stops Clara before the tree, places the Nutcracker in her arms as if it were a newborn babe, and crouches by the bottom branches as if searching for yet another present. Clara cradles the Nutcracker and peers up at the star beaming down from the treetop.

Everything is as I've seen it countless times... until it isn't.

Unseen by anyone but me, the Nutcracker doll's head turns in my direction. A hideous grimace carved into its features, one wooden eye winks at me while the other gleams with mischief. The oaken teeth part, as if to bite. Before I can stop myself, I rush at Clara, frantic to save her from the strange doll cradled in her arms. Though she draws away in sudden fear, I'm too quick for her and seize the Nutcracker's head.

The ferocious tug-of-war is over almost before it begins, as with a yank, the doll's head comes away in my hands. I look down into the decapitated Nutcracker's face and find there only the snarling features carved into its woody visage. Fear turns into guilt as tears well in Clara's eyes and my guilt into utter shame as I meet Drosselmeyer's angry gaze.

Mom may have always been the disciplinarian in the house, but nothing ever motivated me like the unmistakable disappointment that all but pours from the magician's eyes.

My father's eyes.

Drosselmeyer holds out one gloved hand, and without a second's hesitation, I place the Nutcracker's head in his palm. With a grim nod and a pointed finger, he banishes me to the next room and I comply.

At least for the most part.

As before, I leave the door cracked.

I'm not leaving Mira alone in there with whoever or whatever hides behind the Nutcracker's twisted scowl.

Balled up in a corner beside the Christmas tree, a despondent Clara weeps into her hands. Drosselmeyer regards her with compassion as, with the grace of a skilled watchmaker, he deftly replaces the Nutcracker's head. Tiptoeing up behind his goddaughter, he gently taps her on the shoulder and returns the doll to her arms. Gazing down at the damaged doll, her face shifts from sadness to anger to confusion. In response, Drosselmeyer pulls a bright blue cloth from his sleeve and applies a makeshift bandage to the wounded Nutcracker's neck, a move that appeases Clara and returns a smile to her face.

A gentle tune of flute and muted brass fills the air, sending Clara dancing around the room with the Nutcracker in her arms. This time, however, the innocence in her gaze is tempered with the watchful cast of a mother lioness, a look I've seen countless times in the eyes of Mira Tejedor.

The smooth flute melody soon gives way to a trumpet fanfare, and before I can stop myself, my body again leaps into action. I rush back into the room with a trio of boys in tow, the toy cutlass in one hand and the stick horse held in the other. Though I have no desire to terrorize poor Clara further, we charge at her and send her sprinting from the room with the Nutcracker doll. A strange glee fills my heart at her terror, though the part of me that is still Anthony Faircloth drowns in a reservoir of shame at the cruelty I am being forced to inflict on a woman who has never been anything but kind to me.

The remainder of the party passes without event. The grown-ups dance, the children play, the drunkards drink, and general merriment is had by all. I've all but forgotten where I am when a chime sounds from the room's far corner. There, a grandfather clock topped with a carved owl's head peals ten times, causing everyone to stand frozen until the clock is silent again. My gaze locks with the wooden gaze of the owl for the duration. Images of the dark sorcerer from *Swan Lake* flit through my memory, sending chills up my spine. With all my might, I push the memories of those haunting yellow eyes to the back of my mind and carry on as the party returns to life.

Not long after, the festivities begin to draw down, and I line up with Clara and the Stahlbaums by the door to wish the line of departing revelers a pleasant evening. Drosselmeyer, the last to leave, shoots me one last glare before sweeping Clara into a tight embrace and bidding us all a good night.

No sooner has the door clicked closed behind him than our "father" sends me to my room. As I head for the stairs leading to the second floor, the woman wearing Rosa Tejedor's face takes the Nutcracker from Clara. Placing the doll back on its shelf, she pulls her daughter close and strokes her hair, calming her as she prepares the girl for a good night's sleep. From the door, I watch as Clara and Mrs. Stahlbaum extinguish the lights on the beautiful Christmas tree one by one, a part of me wishing I could be included in the family moment.

As the last light goes out, my eyelids slide closed for somewhere between a second and a millennium. When my eyes again open, I find myself in a place far more familiar.

Though I fell asleep on top of the covers before, my favorite blanket now envelops me like a shroud. Captain America, Frodo Baggins, and Neo stare down at me from my wall of movie posters. The digital clock on my nightstand reveals I've been out for over two hours.

And I feel like I just swam a hundred miles through molten lead.

"Mom?" My first attempt at speech doesn't go well, the word a barely comprehensible grunt escaping between lips that don't want to move. "Mom?"

Footsteps outside my door end in Mom's inquisitive stare into the darkened room.

"Anthony?" she asks. "Was that you?"

"Yeah." Better. That actually sounded like human speech.

"Did you sleep well?" she asks.

"It happened again."

"No." Mom's hand clenches around the doorknob, the hinges creaking as my mother's full weight pulls down on the door. "What happened?"

Sparing her as many details as I can, I share an abridged version of the events that just transpired. My part in the drama. Mira's role as Clara. My father as Drosselmeyer.

I hold off telling her about the appearance of the dolls from *Petrushka*.

I'm not sure she's ready for that.

And as for the Nutcracker doll shooting me the evil eye? I keep that to myself as well.

"Your father was there?"

"And Mira's mother."

Mom takes a minute to digest all I've told her. "So, *Swan Lake* and *The Nutcracker*. Just like last time, we're waging a war on two fronts."

"Not sure I'd call it a war." I pull myself up into a seated position and hug my pillow to my chest with arms that ache to the bone. "At least not yet."

She skewers me to the spot with a perturbed look only my mother can mount. "What would you call it, then?"

"I'm sorry, Mom. I don't know how any of this works." I sigh. "But neither did Mira."

Mom brushes a lock of hair from her face. "And look where she ended up."

The chirp of Mom's phone startles both of us. She steps out of the room and pads down the hall to answer. I strain my ears and manage to catch most of her side of the conversation.

"What?" she whispers. "No." A sharp intake of air hits my ears. "I suppose that makes sense. Anthony was just telling me a similar story." Another pause. "Of course. We'll be right there."

Mom steps back into the room. "That was Dr. Archer. He's asked if we can come by his office as soon as possible."

I squint my eyes, trying to read her expression in the dim light. "I thought he was coming here."

"That was the plan." Her head drops. "He's not feeling up to driving at the moment."

"Why?" I ask. "What's wrong?"

Wait.

The Harlequin.

No.

"It really did happen again, didn't it?" A terrifying notion grips my heart like a vise. "Did I... hurt him?"

She meets my gaze, her face shifting into her most comforting mother's smile. "Dr. Archer is fine, Anthony. He just had an episode like Detective Sterling's earlier today."

As I contemplate our ever-shifting definition of the word "fine," Mom's phone rings again. She glances down at the screen, her brow furrowing.

"And speaking of the good detective..." She taps the screen and pulls the phone to her ear. "Hello?"

She listens intently, and tries to keep the horror from her face as Detective Sterling no doubt shares an increasingly familiar story.

"Again?" she whispers. "I'm so sorry." Her eyes shoot to me. "No, he's right here." Her head shakes subtly from side to side. "I understand that, Detective, but there's nothing I can do." Her head shakes subtly from side to side. "Unfortunately, I just received a similar call from Thomas. Anthony and I are headed to his office if you'd care to join us."

She taps the screen again and places her phone on my dresser. "Well, Anthony, this Christmas party you were telling me about managed to reach out and touch both Dr. Archer and Detective Sterling."

The fist of ice around my heart grows even tighter. "They're both all right?"

"From what I can tell. Each of them was out for over an hour, but they were both in a safe place when they went under." She studies me before continuing. "As you can probably guess, they want to talk to you." Her eyes narrow. "And from what they said, there's a part of the story you conveniently forgot to tell me about."

"Mom." My heart threatens to explode out of my chest. "I'm sorry."

"It's okay, Anthony. I know you were trying not to worry me." She steps into the hallway. "We can talk about it on the way to Thomas' office."

"Are you sure you want to know?"

She turns for her room, muttering just loud enough that I'm not sure if she means for me to hear it or not. "Anything, as long as it keeps you awake."

Dr. Archer stares across his massive desk at me through bleary, half-closed eyes. "Anything you want to tell us, Anthony?"

Jason, who insisted on coming with us, bristles at Dr. Archer's tone, but a simple tilt of Mom's head convinces him to keep quiet.

It's only the second time we've ever been invited to Dr. Archer's actual office, but there's little question why. If my third trip today into the worlds of Tchaikovsky hit me like a runaway truck, it's left him totally wasted.

And compared to poor Detective Sterling, Dr. Archer looks positively well rested.

"Anthony was just taking a nap." Mom rests a hand on my shoulder and pulls my head to her side. "He didn't mean to do any of this."

"Doesn't change the fact that my body's been hijacked twice today." Detective Sterling rubs at his temple as if the headache pounding above my right ear is broadcasting like a radio station. "No offense, kid, but you need to lay off."

"I'm not doing any of this." Unbidden tears well at the corners of my eyes. "At least not on purpose." My eyes flick from the exasperation in Detective Sterling's gaze to the utter fatigue in Dr. Archer's. "I swear."

"Don't forget, gentlemen," Mom interrupts. "In only one of the three instances today was Anthony trying to do anything. During the other two, he was fast asleep." Her grip on my shoulder clamps down like a vise. "He's no more culpable for these attacks than he was a year ago when he was... away."

"Attacks?" I pull away from Mom's stifling grip and go to the window. "I'm not attacking anyone. I'm trying to help Mira, like everyone asked."

"I'm sorry, Anthony." Mom's cheeks grow a shade darker. "I didn't mean—"

"I told you this was a bad idea." Jason, who has miraculously held his tongue till now, joins me by the window. "This thing Anthony can do isn't some video game where you can hit the reset button if things go bad." He takes a few deep breaths through his nose, no doubt trying to keep his cool. "You're all so gung-ho to send Anthony back into this insanity that took a month of his life last year despite the fact we still don't have the first idea how any of this works."

"Jason..." Mom murmurs.

"No. Mira barely understood what was going on, but she kept poking the bear, and now she's lying in a coma in worse shape than Anthony ever was." He rests a hand on my shoulder. Despite the righteous anger in his voice, his grip is gentle. "Look. The kid just turned fourteen and has already been through more than most of us will ever experience. Can't we at least try and find another way to help Mira?"

Detective Sterling inhales to speak, but Dr. Archer beats him to the punch. "I hate to say it, Jason, but as much as the events of today have proven terrifying and beyond any of our understanding, I still believe your brother is Mira's best shot." He forces himself out of his chair, his knees wobbly, and rounds his enormous desk to stand by my side. "We all understand this is dangerous, Anthony, you more than any of us. Still, the Exhibition, or whatever this thing is that ties you and Mira together, is what got her into this and unless I miss my guess, it's the only thing that's going to get her out."

"That's all fine and good," Detective Sterling interrupts, "but what happens if the kid starts dreaming about a hundred-year-old ballet when I'm cruising down I-77?"

Dr. Archer inhales sharply, and lets out a quiet sigh as he turns me around to face the rest of the room. "First thing, I suppose, is no naps." He glances over at Mom. "Until this is over, Detective Sterling and I will need to be kept abreast of Anthony's sleep schedule to ensure we are not in a position to endanger ourselves or others should his mind take us again."

Mom lowers her head in a subtle nod. "I... can do that."

Dr. Archer shifts his gaze to Detective Sterling. "I'd suggest you stay off the road as much as possible." He actually laughs. "And no climbing on the roof for the time being."

Detective Sterling raises an eyebrow, clearly not amused. "Shouldn't be a problem."

"Lastly," Dr. Archer continues, "we need to wrap this up as quickly as possible." His gaze returns to me. "This thing with Anthony and Mira leaves all of us in a pretty precarious position, so till this is over, we all stay in close contact, agreed?"

Detective Sterling, Mom, and I all nod. Jason, on the other hand, finally boils over.

"So we're supposed to tell you when Anthony goes to sleep, when he wakes up, and make sure he never dozes off or daydreams." He shakes his head, his arms crossed. "Should I text everyone every time he goes to the bathroom? Takes a shower? Eats a sandwich?"

"Jason," Mom whispers. "Don't."

"No," Detective Sterling says. "Jason is right. Dr. Archer is asking a lot, and we all get that. Still, if the kid's dreams or whatever they are can reach across town and incapacitate either or both of us, we need to take precautions."

"Of course we do," Mom says. "We don't want anyone to be hurt." She takes a step in my direction but stops midstride. "Isn't that right, Anthony?"

Each of them gazes at me through a different filter. Mom's eyes appear sad and apologetic, Detective Sterling's angry but composed, Dr. Archer's exhausted but compassionate, and Jason's simply fuming.

There is, however, one common element in each of their expressions.

An untempered emotion I feel as much as see.

Fear.

VII

TROIKA

I **awake with a start the next morning. The sky has just turned** pink outside. Last night, I set the alarm for eight, but I've beaten the clock by over an hour.

I waste no time climbing out of bed and starting the day. A splash of water from the bathroom sink washes the sleep from my eyes as well as the last vestiges of a dream that bordered on nightmarish. Unlike the various images that haunted me yesterday, however, this particular series of visions revolved around cyborg warriors from a war-torn future fighting dragon-riding knights from a forgotten past, all over the fate of a Pokémon hidden inside the idol from the opening scene of *Raiders of the Lost Ark*.

In other words, normal. At least for me.

More importantly, anything but the stuff of nineteenth-century Russian ballet.

I creep down the hall for Mom's room, hoping the relatively benign subject matter of my dream means Dr. Archer and Detective Sterling both got a decent night's sleep.

I crack the door and find Mom also awake despite the early hour. The sun barely peeks through her drawn blinds, the pale light revealing her hunched over her phone. She glances up at me, her furrowed brow smoothing as she fakes a smile.

"Good morning, Anthony."

"Hey, Mom." I step further into the room. "Did you sleep?"

"A few hours." She chuckles and glances down at the well-worn "Paris is for Lovers" T-shirt Dad gave her a year before I was born. The logo is all but completely worn away by countless trips through the wash. "I dozed off a little after two." She pats the bed by her side. "How about you?"

"Not too bad." I join her on the bed, flopping down atop the old down comforter. "Any word from Dr. Archer or Detective Sterling?"

She peers down at her phone. "Not a single call all night, thank God." She rests a hand on my leg, the slightest tremor in her fingers. "Why? Did something happen?"

"Not that I can tell." I swallow back the fear and dread rising in my throat. "It's a lot to take, you know."

Her head tilts to one side. "What are you talking about, Anthony?"

"This." I bite my lip to keep the tremor from my voice. "Dr. Archer says I'm the only person who can bring Mira back, and yet all I've ended up doing is hurting people." I swallow back a quiet sob. "Again."

"Anthony—"

"Awake or asleep, conscious or dreaming, it doesn't matter." My eyes squint as a ray of sunlight sneaks between the blinds and hits me full in the face. "Detective Sterling said it yesterday. I'm like a ticking time bomb."

Even in the dim light, I can tell Mom's cheeks shift to a deeper hue of red. "You weren't supposed to hear that."

I collapse on the bed. "At least with the Exhibition, the only person I was hurting was me. Then it was Rachel, Isabella, and all those poor girls. Now it's Dr. Archer and Detective Sterling, and worst of all, Mira herself." I stare up at the ceiling fan. The gentle breeze from its spinning blades brings goosebumps to my arms. "It just gets worse and worse, and it's all my fault. What am I supposed to do?"

"You fight, Anthony. You fight for what's right and you win." Mom pulls me up beside her to wrap me in a tight hug, and though a part of my brain rails against the sudden closeness, I let it happen. "I've thought about this a lot," she whispers. "All the times I told Mira to leave, no matter how hard I pushed her away, she never backed down. Not once." She pulls back and holds me at arm's length, regarding me with surprising pride. "You and she are cut from the same cloth, you know. Mira always found a way, and so will you."

"What about what Jason said?" My eyes shoot to the door, where down the hall, my brother likely still sleeps. "He thinks this is all too dangerous."

"We've already been through something like this, Anthony." The corners of her mouth turn up in an ironic smile. "Twice now, in fact, and if there's one thing I've learned, it's that the link between you and Mira is unlike any other."

"What are you saying?"

She shakes her head and even laughs a bit. "Even if Thomas hadn't asked you to help Mira, I'm guessing we would have ended up in the exact same situation." She squeezes my shoulders. "Don't you see? What you and Mira have is in a weird way, a marriage of the minds."

"A marriage?"

"You probably remember back before he died how your father and I would finish each other's sentences? How I knew what he was thinking sometimes before even he did? I understood William better than I did myself at times, and still the degree of intimacy we shared is nothing compared to what you share with Mira." Any semblance of a smile leaves her face. "As hard as it might be for me to accept, you've literally walked each other's minds. I'm not sure a bond like that can ever truly be broken." She bites her lip. "You may not remember all the things the two of you shared, but from what Mira has told me..."

I've got to tell her. She needs to know.

"Mom, there's something I need to—"

The phone lying half beneath my leg comes to life, chirping with Mom's distinctive ringtone. The sudden noise scares me and nearly sends me rolling off the side of the bed.

Mom grabs the phone and squints down at the screen. "It's Detective Sterling." She rises from the bed and answers the call. "Good morning, Detective. You're calling awfully early. Is everything all right?"

Mom keeps the phone pressed to her ear, but I do catch the occasional word or two from Detective Sterling's end of the conversation.

And then, a name.

One I'm pretty sure I'm not supposed to know.

Sarah Goode, the kidnapping victim Mira helped find a year and a half before she entered our lives and the only reason Mom had ever heard of a psychic who lives almost two states away.

The details of the case are way beyond anything Mom wants me to know about, I'm sure, but I've done my research. Cross referencing the names Mira Tejedor and Sarah Goode leads down a particularly deep rabbit hole. I doubt even Mira knows some of the stuff I uncovered visiting a few darker parts of the internet.

There is, however, another name neither Mira nor Mom is aware I know. A name that riveted the nation a couple years ago when I was theoretically too young to be watching the news.

A name that, once Mira Tejedor is a part of your life, you cannot forget.

"Wendell James Durgan." Detective Sterling sits behind his desk at the police station. "Do you know that name, Anthony?"

Mom grabs my hand. "Why would my son know anything about that monster? He's—"

"It's okay, Mom." I was expecting the question, even if Detective Sterling seems to have taken off the kid gloves in the way he asked it. "Durgan is the man that kidnapped Sarah Goode two years ago."

Mom gasps. "How do you know about that?"

"We've known Mira for months, Mom." I try not to wilt beneath her incredulous stare. "How could I not know?"

"Kid's got a point. Durgan is national news." Detective Sterling slides a manila folder across the desk. "Take a look. And by the way, there's nothing in there Anthony shouldn't see."

Mom grabs the folder up from the battered metal surface. "I'll be the judge of that."

She peruses the contents for a few seconds, her eyes flicking in my direction more than once, before speaking again. "I'm assuming, Detective Sterling, that there's a reason you've dragged us down to the police station before breakfast to look at pictures of a kidnapper and child molester who, last I heard, was rotting in jail?"

"Well, that's the thing." Detective Sterling clears his throat. "I received a call two hours ago from the police department up in Fredericksburg, Virginia." He takes the folder back from Mom and rests it on the desk, open to a picture of a man in an orange jumpsuit. "Effective 3:32 a.m. today, Durgan went missing from custody."

"Missing? How is that possible?" Mom draws close to me, her maternal instinct no doubt kicking in, though I'm not exactly sure what's got her hackles up.

The man in the picture doesn't even know I exist.

At least I hope he doesn't.

Detective Sterling closes the folder. "According to the call from Fredericksburg this morning, Durgan's case was finally slated to come up for trial next week."

"Next week?" Mom asks. "The Goode abduction was two years ago."

Detective Sterling lets out a quiet sigh. "As I understand it, Durgan has been held without bond for the last two years as the various lawyers and mental health professionals involved have tried to figure out what to do with him." His eyes glaze over. "No one is arguing the fact he's one sick individual, but does that 'sickness' buy him the insanity plea? That's the question everybody is trying to figure out."

"But how did he escape?"

"That, Ms. Faircloth, is where it gets interesting." Detective Sterling sits back down and steeples his fingers beneath his chin. "For the last couple of weeks, after months of relatively normal behavior, Durgan has been experiencing debilitating nightmares bordering on psychosis to the point of needing medication on a regular basis."

"And?" Mom asks.

"Last night, he apparently had the worst episode yet. Despite the risk, the police decided to transport him under heavy guard to the state psychiatric facility."

"If he was under guard, how did he escape?" I ask, although a part of me already knows the answer.

"A couple minutes before the car arrived at the hospital, Durgan had a grand mal seizure." Detective Sterling shakes his head. "One of the guards stayed with him to keep him from choking while the other ran inside to get help. When he returned, the first guard was found down and Durgan had vanished into the night."

Mom taps her fingernails on the desk. "Is the guard that stayed with Durgan okay?"

Detective Sterling's eyes flick to me and then back to Mom. "That officer has, unfortunately, not regained consciousness yet."

"So the man Mira helped put behind bars two years ago is on the loose." Mom's eyes narrow as if she's trying to peer through to Detective Sterling's soul. "I can see why you'd want to beef up security around Mira, but I still don't understand what any of this has to do with me or my son."

"Honestly," Detective Sterling murmurs as he runs his thumb along the edge of the closed folder, "it was something the officer that called this morning said." He hands the folder to me. "Anthony, take a look at the picture clipped on top."

I open the folder and stare down at the photo of the man in the orange jumpsuit. He's white, roughly the same age as Detective Sterling, tan with thick dark eyebrows, a well-trimmed goatee, and a shaved head. Neither smiling nor frowning, the man in the picture looks into the camera with calm assurance. This monster is patient, calculating, relentless.

And, apparently, loose upon the world at large.

"Have you ever seen this man before, Anthony?" Detective Sterling asks.

"Only on television and the internet."

"That's not what I'm talking about." He taps the side of his forehead. "I mean up here."

"Wait." Mom steps over to Detective Sterling. "You think Anthony has something to do with Durgan escaping?"

Exasperated, he turns to Mom, his fingers clenching and unclenching at his sides. "The officer I spoke to in Fredericksburg said there have only been three documented periods of Durgan having these spells. The most recent was the episode from last night. Before that was three weeks ago, a series of spells that lasted for just a couple of days. There was, however, one other time Durgan suffered from crippling nightmares—a period that lasted a week." He takes the folder from my hand. "Care to guess when that was, Ms. Faircloth?"

"Last September." Mother whispers the words so quietly they barely register. "And these nightmares. Did they have a common theme?"

"You're catching on." He flips through some faxed records at the back of the chart. "These are a few notes from the physician that works in the jail. All the notes regarding Durgan's nightmares from last year seem to revolve around references to witches and monsters and dark catacombs, but more recently, the subject matter has been a bit... different."

Mom eyes the folder. "Dark sorcerers," she whispers. "Evil magicians." She sucks in a breath. "Dancing puppets."

"See why you're down here now?" Detective Sterling pushes the chart back into my chest and points to Durgan's picture. "Now, I've got to know. Have you seen this man before in your Exhibition or wherever it is you and Mira have your meeting of the minds?"

"Anthony can't help you, Detective. He doesn't remember any of the—"

I gently grab Mom's arm. "It's okay, Mom. Let me try."

I stare again into the two-dimensional representation of Durgan's cool gaze, the man's eyes sending shivers through me. Still, though I study his every feature, nothing seems familiar beyond what I know from searching the internet for every scrap of information on the man I could find. I think back over every face from the Exhibition, every character from *The Firebird*, every staring face from *Petrushka*'s Shrove-Tide Fair. I even race back through my latest experiences. My walk by the waters of *Swan Lake*. The crowded party from the opening of *The Nutcracker*. And... nothing.

If Durgan has been a part of any of this, he's been hidden well.

"I'm sorry, Detective." I rest the folder back on the desk. "I don't think I can help you."

"Hold on a minute." Mom's hand trembles as she takes mine. "You're concerned Durgan might come here, but what about Sarah Goode? Has anyone warned her family her kidnapper is on the loose?"

"That's where it gets sticky." Detective Sterling palms his forehead with his massive hand and massages his temples with his thumb and pinky finger. "By the time the police got in touch with Sarah Goode's family, she had disappeared as well."

"My God." Mom nearly breaks a couple of my fingers. "Was she abducted?"

"No one knows." Detective Sterling sits back down behind his desk. "All reports indicate that even after all these months he still maintains a weird obsession with the girl." He pauses. "And her savior as well."

"So." I swallow back the fear at the back of my throat. "You think he has Sarah and now is coming for Mira."

"That's one theory. Virginia and surrounding states have put out an AMBER Alert for Sarah Goode, there's an APB out for Durgan, and I've put Mira's room at the hospital under around-the-clock guard until he's apprehended."

"I just hope that's enough." My response nearly sends steam pouring out of Detective Sterling's ears.

"And what exactly is that supposed to mean?" he asks.

I study the ground beneath my feet. "Just that everything I've read and heard about Durgan says he's already as focused as they come. Driven. Single-minded. If he's coming after Mira, he's coming big time." I peer into Detective Sterling's questioning gaze. "Add to that the fact that there may be an actual psychic connection between the two of them." An image of Sarah Goode's face framed in blonde ringlets flashes across my memory. "Or even all three."

"Once Mira started with Anthony, there was no stopping her." Mom brings her hand to her chest. "As good as her intentions were, there's no doubt she was obsessed with helping him, no matter the cost."

"One obsession fueled by another." Detective Sterling scratches his chin and picks up the phone. "I'll double the guard on Mira's room." He meets my gaze, the irritation I found there before replaced with nothing but concern. "As well as increase the patrols in your neighborhood." His eyes shift to Mom's gaze. "You have to know I'm doing all I can here, Ms. Faircloth."

"Understood." Mom clutches her handbag in two white-knuckled fists. "I have to agree with what Anthony said, though." Her eyes flick in my direction. "I pray it's enough."

VIII

BLACK SWAN

The rest of the morning goes by like pretty much any other morning. Mom and I head back home where we find the house still dark and silent. It's not long before Rachel is up, and not long after that when her high-pitched voice raises Jason from the dead. The four of us gather around the kitchen bar where Mom does her best to send us all into food comas with all-you-can-eat pancakes, scrambled eggs, and bacon. We're all pretty used to fending for ourselves in the morning and dealing with cold cereal, but I have a feeling this rare treat is nothing but a prelude to a serious family discussion.

I'm not disappointed.

"Jason," she starts. "I know you're not a big fan of everything Anthony is doing to help Mira, but—"

"What I'm not a fan of is my brother being put into a dangerous situation none of us can even begin to understand."

Mom takes the interruption in stride. "And you know in my heart of hearts I agree with you on that, don't you?"

"I suppose." The words come out as more grunt than speech. "What about it?"

"Well…" Mom shoots a glance in my direction. "It seems the situation may be even more dangerous than we knew."

Mom launches into an explanation of where we've been all morning and what we learned from Detective Sterling. Toward the end, especially when the subject of Durgan's appearance comes up, Rachel begins to tremble and Mom steps around the island to comfort her.

"Now, now, Rachel. I didn't tell you all this to scare you." She wraps Rachel in her arms and squeezes her tight. "For the next little bit, though, I'm going to need you to stay close to home. Don't go anywhere unless me or Jason is with you, understand?"

Her head pulled close to Mom's chest, Rachel gives a single nod.

"One thing I don't get," Jason mutters. "Say this Durgan guy does come for Mira. Why in the world would he give us a second thought?"

"Detective Sterling thinks Durgan may be looped in on everything that's going on between Mira and me." At Jason's incredulous stare, I add, "I think he might be right."

Rachel's eyes widen and Mom shoots me a perturbed look. "Rachel, maybe you should go to your room and let me and your brothers finish talking."

"No." I speak up despite my heart hammering in my throat. "Let her stay."

"She's too young, Anthony."

"She's eleven, Mom, and already a part of this, maybe more than we understand."

"I'm okay, Mommy." Rachel wipes a tear from her eye. "Don't send me away."

"Fine." She levels a no-nonsense glare in my direction. "But just so you know, when she wakes up at two a.m. with nightmares tonight, you're coming with me, do you hear?"

As if nightmares were the worst thing that could happen. "Got it."

"So," Jason says. "We're going to keep poking the bear."

"We're going to continue working to help Mira and keep our heads down until this thing with Durgan blows over." Her hands go to her hips. "In fact, you're watching Rachel this afternoon while I take Anthony to see Mira and Thomas."

"But—" Jason shuts down his retort before the second word is out of his mouth. For all his tough guy exterior, there's not a thing he wouldn't do for Rachel. Or me. Or Mom, for that matter. "Sure," he amends. "What time are you meeting them?"

"One o'clock." She checks the time on the microwave. "It's a little after nine. If you have stuff to do, can you be back by noon?"

"No problem." He gives Rachel's shoulder a playful squeeze. "So, kiddo. Lunch and ice cream later?"

Rachel's eyes go wide with excitement. "Can we get gelato?"

Jason flashes her a winning smile. "Of course."

"Yay!" Rachel speeds to the other end of the house, most likely to pick out her outfit for the day, and Jason follows, no doubt to grab a shower.

The two of us left alone, Mom turns to me. "You ready for today?"

I wipe the remainder of sleep from my eyes. "Do I have any choice?"

"Back into the breach. That's what she would say." Dr. Archer glances over at Mira's sleeping form and then brings his penlight up before my face. "Tell me, Anthony. Where shall we go today?"

"Back to *Swan Lake*, I suppose, as long as everyone is okay with that."

Detective Sterling sits in the corner fidgeting with his phone. He's trying to look cool and composed, but losing control of his body—not once, but twice—yesterday has left him visibly shaken. I feel for him, but only so much.

When he's had weeks of his life taken from him and has to do physical therapy for a couple months to get his legs strong enough to walk again, then we'll talk.

"Detective Sterling?" Mom asks when he doesn't say anything. "You in?"

His head bobs in a quick nod. "I'm in."

"And you, Thomas?" Mom asks. "There's no guarantee you won't get sucked in as well."

Dr. Archer tries to cover his trepidation with a smile. "There's no guarantees with any of this." He looks around the room, meeting each of our gazes. "For any of us."

"Can we just get started?" I interlace the fingers of both hands to stop them from shaking. "I'm not sure how much more waiting around I can stand."

"Very well." Dr. Archer begins the hypnotic ritual we've practiced together dozens of times over the years. The swaying penlight and his smooth baritone work their magic, the subtle back-and-forth of each playing at the edge of my mind like the lapping of waves along a distant lakeshore no man will ever see.

The rhythm of the waves soon fades into music.

The mournful theme of *Swan Lake* echoes in the darkness, and I'm immediately taken back to my last moments by the placid water. Barely healed wounds in my soul from witnessing the painful separation of Siegfried and Odette at the hands of the villainous von Rothbart are flayed open anew. Wallowing in despair, I pray for someone or something to end the loneliness, the isolation, the utter misery.

And then, in a blink, my prayers are answered.

The darkness dissipates.

The music shifts from sad to joyous.

And I find myself in another place entirely.

It starts with tympani, then drums and trumpet and woodwinds.

If the previous theme was a dirge, this new melody is a celebration.

An ornate palace forms around me, the intricate stonework and fine statuary indicative of royalty and wealth. Along one wall, an intricately carved double throne materializes, the shared back in the form of an all too familiar bird of fire and smoke and the double set of armrests fashioned to resemble a quartet of angry badgers. Fine tapestries roll down the walls depicting a long history of victories on multiple battlefields. Plush carpets of every color, shape, and size break up the monotony of the otherwise cold stone floor.

One moment, the throne room of this opulent palace stands empty and the next, clusters of courtiers fill every corner of the space. Paired off, the various lords and ladies gossip as if awaiting the commencement of some grand event. No sooner have I adjusted to the sudden appearance of all these strangers when, from an adjoining hall, a crowd of young maidens rushes at me. The six of them surround me, dancing in synchrony as each offers me some small token of their affection. Flowers, chocolates, trinkets. At first I don't understand, but then I remember in whose palace I stand and what that means.

In this part of the ballet, Siegfried's mother has arranged a lavish party and invited the loveliest maidens of the land to come and offer the prince their hand in marriage. In the real world, I may be just a kid, but here, I am Benno, best friend of Prince Siegfried, one degree of separation from the most eligible bachelor in the history of ballet.

No wonder these women are trying to curry my favor.

The six maidens clearly have traveled from every corner of the earth. One boasts skin as black as night. Another is so fair it appears her flesh has never seen the sun. Still another's features mark her as hailing from the Far East. Each of them dances to the same music, yet their movements couldn't be more disparate. Elements of every dance I've ever seen play out before me, from the formal to the casual to the tribal to the height of refined. The six maidens seem as real as any person I've ever encountered, and I have to remind myself they are nothing but flitting figments of my imagination.

And that begs another question. Do these women represent aspects of

Mira's subconscious or my own? Perhaps a combination of the two? Does it even matter?

Each more beautiful than the one before, the six women dance around me, their intricate gowns of black silk and gossamer white flowing like a gentle breeze as their disparate dances form a cohesive whole. As they pass before me, each one smiles and beckons me to draw closer. At the back of my mind, however, I never let go of one simple fact: in this story, I am merely a steppingstone to the real prize.

The unseen orchestra shifts from bombastic to a formal fanfare, announcing the arrival of the royal party. I raise an arm and motion for the women to follow me to the far corner of the room. No sooner have we cleared the floor than four couples dressed in finery fashioned of white silk with gold trim precede Siegfried and his mother through a grand door.

Leading her son to the center of the enormous room, the queen glides across the floor, dazzling in a gown of ivory with black embroidery, the full-length skirt billowing beneath an empire waist. Her elaborate crown of platinum and gold rests atop a full head of jet-black hair that spills down her back like a dark waterfall. She surveys the crowd, her kind eyes stopping briefly on me and the collection of six hopefuls.

Siegfried's gaze follows the queen's, and with a smile I've rarely found on the detective's face, he winks in my direction. The prince's royal garb matches his mother's, an ivory tunic with black embroidery at the sleeves, waist, and chest. I wonder if the woman beside him is a fabrication, like the various courtiers and maidens populating the space. Seeing the resemblance, however, I suspect Detective Sterling would find the dark-skinned woman's face all too familiar.

After a full circuit of the room, Siegfried and the queen spin as one and move toward the firebird throne as another fanfare sounds. Taking their cue from the musical shift, the six women surrounding me form up into two lines of three and put on their most winsome smiles. The melody reaches its end and Siegfried and the queen take their seats.

I rush to Siegfried's side. "Today, it would seem, is the day."

"It seems so, indeed." Siegfried's downcast gaze punctuates his frustration.

"The maidens your mother has summoned are breathtaking." I chance a glance at the collection of women in the far corner of the room who are all doing their best to not look in our direction. "They are eager to meet you."

"How has this happened, Benno?" He lifts his eyes to glance in the direction of the women. "Just yesterday, I would have been elated at the prospect of choosing a wife from among such beauty, and now all I feel is dread."

"Dread, Siegfried?"

His gaze locks on mine. "I cannot give my heart to any of these women. My love is spoken for."

"The Swan Princess?"

He nods grimly. "None other will hold a candle to her beauty, her elegance, her perfection."

Little does he know his reunion is coming sooner than he can imagine.

Or so he will be led to believe.

Von Rothbart, as we speak, plots against both Prince Siegfried and Odette. If the story goes as I recall, at this very event, the sorcerer will arrive with his own daughter, Odile, disguised as Odette the Swan Princess and trick Siegfried into swearing his undying love to an imposter. This betrayal, however unintentional, will cement von Rothbart's spell, leaving Odette forever cursed to a fate of swan by day and maiden by night.

Do I warn Siegfried? And if I change something so substantial as the outcome of this event, what effect will that have on saving Mira from her fate back in the real world?

The rules of this game, though set in some bizarre way by my own mind, remain hidden from me.

On the other hand, without knowing whom von Rothbart represents in this drama, does playing along merely play into his hands? If Siegfried chooses Odile and dooms Odette, does that also doom Mira forever?

How did Mira do this?

"Siegfried?" I whisper. "A word of advice."

"Of course, Benno." A genuine smile blossoms on his face. "There is no one I trust more than you."

"Then hear me and hear me well. Your heart and troth are serious matters. Even should the opportunity present itself, perhaps a moment of consideration before—"

"I already told you. My heart already belongs to one and one only."

"Not everything or everyone is what they seem, sire." I offer him a slight bow. "I merely suggest you consider carefully before making any rash decisions." I draw close. "Particularly if what is put before you appears to be everything you've ever dreamed of."

His expression darkens. "Do you know something I don't, Benno?"

"Merely giving out the best advice I can, sire." I repeat my bow. "Appearances can be deceiving."

"Come, Siegfried." The queen rises from her throne. "The time has come for us to meet our invited guests."

"Of course, Mother."

Siegfried and his mother take their place at the center of the room. At the queen's silent command, the invisible orchestra shifts to a waltz and the six maidens form a circle and begin another tandem dance. The queen returns to her throne and Siegfried walks among the six women vying for his affection, searching each of their faces for Odette's features.

Failing that, Siegfried steals away to his mother's throne, his heart and mind clearly a million miles away. His mother's glare, however, sends him back to face the women gathered at her royal invitation.

Their dance over, the six beautiful maidens line up from one end of the room to the other. The waltz shifts again to a pleasant yet repetitive tune that no doubt mirrors Siegfried's thoughts. With little art and only the bare minimum of energy, the prince greets the women one by one, taking each by the hand and allowing each a cursory spin before moving on to the next. Less than a minute later, he comes to the other end of the gauntlet, his eyes forlorn and his fist before a heart that already belongs to another.

Rising from the throne, the queen beckons me to come close. Instinctively, I rush to a far corner where a beautiful bouquet of flowers awaits. Pulling the tight bundle of lilies and other blooms from their vase, I gracefully approach the queen and offer the flowers with a deep bow. The queen, in turn, hands the bouquet to Siegfried.

The time has come for him to make his choice.

His choice, however, was made last night.

Siegfried brings the bouquet before each of the six maidens one by one, sizing each up with a glance before moving on to the next with a glance just shy of dismissal. As he passes the sixth, he hands the bouquet back to me.

"This is a farce, Benno." He holds aloft the symbol of his love, the extended index and middle finger of one hand before him as the other hand hovers over his heart. "You know as well as I my troth belongs to another."

And now, the moment of truth. Do I warn him the Swan Princess destined to arrive at any second is an imposter? That the woman who has stolen his heart pines for him back at the lake and that his actions could doom her to an eternity of torment?

The rules of this place are particular.

And I should know.

Still, I cannot let evil win. I must fight for what's right.

It's what Mira would do.

"Siegfried."

He turns to me. "Yes, Benno?"

"There is something you must know. Something I have to tell—"

An unseen force closes about my throat, leaving me unable to speak or even breathe.

A trumpet fanfare sounds in the distance.

From the hall's grand doorway enters von Rothbart, his feathered cloak traded for a lavish cape and ornate clothing befitting royalty, the owl features he wore by the lake now transformed into a human face.

A terrifyingly familiar face.

The face of Wendell James Durgan.

I only have a moment to process this, however, as my eyes drift to the woman on his arm.

Mira.

Or at least someone wearing Mira's face.

With dark brown hair pulled back in a tight braid beneath a shining crown and her face painted to accentuate her already striking features, the woman strides into the room in a form-fitting tutu the same design as the one Odette wore by the lake, though the white bodice and skirt have been traded for something a bit more... dark.

The Black Swan, in all her majesty, has arrived.

IX

ODILE

S he's here." Siegfried's eyes come alive. "My love has come."
I attempt to speak, but fail at even taking breath. I fall to one knee, struggling to remain conscious, and shoot a frantic glance in von Rothbart's direction. Not surprisingly, I find his eyes already fastened on me. An amused smirk spreads across his face as he waggles a finger back and forth and tauntingly shakes his head.

The pressure on my windpipe doubles and my hands come to my throat in a panic. Still, everyone other than von Rothbart seems oblivious to my plight. Darkness encroaches on my vision from every side and my mind flirts with giving in to sweet oblivion. I close my eyes in surrender and the unseen fingers around my neck release. As I fall to the ground gasping, the crowd surrounding me acts as if nothing is amiss.

Von Rothbart draws close to me and the entire room freezes in place. He hums a familiar tune before dropping a line from one of my favorite musicals, no doubt stolen from my very own mind.

"Those who speak of what they know find, too late, that prudent silence is wise."

The haunting tones of the owl-sorcerer's sung words are punctuated by the icy fire in his stare. No amusement. No humor. Just cold, cold hate. And all of it for me.

"Consider this your first and only warning, young Benno. This plot was set in motion a century ago, and interference on your part might have consequences you do not intend." He waves an arm in a magician's flourish. "Observe."

The far wall of the palace comes to life like the big screen at Charlotte Knights ballfield. Depicted there, Odette/Mira in her costume of purest white stands by a dark lake, alone. In the distance, a menacing storm brews.

A blink, and I'm no longer merely an observer, but within the scene. On my hands and knees, the cool, wet grass beneath me chills my fingers. Whispers on the wind fill my ears even as an overpowering ozone stench threatens to choke me. A copper tang invades my taste buds, followed by an earthy flavor that brings to mind an open grave.

Without warning, Odette turns her head and screams at the sky as a bolt of blue lightning splits the heavens and strikes her, sending her body into convulsions.

"*Stop it*," I scream. "Leave her alone."

Another blink, and I'm back on the floor of Siegfried's palace. All around me, the crowd continues to stand perfectly still, von Rothbart's magic keeping them immobile as he completes his warning.

"Up from the floor, Benno." He waits for me to get to my feet and brush myself off, and then draws close, his voice dropping to a gruff whisper. "Now, listen very carefully, boy, for I shall not repeat myself."

I give him only the slightest of nods, wisely keeping my silence.

Von Rothbart studies me like an insect pinned beneath glass. "It is clear you know precisely where this little drama is headed, at least as well as I do. Understand that you will not interfere with the events as they unfold unless you wish the Swan Princess to pay the price for your meddling." He steps back and looks me up and down, his gaze filled with utter derision. "Do we have an understanding?"

In command of my voice once more, I mutter two simple words as my eyes cut to Siegfried's hopeful gaze, the prince frozen midstep just a few feet away. "We do."

"Good." Von Rothbart claps his hands together and everyone else in the room returns to life as if no time has passed. Siegfried and the false Odette gaze at each other with an intensity rarely seen outside of movies. Meanwhile, the queen looks on with cautious joy, no doubt unsure exactly what to make of the beautiful creature clothed in black commanding her son's attention.

My heart hammers in my chest as I wrestle against my instinct to rush to Siegfried's side and warn him of von Rothbart's trickery. I have no doubt, however, that this sorcerer who wears the face of the man who turned Mira's entire world upside down will gladly carry through with his threat if I do anything other than smile and play along with the deception.

Von Rothbart rushes back to this false Odette's side and escorts her forward to meet the queen before allowing himself to fade into the background.

As if anything he did mattered. Every eye in the place is on Odile, the Black Swan.

This dark doppelganger of the Swan Princess drops to a low curtsy before the queen and then circles the room, her every movement demonstrating a level of grace and finesse the other six maidens can only dream of. But it's more than just elegance. Though both Odette and Odile move with refinement bordering on perfection, the White Swan's dance always suggests purity and innocence while the Black Swan's every turn, step, and glance exudes sheer seduction.

The misery on Siegfried's face from before already a distant memory, he watches Odile's every step with awe and wonder, as if he were watching the birth of a nascent star.

Unfortunately, the light into which he's staring is actually an oncoming train.

A fact I'm forbidden to share.

One moment the infatuated couple stand among us and the next Siegfried and Odile have disappeared into one of the many halls off the main room, leaving von Rothbart, the queen, and me with the remainder of the court.

The dominos are all in place. All that remains is to let them fall.

Von Rothbart takes Siegfried's seat by the queen on the double throne as the six rejected maidens and two trios of men from the court come together to entertain all present with a series of ethnic dances. Their performances bring flavors of Hungary, Spain, France, and Poland, each more impressive than the one before. Throughout, the queen maintains a quiet conversation with von Rothbart, her royal bearing betrayed only by eyes that constantly scan the room for the return of her son and the mysterious woman in black.

And with every passing moment, the sorcerer's smug grin grows only wider.

As the Polish Mazurka draws to a close, von Rothbart rises from the throne, and with a wave of his dark cloak, the music shifts into another fanfare that draws Siegfried and Odile back into the room. Absolute adoration beams from the young prince's face as he revels in the false belief that he has been reunited with the love of his life.

And still, I keep my tongue.

At least, for the moment.

Together the pair strides to the center of the room, arms held high above their heads, as they prepare to dance one of the most famous sequences in all of ballet.

The Black Swan Pas de Deux.

Exultant in the triumph of love, Siegfried's face glows with happiness I know good and well is destined to be, at the end of this dance, crushed like a flower beneath von Rothbart's heel. My gaze flicks to the sorcerer, and again I find his eyes already on me, a dark reminder of what will come if I speak a word of what I know.

And so begins a courtship in dance.

Odile goes first, every fluid movement more hypnotizing than the one before. The queen looks on in admiration as the mysterious woman in black enchants all present with her flawless performance. Spellbound by the Black Swan's beauty and grace, Siegfried soon joins her, putting Odile through a series of spins and carries that show off his new love to the world. At times coquettish and at others confident, this woman wearing Mira's face makes the most of her moment in the sun. Even my confused heart quickens as she draws near to the corner where I try to blend into the crowd.

With every measure of Tchaikovsky's score, Siegfried falls further under Odile's spell and further into von Rothbart's web of lies.

Throughout the dance, Odile toys with Siegfried's emotions, drawing close only to pull away, returning to von Rothbart's side time and again. The naive frustration grows in Siegfried's expression with each repetition of this ploy, and I wonder at how effortlessly von Rothbart's plan is coming to fruition.

Separated from the prince, Odile stops at one end of the room by her sorcerer father with Siegfried at the opposite. She and von Rothbart share a knowing glance, and then, with consummate skill, Odile pirouettes to the center of the room where a joyous Siegfried greets her with open arms.

Every eye in the place is glued to the drama playing out between the young lovers. Their dance grows more romantic with every bar of music, and yet at every instant when the pair's passion seems set to consume them, von Rothbart steps in and dances with faux Swan Princess himself. With each brief separation, the discontent in Siegfried's face grows, his desire boiling into dangerous obsession.

Obsession that is about to burn him worse than any fire could.

One moment worshipped and the next spurned, Prince Siegfried rides the emotional rapids of this public courtship as best he can, but in the end he is being played no less than any of the invisible instruments providing the music for the heartbreaking performance. Again and again Odile falls into the prince's arms, her body bending to his every touch and desire, only to return to von Rothbart's side.

I tremble with frustration, but the fate Odette/Mira will face if I breathe a word of what I know forces my continued silence.

Love, jealousy, infatuation, and anger all play across Siegfried's features. As if sensing he is losing the prince to the frustration of the game, von Rothbart returns to the throne next to the queen and allows the pair to continue their dance uninterrupted. Back and forth, Siegfried dances in the throes of young love while the Black Swan continues to beguile everyone in the room with her magical grace. Both performances demonstrate a mastery of human motion all but unattainable in the real world, Odile's maintaining the elegance of her avian namesake and Prince Siegfried's every movement capturing the energy of a puppy on the best day of its life.

As the pair again comes together, the moment of truth approaches like a dark tsunami even as the music turns playful and boisterous. Siegfried looks on with utter adulation as Odile puts herself through what seems an infinite set of pirouettes and answers with a full lap of the room, his every step a spinning leap. Odile responds in kind, spinning herself around the entire circumference of the room before leaping into Siegfried's arms to be held aloft before the queen, von Rothbart, and the entire court. The music crescendoes, capturing the emotion in an explosion of brass, woodwind, and percussion, as Siegfried lifts the beautiful girl in black to the sky in celebration of love fulfilled.

The queen stands, her hand raised in approval.

The crowd applauds.

And von Rothbart stands to one side, his lips turned up in the same perverse smile.

It's all a lie, and there's not a thing I can do about it.

Held aloft in arabesque position, her back arched and her leg pointed to the heavens, Odile's victory is nearly complete.

And therefore, von Rothbart's.

The enraptured prince lowers Odile to the ground only for von Rothbart to sweep her again from his arms and sequester in a far corner of the room. Siegfried is too caught up in the excitement, however, to realize the endgame has begun. He rushes to his mother's side, flushed with emotion, and whispers in her ear. The queen in turn scans the crowd for my gaze. At first, I have no idea why, but a glance down reveals I still hold the bouquet Siegfried is meant to present to the woman he chooses as his mate.

And so it comes to this. To hold my tongue, a lie of omission, is bad enough. But to hand the very instrument of love's destruction to a man who in this place is my best friend?

The ultimate betrayal.

And I have no other choice.

Von Rothbart has seen to that.

I arrive at the queen's side as Siegfried takes Odile from von Rothbart's arm and escorts her to stand before his mother. She is allowed a single curtsy before the sorcerer again pulls her away to the room's far corner.

He's making Siegfried work for every second of his own destruction.

I have never seen anything so cruel.

And considering the year I've had, that's saying something.

Siegfried pleads with his mother to accept this strange woman in black and with only a brief debate, she capitulates. Together they turn to me, and despite my every instinct screaming to run, to warn, to do anything else, I hand the bouquet to the queen and offer a bow.

I even wear a smile as I commit the treacherous act, thinking all the while of poor Odette/Mira waiting by the darkened lake for a lover who is about to pledge his love to another.

The queen hands the bouquet to Siegfried who wastes no time in crossing the room to bestow the token of love to the woman he believes to be the Swan Princess. Dropping to one knee, he holds the cluster of white blossoms up to Odile who gladly accepts the bouquet from the hapless prince.

The bouquet is not sufficient for von Rothbart, however, who separates the pair and stands between them. The sorcerer motions first to Siegfried, then to Odile, and then lifts his arm high, his index and middle finger extended in imitation of the prince's gesture of love. Without hesitation, the prince raises his own arm and pledges his eternal troth to the woman he believes to be Odette.

In that moment, von Rothbart has won.

The room goes dark as one entire wall becomes the edge of the dark lake where Odette languishes in agony. Falling to one side, the Swan Princess writhes on the ground, her last hope of freedom from von Rothbart's curse dashed on the rocks of Siegfried's unwitting betrayal.

Not to mention, my own.

The sorcerer sweeps Odile beneath his cape and the pair rush laughing for the nearest exit, though Odile does make a point to look back long enough to catch Siegfried's eye as she tosses the destroyed bouquet into the air.

The scattered petals break into a thousand points of white.

Odette's shattered heart, for all to see.

Sorcerer and daughter flee the room and I follow. The queen rests on the precipice of losing consciousness while Siegfried remains far too stunned by the abrupt reversal to do more than stare at the agony he has caused. Von Rothbart, however, is more than ready for me. Door after door slams itself in my face as I sprint down the longest hallway in the history of architecture, and yet, I somehow manage to stay no more than a few paces behind the fleeing pair. As the portcullis that guards the entrance to Siegfried's palace begins to fall, however, I stop in my tracks. This may be a realm of dream, but I'm not feeling especially suicidal today.

As the enormous iron gate slams into the ground at my feet, Von Rothbart peers back through the iron latticework and winks deviously before racing away with a grinning Odile by his side. Just as the pair is nearly out of sight, however, the sorcerer's daughter finally makes her first mistake of the evening.

Apparently weary of her guise as Odette, she rips her false face away and casts it aside. I catch but the briefest glimpse of the back of her head before she and von Rothbart round a bend in the road, but a glimpse is enough to see the shock of wavy blonde locks that courses down her back.

My heart freezes.

The list of villains in this realm sporting such a head of hair is notoriously short.

As Von Rothbart and Odile are beyond my ability to stop or even slow down, I return to the throne room where I find a despondent Siegfried wailing at his recovered mother's feet as she strokes his hair in a moment of sympathy.

But just a moment.

This is Siegfried a la Detective Sterling, after all.

Stepping to the center of the room, he holds aloft the symbol of his troth once more. Brass and tympani pound at our ears as the unseen orchestra echoes the beating of Siegfried's noble heart. The prince brings his hand down to his chest before rushing from the room. I sprint after him, not sure if I plan to help or stop him, to confess or keep secret my own part in this tragedy.

If I had trouble catching von Rothbart, however, I have no hope of catching the prince as he races to save the love of his life from certain death. This palace is his home, and he loses me in the maze of halls and doorways as he escapes to the countryside beyond the outer walls.

In defeat, I return to the throne where the other courtiers have surrounded the weeping queen. I drop to my knees by her side and look into the face of a woman I have no doubt is an exact doppelganger of Detective Sterling's mother a million miles away from here.

As the unseen orchestra pounds at me with explosive force, a voice cuts through the din. A voice that calls my name again and again. But not my name in this place.

Not Benno the coward, but...

X

STORM

Anthony."

Dr. Archer's voice, not nearly as soothing as when he was putting me under, hits my ears like a thunderclap, pulling me from the sudden darkness that precedes the final act of *Swan Lake*. My eyes close on the dimly lit interior of Siegfried's palace, the entire court lamenting the fate of their prince and his love, and open on Mira's room at the hospital. Standing hunched over me, Dr. Archer shakes my shoulders as he shouts my name again and again. Past him, I spy Mom trying to force a slumped Detective Sterling awake.

Most disturbing, however, is what I find when my still groggy eyes wander to the other side of the room. There, a team of nurses and doctors surround Mira's bed where the woman we've all come here to save suffers in agony. Her back arched like that of the dark ballerina who wears her face, her lungs work like a bellows. Her arms, stretched out to either side, writhe like serpents, though I know exactly what the movements actually represent.

The gentle up and down of the swan dancers' arms from *Swan Lake*—that is, if those dancers were being tortured within an inch of their life.

"How long has Mira been doing that?" I ask, my voice a raspy croak.

"Just a few minutes." Dr. Archer cranes his neck around. "Anthony is awake, Caroline. Any luck with Detective Sterling?"

"I'm trying," Mom answers. The abrupt crack of a slap echoes in the small space. "Are those smelling salts going to get here any time soon?"

"Any moment now," shouts one of the nurses by Mira's bed. "Will one of you please tell us what the hell happened here?"

"Just keep her stable," Dr. Archer shouts. "If we get the detective conscious, all of this should stop."

"Never seen shit like this in seventeen years," another nurse grumbles.

"Like something out of *The Exorcist*," the doctor at the head of the bed adds.

"Odette," Detective Sterling shouts as he starts awake. "I'm coming for you."

Immediately, Mira's contorted form relaxes and falls into the bed. The nurse rests her first two fingers below the angle of Mira's jaw and lets out a sigh, her relief echoed in the faces of the entire medical team. The doctor, not one I've seen before, takes a few minutes to check Mira and then steps over to speak with Dr. Archer. To say he looks displeased would be the very definition of understatement.

"Exactly what the *hell* are you people doing in here?"

Dr. Archer pulls himself up straight. "I've reviewed with Mira's attending physician exactly what we're trying to do. Her reaction today was unforeseen, but—"

"Look, Mr. Archer," the doctor begins, ignoring the vexed expression that crosses Dr. Archer's face at the deliberate besmirching of his title. "We've given you lots of latitude with visitation and guests, both based on your background and your relationship with Ms. Tejedor." He waves an arm at Mira's bed. "This, however, is unacceptable. I'm not sure what just transpired here, but it is not to be repeated." His eyebrows rise and his head shifts to one side. "Are we clear?"

Dr. Archer lets out a frustrated sigh. "As a midsummer sky."

The doctor looks over at me. "You feeling all right, kid?"

"I'm okay." I project as much confidence as I can, though my weak voice still sounds like I've been gargling battery acid.

"And you, Detective?" The doctor turns to Detective Sterling. "I knew you were in charge of the guards outside the door, but I wasn't aware you were a part of... this."

Detective Sterling attempts twice to stand and makes it to his feet on his third try. "It was news to me too, Doc." He strides clumsily over to the bed where the nurses are tucking Mira back in. "Can you tell if she's going to be all right?"

"Ms. Tejedor seems to be returning to her previous state, which, as you know, isn't optimal." He shoots a perturbed gaze in Dr. Archer's direction. "Still, at least her pulse is out of the 200s."

"We're just trying to help her." Mom's eyes drop. "The only way we know how."

The doctor lets out an exhausted sigh. "Not sure what went down with your little séance or whatever this was supposed to be, but another episode like this and the only thing you'll be helping her toward is an early grave."

All but one of the team of nurses files out of the room, the remaining tucking a lock of red hair behind a pale ear as she sits by the bed. "Want me to watch her for a while, Dr. Friedman?"

He nods. "The next few minutes should tell us what we need to know. Make sure her vital signs stay stable and that nothing else... untoward happens." They both shoot irritated glares in Dr. Archer's direction and then the nurse returns her attention to Mira as the doctor steps out of the room.

Detective Sterling, Dr. Archer, and Mom wait for the nurse to leave and then huddle around me to discuss what happened to Mira.

"Well, Anthony?" Mom asks. "Anything to tell us?"

Detective Sterling steps in before I can say a word. "He has her." His gaze shoots to me. "You saw him, didn't you, kid?"

My head drops in a subtle nod. "Durgan."

Mom gasps. "He was there?"

"He's more than just there." My shoulders fall. "He's von Rothbart."

I'm not sure who appears more flabbergasted by my words, Mom or Dr. Archer.

"Are you sure?" Dr. Archer asks.

"Wherever Anthony and I just were," Detective Sterling answers, "Durgan was there, and he had Mira under his control."

"That wasn't Mira." I bite my lip to keep it from trembling. "At least not the one in black."

"But..." Detective Sterling considers my words. "Wait. An imposter?"

"Just like in *Swan Lake*." I take a deep breath, trying to force down the fear building in my chest. "I didn't see her face," I whisper as I lock gazes with my mother, "but underneath her Mira Tejedor masque, she sports a full head of blonde hair."

"No." Mom steps back and grabs the bed railing as if she's about to faint. "It's not possible."

"Caroline..."

"No, Thomas. It's not fair. Mira has already destroyed her twice, sacrificed everything to save us from her insanity." Her hands tremble. "How many times must we face Madame Versailles before she's finally out of our lives?"

"First, we don't know for certain Versailles is behind this." Dr. Archer strides over to the door leading to hallway and peers out to ensure we're not being listened to before rejoining the circle. "Since Veronica Sayles died, I figured that was a name we'd never hear again, but seeing as how none of us know exactly how any of this works—"

"We need to keep an open mind." Detective Sterling shakes his head, chuckling at his own words. "Pardon the pun."

"So," Mom whispers. "What you're all saying is that it's possible a child molester from a state away might be loose inside Mira's head and running around with the psychopath that killed a pregnant high school student and tried to smother my child with a pillow? And you want Anthony to keep going in there?"

Dr. Archer raises his hands before his chest in surrender. "Perhaps, but it's just as possible Anthony superimposed Durgan's face on von Rothbart's form while in the dream state he and Mira share." He turns to me. "In fact, the same could apply to the blonde hair you saw Mira's doppelganger sporting."

"Come on, Thomas. This isn't our first rodeo." She jabs a thumb in Detective Sterling's direction. "The reports from the prison said Durgan had nightmares coinciding with each of Anthony's spells and now the creep starts showing up in Anthony and Mira's headspace? I know you're trying to help me stay calm, but nothing in Anthony's world of dream is ever coincidence."

"Caroline." Dr. Archer slides into his most soothing psychologist voice. "You have as much idea as I do about all of this. We're all of us making it up as we go along." He shakes his head. "All we know is this: Mira is comatose, Durgan is loose, Sarah Goode is missing, and Anthony, Detective Sterling, and I are the recipients of an all-expense-paid tour through the works of Tchaikovsky."

Mom massages her temple the way she does when a headache is coming on. "Why does this keep happening to us?"

Dr. Archer holds back the words I know are sitting on the tip of his tongue, so I voice them instead.

"It's all my fault."

"Anthony…" Mom tries to cut me off, but there's no stopping the flood now.

"Mira's current state—my fault." I lock gazes with Detective Sterling, then Dr. Archer. "All the stuff happening with you two—my fault." I turn my attention back to Mom, the heartbreak in her eyes somehow doubling the pain in my own chest. "Rachel, Isabella, all those poor girls that suffered under Madame Versailles, Durgan, Sarah Goode—it's all because of me and what I can do."

The room is silent. I figure either Mom or Dr. Archer will be the one to speak next, but the words of comfort I'm expecting come from an unexpected source.

"Listen, kid." Detective Sterling pats my shoulder. "I've brought in more than my fair share of monsters guilty of crimes so heinous you can't imagine. I've looked into the eyes of the innocent and the guilty. Trust me, your brain may be the catalyst for all this crap, but you are not at fault."

"But—"

Detective Sterling raises a hand, silencing my rebuttal. "Not. Your. Fault."

"Listen to the man, Anthony." Dr. Archer gently musses my hair. "There's no doubt a part of your mind is contributing to all of this, but as much as you're a part of the problem, you're also a part of the solution. A big part."

"We need you." Mom kneels before me. "Everyone you just named, maybe even Mr. Durgan himself, needs you to be strong. Can you do that, Anthony? Can you be strong?"

"I suppose." Words I've heard Mira say a good dozen times pass my lips. "What other choice do I have?"

Mom and I arrive back at the house a couple hours later. Dr. Archer felt everyone could use the rest of the day off, and Detective Sterling couldn't have agreed more.

When we get back, Jason's car sits in the driveway.

He and Rachel must be back from lunch.

If I'm expecting the third degree first thing when I walk in the door, I'm sorely disappointed. Instead, the house is silent. The hallway leading to the bedrooms is dark and the only movement is the ceiling fan in the den, which turns lazily above our heads.

I cast a glance at the empty kitchen and then shoot down the hall to check first Jason's room, then Rachel's. Both vacant.

"Mom?"

No answer.

I steal back into the main room and find the door to the backyard standing open.

"Mom?"

I race to the open doorway, my heart about to explode out of my chest.

"Hi, Anthony," Rachel squeals as she rockets down the sliding board and into the high grass, the yard in desperate need of a good mow. Jason, in turn, scoops her up from the ground and returns her to the top of the slide as if she were a sack of potatoes. Laughing, Mom turns and smiles in my direction, the first time I've seen the expression on her face in at least two days. She deserves this moment, even if that's all it is.

I trudge over to the swing set and grab my favorite seat. Jason shoots a nod in my direction and flashes me a smile before returning his attention to Rachel. Mom gives me a few seconds to myself as I do my best to process all that's happened since we awoke this morning. In the distance, someone is hammering—probably the new house going in down the street. The scent of smoked meat hits me, and my stomach, tied in knots till now, rumbles to life.

"Hey, Mom?"

She steps over to my side. "Yes, Anthony?"

"Can we have spaghetti tonight?"

"Of course, sweetheart." Her laugh warms my heart. "Of course."

Not only do we get spaghetti, but buttered croissants, and for dessert, chocolate pie.

All my favorites.

It's a good night. We don't discuss Mira as even the mentioning of her name makes Rachel cry. We completely avoid discussion of *Swan Lake* and *The Nutcracker*, as neither Mom nor I want to upset Jason again. For ninety minutes, we somehow keep the darkness at bay, enjoy each other's company, and keep up the facade of a normal family.

Not that normal has ever been the case in this household.

After Jason takes Rachel to bed, however, the kid gloves come off.

"So," Jason seethes as he steps back into the kitchen and sits across from Mom and me. "What mountain did we choose to die on today?"

"Jason," Mom whispers. "Don't start."

"*Swan Lake,*" I answer. "The part where things go all to hell."

"Sounds about right." Jason stares pointedly at Mom. "Anybody's head explode?"

"That's not funny." Mom stands and pours herself a glass of water. "Can you at least try to keep this civil?"

"Sure, Mom." Jason shakes his head and chuckles. "Civil it is."

Jason manages to keep the commentary to a minimum as I catch him up on everything Detective Sterling and I encountered in the dreamworld where my mind and Mira's have conjured one of Tchaikovsky's favorite works. Despite his sarcastic outer shell, however, the brother who has always listened to me when it's been important takes in every word with a mind sharper than most of his peers or even teachers ever gave him credit for.

"Wait." Jason stops me mid-sentence. "You saw Durgan there?" He turns on Mom. "The freak Detective Sterling was talking about that just broke out of jail like a couple hundred miles from here?"

"Jason," Mom says, "calm down."

"You calm down." Jason gets up from the barstool and paces the room like a caged tiger. "We've already had one psychopath come into this house and try to kill all of us." He massages the shoulder that took a bullet from Veronica's Sayles' handgun nine months ago not twenty feet from where we're sitting. "Call me crazy, but I'm not too keen on inviting another monster into our lives."

"No one is inviting anyone." Mom goes to the refrigerator, pulls out a half-empty bottle of white wine, and pours herself a tall glass. "Anyway, Thomas said it's possible Anthony's mind is just using Durgan's likeness as the face of the villain."

Jason's eyes narrow at Mom. "And from the look on your face, I can tell you believed that load of crap about one second longer than I did." He glances over at me with more than a hint of trepidation in his gaze. "There's another shitstorm coming. I can feel it."

"Jason." Mom lets out a defeated sigh. "Watch your language."

"Seriously?" He stretches his muscular arm in my direction. "Anthony's been stuck in a coma for a month, almost murdered by one of his teachers, attacked a year later by her psychic ghost, and now is being stalked by a known child molester and kidnapper both in the real world and his dreams, and you want me to watch the four-letter words?" Jason shakes his head and lets out a quiet groan. "Priorities, Mom. Priorities."

Mom raises a finger to shoot back, no doubt with all the anger and frustration of the day, but in the end, lowers her arm and mutters a quiet, "Know what? You're right."

"Mom." I go to her and wrap my arms around her waist as she tries to bring the glass of wine to her lips with trembling fingers. "It's okay."

"It's not okay," she answers. "None of this is okay."

"I'm sorry, Mom." Jason joins us, his strong arms around us driving away the fear of the moment. "I just want all of us to keep it real till this is over."

"Like we have any choice about that." Mom squeezes my shoulder. "Anthony and Mira both have said it a hundred times. This is happening, whether we like it or not." She kneels before me and takes my face in her hands, one warm and one chilled from the wine glass. "That's why we have to stick together." Her eyes lock with Jason's. "All of us."

"I'm not going anywhere." Jason squeezes us both tight. "You can count on that."

XI

BATTLE

When bedtime rolls around, Mom makes a point of tucking me in like I'm in first grade and leaves the hall light on, even though I know how much she hates the light pouring beneath her door when she's trying to sleep.

Like my mom needs an excuse to be overprotective. Yet another reason to hate Durgan.

Falling asleep should be difficult, considering everything that happened today, but within seconds of my head hitting the pillow, I'm fighting to keep my eyes open. Faces flash through my mind as I try to put all the pieces of the day together before sleep takes me.

Mira's. Detective Sterling's. Durgan's. A kaleidoscope of identities swirling together.

I pray for a normal night's sleep, for dreams based on nothing but the random firing of neurons processing the day's events, for one moment of peace.

As my eyes open on the darkened Christmas tree from the Stahlbaum house, one thing becomes exceedingly clear.

There will be no rest for the weary tonight.

A glance down reveals I'm trapped inside the body of one of Fritz's toy soldiers, the carved and painted torso, arms, and legs just visible in the dim moonlight that filters through the curtains. I ponder why the forms I take in the dreamworld are so often wooden. Something to discuss with Dr. Archer if I make it out of this alive, I suppose.

The doll form I now possess lies on the floor beneath the Stahlbaum's Christmas tree. I attempt to rise from the ground and find myself unable to move.

Paralyzed, every bit a discarded toy.

Except for my eyes. They seem to be working just fine.

I try to breathe but can't so much as open my mouth.

Stay calm, Anthony. This is all a dream. You can't suffocate in a dream.

And yet, I couldn't be any more afraid if Veronica Sayles herself was hunkered over me a second time, forcing the pillow into my face and screaming for me to hurry up and die.

Yes, Mom. I remember that part too.

The owl carving crowning the grandfather clock in the corner stares at me through the near darkness as the minute hand overlaps the hour hand at the top of the dial. Twelve chimes sound in the dim, the clear tone echoing from every corner of the room.

Midnight.

The witching hour.

With each strike, mice that walk like men appear one by one at the periphery of the room. Dressed in Victorian topcoats replete with military ribbons and accoutrement, their eyes flash a sinister red as they scan the dim. With the last peal of the clock, the twelfth and final mouse materializes from the darkness and they all freeze in place as if awaiting further instructions.

A moan from across the room captures my attention, followed by a hint of movement in the dark. I struggle to move, to shout, to breathe, and again meet with utter failure. Another moan and a previously invisible form beneath the tree sits up with a loud gasp.

Clara, the Nutcracker cradled beneath her arm, starts awake and peers through the darkness in every direction as if she's awakened from the most horrible of nightmares. Clearly, she fell asleep beneath the tree with her wooden guardian at her side, hoping no doubt for a night filled with visions of sugar-plums dancing in her head.

God willing, that's exactly where we're headed.

But first, of course, we'll have to battle for our lives.

Like a scene out of *Alice in Wonderland*, Clara begins to shrink, though to her innocent eyes, everything—the tree, the presents, the entire house— must appear to be growing. Suddenly too large for her to hold, the Nutcracker falls from her hands and rolls into the shadows beneath the tree's lower branches. In the low light, the mouse-soldiers encircle Clara, gleeful as their prey becomes more bite-size by the second, and pace in synchronous step with sinister music provided by the ever-present unseen orchestra.

Too panicked to even scream, Clara merely stares out into the darkness, eyes wide with terror, as she falls further and further into this dream within a dream. The mice close the circle around her, leaving the ever-shrinking Clara with her back to the tree and otherwise surrounded by fur and fang. Even then, she still can't see her assailants, their gray bodies blending into the shadows and only their flashing eyes visible. I attempt to inhale to shout a warning, and again find myself paralyzed. Even my eyes only obey the simplest of commands.

A front row seat and still helpless to intervene. The very definition of torture.

As Clara finally reaches the size of the toys laying discarded about the room from the Christmas party, she inspects the suddenly giant tree before her, the music swelling as she finds herself caught up in the majesty of the dream.

Taking advantage of her distraction, the mice rush at Clara from every corner, bringing a scream ripped from the very depths of her soul. She backpedals away from her attackers until she can go no further, the Christmas tree's lower branches blocking her only avenue of escape. Falling at her feet on every side, the mice alternate between gnashing their rodent teeth and stretching out their razor claws for her bare legs. The music builds and builds as they draw ever closer. With nowhere left to run, Clara drops to her knees and prepares for the inevitable.

The lead mouse charges Clara, eyes flashing red and canines gleaming in the dim light, only to draw back a moment later with a stump where its clawed hand had been.

From the shadows beneath the darkened Christmas tree steps the Nutcracker, its white-and-gold uniform iridescent in the gloom. Its wooden eyes wide and unblinking, its wooden jaw clacks down with a sound like the hammer of a gun. The unseen orchestra swells at the arrival of Clara's champion, and the mice all draw back together in fear.

But not for long.

The dozen mouse-soldiers pull together, and as one, rush Clara and her protector. In answer, the Nutcracker produces a gleaming curved saber from thin air and with clockwork precision cuts down the nearest mouse-soldier with a single blow. Two of the mice pull their fallen comrade to one side and then the eleven remaining resume their ominous dance. The Nutcracker launches into a series of leaps and thrusts, each more impressive than the one before, as the rodent army keeps a safe distance, ever watching, pacing, plotting.

And then, in the space of a heartbeat, the mice adopt a different strategy.

The mouse-soldiers reform their circle and like a noose around a hanged man's neck, draw tighter with each measure of music, each crescendoing note, each bated breath. The Nutcracker jabs at them, but the mice remain ever an inch beyond the tip of his blade.

Then, without warning, an explosion at the center of the room fills the air with smoke, signifying the appearance of a thirteenth mouse. A head taller than the rest, the enormous rodent on two legs boasts royal robes and an ornate crown of gold sparkling with a smattering of sapphires, rubies, and emeralds. The eleven remaining mouse-soldiers abandon their pursuit of Clara to kneel and bow in delight at the feet of the latest player in this drama.

The Mouse King has arrived.

Flush in his power, the Nutcracker's nemesis rides atop the shoulders of two of the mouse-soldiers, surveying his troops as if he were some rodent Genghis Khan. Clara buries her face in her wooden guardian's shoulder, the usual courage and confidence I've always found in those eyes replaced with abject terror. Undaunted, the Nutcracker brandishes its sword, taunting its tailed adversaries to draw near enough to taste steel.

Tympani drums roll, trumpets sound, and violins scream as the impasse between good and evil plays out.

And still, I lie here, useless.

His feet again on the ground, the Mouse King gathers his soldiers close and prepares for a new assault. In answer, the Nutcracker pushes Clara away, back into the shadows of the Christmas tree, and brings its saber before its chest as if it were a general directing troops.

The comparison, it seems, is apt.

As the stalwart Nutcracker holds its position, ready to filet any mouse, crowned or otherwise, that comes within range of its blade, a trumpet sounds in the distance, followed by the boom of a different cannon.

From the shadows opposite me, an army of toy soldiers appears. Dressed in the same blue coat, white pantaloons, and black boots that clothe my wooden form, the soldiers form a double line behind the Nutcracker, muskets at the ready and sabers at their sides. As the lone cannon, still smoking, comes to the fore, the Nutcracker turns in my direction, its enormous jaw and teeth turned up in a gruesome grin.

In an instant, strength flows into my limbs. Before our enemy can cut me off, I leap up from the floor and rush to join the front line of the Nutcracker's soldiers who readily accept me into their ranks. One sits atop a brown stick horse and the rest march on foot like me, yet all of us quiver in our boots as we steel ourselves for the coming onslaught. Across the floor, the Mouse King's troops stare in our direction, red hunger shining in their beady eyes, the crimson gleam echoed in the ravenous gaze of their crowned leader. With Clara at the center of the conflict, both sides prepare to wage a battle that has played out on stages around the world every Christmas for the better part of a century.

The irony?

In every version ever produced, the forces of good eventually win. Every single time. That's just how the story, music, and choreography go.

In this iteration, however, there are no such guarantees.

The Nutcracker raises its sword and sends its front line to engage the mouse army. The lone soldier on horseback charges the Mouse King, though his rush is cut short as a pair of mouse-soldiers pull him from his steed and hurl his shattered form beneath the Christmas tree.

The Nutcracker may have drawn first blood, but the Mouse King has answered in kind.

As a trumpet sounds in the distance, I with half a dozen others charge the mouse front line, the Nutcracker leading from the front. Our leader and his slashing blade makes short work of two of the mouse-soldiers before he is knocked to the floor by a single swat from the Mouse King's outstretched paw. As toy soldiers fall to my left and right, I fight to break through to help our downed general but find my way blocked by the gnashing teeth of a towering rodent that will make me think twice about ever visiting a Disney property again.

That's when I spy it—the discarded stick horse left behind by the dispatched toy soldier. In a move that would make Jason proud, I rush for the lost steed, slipping beneath the grasping claws of two mouse-soldiers like I'm sliding into third base.

I jump to my feet, grab the stick horse, and hurl it at the Nutcracker.

"Catch!"

For half a second, I fear my gambit has accomplished nothing and that I'm about to witness the Nutcracker's end.

I needn't have worried.

A wooden hand shoots up from the ground and snags the stick horse in midair. In a heartbeat, the music changes as a classical riff reminiscent of the *William Tell Overture* fills the space. Empowered by the imaginary horse held between its muscular thighs, the Nutcracker finds new strength to stand against the army of mouse-soldiers.

The battle rages on, with soldiers on either side falling prey to the utter violence.

When all is said and done, only four remain.

The Mouse King, eyes narrowed at his enemy with unmitigated anger.

The Nutcracker, its steed lost in the raging combat and its slashing blade directed at the Mouse King's whiskered snout.

Clara, her tear-streaked face twisted with horror.

And me, the lone soldier still standing amidst the carnage.

The Nutcracker and the Mouse King circle each other like wounded jungle cats, neither willing to look weak before the other. Enraged, Clara's defender charges its enemy, saber held high and powerful jaw agape, as if it can't decide whether to run the Mouse King through or simply bite him in half. The Mouse King, in turn, draws a scimitar from a sheath at his side, the first time he's deigned to use a weapon beyond his own powerful claws.

Steel clangs on steel as the two combatants commence their final battle. A terrified Clara looks on helplessly as the far stronger Mouse King drives the Nutcracker back again and again, parrying the wooden soldier's best blows with ease and finally knocking the animated toy to the ground.

Grabbing up a musket from the ground, I raise the weapon to fire on the Mouse King when rough hands fall around my neck. A forgotten mouse-soldier throttles me with one arm and knocks the weapon from my hand with the other. My vision darkens at the edges as the muscular forearm at my throat grows tighter and tighter.

Across the room, the Nutcracker scrambles to escape the deadly arcs of the Mouse King's slashing scimitar.

And Clara. Poor Clara.

She stands paralyzed, frightened beyond the ability to do more than simply stare.

This is her moment—the decision point around which all of this turns—and it's going to pass us by and leave both Mira and me at the mercy of a monster.

With the last vestige of strength left in me, I pull my elbow up and slam it straight back, hoping to drive the air from the mouse-soldier's lungs. The hairy paw around my neck loosens just long enough for me to get out three grunted words.

"Clara, your shoe."

At first, I can't tell if she's heard what I said, but as her head slowly turns my way, I give her one vigorous nod and train my eyes on the Mouse King like twin laser beams.

"Now."

Clara pulls the shoe from her foot and hurls it at the Mouse King. Timid though she may be, her aim is true and the heel of her shoe strikes the monster's skull, giving the Nutcracker the half-second opening it's needed since the fight began. A singular thrust upward with its saber pierces the Mouse King's belly just below his ribcage. The Mouse King howls in pain, but even in defeat, a glimmer of malice fills his rodent gaze.

"Don't," I scream despite the mouse-soldier's grip still at my neck. "Please."

With a low grunt, the Mouse King grabs the Nutcracker's shoulder and pulls himself further onto the blade protruding from his midsection. The Nutcracker's face twists into a pained grimace as it attempts to pull free, but the Mouse King's grip doesn't yield an inch. Despite the blood seeping between his razor-sharp teeth, the Mouse King's whiskered lips pull back into a smile as he brings the scimitar down and nearly takes off the Nutcracker's arm at the shoulder.

The Nutcracker bellows in agony.

Clara screams in terror.

The Mouse King howls in triumph.

As one, the Nutcracker and his opponent fall to the floor and do not move again. The mouse-soldier releases me and rushes to drag away the Mouse King's body as Clara collapses. I sprint to her side and catch her head before it hits the unforgiving floor.

"Clara," I whisper in her ear. "Stay with me."

"Who?" she murmurs, peering out from beneath half-shut lids. "You're—"

"It's me..." I search my thoughts for any name that might reassure her. "Fritz."

"Fritz?" Her eyes flutter open. "But why do you look like..."

"A toy soldier?" I point at the gigantic tree standing like a skyscraper before us. "Why have you shrunk to the size of one of your rag dolls? Why have my toy soldiers come to life to battle mice dressed in army uniforms?" My gaze flicks over to the fallen Nutcracker doll. "Does any of this make sense to you?"

Her entire body shakes as the tears start to flow. "My Nutcracker. That thing killed it."

"Wounded?" comes a deep voice that used to read me bedtime stories a million years ago. "Yes." Drosselmeyer, shrunk to the same size as Clara and me, stands over us, his eyes just visible above the folds of his dark cloak and beneath his coned hat covered in shimmering stars and magical sigils. "But killed? Not quite."

Drosselmeyer produces his wand from within the voluminous cloak and waves it over the Nutcracker's fallen form. Like a marionette whose strings have found a new puppeteer, the wooden doll pulls itself up from the ground and assumes a position of attention.

"He can no longer exist in this state." Drosselmeyer's mouth forms the words exactly the way my father's would have. "But perhaps with a few minor modifications, he can be made whole." His gaze drifts over to this place's juvenile version of Mira Tejedor. "Clara, if you will?"

As if she's rehearsed her entire life for this moment, Clara stands and positions herself next to Drosselmeyer opposite the wounded Nutcracker. The mysterious man wearing my father's face raises his arms above his head and for seconds that seem to last an eternity, all light leaves my vision and utter darkness rules my senses.

When I can again see, Drosselmeyer stands unchanged between two familiar figures.

Where young Clara was poised before now stands Mira Tejedor in all her full-grown glory. The nightgown she wore as her younger self replaced with a simple white dress and her bedroom slippers with ballet shoes, the woman standing before me appears exactly as I've known her for months. Her face beams with radiant happiness, and it's not hard to figure out why.

On Drosselmeyer's other side, where before stood a grotesque doll, now stands a man. The Nutcracker's tattered soldier's uniform has transformed into the fanciful ivory and silver of ballet royalty, the worn boots now pristine white tights over a dancer's legs.

No injuries, no weapons, just a man, his steady gaze confident and sure.

Gone as well is the hideous carved head I tore from Drosselmeyer's gift when I played the role of Clara's brother, Fritz, though the eyes of this new face aren't new to me.

The Nutcracker Prince looks upon us with the kind wit and wisdom of one Dr. Thomas Archer.

XII

SNOWFLAKES

Two worlds from the mind of Pyotr Ilyich Tchaikovsky.
Two women, each who wear the face of the second most important woman in my life.

Two princes struggling to save her from two disparate fates, each bearing the features of two men who, in the real world, would do anything for her.

It may be cliché, but history certainly seems to have a bad tendency of repeating itself.

Clara, flush with the rapture of her transformation, and the Nutcracker Prince, filled with the vigor of his rebirth, gaze at each other with both the wonder of first introduction and the intimacy of years.

Soul mates, as they always say in those movies Mom loves to watch.

Drosselmeyer steps from between the pair, allowing Clara and her prince to come together, and waves his wand. In an instant, the gigantic Christmas tree silently explodes with each branch forming a new tree around the periphery of the room. In a blink, the Stahlbaum house vanishes, and the four of us stand in a glade not unlike the clearing by the lake where I met Odette. Another blink, and snow begins to fall from the sky and covers the ground in seconds.

Pleased with his conjuration, Drosselmeyer flips the wand in his grip and holds it out handle first to the Nutcracker Prince. With a bow, the Prince takes the generous gift and in turn bestows it upon Clara with a wink and a joyful grin.

Another step back and Drosselmeyer disappears into the forest, his dark cloak blending in with the shadows between the trees. Clara and the Nutcracker Prince come together at the center of the clearing, my presence forgotten, and embrace like lovers kept apart for centuries. Invisible woodwinds and strings swell as the Prince falls to one knee and rests his head against Clara's hip, the longing in his expression matched by the elation in hers.

Their dance begins, a dance of love. Together, apart, and together again, they orbit each other with unmitigated faith that each separation is but temporary. At times, she moves with grace in the Prince's gifted hands, spinning *en pointe* like a whirling dervish or held aloft in lifts that challenge the laws of physics. At others, the two dance on opposite sides of the glade, their movements in tandem as if they were on either side of some enormous mirror. Most importantly, whether held in her Prince's hands or momentarily apart, there is no doubt that this pair, Clara and the Nutcracker Prince, are destined to be one.

Snow continues to fall, picking up with each passing minute until it becomes difficult to see. The music shifts and Clara leaps into her prince's arms to be held aloft in a position of triumph just as more dancers enter the glade. All female, each is dressed in the same white bodice and tutu and bears a wand that terminates in glistening white radiance.

The Snowflakes have come to lead their Prince home.

Clara looks on enraptured as one quartet after another of ballerinas enter the clearing until sixteen dancers surround them. She and her prince retire to one corner of the glade as the Snowflakes play out a gathering blizzard. The music turns whimsical and the dancers in white flit in and out of the space like the snowstorm they represent. All the while, Clara and the Nutcracker Prince fall deeper and deeper in love, their every glance in the other's direction ripped from the covers of books from the romance aisle at the local bookstore.

More and more Snowflakes appear until their number is higher than I can easily count, their performance growing more intricate with every passing moment. An eternity later, the synchronous dance ends with the pounding of tympani drums. In time with the martial beat, the Snowflakes all pirouette, leap as one into the air, and fall to the earth. In their midst, where only empty ground had been before, rests a wooden sleigh decorated in white with silver bows at every corner. No beast of burden stands shackled to the archaic sledge, but if I know this ballet as well as I think I do, none will be required.

Clara and the Nutcracker Prince come to the front of the sleigh from opposite directions and kneel before the silver wreath hung there. A lone harp sounds in the distance, followed by a swell of voices like the choir of Heaven. The countless Snowflakes surround the couple and bow to them in concentric circles three and four deep as if blessing their trip.

The Nutcracker Prince helps Clara onto the sleigh and then joins her inside. Clara returns the wand to her prince. With a single wave of Drosselmeyer's implement of power, the sleigh takes to the sky. Brass and woodwind and percussion crescendo into a tympani roll that threatens to make my ears bleed.

Then, for the first time in any realm Mira and I have visited, a curtain falls, fashioned from deep red velvet with gold embroidery and tassels decorating its fringes. Strangely, the expanse of fabric appears at first a normal curtain from any of a thousand theaters all over the world. However, no matter which way I look, before or behind, left or right, up or down, all I see is burgundy, the color unfortunately forever paired in my mind with drying blood.

And with that unfortunate association, this latest visit to the revolving door prison Mira and I share comes mercifully to a close.

Morning light peeks between the blinds.

That means I spent an entire sleep cycle in the world of *The Nutcracker*.

If that's the case, I'm betting I didn't go alone. Who did I take with me this time?

As if on cue, Mom's cell phone down the hall lets out a shrill tone, the sound sending a wave of cold down my back. It only gets halfway through the second ring before she answers. Her voice, barely audible through my closed door, suggests she's still in bed.

I check the clock. Almost eight a.m. A good ten hours unconscious, and yet I ache like I just ran a marathon before getting hit by a runaway train.

And if I feel this horrible...

Footsteps in the hall. A gentle knock at the door.

"Anthony?" Mom's voice. "Are you awake?"

"For about a minute." My voice comes out as a rough whisper. "Is that Dr. Archer on the phone?" I sit up, rub my eyes, and reach for my glasses as Mom cracks the door and peers inside, her face lined with worry.

"How'd you guess?" A haunted cast fills her eyes. "He wants to talk to you."

She sits on the corner of the bed the way she does when it's time for one of our patented mother-son talks and places the phone in my hand. "If you need me, I'm right here."

I bring the phone to my ear and before I can say a word, the raspy breathing on the other end sets my nerves on edge. "Hello?"

"Anthony." Dr. Archer's voice sounds deep and husky, as if he's been gargling thumbtacks. "Thank God. Are you all right?"

"I'm fine," I answer, my voice just as raw as Dr. Archer's. "Are you?"

"Still breathing if that counts." He pauses, no doubt trying to figure out his next question. Dr. Archer speechless—a rare event in my experience. "Did I just—"

"Travel to the world of *The Nutcracker*, fight the Mouse King and his legion of minions, and then dance in the snow with Mira in the form of Clara Stahlbaum? Yes."

Surprisingly, Dr. Archer answers me with a quiet chuckle. "You make dream analysis seem so easy."

I answer with a laugh of my own. "The front row seat tends to help."

I'm not sure which is stranger—the fact that I just shared a dream with the psychologist who's been helping me the majority of my life, or that we're suddenly talking like peers rather than therapist and client.

"What do you think?" he asks. "It's been a while since I've seen *The Nutcracker*, but unless I'm missing something, we just won, right?"

"If the events follow those of the original ballet, then yes." I swallow back the bile at the back of my throat. "Let's not forget about *The Firebird*, though. Mira followed that path all the way to the end and we almost lost everything."

"I did lose everything." Dr. Archer's voice, already little more than a grunt, grows quiet. "So," he asks when he has regained his composure, "what's next?"

"The Nutcracker Prince takes Clara to visit his kingdom," I answer, "a land of fairies and magic, music and dance, before returning her home. She awakes the next morning and finds the entire evening of adventure and romance has been nothing but a dream."

"But you don't believe that's how it's going to go down." Flat. Matter of fact. And most importantly, correct.

"Until we have Mira back, I wouldn't count on anything, Dr. Archer."

"Anthony," he whispers. "You're risking everything to help me save the woman I love and are braver than most of the grown men I've met, including me." He pauses. "I think you can drop the whole Dr. Archer thing and just call me Thomas."

I look over at Mom who has no idea what Dr. Archer has said. I roll the whole thing over in my mind and then answer simply, "Thank you. I'll give that some thought."

"All right." His exhausted sigh comes across the phone line loud and clear. "Can you put your mother back on? We should probably get together later this afternoon."

"Don't you have appointments?" I ask. "Other clients?"

Another laugh. "I feel like I haven't slept in days. I don't think I'd be doing anyone any good seeing them in this shape." He clears his throat. "Until we get this thing sorted out, it's just me and you, Anthony Faircloth."

"Just me and you."

And Detective Sterling. And Mira.

And Durgan.

"Got it." I pull in a breath. "Here's Mom."

I hand the phone back to Mom as the chill rolling up my spine drops another few degrees. Her expression more pensive with each passing second, she eventually raises a lone finger and excuses herself from the room. I can't imagine what Dr. Archer would tell her that he hasn't already told me, but then I remember the one thing that always trumps everything else.

In Mom's mind, she and Dr. Archer are the grown-ups. No matter how smart I am or how involved in this thing I already may be, I am still just her baby boy.

And this is Caroline Faircloth we're talking about.

Some kids may have tiger moms, but a small part of my mother lives in a house on chicken's legs and rides around on a magical mortar and pestle she uses to grind up and literally eat those kids for breakfast.

It's odd. We're all afraid of this Wendell James Durgan creep, but if he runs into my mom, it may be Durgan who needs rescuing more than Mira.

Mira.

In one reality, she is the Swan Princess, and her fate hangs in the balance between Siegfried's bravery and skill and von Rothbart's cunning and magic.

In the other, she and the Nutcracker Prince have just survived the Mouse King's onslaught and ostensibly are on their way to a land of dancing candies.

Von Rothbart wears Durgan's face.

His daughter Odile? Mira's, at least on the surface. What I saw suggests a certain teacher from *Tuileries* may have somehow yet again escaped death.

And as for the Mouse King? God only knows what hides behind those soulless eyes and matted fur. Can't anything just be simple? Just once in all of this?

Mom pokes her head back in. "Hungry?"

I climb out of bed. "Like I haven't eaten in weeks."

"Come on, then," she says with a grin. "Pancakes and strawberries it is."

Over breakfast, I do my best to relay to Mom everything that happened last night, ending with the Nutcracker's miraculous transformation and his spiriting Clara away in his sleigh through the most beautifully choreographed snowstorm I've ever seen.

"So," she asks, "that's it? Story's over?"

"Not exactly."

"And what do you mean by that? You think there's more?"

"Dr. Archer asked the same question." I take a bite of my pancake and wash it down with some milk. "The second act of *The Nutcracker* is supposed to be filled with nothing but goodness and light. Clara and her prince go off to the land of the Sugar Plum Fairy, the entire court dances for them, and everything is wonderful."

Mom's eyes narrow, studying me. "But you don't believe that's where the story is going, do you?"

"Have you seen what comes out of my imagination?" I pull a deep breath through my nose. "Not to mention if Durgan's mind really is somehow involved in all this..."

"We don't know that." Mom takes one last gulp of coffee and pours herself another cup. "That could all be simply the power of suggestion. You had just looked at all those files at Detective Sterling's office. Isn't it possible you're— what's the word—projecting?"

"After everything that's happened, I don't think we should assume anything."

"Then what?" she asks. "Say Durgan *is* coming for us and that he wants Mira and maybe even you dead. What else can we do? The police are already doing all they can to keep us safe."

I step to my window. The unmarked police car that's been across the street for the last day or so sits exactly where I last saw it.

"They'll do their best." I tap my temple. "But if Durgan is up here and inside Mira's head as well, he's got one up on all of us." I bite my lip. "Especially if he's somehow found a way to bring back Madame—"

"Don't speak her name." Mom downs a hunk of pancake. "I've heard enough about her to last a lifetime."

"Fine." I spear a strawberry and bite into its ripe sweetness. "Still, if she and some part of Durgan are working together..."

"Then this time around is more dangerous than anything that's come before." She stares down at the rest of her breakfast and then chucks it all in the trash. "Funny. I seem to have lost my appetite."

Me? Not so much. I wolf down the rest of my plate while Mom sips at a fresh cup of coffee.

I'm glad she decided to quit cigarettes long before I was born. If anything would drive someone to chain smoke, it would be the last month.

Jason, awake uncustomarily early, stumbles into the room in a pair of boxers and an old Foo Fighters concert shirt, his hair askew and his face bearing a couple days of stubble.

"You two are up early." Jason pours himself a cup of coffee, black, and gulps half of it down before joining us at the kitchen island. "Did I hear a phone before?"

"That was Thomas," Mom answers. "Anthony had another episode last night."

As if he's just received news that grass is still, in fact, green, Jason shoots me a sidelong glance. "You okay?"

"I'm fine." My voice is almost back to normal. "Dr. Archer sounded a little rough, but I think we both made it through this one all right."

"This one." Jason shakes his head, his usual glower firmly in place. "What was it this time?"

As I go over the events of last night's mental escapades, Jason listens intently, as does Mom, even though I just told her the exact same story half an hour ago. I know she's worried and understandably freaked out by all of this, but a part of me can't help but feel like I'm in the middle of an interrogation and that Mom is trying to catch me in a lie.

When I'm finished, Mom clears her throat and rests her elbows on the island's granite surface. "Tell him the rest."

Jason rests his empty mug by the sink. "There's more?"

"Just a feeling." My gaze wanders from Jason's concerned eyes to Mom's. "As it stands, I'm currently a minor character in two stories. *Swan Lake*, depending on the production, ends in either triumph or tragedy while the outcome of *The Nutcracker* is quite literally syrupy sweet."

Jason raises an eyebrow. "You're saying we've got a fight on our hands to make sure both stories end up the way we want?"

"No." My head drops. "I'm saying the stories in my head never seem to have happy endings and we should prepare for the worst."

"Anthony..." Mom pulls up beside me and does her best to comfort me with a reassuring hug. "Everything is going to be all right."

I pull myself from Mom's embrace and head for my room. "That's what Mira thought."

XIII

REUNION

I'm back asleep in minutes. My brain exhausted from a full night in the ether between Mira Tejedor's mind and mine, the hours I spend unconscious are dreamless. Though I awake feeling physically refreshed, the fragmentary sensation of things left unfinished, ideas unresolved, decisions unmade, won't leave me.

I drag myself from beneath the covers. My clock shows it's a little past one and the brightness beyond my drawn blinds suggests it's afternoon.

But the same day? I have no idea.

I wander into the family room where Mom, Jason, and Rachel are watching a movie on the DVR.

"Mom?"

"Anthony." She rises and comes to me. "You're awake."

Shrugging off her hug, I ask, "Are we still going to visit Mira today?"

She takes a step back. "Do you feel up to it?"

"Does it matter?" I glance over at Rachel, caught up in the bright images pouring off the screen, and Jason, who pretends to watch the movie but is no doubt listening to every word we say. "Nothing has changed. Mira still needs help and I'm the only one who can reach her."

"I'm just looking out for you." Mom looks away, a hint of tears at the corners of her eyes. "Understanding with my head that you're doing what needs to be done doesn't make it hurt my heart any less."

"I'll be okay, Mom." I steel myself and allow her to hug me. "I promise."

Mom calls Dr. Archer and he agrees to meet us at the hospital at three. Another call and Detective Sterling is on board as well.

As we get off the elevator, one thing is clear.

When Detective Sterling puts someone under guard, he doesn't mess around.

One officer patrols the halls while a pair of CMPD's finest, as Jason always calls them, stands at either side of her door. I've never seen either of them before, but they seem to recognize both of us. Regardless, they still ask us for identification.

Good to know they're taking this seriously.

Inside the room, Detective Sterling, Dr. Archer, and Mira's treating physician, Dr. Friedman, are in the midst of an argument.

"I'm not sure what went down in here yesterday," Friedman says, "but we cannot have a repeat of that. You put Ms. Tejedor's life at risk, not to mention your own, the detective's," his gaze shoots to me, "that young man's."

"You think I don't know that?" Dr. Archer throws his hands in the air. "In case you haven't noticed, Mira is in a coma and being fed through a tube. Her life is already at risk, and if we can't wake her up..."

Friedman turns to Detective Sterling. "Not to mention I still don't understand the increased police presence on my floor. You do know you're frightening the other patients, right?"

"Just routine security precautions." Detective Sterling looks away, no doubt hoping the interrogation will end there.

He is sorely disappointed.

"Routine security? Against what?" Friedman's mouth turns down in a frown. "Or who?"

Detective Sterling crosses his arms. "I'm sorry, but I'm afraid I can't tell you that. Trust me, though. CMPD has this well in hand."

Friedman's eyes narrow. "Somehow, I don't find that the least bit reassuring."

Dr. Archer steps in. "Let us keep working with her. Please. If we manage to bring her out of her comatose state, Detective Sterling plans to put her in a safe house far from here. Until then, however, the hospital is the safest place for her."

Friedman lets out a frustrated sigh. "So we can clean up the mess next time all this 'psychic' nonsense sends everybody in the room into a seizure again?"

"It's not nonsense." Mom's voice, just above a whisper, commands the attention of everyone in the room. "You may not like it, Dr. Friedman, but you can't possibly believe we're faking all of this. For God's sake, you saw Mira before. Do you think she's in on it too?"

Friedman backs down. A bit. "No one is saying Ms. Tejedor isn't ill, but if we continue to find nothing medically wrong with her, the only explanation that makes any sense is a form of conversion disorder, where she truly believes herself to be comatose and her mind follows suit."

"You think this is all in her head?" Detective Sterling asks.

"Not too far from the truth," I mutter to sharp looks from both Mom and Dr. Archer.

"And how would you explain Detective Sterling's unconscious state?" Mom's eyes shoot in my direction. "And Anthony's?"

Friedman shakes his head, his lips tight. "A shared delusion? Or perhaps... hypnosis?" His eyes narrow. "You are, after all, a licensed hypnotherapist, aren't you?"

Dr. Archer pulls back as if struck. "You think I'm responsible for this?"

Friedman's head tilts to one side, his gaze turning derisive. "Your version is that you, the detective, the boy, and Ms. Tejedor share a psychic link and that you and the others are entering her mind again and again in an effort to bring her out of a coma. I'm merely suggesting that making someone fall into a deep trance or flap their arms like a bird is well within the skill set of a hypnosis expert such as yourself. You tell me, Dr. Archer. Which is the more plausible explanation?"

Dr. Archer's nostrils flare, though he manages to keep his voice even. "That's quite the accusation, Dr. Friedman."

"Now, hold on." Friedman raises his hands before his chest. "I'm not accusing anyone of anything. I'm just... broadening my differential."

Detective Sterling shakes his head. "Sorry to shoot holes in your theory, Doc, but Archer here is on the up-and-up. I can assure you of that."

Friedman shoots him a withering look. "Says the man that had to be awakened out of a trance state not twenty-four hours ago."

"Dr. Friedman." Mom gently pushes Dr. Archer out of the way and comes nose to nose with the man. "Dr. Thomas Archer has cared for my son for years. He's spent countless hours helping him with his unique issues, even to the detriment of his own health." She glances in Dr. Archer's direction and then locks gazes again with Friedman. "In fact, if you check his medical record, you'll find *he* was the one lying comatose in this very hospital not three weeks ago—"

Friedman clears his throat. "I am well aware of what happened with—"

"I'm not finished." Mom puts her finger in Friedman's chest. "We've never out and out discussed it, but you know good and well Mira Tejedor fell ill the very same day both our daughters as well as ten girls in the pediatric hospital and Dr. Archer all miraculously recovered from a mysterious ailment not one doctor in this hospital could diagnose."

"Ms. Faircloth…"

"Interrupt me again, and we will be asking for a new doctor to take over Mira's care. Am I making myself clear?"

Friedman's face relaxes into a placating smile I've seen more than my fair share over the years. "Please. Continue."

"Try as you might, what happened here last month is beyond anything that can be explained by medical science or found in your textbooks. Explain it away as you must, but what Mira and Anthony can do is real. I've seen it. I've felt it. If you don't let us keep trying, you're dooming her to spend the rest of her life this way. Is that what you want?" Mom crosses her arms, defiant. "Is it really more important for you to be right than to help this woman who sacrificed everything to save thirteen people's lives, ten of whom she'd never even met?"

"Of course not, Ms. Faircloth, but—"

"I certainly hope you don't think I'm under some sort of hypnotic spell, Dr. Friedman."

A bitter chuckle escapes Friedman's lips. "No, Ms. Faircloth. You seem quite awake to me."

"Good." Her gaze wanders to Dr. Archer's, then to Detective Sterling's, then to mine, before lighting on Mira's still form. "Then please. You and your team continue to keep Mira physically sound, and we'll keep working on the problem at hand."

"Very well." Friedman heads for the door. "But another incident like yesterday, and per hospital protocol, I will have to limit visitors to family only. Am I making myself clear?"

"Perfectly," Dr. Archer murmurs. Mom, on the other hand, only raises an eyebrow before returning to Mira's side. After Dr. Friedman shows himself out, Detective Sterling joins her at the bedside with Dr. Archer close behind.

"That was incredible." Detective Sterling studies Mom with a newfound respect. "Have you ever considered a job in law enforcement?"

Dr. Archer lets out an ironic laugh. "I was thinking more drill sergeant."

I come and sit at the foot of the bed. "Enough jokes. We're here to help Mira, and we just won the right to do so. I say we get started before Dr. Friedman changes his mind."

"Ah, my brave, brave child." Mom looks at me, her lips parting in a radiant smile. "We're ready whenever you are."

We're almost ready to start when Mrs. Tejedor brings Isabella by for her daily visit with Mira. We drop our preparations immediately and work to keep the conversation light to avoid upsetting the poor girl for the few minutes she gets to see her mother. Once she's gone, however, we begin again, as every hour that passes makes the chances of Sarah Goode's survival more and more remote.

Dr. Archer and Detective Sterling take positions on either side of Mira, each sitting in chairs we borrowed from the waiting room down the hall. That leaves me the lone hospital-issued recliner in the room, now positioned at the foot of the bed. Mom, far too busy pacing to sit for more than a minute, watches from the corner, trepidation etched into her features.

One of the nurses who was present for the big event yesterday comes into the room and adjusts the settings on Mira's IV. She tries to ignore us and pretend like everything is status quo, but I catch more than one furtive glance out of the corner of her eye.

To be honest, I can't blame her. I don't imagine nursing school has a class on psychic phenomena.

Once the nurse leaves, we get started. Detective Sterling takes a few deep breaths, steeling himself for what's to come. Mom, ever the caregiver, strokes Mira's temple with a damp washcloth. Dr. Archer, studying me from his chair, pulls out his penlight, but I motion for him to put it away.

"We won't be needing that today." I close my eyes and incline my head to one side. In the distance, and no doubt audible to no one but me, an unseen orchestra already plays a hauntingly familiar tune. "It's already begun. Tchaikovsky is playing in my head as clearly as if I were wearing headphones." I open my eyes and fix my gaze on Mira's placid features. "Look out, Mira. Here I come."

"Be careful, Anthony." Mom's hand shakes as she dabs at Mira's brow. "And come back to us."

I force a smile. "Don't I always?"

One of my teachers always says you can never truly understand someone until you've walked a mile in their shoes. If the last few days have taught me anything, it's that I had no idea of the bravery Mira Tejedor showed each time she helped me till I was the one who had to go walkabout in other people's heads. Still, no matter how terrified she was or how much it cost her, she never let it show.

At least not to me.

I owe her the same courage.

As easy as walking through an open door, I step into the space between my mind and Mira's. A glance down confirms I again wear the blue-and-white-clad form of Siegfried's best friend, Benno. Booming percussion pounds at me like a prizefighter while an army of flutes and clarinets run up and down mysterious arpeggios written more than a century ago. The screech of countless violins rails against my nerves while blaring brass deafens me with the raw power of a thousand trumpets.

The final act of *Swan Lake* has begun.

Things are about to get interesting.

Out of the darkness comes Siegfried, exhausted from his run and drunk with despair. In this place, mere moments have passed since I walked the royal hall of the prince's palace. The shock and sorrow on his face left by his own unwitting betrayal of his true love remains fresh. He stumbles through the clearing by the lake, searching for Odette to beg her forgiveness.

From the treeline, a pair of swan dancers rush by to a fanfare of horns, knocking Siegfried to the ground as they pass. Another pair charges past him, then another and another, until the embattled prince is surrounded by an octet of a ballerinas. Closer and closer they dance, their eyes cruel and filled with anger

When Siegfried betrayed Odette and cursed her to live the rest of her days as a swan under the control of an evil sorcerer, so too did he curse her flock.

Swans may be one of the most beautiful of God's creations, but they are not creatures you should cross.

The eight swan dancers stand poised to descend upon Siegfried when a roll of tympani accompanied by a triumphant swell of the invisible orchestra heralds Odette's return. Atop a jagged boulder by the lake's edge, she arches her back and reaches to the sky in lamentation of her fractured love. Siegfried spins to find her lithe form silhouetted against the rising moon. She turns her gaze in the prince's direction and her face fills with sadness and hurt.

Undeterred, Siegfried runs to her, his arms held out in contrition even as his eyes brighten at being again in the presence of such beauty and grace. Odette draws back at first but even her spurned heart can't resist the pull of her true love's fervent gaze. Descending from the enormous stone with the grace of her namesake, the Swan Princess joins Siegfried at the center of the clearing.

They move as one, their dance one of longing and regret, of heartbreak and apology, of anger and forgiveness. The lovers reunited, they grow closer and closer as the music slows. Their every movement in concert, Odette's expression vacillates between absolution and remembrance while Siegfried's eyes remain steadfast throughout. Together and apart more times than I can count, the remorse in Siegfried's every step, every gesture, every glance eventually wins Odette back to his side. Soon they dance again as they did upon their first meeting, he the skilled potter and she the clay in his supple hands. As the dance of sweet reunion concludes, Siegfried rests his head on her bare collarbone, enraptured, though the tragedy that looms remains etched in his features.

The music shifts to a mysterious back-and-forth between strings and woodwinds as the octet of swans returns to the glade. Gathering around the pair of lovers, they bear witness as Siegfried again holds aloft his two-fingered salute, pledging his undying love for Odette. In response, the Swan Princess holds aloft her arms and spins in an excited pirouette before falling again into Siegfried's embrace. The clearing by the lake fills with the entire flock of swan maidens, all in celebration of the triumph of love. Happiness fills the darkened glade, and for a moment, it's as if von Rothbart's deception and the prince's resultant betrayal never occurred.

A moment, unfortunately, that cannot last.

I came into this whole thing already knowing more about the works of Tchaikovsky than the average person, and in the last few days I've researched countless references to *Swan Lake* and *The Nutcracker* on the internet and even had Mom run me by the three libraries in our area to pick up as many books and magazines on the two ballets as I could find.

The one thing I've learned from all this research?

Swan Lake has nearly as many endings as it's had productions over the last century. A scant few end with Siegfried and Odette's love conquering all and the pair living the happily ever after of every Disney movie ever made. The majority, however, end in disaster of varying degrees. In most of these, good still somehow triumphs in the end, but almost always at the cost of the lives of the two leads.

And even that cold comfort isn't guaranteed in this place.

The worst part? From my vantage here at the forest's edge, there is little I can do but stand by and bear witness.

Benno's part in this story is done.

A lone flute plays in the distance as Siegfried and Odette come again to the center of the clearing. The entire complement of swan maidens lines up on either side as if they were the bridesmaids at an impromptu wedding. The prince allows his princess to spin in his hands once, twice, three times. Then, as the unseen flute warbling resolves into a single curt note, Odette arches her back and neck until it nearly touches a leg held back in arabesque pose and Siegfried raises an arm to the sky in triumph.

Before I can take so much as a breath, the music begins anew. The ominous tremolo of a swarm of violins fills the air with dread as von Rothbart, his features that of the wide-eyed owl, steps from the shadows of the boulder by the lake's edge. The main theme from *Swan Lake*, voiced by a lone oboe, begins in earnest as the furious sorcerer pushes through the line of swan maidens to confront the determined prince.

Forcing himself between Siegfried and Odette, von Rothbart spreads his dark owl's wings wide as the final conflict of *Swan Lake* simmers on the edge of a boil. The sorcerer's back to me, an image flashes across my imagination, of Benno sprinting across the clearing to attack the villain, saving his best friend's life and leaving behind his fear, his cowardice, his shame.

My shame.

I tense to leap from the shadows, but before I can make a move, von Rothbart's owl's head turns fully around to gaze in my direction. My heart freezes. Can the sorcerer see me in the dank darkness of the forest's edge? I don't have long to ponder the question as one of the round yellow eyes slides closed in a cruel wink.

That's when everything becomes perfectly clear.

He doesn't just know I'm here.

He wants me to watch.

XIV

SWAN SONG

Nose to curved beak, Siegfried and von Rothbart face off, the prince's features filled with righteous anger and the sorcerer's with smug victory. The flock of swan maidens trembles in fear, but at a single wave of von Rothbart's hand, they become perfectly still. Even Odette, her face frozen in terror, moves not a muscle as she falls even deeper under the sorcerer's thrall. My heart racing, I step from the shadows to help Siegfried only to have my own limbs betray me as von Rothbart's spell immobilizes me as well.

In silence, the sorcerer motions to the transfixed Swan Princess and then holds aloft a mocking imitation of the prince's two fingered salute, reminding Siegfried of his broken vow to Odette and the repercussions of his rash decision.

Siegfried's eyes fill with regret, and more than a little fury. He brings his hands over his heart and begs for Odette's freedom, but von Rothbart ignores the prince's pleas. The sorcerer's trickery has brought him victory, and he knows it.

As a sign of his power, von Rothbart sets the entire flock of swan maidens to dancing in two large circles, their arms fluttering up and down like the graceful waterfowl that have captured their souls. Siegfried takes advantage of the distraction to pull Odette to one side in an attempt to break her from her trance, but von Rothbart is on them in an instant, his power not to be denied. His love torn from his arms by von Rothbart's magic, Siegfried remains relentless in his pursuit of Odette, but even the unbridled passion found in the prince's heart cannot withstand the sorcerer's indefatigable resolve and cruelty.

Von Rothbart sends Odette to dance in line with the rest of the swan maidens, her heart, mind, and soul bent again to the urges of her dark master. Again and again Siegfried valiantly attempts to get to her, and each time von Rothbart mercilessly blocks his path. The prince's incessant efforts, however, tax even the considerable resources at von Rothbart's command.

First one, then another, of the swan maidens disengages from their coordinated dance, their movements and minds momentarily their own. As a third breaks away from the tight formation, von Rothbart's eyes go wide, his absolute sway over his flock diminished.

The sorcerer's attention again divided, Siegfried dives beneath von Rothbart's outstretched wing and again takes Odette in his arms, lifting her body above his head. At first she remains as stiff as a mannequin, but with each passing second her form becomes more supple, more responsive, more alive. Her leg straightens into arabesque position, her arms stretch out to her sides, and her graceful neck arches back in triumph.

Despite von Rothbart's machinations, Prince Siegfried and his Swan Princess are together once more.

Von Rothbart exerts his inescapable will and brings the entire flock—save Odette—again under his control before returning his attention to the pair of lovers. Finding them in a passionate embrace, the sorcerer's simmering rage finally boils over. He rushes at them and, with a blow from one mighty wing, hurls Siegfried to the unforgiving ground and sends Odette's body flying end over end to the far end of the glade.

Tears run down my cheeks like twin rivers, but despite my every effort, my feet remain frozen to the spot as von Rothbart gathers himself to finish the battle once and for all.

His dark pinions spread wide, the sorcerer descends upon the winded prince like the bird of prey whose form he wears. Siegfried brings his arms before his face in a futile effort to protect himself from von Rothbart's slashing beak. The unseen orchestra crescendoes into a dramatic clash of brass and percussion and all seems lost.

As Siegfried suffers beneath von Rothbart's brutal attack, a change overtakes Odette. As if waking from a horrible nightmare, her taut muscles relax and her glassy eyes come into laser focus. Her angry gaze leveled at her cruel tormentor, I fully expect Odette to leap upon von Rothbart's feathered back and pull the crazed man-bird from her lover's twisted form. Instead, she flees to the boulder by the lake's edge.

His owl's eyes wide, the sorcerer leaps from Siegfried's bloodied form, spins in Odette's direction, and raises his arms high. The entire flock of swan maidens answers in kind, with each raising a curved arm above their head, allowing their bodies to adopt the graceful silhouette of the majestic bird that overtakes each of their forms at daybreak each morning. Feathers sprout from every inch of alabaster skin, full crimson lips extend into black beaks, and lithe arms transform into mighty wings. Within seconds, the entire entourage of enchanted maidens have become true swans, their plumage the brilliant white of a fresh snowfall, the beauty of their doom made manifest.

Of all the swan maidens, only Odette remains in human form, a fact that gives even von Rothbart pause. He rushes at the boulder where the Swan Princess stands, the smugness in his gaze tarnished, as she steps closer and closer to the edge.

Standing at the precipice, Odette turns, tears coursing down her face as her eyes fall upon Siegfried's wounded form. Von Rothbart halts beneath the enormous stone, tracing mystic sigils in the air as he tries to once more enrapture the Swan Princess, but to no avail. The *Swan Lake* theme fills the air once more, the oboe replaced with blaring brass and thundering percussion. With one last glance in her love's direction, Odette raises her arms to the sky and leaps into oblivion.

"No!" I scream, my raw emotion echoed in the sorcerer's silent rictus of pain. As if struck by an invisible bolt of lightning, von Rothbart falls to his knees in agony, the first sign of weakness he's shown. Despite all his power and influence, Odette has freed herself at last from his dark machinations, and the loss clearly takes its toll.

Good. May the bastard rot in hell.

I suck in a breath, the first I can remember taking since von Rothbart shut me down with no more than a wink of his round owl's eye. Sensation and strength flooding my limbs, I rush from the shadowy forest and make my way to Siegfried's side, but look away from his slashed face and throat before my stomach rebels.

Though I stand in a dreamworld formed from a bizarre interface of my mind and Mira's, Detective Sterling's maimed features appear as real as anything I can imagine.

"Benno?" he murmurs.

"Siegfried," I whisper as I look down into his pained features. "You're alive."

He coughs a streak of blood onto his royal tunic. "Am I?"

I attempt a smile. "For the moment."

Something tickles my brain. Something I'm missing. Something important.

"What now?" he asks.

"Now," comes von Rothbart's guttural tone, "you both die."

Both our gazes shoot in the direction of the sorcerer. Recovered, he stalks toward us, the self-satisfied air that's surrounded him since our first encounter replaced with utter fury.

"Come, my prince." I slide my hands beneath Siegfried's arms and attempt to pull him to his feet, though his body has become so much dead weight. "If we don't run, he'll kill us both."

"I can't move." His grunted whisper fills my heart with terror. "My arms. My legs. It's like they're not there."

"Fear not, Prince Siegfried." Von Rothbart looms over us, a gleam in his predator's eyes. "You have but seconds left for such concerns."

"Come on," I grunt, tugging at Siegfried's arms. "We've got to go."

"No." Siegfried groans in anguish. "It's over."

"Not yet," I answer as a subtle smile overtakes my features. "Not by a long shot."

A stir of movement all around us captures my attention, as does the not-so-subtle shift of the *Swan Lake* theme from minor to major key. I remember something Mira told me months ago, when she first explained to me why she was a part of my life.

"Even in your worst moment," I whisper, "you must find hope."

"The only hope you have remaining, boy, is that I grant you a quick death." Von Rothbart descends on us, his yellow eyes flashing with fury, only to be knocked to the ground by a rushing mass of swans.

"What?" he grunts. "How is this possible?"

The army of swans becomes just that. Freed from von Rothbart's influence by Odette's sacrifice, they flail their feathered forms at their dark master, colliding with his body, nipping at his wings, and scratching at his eyes.

The dark sorcerer may outstrip the swan maidens in raw power, but against their combined strength, even the mighty von Rothbart must take heed.

I drag Siegfried toward the lake as three dozen swans descend upon the sorcerer. Sparing but one glance back at the carnage, I channel the rest of my energy into getting the prince to our destination in hopes the enchanted waters there can somehow return the strength to his limbs. After what feels like a year, I drop exhausted onto the lake's bare shore with Siegfried by my side.

"Here." I dip a cupped hand into the cool water and bring the refreshing liquid to his lips. "Take this."

"The very water that took my beloved?" With the last ounce of strength in him, he swats my hand away and clenches his eyes shut in defiance. "I'd rather die of thirst."

Apparently, nothing today is going to be easy.

"My prince, the legend states this lake was born from the tears of all the mothers who lost their daughters to von Rothbart's madness. Surely you wouldn't have your own mother's added to its expanse, would you?"

He glares at me and then offers a grudging nod. I gather another palmful of the cool water and deliver it to his open mouth.

"Another," he whispers.

Mouthful after mouthful, he gulps down the frigid liquid. Slowly, the color returns to his cheeks and even the wounds of his face and neck begin to close. Soon he is strong enough to scoop his own water from the lake and by the time his thirst is finally slaked, Siegfried is healed.

Together, we turn in time to see the result of the battle between swan and sorcerer. Von Rothbart flees the glade in defeat, his winged cloak torn from his shoulders and left in tatters on the ground. As he hits the tree line, he looks back with one yellow eye, the other now a gaping hole, and disappears into the shadows. In answer, the army of ivory waterfowl honks in victory.

Then, in a flash of silver, they are swans no more, but maidens, unfettered at last. Freed of von Rothbart's influence, they gather in small groups to comfort each other, seemingly oblivious to our presence. One of the maidens, however, her face and movements strangely familiar, strides in our direction.

"Prince Siegfried," she says, "though all gathered share in your undoubted sorrow, let it be known we owe you a great debt. Thanks to your and Odette's sacrifice, we are finally freed from von Rothbart's foul sorcery. For all you've done and all the suffering this day has caused, we can never repay you."

"I did nothing." The prince stands and offers the maiden a polite bow. "Nothing, that is, save betray my love and watch her die as a result of my recklessness."

"Do not blame yourself for falling victim to the sorcerer's deception." She waves an arm in the direction of the gathered maidens. "You look upon centuries of young women von Rothbart has duped into his clutches. Odette may have been his favorite, but she was far from his first." Her eyes dart in the direction of the woodline where von Rothbart disappeared. "He is as much trickster as enchanter, that one. Would that we could have destroyed him today, but I fear my sisters and I have merely given the world a brief respite from his evil."

"But all of you are free now," I ask, "aren't you?"

"And will remain so," she answers with a nod, "though each of us will likely remain on our guard for the rest of our days." Her eyes grow distant. "I fear more for the world, full of innocent young girls just waiting for the right words to lure them away from the safety of their homes and into the sorcerer's web of lies."

I flash briefly back to the scene from the palace, where von Rothbart shed his owl facade and his true face stood revealed. My stomach turns as I recall what the man with those selfsame features did in the real world, and more importantly, what he is capable of now. I pray what I saw was indeed just some game my psyche is playing with me, but if we really are facing off against Wendell James Durgan, then today's battle was just the first of many.

I motion to the crowd of young women in white. "If any of the other maidens are injured, you can bring them to the lake." I motion to Siegfried, who continues to look stronger by the second. "The water of the lake has healed the prince. Its frigid currents might help them as well."

The maiden's gaze drops. "That's not how it works, I'm afraid."

"Pardon." Siegfried's brow furrows. "What do you mean by that?"

The maiden steps closer and takes Siegfried's hand. "Simply that these waters don't heal. In fact, the placid waters before us represent a large part of the enchantment that held us all in thrall for all these years. I hope to never set foot in the damned thing again."

"But look at him," I stammer. "He's fine. How do you explain that?"

The maiden's eyes narrow at Siegfried, as if she's measuring whether he can handle the truth. "Oh, the prince has been healed. There is no doubt about that." She turns and walks away, shooting one last glance in our direction. "His one true love just drowned herself in that lake because the idea of living without him was unimaginable. If anyone is going to find succor in its cruel expanse, it's him."

As she rejoins the cluster of young women at the center of the clearing, the bob of her wavy red hair gives me the final clue as to her nagging familiarity.

Her knowing eyes.

The subtle freckling of her nose and cheeks.

Her voice.

Though a good decade older than the girl I ate breakfast with this morning, the maiden clearly is an avatar for Rachel, though whether we were actually speaking with my sister just now or her face was merely another I've created in this funhouse between my mind and Mira's, I have no idea.

I scan the crowd for any other familiar faces, and failing that, return my attention to a grief-stricken Siegfried who stands there on the verge of tears.

"She gave her life for me," he whispers between choked sobs. "And now she's gone forever."

"Perhaps." I glance across the lake where the sun is just peeking above the water and catch just a flash of a pirouette before the first full rays of sunshine blind me. "Perhaps not."

I turn my head away from the ever-growing ball of light and survey the crowd of maidens as they gather together to return to whatever remains of their various homes and families. Each dressed in the same identical white bodice, tutu, and headdress, telling one from another seems all but impossible. Try as I might, I can't find the one that resembled Rachel, but in my search for my sister's familiar eyes, I catch a glimpse of something else important I might have otherwise missed.

In the forest edge, beyond the crowd of young women in white, stands a lone girl in a black tutu. Something about her, like the maiden who spoke with us, seems strangely familiar, though the distance makes it difficult to make out her features. One aspect, however, is unmistakable.

Her full head of long blonde hair, reminiscent again of a certain teacher from *Tuileries*.

I rise from the ground to confront her when a lone yellow eye, round and as big as a saucer, appears in the shadows directly behind her and narrows at me.

"What is it, Benno?" Siegfried stands and peers across the clearing with me. "What is it you see?"

When I look again, both the girl and the hate-filled eye are gone as if they were never there.

"Nothing to speak of, my prince." I fight to keep the tremor from my voice. "Nothing at all."

No drama accompanies this awakening. No rush of doctors. No alarms.

Just the bleary eyes of a nap that went on a bit too long and the disorientation of waking up in a place that isn't my bed. As my vision clears, I hope against hope that the first eyes I meet will be Mira Tejedor's. As my gaze settles on her still comatose form, however, my heart sinks.

"It didn't work," I mutter. "All that, and nothing."

"Welcome back, Anthony." Mom's whisper, close by my ear, wavers with emotion as her hand, cold as ice, falls on my neck. I turn and gaze into her face, a face that seems to have aged a decade since we ate breakfast.

"I found her, Mom." The quiet beep of Mira's heart monitor, even and steady, does little to raise my hopes. "She won. Von Rothbart was defeated and the swan maidens were freed. Why didn't she wake up? What did I do wrong?"

She doesn't answer.

"Mom?"

"I don't know, Anthony." Her hand falls away, leaving my neck somehow even colder. "I just don't know."

I focus on the two chairs positioned on either side of Mira's head. Detective Sterling, still coming awake to my right, appears none the worse for wear from the punishment his doppelganger just sustained in the dreamworld. The chair where Dr. Archer sat, however, rests empty.

"Detective Sterling?" I whisper. "Can you hear me?"

"Give him a minute." Dr. Archer's deep baritone echoes from somewhere to my rear. "As deep as you went, Anthony, Detective Sterling went deeper." He brushes my left arm as he passes and plants himself at the foot of Mira's bed. Fixing me with a humorless gaze, he utters two words that ask a million questions.

"*Swan Lake?*"

"Yes."

"Is it… finished?"

I swallow. "Yes."

His eyes narrow. "What happened?"

I tell him everything. Every horrifying detail.

Halfway through my tale, Detective Sterling comes around. He doesn't interrupt, though more than once as I finish the story, he offers a solemn nod.

When I finally get to the part where Odette leaped into the lake, Mom lets out a small gasp, Dr. Archer winces, and Detective Sterling's head drops in shame.

"Another sacrifice." Mom goes to Detective Sterling's side. "And this one to save *you*."

"It's not the same." Detective Sterling searches my face for support. "Right, kid?"

"That wasn't Mira," I mutter. "At least, not exactly."

"What do you mean by that, Anthony?" At Dr. Archer's question, he, Mom, and Detective Sterling turn the same baffled gaze at me.

"Simply that while Odette may have worn Mira's face and is no doubt linked to the woman we all know and love, the Swan Princess who just died before our eyes was not Mira in the same way the others were. As I understand it, even when she was Scheherazade, Ivanovna, the Ballerina, or the Spring Maiden, she maintained some part of her true identity and could act upon the events at hand. As Odette, though? She was merely acting out a role." My gaze drops. "I didn't see even a glimmer of our Mira in those dark eyes."

Dr. Archer strokes his chin. "She doesn't know who she really is."

"And therefore," Mom whispers, "she can't liberate herself." Her gaze shoots to me. "She's trapped in her own story, just like you were last year."

"I didn't do enough." I take a long cleansing breath in an effort to clear my head. It doesn't help. "And that story is now over."

"There's still *The Nutcracker*," Dr. Archer says, allowing himself a moment of hope. "Perhaps the answer is there."

"We'll see." I rise from the chair and go to the window where a gentle rain has begun to fall. "Though from what I've seen Mira is just as lost inside Clara Stahlbaum as she was inside Odette."

"It's up to us, then," Dr. Archer mutters.

"No. It's up to me."

I glance back at Dr. Archer, Mom, and Detective Sterling.

Mira.

"This time around, *I'm* the free agent." I return my attention to the dismal sky beyond the glass. "Which is funny, because I feel anything but free."

XV

Autumn Song

Dinner is quiet.

Mira's mother, Rosa, has again taken Rachel for the day. Mom barely had the energy to warm up the pizza we're eating, Jason is being his usual surly self, and I'm too exhausted to do anything but chew.

Every time Rosa comes around, I can see in her eyes how devastating all this is for her. At first, I thought it was strange how she seemed so content to leave Mira's care and recovery up to us, but with each passing day it makes more and more sense.

Considering everything her granddaughter went through last month, she wants to shield Isabella from as much of this as possible.

By taking Rachel, Mom and I are free to help Mira, unencumbered with worrying about my little sister.

But most of all, if I, the only other person we know who can walk minds, feel so helpless after everything that's happened the last few days, I can only imagine how useless she must feel.

Her very own daughter, and all she can do is watch her lie there and suffer.

Pretty sure I wouldn't hang around.

The doorbell rings and Mom jumps up from the table. Rosa, Isabella, and Rachel were supposed to hit the Uptown kid's museum this afternoon and then head back in time to join us for dinner, but if I know my sister as well as

I think I do, I wouldn't be surprised if she talked Rosa into taking her and Isabella out for burgers and milkshakes.

Girl's almost as persuasive as me.

An unexpected deep voice from the next room captures both my attention and Jason's.

"Who is that?" Jason asks as he rises from the table. "Detective Sterling?"

"Not with that accent." I perk my ears up to listen more carefully and catch Mira's name. "New Yorker... maybe with a hint of world traveler?"

"What now?" Jason disappears into the next room and I follow, hot on his heels.

As we round the corner, we find Mom standing in the foyer with a man and a woman I've never seen before.

Square-jawed and handsome, the man is dressed in a button-down shirt and dark jeans, his expensive haircut fading past his ears into three days' worth of stubble. Like some sort of Hollywood demigod, he flashes me a grin and puts his well-muscled arm around the woman at his side.

As beautiful as any of the models featured on the glossy magazine covers down at the supermarket newsstand, the woman raises an eyebrow when her gaze meets mine. Even the quizzical expression looks like something lifted from a movie poster. A full head of blonde locks flows well past her shoulders and her toned legs pour from beneath a designer dress into shoes I have no doubt cost more than our monthly mortgage payment.

Jason shoots me a quizzical glance. At my casual shrug, he strides over and posts himself at Mom's side.

"Everything okay?" he asks.

Mom glances back at Jason and me, her brow furrowing. "Jason, Anthony, this is Dominic MacGregor and his fiancée, Autumn."

Mira and I have never discussed her personal life in any detail. I'd have to be blind to not notice that she and Dr. Archer are involved in a serious relationship and pretty dense to not realize that things with her and Detective Sterling are also complicated. But all I know about her ex-husband is from an accidentally half-heard phone conversation between Mira and her mother a few weeks ago.

Mr. MacGregor is Mira's ex-husband and Isabella's dad. Autumn, as far as I know, is the woman he left Mira for. Neither of them rate very high on Mira's list of favorite people, but from what I overheard, it sounds like she's doing her best to make the situation work for Isabella's sake.

None of this explains what the two of them are doing standing in the foyer of my home.

"You and Mira," Jason asks. "You used to be married, right?"

"That's right." Mr. MacGregor allows himself a chuckle and shifts his attention to me. "I'm Isabella's dad."

"Nice to meet you." I put on the smile Dr. Archer taught me to use when meeting someone new, especially someone I'm not sure I'm going to like. "What are you doing here?"

"Anthony," Mom whispers, "what have we said about being polite to people we've never met?"

"Give the kid a break, Mom." Jason reaches out a hand to Mr. MacGregor. "Hi. I'm Jason, Anthony's older brother."

Mr. MacGregor takes his hand and gives it a brisk shake. "Pleasure."

"Sorry if Anthony's question seems a bit brusque," Jason says, "but I'm kind of wondering the same thing."

"Boys." Mom rolls her eyes and jumps in. "Like he said, Dominic is Isabella's father. He and Autumn have been out of the country, but have returned from... somewhere in Africa?"

Mr. MacGregor smiles. "I've been on a shoot in Zimbabwe since May. Took a few days to get back stateside."

Autumn steps up. "Rosa called us." If her fiancé's accent hints of upper crust Manhattan, then Autumn's reeks of it. "She wanted to know if we could come to Charlotte and help care for Isabella while Mira is..."

"Incapacitated," Mr. MacGregor finishes. "We came as soon as we could get away."

My brow furrows. "But why are you here in our house?"

As if in answer, the doorbell rings again. This time Jason answers the door and is nearly bowled over as Rachel leaps into his arms. Close behind, Rosa and Isabella step inside.

"Daddy," Isabella shouts as she rushes to her father's side and wraps her arms around his waist. "You're back!"

"Wild elephants couldn't keep me away." He shoots Autumn a wink. "And they definitely tried."

Rosa surveys the situation and then offers the couple a perfunctory smile. "Dominic," she intones with a subtle nod. "Autumn."

"Nice to see you again, Rosa." Autumn holds out her hand and Mrs. Tejedor gives it a quick shake. "We just flew in from Africa. We had a couple hour layover in Atlanta, but we're here."

Mr. MacGregor pulls Isabella up to his chest and envelops her in a bear hug. "Mira?" he asks Mrs. Tejedor with a questioning look.

Rosa puts her finger to her lips and inclines her head in Isabella's direction. "Later."

"It's good to see you, Isabella." Autumn drops to one knee and holds her arms out. "Did you miss me?"

"Of course I did." Isabella drops from her father's arms and scoots over to give Autumn a perfunctory hug. "Did you and Daddy bring me a present?"

"Actually..." Autumns face breaks into a wide smile. "We got you three presents." She flashes a quick look at Mr. MacGregor and then returns her attention to Isabella. "They're out in the car. Do you want to see them?"

She looks up at her father so excited, I'm afraid she might explode. "Can I, Daddy?"

"Sure. Just don't open them until I can watch, okay?" Mr. MacGregor shoots his daughter a wink. "Especially the big one."

"The big one?" Isabella grabs Autumn's hand and all but drags her to the door.

No sooner are they outside than Mom shoots my brother a knowing glance. "Jason, why don't you take Rachel into the kitchen and get her something to drink."

"But I'm not thirsty," Rachel complains.

"Come on, kiddo." Jason heads for the kitchen with Rachel on his hip. "There's a juice cup in the fridge with your name all over it."

No sooner are they out of the foyer than the mood shifts deadly serious.

"All right, Rosa," Mr. MacGregor whispers. "What the hell is going on? What happened to Mira? Is she all right?"

Caroline steps between them. "Mr. MacGregor, come join Rosa and me in the den." She meets my gaze for half a second before leading us all beneath the arch of the foyer and into the next room. "This is probably going to take a minute."

Mom and Rosa take seats on the couch, Mr. MacGregor sits on the recliner nearest the fireplace, and I flop down on one end of the loveseat.

"No offense," Mr. MacGregor says, studying me with a raised eyebrow, "but should the kid be in here for this discussion?"

Mom bristles at the question but keeps her silence at Rosa's raised hand.

"Dominic," Rosa whispers, "this is Anthony Faircloth, the boy Mira was helping last fall when you and Autumn were last on this side of the Atlantic."

Mr. MacGregor's eyes narrow as he peers at me. "The kid that was all screwed up?"

"That's me." I raise my hand in a simple wave and hold back a sarcastic laugh as a line from an old Monty Python movie plays through my mind. "I got better."

"Wait." Mr. MacGregor shifts his attention back to Rosa. "You had me meet you here to pick up Isabella. Does Mira's condition have something to do with what happened last year?"

"I'm afraid it has everything to do with it." The color drains from Mom's face. "Mira put everything on the line for my family, and now, unless we can somehow help her the way she helped Anthony..."

"What the hell is going on here?" He turns on Rosa. "You said Mira was sick, but that's not it at all. She's gone and gotten herself swept up in another one of these psychic things and screwed up her head again, hasn't she?"

Rosa nods solemnly. "She's in a coma, Dominic."

"A coma?" His face blanches. "For how long?"

"A couple of weeks." Rosa breaks her gaze away. "We tried to contact you sooner, but you haven't been the easiest person to get in touch with lately."

His eye's narrow in anger. "Mira and I may not be married anymore, but she's still Isabella's mother. You should have tried harder."

Rosa's patient expression drops into an exasperated glare. "Perhaps you could be a bigger part of your daughter's life if you didn't spend half the year on the opposite end of the globe."

Mr. MacGregor shoots out of his chair. "That's between me and Mira."

"And were she able to so much as open her eyes, I'd be happy to let the two of you work this out without my involvement." Rosa's lips curl into a beatific smile. "For the time being, however, in matters regarding my only granddaughter, you will deal with me."

Mr. MacGregor appears ready to fire back with anger and venom until a look of cool understanding overtakes his features. "Wait. Isabella doesn't know, does she? You haven't told her."

"She knows her mom is sick and can't see much right now." Rosa rests her forehead in her hands. "It's been hard keeping her busy."

"Has Isabella seen her mother?" he asks.

"A few times," Rosa answers. "We've told her Mira is sleeping and can't be disturbed."

Mr. MacGregor's eyes narrow. "You've been lying to my daughter."

"We've been protecting her." Rosa crosses her arms and shoots her daughter's ex a look that in many cultures would be considered the Evil Eye. "But if you think telling an eight-year-old girl her mother is in a coma is a good idea—"

"A coma?"

The quiet voice from behind us steals the air from the room. As one, our attention shifts to the house's front foyer where Isabella stands holding a carved wooden mask in her trembling hands. Directly behind her, Autumn wears a mortified stare, her mouth agape.

"Isabella..." Rosa shoots up from the chair and rushes to her granddaughter's side. "Don't you worry. Your mami is going to be just fine, isn't that right, Dominic?"

He joins Rosa. "Of course, sweetheart. Your mother just needs her rest."

"I'm not dumb, Daddy." Isabella's face twists into an accusing scowl. "I know what a coma is." And before anyone can say a word, she heads down the hall, no doubt heading for my room. She's napped in my bed more than once when Mira was visiting, and with all the posters and toys, it's by far her favorite place in the house.

Rosa disappears down the hallway after her granddaughter, leaving me alone with Mom, Autumn, and Mr. MacGregor. None of us have any idea of what to say to each other, so we all just sit and stare at each other for well over a minute until Autumn finally breaks the quiet stalemate.

"I'm so sorry," she whispers in her fiancé's ear. "I tried to keep Isabella occupied outside, but she was desperate to come inside and see her dad. She's really missed you"

"Hey." Mr. MacGregor wraps an arm around her, his expression softening. "It's not your fault, honey." He shoots Mom and me a conspiratorial wink, the first sign of a truce. "Mira is in a bad way and Izzy was going to find out at some point."

"The whole thing is an impossible situation." Mom follows Mr. MacGregor's lead. "We were hoping Mira would get better quickly and that Isabella could move forward without having to go through the trauma of knowing how bad her mother's condition really is. Apparently, that wasn't the best thought-out plan."

"And what exactly are all of you doing to help Mira anyway?" Mr. MacGregor motions in my direction. "Last I heard about you and your family back in the fall, Mira was trying to work her mojo to help bring your kid back from the edge."

"She did." Mom shakes her head. "And now that the shoe's on the other foot, God help us, Anthony is trying to do the same for her."

"Wait." It takes Mira's ex all of three seconds to do the math. "Your kid. He's..."

"Special." Mom bites her lip. "Like Mira is special."

Mr. MacGregor studies me as if I'm some sort of exhibit in a museum while his fiancée stares in my direction as if she's seen a ghost.

It would seem that regardless of what Mr. MacGregor told Autumn about his first marriage and why it ultimately failed, she doesn't know much of anything about Mira and what she can do.

He leans across the coffee table and offers a cautious smile. "And what exact talents do you bring to the table, Anthony?"

"My apologies," Mom intercedes, "but that's not exactly any of your business."

"I disagree." He jets out of his seat and begins to pace. "As I understand it, my ex-wife and the mother of my only child is lying in a hospital across town in a near-vegetative state. Unless I miss my guess, it has something to do with her coming here to North Carolina to help you and your family." He stops in his tracks and studies me anew. "You say your boy can do the things Mira can do. Call me crazy, but if he was the brain surgeon doing Mira's operation, don't you think I'd have the right to know if he had at least graduated from medical school?"

"Now, see here—"

"Mom," I interrupt, "it's okay." I wait for Mr. MacGregor to return to his chair and then shoot a glance in Autumn's direction. "Just curious. Are you okay with talking about this in front of her?"

"Dominic and I don't keep any secrets." Autumn crosses her arms, a huff escaping her pursed lips. "Say whatever you want."

No secrets. A nice sentiment, but I've got news for the woman that stole away Mira's husband while he lied to his wife and the mother of his child.

We all keep secrets. Every last one of us.

I search Mr. MacGregor's eyes to see if I should go on, and at his exasperated nod, I begin.

"You know part of this, but not the whole story. In the last year, Mira has helped me and my family not once, but twice. Last year, she came into our lives at a particularly dark time and helped pull me out of the quicksand my mind had become. The victory cost her dearly, but she eventually recovered and things were fine for a while. Or so we thought."

Mr. MacGregor watches my every move like a hawk. "And the second time?"

"Just a few weeks ago, everything we thought had been resolved last fall came undone and Mira was forced again to intervene. The first time, she got lucky and made it through for the most part unscathed." I swallow back the emotion building up in my throat. "The second time? Not so much."

"What happened to her?" Autumn's pleading eyes lock with her fiancé's. "You told me Mira was a professional psychic, Dominic. I figured she just had good intuition and charisma to spare, but what this kid is talking about sounds really scary."

"Excuse me," Mom leaps to my defense, "but the *kid's* name is Anthony."

I raise a hand, letting her know to back down. "It is scary. Scarier than anything you can imagine. And Mira faced it all without a second thought and saved us all." I meet Dominic's cool gaze. "I owe her everything."

"But you still haven't answered my question." Dominic takes Autumn's hand, almost as if he's hedging his bets that she'll run when I finally tell him what he wants to know. "Mira was good at reading people and finding things, but I don't understand how that's led to her being in any sort of trouble. What can you do that makes you think you can help her?"

I lock gazes with Mom, asking permission to answer truthfully. With a defeated wave, she consents, though I have no doubt she already thinks it's a mistake.

"Mr. MacGregor." I do my best to keep my voice from cracking as I address this man who has traveled to every corner of the world. "Your ex-wife can do far more than simply read people's emotions. She can walk minds." I take a breath. "Or at the very least, she can walk mine."

"Walk minds?" He studies me, his eyes flicking from me to Mom and back as if he's trying to decide if we're playing a game. "What the hell is that supposed to mean?"

"It's difficult to understand, but as best we can tell, Mira's mind and mine communicate in a way that's unique in both our experiences. Somehow in our first encounter, we forged a common ground between us, a space either of us can visit where we interact with the other via aspects of each other's thoughts, some friendly and some... not so much."

"So," Dominic answers slowly as he attempts to process in seconds what's taken the rest of us months to understand, "she walked your mind, encountered something that hurt her, and that experience has left her in a coma?"

"More or less." To say any more right now will just muddy the water. "As far as we know."

"I never knew." The quizzical nature of his gaze fades into something akin to wonder. "What exactly are you doing to help her now, Anthony?"

"Mira Tejedor explored every corner of my imagination until she found me in my darkest hour and dragged me out into the light." I puff up my chest with a deep breath. "With everything I've got, I intend to do the same."

XVI

SNOWDROP

I **pass the night dreamless, my sleep that of the dead.**
The next morning, I awake slowly, my mind as sluggish as half-dried glue, a far cry from the rushing thoughts that kept me awake way past midnight.

The meeting with Mira's ex-husband and his fiancée may have been the very definition of awkward, but by the end of the evening, it seemed we all reached an understanding. Mr. MacGregor plans to stay in town, at least for the foreseeable future, and help Rosa take care of Isabella while the rest of us continue to work with Mira. Autumn doesn't seem too pleased at having her summer in Africa cut short, but despite her frustration, it's clear she understands that family is family. After Jason took Rachel to bed, he joined us in the family room and similarly offered to watch our little sister until things with Mira get straightened out.

Throughout the discussion, no matter who was speaking, every eye was on me. Be it Mom's proud yet frightened glances, Mr. MacGregor's incredulous stare, or Autumn doing her best to avoid my gaze altogether, being the center of attention in a room filled with adults was odd. And not just that, but to know that each of them was and is counting on me in one way or another. Dr. Archer and Detective Sterling were never far from my thoughts, and there at the center of it all, Mira Tejedor's face.

The closed eyes and slack features of her forced slumber leave a dark blot on my soul.

I'm the first one up this morning. No one stirs as I step across the hall to shower and brush my teeth. I'm halfway through a bowl of cereal when I hear a door open from the other end of the house. The pitter-patter of tiny feet is quickly followed by my sister's quiet yawn as she steps into the kitchen.

"Good morning, Rachel," I whisper, keeping my voice low. "Want something to eat?"

"I'll get it." She rummages in the pantry and grabs a box of cereal before heading to the refrigerator. "Can you help me?" she asks. "Jason put the milk on the top shelf again."

We're both down to the last dregs of our bowls when Jason saunters in from the family room. He doesn't say a word as he drops a couple slices of bread into the toaster and cracks half a dozen eggs into our big glass bowl. Soon, he drops two steaming plates of scrambled eggs with cheddar and toast covered with grape jelly in front of us, his face breaking into a mischievous smile.

"Figured you two might want something besides corn flakes."

Rachel and I dive into what hobbits would call *second breakfast* and devour Jason's offerings in less than a minute. The conversation that follows stays pretty superficial with Jason and I doing our best to keep Rachel from learning anything that will make her worry more than she already is. Jason and I, on the other hand, share frequent concerned glances as we both know what's coming for me today.

Another trip through Mira's mind.

The most likely scenario is a return to the world of *The Nutcracker*, where if everything proceeds as written, the danger is passed and all that awaits us is a magical court filled with dancing candies.

Somehow, I think the powers that be have a different idea.

Mom eventually joins us, the dark circles under her eyes evidence she was up hours past my final nodding off. She starts the coffee maker and quietly gives each of us a hug and a kiss, but the hubbub of morning energy normally found in our home remains absent.

"Are you all ready for the day?" she asks me once she's finished her second cup. "We need to leave soon to meet Thomas at the hospital."

"Just need my shoes." I slide off my stool and head for the family room where my sneakers rest haphazardly beneath the coffee table. "Is Detective Sterling joining us today?"

"We'll see," she calls after me. "Yesterday seemed to take a lot out of him."

"He's not the only one," I mutter. "And unless I'm way off base, today is going to be worse."

Two new officers guard Mira's door today. Like the ones we met last time, they know who we are but still ask Mom for identification before letting us past the door.

If Durgan does have his sights set on Mira, the cops aren't going to make it easy.

Like yesterday, Dr. Archer awaits us, though Detective Sterling is absent.

"Good morning, Caroline." His eyes drift over to me and he tries to fake a smile. "Anthony." He beckons us away from Mira's bed and over to the window. "Detective Sterling can't join us today. He called earlier. Said he needed a day to recuperate."

Mom's lips draw down to a narrow line as she nods her understanding. "If yesterday was hard on him, should we even be working with Mira today? I mean his doppelganger may have had a rough time of it, but Mira—or Odette, I suppose we should call her—died."

"To be honest, I have no idea." Dr. Archer shakes his head slowly. "Like I've said a thousand times, we're all making this up as we go along." He glances in Mira's direction. "According to Dr. Friedman, she's medically stable, but with each day that passes, her body gets more deconditioned, and I'm afraid if we don't bring her around soon—"

"That her mind will follow." I walk to the bedside and take Mira's hand. "Trust me. I've been there." I pull a chair over to the bedside and take a seat. "Shall we get started?"

Today is different. Entering the space between Mira's mind and mine yesterday was as easy as falling out of a boat and hitting water. The orchestra all but greeted me with symphonic open arms and my final trip through the world of *Swan Lake* began, at the very least, without event.

Today? A half hour in, and nothing.

Dr. Archer breaks out his pen light in an effort to help me relax, for all the good it does.

I suppose the possibility of seeing Mira die yet again, albeit in a dreamworld of our own making, is more than my mind is willing to accept without a little coaxing. A few soothing words and the flashing LED, however, and my entire body eventually loosens. My mind wanders for the first time since I awakened this morning as the familiar melody of *The Nutcracker*'s second act fills the ether between my thoughts and the maze Mira Tejedor's have become.

My heavy eyes drift closed and open anew on the inside of the Nutcracker Prince's sleigh. My body, still the carved wooden form of one of Fritz's toy soldiers, lies splayed across the cold oaken floor of the magical carriage. As with my previous trip to this place, I can't move anything but my eyes. Last time, it was the Nutcracker's attention that brought me around and allowed me to act, and yet, here I am, so close I could reach out and touch his tunic, and my limbs remain useless.

A gentle snow falls as we fly on invisible wings to, I'm guessing, the Land of the Sugar Plum Fairy. The ride is smooth and silent, the only sounds the delightful tinkle of Clara's laughter and the Nutcracker Prince's deep-throated chuckle.

That is, until the screaming starts.

Something big hits the side of the flying sleigh, knocking Clara and the Nutcracker Prince from their seats and sending me careening into the side of the carriage like a wooden missile. Fortunately, nothing breaks.

Nothing that I'm aware of, at least.

The horizon, steady in my previous line of vision, flips end over end. Unbelievably, neither I nor the other passengers are thrown from the sleigh.

Good thing the laws of physics don't always apply in this world of dream.

We plummet toward the forest below us, the snow-covered canopy flying at us faster and faster with each flip of the sleigh. Only a miracle keeps us from careening into the side of one of the many trees that fly past. As the sleigh crashes into the forest floor, I can't help but notice we land sunny side up.

That's two for Team Nutcracker and zero for the catapulted rock or guided missile or whatever it was that knocked the sleigh from the sky.

"Are you all right?" the Nutcracker Prince asks Clara as he offers her his hand.

"I believe so." She grasps his outstretched arm and steps out onto the snow-covered ground. "What happened?"

The Prince leaves Clara by the front of the sleigh and steps around to the side to inspect for damage, his face turning up in disgust as he comes to the rear quarter of his magical carriage.

"Clara," he whispers. "Stay where you are. You don't want to see this."

"What is it?" The word shoots out of my mouth before I even realize I've regained the power of speech. "What hit us?"

"Who said that?" The Prince's hand goes to the hilt of his blade. "Show yourself."

"As you wish." The strength again flowing into my limbs, I climb from the enchanted sleigh and pop my head above the side. "It is I, my prince. Fritz, your soldier and—"

I peer down from my perch at the fractured side of the carriage and a shiver races through my wooden body. The Mouse King's head, torn from the monster's torso with crown intact, rests all but pulped in the splintered wood of the sleigh's outer bed, the missile that knocked us from the sky. Despite this, I get the distinct impression that even headless, we haven't seen the last of the Nutcracker Prince's nemesis.

"Fritz," the Prince commands. "Come out of there and keep Clara safe while I scout the area." His eyes shift left and right. "It would seem we are neither as alone nor as safe as I thought."

As the Prince steps into the surrounding woods and disappears from sight, I climb out of the sleigh and take my place at Clara's side. I'm not sure which pains me more, the terror I find in the eyes of the woman I've come here to save or my helplessness to do anything even remotely useful.

"Fritz?" she asks. "That is still you in there, isn't it?"

"Don't worry, Clara." I hold up my curved sword before my face. "No one will harm you while I and your Nutcracker Prince are guarding you."

"But, my prince defeated the Mouse King." She peers around the side of the carriage with a curiosity I've seen in Mira's features on more than one occasion. "What enemy could we possibly be facing now?"

I step into her line of sight to spare her the gory visual of the enormous rodent head protruding from the side of the sleigh. "Let's just say the Mouse King and his forces may not be quite as vanquished as we'd like to think."

Together we wait in the cold, Clara shivering and me standing stock-still as the chill radiates up my wooden legs. I don't even have a coat to offer her, as every part of me is carved from the same hunk of oak or hickory or whatever this strange body is made from.

A few minutes pass before the sound of cautious footsteps from the dark forest captures both our attention. I step in front of Clara to fend off whatever new enemy awaits and am relieved when the Nutcracker Prince emerges from the undulating shadow.

"Ho, Fritz," he shouts. "Is everything well?"

"Other than Miss Clara's lips and fingers turning blue, we are both fine, my prince."

"Fear not," he proclaims with a smile. "I found no trace of our enemy anywhere in the vicinity and determined that even with our unexpected fall from the sky, we have nearly arrived at our destination." He stretches out an arm at a rise of land to our forward right. "The home of the Sugar Plum Fairy is just across that ridge." He comes forward and takes Clara's hand. "We should be there within the hour."

The three of us trudge through bank after bank of knee-deep snow. The ridge far steeper than it appeared from the site of our crash, it takes all our effort to help a trembling Clara, covered only by her ivory shift and pointe shoes, across the ice-covered crag. As we reach the precipice, the castle of the Sugar Plum Fairy comes into view. Pastel pink and blue, each piece of architecture seems to be fashioned from different types of cake or candy. Every column a swirled candy cane, every sconce a gumdrop, and every parapet a cupcake, it's a child's fondest dream made manifest.

That being said, after a steady diet of fairy tales over my first few years on the planet, I know all too well what kind of people live in candy houses in the middle of the woods.

We make our way down the ridge following a serpentine path carved into the rock. Between the snow hiding the stone below our feet and the black ice clinging to the exposed granite, the descent is nigh impossible. Still, we eventually make it to level ground and after another few minutes of hiking a snow-covered road of M&M cobblestones, the wood opens up on an enormous courtyard filled with trees dripping with candied fruits and sugary treats of every shape, size, and color. Across the open space, the castle looms in all its confectionery glory. This close, the unbelievable detail of the massive edifice boggles my imagination, which is ironic, as every inch of what I'm looking at represents exactly that.

As we cross a hanging bridge fashioned from Kit Kats and red Twizzlers, a flurry of motion at the castle's main entrance pulls my attention. There, beneath an arch formed of enormous triangular bricks of candy corn, a quartet of noblemen wait in eighteenth-century French dress of blue, red, and white, all trimmed with gold. In perfect synchrony, they dance before the gate in time with a pleasant melody. Though their movements are fluid and graceful, it's clear the quartet represent the guards of this place.

It seems even here we should proceed with caution.

Any fear I have about an attack dissipates when I see the quartet's reaction to the Nutcracker Prince's royal wave. They surround us in seconds and, as one, offer a low bow to their missing master. Then, before I can utter a word, they initiate a new dance to celebrate his return. With a wave of his arm, the Prince silently announces Clara, and in response, the four guards sweep her off her feet and hold her high above their heads. An intricate dance ensues, a dance that apparently doesn't include me.

Gliding from one pair of guards to the other to the Prince and back, the thrilling performance brings a smile to Clara's face and color to her cheeks. Meanwhile, I remain on the bridge, all but ignored as a river of butterscotch flows beneath my feet. But that's for the best.

Having a body made of wood does not lend itself particularly well to anything requiring agility or grace.

In dance, Clara and the Nutcracker Prince relay the events of the battle with the Mouse King and his forces, much to the delight of the guards. As the dance draws to a close, however, the Prince's expression grows dark as he points in the direction of our downed sleigh and communicates in no uncertain terms that danger has come home to roost. Two of the four soldiers return to their post at the palace gate and arm themselves with shields formed from waffles and candy cutlasses.

I'd rather they be armed with cold steel, but I don't make the rules around here.

And yet, if I'm not the one making the rules, who is?

Something to think about.

The remaining guards lead us inside the castle to a throne room constructed from various sweets. Cotton candy tapestries cover the walls, frescoes fashioned from every color of jellybean imaginable fill the ceilings, and beneath our feet, the stones of the floor are swirled lollipop heads surrounded by mortar composed of innumerable jawbreakers, fireballs, and petrified frosting.

The guards show their prince and his companion to a pair of thrones fashioned from candy canes and gumdrops at the far end of the room. I, conversely, am left by the door with one of the guards, a nobody among royalty.

The celebration of the Prince's return continues as the second act of *The Nutcracker* plays out before my eyes exactly as I've seen it a thousand times before. Though there are likely as many versions of the ballet as there are stages in the world, I know the sequence well.

Dancers representative of the various indulgences of Tchaikovsky's time come forth one by one to entertain Clara and the Nutcracker Prince.

A pair of dancers in Spanish attire are first, their costumes the brown and tan of chocolate and caramel. The lines of the man's costume remind me of a matador, while the woman's elaborate dress brings images of the perfect flamenco dancer. As muted trumpet, horn, flute, violin, and the occasional staccato rhythm of castanets fill the air, the pair move in concert, spinning to and fro, their elegant dance as sweet as the candy they represent.

Chocolate is soon followed by coffee. A trio of women dressed in blue and white sarongs similar those worn by Mira in her Scheherazade guise converge upon the center of the floor, though unlike the storyteller, they are armed with scarves instead of daggers. Their hypnotic dance consists of slow and sultry steps, their attire and purposeful movements capturing not only the essence of the rich drink they represent but of Arabia itself.

As the trio of coffee dancers leaves the floor, an Asian man and woman sprint in from opposite sides of the room and come together a few steps in front of me. Outfitted in yellow and green raiment befitting the Orient, the tea dancers perform an eclectic dance to trilling flute and plucked violin strings. The polar opposite of the preceding trio, this performance brings a smile to my face and leaves me with a strange gladness in my heart as they end with a simple bow.

Next, the Bouffons take the stage. A man and two women, very clearly dressed as candy canes with diagonal red and green stripes across their white silken costumes, dance clown-like to one of Tchaikovsky's most boisterous and most famous melodies. I take special interest in this, the most Russian of the dances, but the joviality of the Bouffons is over far too quickly.

The candy cane dancers are soon replaced by a young couple clothed in pastel blue and yellow. The man plays a simple reed flute in time with the ever present but never seen orchestra, his every note mirrored in the woman's lithe form. Though beautifully synchronized, his control over her stirs a discomfort in my heart none of the other performances has brought. His eyes fall on me, and for only a moment I see a familiar glint there. A glint I've seen in only one other place.

Von Rothbart's owl stare.

Before I can take a closer look, the Dance of the Reed Flutes is over, and Mother Ginger, a character from Russian folklore, takes the stage. Clothed in an enormous hoop skirt in the shape of a pink-and-turquoise gingerbread house, she struts to the center of the stage. Her offspring, the Polichinelles, pour from beneath the folds of her dress, the octet of boys and girls dressed in the simple brown and red of gingerbread children. Between the rushing boys and girls, reminiscent of the terror of *Tuileries*, and blonde Mother Ginger, her controlling stare hidden behind a perfect smile far too much like Madame Versailles', I look away, my heart in my throat. Only when the children are again hidden and Mother Ginger has left the floor do I return my attention to the performance.

As the Waltz of the Flowers begins, I take some comfort in the fact that no veiled threat presents itself in the elegant dance of the two dozen men and women in French attire and powdered wigs. Strings and woodwinds, bells and chimes, and the occasional interlude of brass fill the air and all seems right with the world again. The men's attire all white and silver and the women's sparkling dresses showing just a blush of pink, the scene appears pure and without agenda. Still, the dread remaining in my heart after the preceding two performances leaves me with the impression I'm missing something.

Like Mom would say, as if I'm being led down the cherry path.

And in this place, all but literally.

The garland of personified flowers parts to allow the passage of a pair I've been awaiting since this all began. She in a pink bodice and tutu with silver trim and he in blindingly white silk with black and gold embroidery, the Sugar Plum Fairy and her cavalier, Prince Coqueluche, take their place as the hosts of this collection of sweets. In the past, their faces would have left me utterly dumbfounded, but at this point, the revelation of their identities barely registers as surprise.

The guardian of this hall wears the face of Mira's ex-husband, Dominic.

And his mistress? A romanticized version of Dominic's fiancée, Autumn.

I look to Clara, expecting to find the consternation I'd find in Mira's eyes at such a revelation, but only find the innocent delight I'd expect from Clara Stahlbaum.

An unseen harp plays arpeggios over quiet violins as the Sugar Plum Fairy and her cavalier begin their performance. Soon triumphant brass comes in as the dance grows more and more demanding, with leaps and spins and holds and carries that would prove all but impossible in the real world.

Is this how Mira sees Mr. MacGregor, all confidence and strength, or is she merely idealizing the life of the man she left behind?

And this flawless interpretation of Autumn—a perfection she could never hope to match?

Prince Coqueluche executes a solo performance, much to the joy of the entire court. His technique perfect, his every step and leap astounds the crowd more than the one before. Though the crowd can't take their eyes off the cavalier in white, my eyes drift to Clara, and this time a hint of subtle longing does color her features. Fortunately, the dance is over almost as quickly as it began.

And then, the moment we've all been waiting for.

The Dance of the Sugar Plum Fairy, a tune known the world over, begins, the plucked strings of an invisible string section guiding the Fairy's every step. As the bell-like tones of the celesta come in, the sound somewhere between piano and glockenspiel, her short pointe steps accelerate, her dance building and building as both music and movement mesmerize the surrounding crowd, not to mention a lone toy soldier with the heart of a little boy from another universe. A virtuoso performance, it seems to go on forever and yet ends all too quickly.

The orchestra launches into a jocular tune and Fairy and Prince dance one last number, their every movement in perfect synchrony. The dance ends in a thunder of brass and tympani, and then all the sweets and flowers return to the stage for the final number of *The Nutcracker*.

Perhaps it's the morbid side of me, but I keep waiting for the other shoe to drop. Yet, nothing happens. Flowers and chocolate, tea and reed flutes, coffee and gingerbread children all dance together, frolicking under the watchful eyes of the Sugar Plum Fairy and Prince Coqueluche. As the invisible orchestra hits its climax, the entire assemblage freezes in place as Clara's dream reaches its ideally pleasant end.

And then, from the shadows, Drosselmeyer appears. He strides confidently to the throne where Clara awaits, utter determination evident in his sage eyes.

Could it be this simple? This man who wears my father's face and who in this place is Clara's godfather... Has he come to take her home?

Silently, he approaches the dual throne. With Clara frozen mid-clap and the immobile Prince looking upon her with the purest of love, Drosselmeyer positions himself between them. Retrieving his wand from the Nutcracker Prince's belt, he circles the throne and takes a position behind the still pair. Holding aloft the implement of his power, Clara's godfather takes a deep breath and—

Behind Drosselmeyer, a velvet curtain parts silently. A lone pair of glowing red eyes stares down at the unsuspecting magician, soon followed by another and then another until the hungry gaze of seven sets of beady rodent eyes converge upon his frail neck.

The Mouse King, the single head torn from his body now replaced with seven like the Hydra of Greek mythology, falls upon Drosselmeyer.

In a sickening display filled with sights and sounds I will never be able to unsee or unhear, the magician is no more.

As the remainder of the court again regains control of their limbs, the Mouse King lifts his seven gore-covered snouts from the half-devoured corpse of Clara's godfather. From beneath his seven bejeweled crowns, his seven pairs of hate-filled eyes lock gazes with mine as he utters a simple, unmistakable command from his seven bloody mouths.

"Now."

XVII

SONG OF THE REAPER

An army of mice appears from every corner of the room and waste no time tearing into the various courtiers of the Sugar Plum Fairy's entourage. Silent no longer, the Mouse King barks commands in a thick French accent from his position on the Fairy's dais. His seven heads, each acting independently, watch with glee at the slaughter being carried out at his command.

The Nutcracker Prince grabs Clara's hand and drags the horrified girl to a far corner of the room where the Sugar Plum Fairy and Prince Coqueluche await. The three of them form a tight perimeter around Clara, and even the bravest of the mouse-soldiers give the trio a wide berth.

The remainder of the Fairy's court, unfortunately, is not granted the same courtesy.

The Polichinelles are the first to fall, the eight of them descended upon by a dozen man-sized mice in military topcoats. Mother Ginger fares a little better, her enormous hoop skirt providing at least a bit of cover at first, but it isn't long before she too succumbs to the unending rush of humanoid rats. The Reed Flutes, the Chocolates, the Coffees, the Teas, the Flowers—they all fall beneath the tide of fur and teeth and sinew. In a matter of seconds, the court of the Sugar Plum Fairy has been reduced to no more than half a dozen still breathing, and even those, not for much longer.

The last of the Flowers, a slim girl in pink, runs at me. The wide eyes of

Isabella Tejedor dart left and right as she dives behind me and begs for my help.

"They're killing everyone," she whispers. "Save me."

I raise my curved saber before me and adopt a fighting stance even as my heart does flip-flops in my wooden chest. "I'll do all I can."

A pair of mouse-soldiers notices us and stalks in our direction. Taking on the slow but steady slasher-walk from every horror movie ever made, they come at us from either side. I take some solace knowing their teeth will only find wood if they attack me. The wilting Flower who trembles behind me, however, will likely not fare as well.

"Hold on, Fritz," sounds the Nutcracker Prince's voice from across the room. "We're coming."

Like a force of nature, the trio of Sugar Plum Fairy, Prince Coqueluche, and Nutcracker Prince push their way through the teeming swarm of mouse-soldiers. The Fairy dispatches her enemies two and three at a time, her martial abilities more than on par with her skills at dance. Similarly, her cavalier fells every mouse that appears before him, the golden mace in his hand shining like a newborn sun. Lastly, the Nutcracker Prince, despite one of his arms being occupied pulling Clara along behind, proves an unstoppable force as time and again he stains his blade with the blood of our enemies.

I manage to hold off the pair of mouse-soldiers set on plucking the last Flower from the Sugar Plum Fairy's bouquet until the cavalry can arrive. A spinning kick from the Fairy sends them both to the floor where they quickly meet their ends at the hands of the two princes.

"How did this happen?" I ask. "How did these monsters come to be here?"

"You brought us, little man of wood," says one of the Mouse King's heads. The mob of mouse-soldiers parts like the Red Sea and allows their ruler to pass.

"As you always do," says another mouth filled with razor teeth.

"As you always will," says a third with an amused laugh.

The French accent coloring every word fills my heart with dread. It's not the first time I've encountered such inflection in this place.

In line with my suspicions about the Black Swan, is it possible the Mouse King is, in fact, a queen? Or, more specifically, a teacher from *Tuileries*?

In seconds, he stands over us, his seven pairs of glowing red eyes set above snouts covered in blood and gore staring at us in morbid glee. "Wherever you go," says yet another head, "you bring death and destruction, do you not?"

"That's not true," I blurt out. "It's not." I peer into the faces of my three defenders, and though in each I find defiance and certitude, I catch more than one of their sidelong glances tinged with a hint of doubt. "You brought this ruin, not me."

"Keep telling yourself that." The Mouse King's central head speaks this time, his tone filled with a mix of mirth and venom. "Tell yourself you're helping the girl, Clara, and not in fact sentencing her to an early grave."

"You don't scare me." I fight to keep my sword hand from trembling, my efforts amounting to nothing. "You're not real."

"Not real?" This time all seven of the Mouse King's heads speak as one.

"None of this is." I bring both hands to the hilt of my sword and manage to hold it still. "This is nothing but a dream, and you, the worst nightmare a frightened boy's mind can come up with."

All seven of the Mouse King's mouths pull wide into bloody grins. "And yet, have you not proven on more than one occasion that dreams can wound?" He takes a step closer as all seven pairs of glowing eyes converge on mine. "That your imagination can kill?"

"What's he talking about, Fritz?" Clara asks. "What have you done?"

"I've done nothing," I retort across my shoulder, far angrier than I intended to sound. "And you're not Clara Stahlbaum, no matter what you believe."

If I expect the Mouse King to recoil from my words like some movie vampire from a crucifix, I'm sorely disappointed.

Instead, he laughs—a deep-throated laugh from seven snarling mouths still dripping with the blood of a man who wore my father's face.

"The truth will set you free, little wooden boy? Is that what you're going for?"

I pull together every ounce of courage in my body and take one small step forward. "Sometimes the truth is all we have."

"The truth?" With a wave of his arm, the Mouse King summons his army. In seconds, the six of us are surrounded, our backs to a wall with no hope of escape. "The truth is this, toy soldier or Fritz or whatever name it is you choose to call yourself—you, the Flower, the Fairy and her cavalier, along with the Nutcracker and the girl are all about to die in as painful and cruel a manner as I can devise and there's not a damned thing you can do about it."

The last Flower, standing to my rear, goes full on shrinking violet and faints to the floor, leaving me, Clara, the Sugar Plum Fairy, and the two princes alone against an army of six-foot rodents decked out in military formal wear led by a seven-headed psychopathic rat.

If we somehow survive all of this, I definitely need to find a new obsession.

"Wait," Clara shouts as the army of mouse-soldiers draws close around us, a rabid hunger in their beady eyes. "It's me he wants." Before I can stop her, she steps out from behind me and stands at my side, defiant and brave before the Mouse King. "Take me if you must, but leave Fritz and the others alone."

"No." I try to pull her back, but it's like gravity has tripled beneath her feet. "Don't do this."

She looks back across her shoulder and locks eyes with me, any semblance of a smile gone from her face. "Listen, Fritz, or whoever resides behind that carved wooden face. You claim I'm not Clara, and yet you stand between me and certain death as a brother would his own sister. I'm not certain what it all means, but there is clearly more to this story than you're letting on."

"Don't listen to her," the Nutcracker Prince whispers, though his voice is undercut with worry I'd expect to hear more from Dr. Archer back in the real world. "We're here to rescue her, not to give her up to darkness."

Clara turns to the Nutcracker Prince. "My prince, you have already given me more this night than I could ever repay. You've sacrificed your body for me, taken me on the ride of a lifetime, and brought me to this place of wonder for a view, however brief, of perfection."

Any hope remaining on the Nutcracker Prince's face is dashed upon the rocks of her quiet declaration and again words I'd expect more from Dr. Thomas Archer than from his dreamworld doppelganger fall from his lips.

"But this time *we* were supposed to save *you*."

Clara cups the Nutcracker Prince's cheek. "Please don't forget me, but for now, this is the way it must be." She turns back to the Mouse King and glares up into his seven pairs of glowing red eyes. "My life for theirs, King of Rats."

The Mouse King attempts to hide his awe at Clara's bravery behind a sarcastic chuckle. "Ever testing the fine line between bravery and stupidity, are we my dear?"

Clara raises a finger. "My life for theirs. Do we have an agreement?"

All fourteen of the Mouse King's eyes squint at once. "I could slay you all where you stand, little girl."

Clara smiles. "And yet, you've stood here bargaining with me instead of doing just that." She crosses her arms. "My life for theirs. Do you accept my offer?"

The Mouse King considers and then raises a fist. The army of mouse-soldiers pulls back a step, confusion replacing the bloodlust in each set of beady red eyes. Once his army has retreated to the shadows, the Mouse King extends a hand. Clara allows herself one last look in my direction, and then places her hand in the Mouse King's outstretched palm. With one last look at the Nutcracker Prince, she admonishes, "Don't come for me." And then, catching my desperate gaze, she adds, "At least not in this place."

She follows the cryptic response with a quick wink, and then the Mouse King draws her lithe form beneath his voluminous cape and disappears into the shadows at the room's opposite end.

The Nutcracker Prince wastes no time tearing into me.

"What have you done?" he shouts. "You let the Mouse King take her."

"First," I answer, "we let him take her." I sheathe my saber. "And second, we did exactly as she asked."

"But why?" The Sugar Plum Fairy, silent throughout the entire negotiation, peers at us incredulous. "Why would she go with that monster? Why sacrifice her life for ours?"

"That's what she does," I mutter through wooden lips as I look down upon the lone remaining Flower, the one that wears Isabella Tejedor's face. "It is the only way she knows."

"What the hell just happened?" Dr. Archer, still struggling with consciousness, stares at me across Mira's still form. "Did we really just let that... thing take Mira?"

"Something..." My mind stretched in a thousand directions at once, I do my best to pull together a coherent thought. "Something wasn't right."

"What is he talking about?" Mom descends on me like a mother hen. "You found Mira?"

"Found..." Dr. Archer pulls himself to his feet. "And lost her again."

"But how?" Mom pushes a cup of water into my hands and helps me take a sip. "Was it *The Nutcracker* again?"

I work to reassemble the countless disparate images warring in my head and attempt to relay to Mom the events of my most recent sojourn into the world of Tchaikovsky. Dr. Archer fills in a few points here and there from what he remembers of our otherworldly encounter, but most of the detail comes from me.

When I'm finished, even Mom looks like she just got off a roller coaster ride.

"The Mouse King took her?" she asks. "And that's what she wanted?"

"I don't think it's what she wanted at all." I catch Dr. Archer's angry gaze. "But in the thick of the situation, it seemed clear any other action was going to leave us all dead." I swallow back the despair building in my voice. "Or worse."

"That monster had us surrounded, and yet it kept talking." A vein in Dr. Archer's forehead pulses with intensity. "It must have been afraid of something."

"Or maybe the Mouse King knew exactly what kind of person it was dealing with." My voice goes so low even I can barely hear it. "What Mira would do if presented with a no-win situation."

"We're talking about the thing like it's a real person." Dr. Archer pounds a fist against the wall. "Like it's not some figment of your and Mira's imagination."

"Unless," Mom whispers, "like von Rothbart, there's someone else involved."

"Von Rothbart." Dr. Archer raises an eyebrow, his understandable anger fading into the cool intellect I've known for years. "If the Mouse King and von Rothbart are related, then it's just like before."

"A two-front war," Mom adds, "but the same enemy."

My heart freezes as I recall the flash of von Rothbart's icy stare from the Dance of the Reed Flutes.

Just weeks ago, Mira battled against Koschei the Deathless in the realm of *The Firebird* and struggled to escape the puppet prison of *Petrushka*. In both instances, the villain hid in plain sight, disguised as an ally in the first and as an innocuous stranger in the second. When her true enemy finally revealed herself, she was forced to humiliate and sacrifice herself before us all to bring the wickedness to its rightful end.

Still, I'm missing something.

Something important.

"So, what now?" Mom paces the room, her face lined with worry. "We had two leads on finding Mira and bringing her back from whatever nightmare has taken up residence between her ears. Unless I'm missing something, both of those leads have come to a, pardon the phrase, dead end."

"We'll find a way," Dr. Archer says. "Mira always did, and we will too." He brushes a trembling hand through her hair. "Right, Anthony?"

"Of course." I meet his apprehensive gaze and fake a reassuring grin. "Back at it tomorrow?"

Dr. Archer returns the smile. His doesn't appear any more real than mine. "See you in the morning."

"You must have been terrified." Mom keeps both hands on the wheel as we coast beneath a yellow light a few minutes from our house. "What would you have done if—"

"If Mira hadn't stepped in and sacrificed herself for me?" I glance out the window at a passing bicyclist and add, "Again?"

"You can't blame yourself for that. As best as we understand it, that was her choice."

"Her choice?" My hands clench into fists. "Were the actions of the various characters along the Exhibition *my* choice? Am I accountable for all that misery?"

Her voice drops to a low murmur. "That was different."

"How, Mom?" I blink away the moisture at the corners of my eyes. "I was unreachable and Mira's in a coma. She walked my mind and now I'm walking hers. How is any of this different?"

Mom's hands clench on the wheel for a second, and then relax as she lets out a defeated sigh.

"I don't know, Anthony." She rubs at her temples with one hand and tries to keep her eyes on the road. "About any of this."

"When I was stuck in the Exhibition, a part of me didn't want to be saved, and that part did everything in its power to keep me there."

Color rises in Mom's cheeks. "You're talking about—"

"The witch." I charge straight ahead. "She did everything to keep me right there, immobile and still."

"And she wore my face." Mom glances over at me, her features wavering between anger and desperation. "What are you trying to say, Anthony?"

Uh oh. I've stepped in it now.

"Sorry, Mom. My mind may have cast you as the witch at the end of the hall, but that's not what I'm talking about right now."

"Then what *are* you talking about?"

"What I'm saying is just like a part of me didn't want to wake up after everything that happened with Julianna and Ms. Sayles, what if Mira's mind has gone into self-preservation mode like mine did?"

"And she's sabotaging every effort we make at freeing her by doing what she's always done in the world of dream."

My eyes return to the world outside the passenger side window. "Sacrificing herself for the good of everyone else."

We're getting closer, but the answer still eludes me.

"We're missing something, aren't we?" Mom asks, as if reading my mind.

I cast my mind back, reliving everything I can remember of Mira's interaction with me along the Exhibition, of our time together in the worlds of *The Firebird* and *Petrushka*, her heart-wrenching sacrifice at *The Rite of Spring*, and every word of our conversations from *Swan Lake* and *The Nutcracker*.

And then, a memory.

The last thing she said to us before she let the Mouse King take her away. *Don't come for me. At least not in this place.*

"That's it." New vigor fills my limbs. "That's the answer."

"What's the answer?" Mom asks as she turns onto our street. "What have you got, Anthony?"

"It's a long shot," I answer, excitement building in my every word, "but maybe we've been dealing too much with the who and not enough with the where."

Mom pulls to a stop a block from our house and looks over at me. "The 'where'?"

"Mira couldn't free me from within the Exhibition itself, but took us all into the maelstrom at the end of the hall to find the Bogatyr Gates. Then, when she couldn't fight her way out of Koschei's realm or the Shrove-Tide Fair, she took us all to another realm to perform the Rite of Spring."

Mom ignores the pickup truck honking at us from behind. "You're suggesting the fight needs to take place on another battlefield?"

"In all the places Mira visited when she was trying to help me, the odds were stacked against her. Only when she moved the struggle to a place of her choosing did she have a fighting chance."

"How would you do that?" Mom takes a moment to show the driver of the truck her favorite finger as he blares past us and then returns her attention to me. "How would you change the rules like that?"

"From what you and she have told me, Mira was the storyteller in my head and both times, she merely decided to tell a different story." For some reason, I continue to hide the fact that I remember everything, though at this point I'm not even sure why I'm doing it. "But all the pieces of the story come from me. The Exhibition. Koschei's garden and palace. The Russian fair. The forest glade where Mira danced *The Rite of Spring*. Even the worlds of *Swan Lake* and *The Nutcracker* we've faced must come from somewhere in here." I tap an index finger against my temple. "The storyteller can decide upon a different page..."

Comprehension fills Mom's face. "But you're the book."

I nod.

"But how would you know where to go?" Mom presses the accelerator and we trudge along the last block before pulling into our driveway. "How would you determine where you could win?"

I consider the question. "I'd need some direction. Mira just led me to one all-powerful sorceress and I could probably start there..."

Mom stares at me from beneath a furrowed brow. "I sense a 'but' in there somewhere."

"The Sugar Plum Fairy would be a step in the right direction, but I'm not sure talking with her is exactly the direction to go."

"Go on."

"If you're up against badness, Glinda of the North may give you some decent tips, but if you want to know the real deal, you go to the Wicked Witch of the West."

"Wait." Mom sees right through me. "You can't possibly be suggesting—"

"That's exactly what I'm suggesting." I rest a hand on the door handle. "Tonight, we rest."

"And tomorrow?" she asks.

"Tomorrow, we search for Baba Yaga."

XVIII

Song of the Lark

Dr. Archer steeples his fingers beneath his chin and raises an eyebrow. "You want me to do what?"

"Not want, Thomas." Mom sits opposite him across our coffee table. "Anthony and I *need* you to hypnotize the two of us so he can converse one on one with Baba Yaga and find a way for us to help Mira once and for all."

"Baba Yaga." His eyes flick from Mom to me. "The witch inside your head who kept you all but comatose for several weeks last fall."

"And then helped to free me, not just once, but twice." At Mom's confused expression, I add, "As far as I understand from what Mira has told me."

His gaze shoots back to Mom. "And you're okay with this?"

Mom actually lets out a quiet laugh. "I'm not okay with any of this, but when you're dropped in the middle of the ocean, you either start swimming or start drowning, wouldn't you agree?"

Dr. Archer stares at us both incredulous for several seconds, his expression shifting from confused to resigned. "And what exactly do you hope to learn from doing this?"

"Baba Yaga, no matter where she has appeared in the various worlds of dream, always seems to possess information no one else has access to." I take Mom's hand and give her fingers a gentle squeeze. "We believe she may hold the key to rescuing Mira."

"But, Caroline," he asks, "you've never had to go under for Baba Yaga to appear before. Why do you think you'd have to do so now?"

"I'm not sure." Her fingers tense in my grip. "You've always told me the witch is just a projection of Anthony's deepest subconscious and that she wears my face mainly because she represents his protector. Still, Anthony's instincts are telling him I need to be a part of this." She releases my hand and crosses her arms. "Whatever my son needs from me, he gets."

Dr. Archer studies us both and sighs, his face breaking into an apologetic smile. "Very well. I can't make any promises, but like you, I'm in this for the long haul." He slides into the practiced clinician's voice I've heard a thousand times. "Before we begin, shall we review all the ground rules?"

For twenty minutes, Dr. Archer goes back over the same set of guidelines he and I have followed for years when it comes to hypnosis. It's like discussing the plot of a movie we've all seen a hundred times, but as Dr. Archer has never before worked with Mom in this capacity, it's basically a whole new ballgame.

In the end, once everyone is on the same sheet of music with what we're doing, Dr. Archer turns off the overhead lights, pulls the penlight from his coat pocket, and we get started.

"All right, Caroline," he breathes as much as speaks. "I want you to listen to my voice and only my voice."

The undulating light passes back and forth before our eyes, Dr. Archer's hand on the instrument and even his mere presence no longer important after a mere few seconds. Soon it's just me and Mom, the darkness and the light, and the soothing tones of Dr. Archer's voice.

And then, it's me, alone at the edge of a wood, resting in a swing crafted from an old board and a single coil of rope tied to the overhanging branch of an old oak tree.

This time, my body is neither the wooden form of Tunny or Fritz the toy soldier nor the full-grown man I embodied as Benno from *Swan Lake*, but an incarnation far closer to home.

I'm me, at least as far as I can tell.

I rush to a nearby pond and peer into the still water at the same reflection that looks back from the mirror each day as I brush my teeth.

Looks like Pinocchio has again become a real boy.

Not to mention, for once, I'm in full control of my body.

A nice change.

Still, I have little doubt I have somehow been translated into yet another entity, an entity I will have to discover.

As with many things in the world of dream, my garb seems simultaneously strange and familiar. A loose white blouse with red embroidery at the sleeves and edges covers my torso, a crimson sash holds the shirt tight at my waist, and blue-and-white striped pantaloons hug my legs. My feet are protected by a pair of leather boots shined to a high luster while a simple brown cap sits atop my head. A bead of sweat courses down my forehead, and I whip out a frayed piece of sackcloth from my pocket to wipe my face.

Why anyone would carry such a rough handkerchief is beyond me.

I add that to the long list of things about the way my brain works that don't make sense.

As I contemplate the implications of my new form, a strange squabble breaks out on the far edge of the pond. A songbird with brown feathers, a yellow breast, and a black throat sits at the water's edge and trills at a white duck as it glides past. The argument goes back and forth, their voices alternating between flute and oboe. As the noisy quarrel continues, a cat enters from beneath a nearby tree and stalks toward the water with clear intent. A smooth clarinet melody fills the air in time with the marauding feline's every step.

Strangely, I perceive this latest addition to the drama as more than just a cat, but as my cat. More importantly, I do not wish to see the orange tabby dine upon either the songbird or the duck.

"Fly from here," I shout to the pair of birds, my warning accompanied by the sound of a lone violin. "Fly and live to debate another day."

With a piccolo trill, the bird flits to a branch high in a tree by the lake while the duck paddles farther out into the safety of the pond's waters, the invisible oboe punctuating its frantic swim. The cat, clearly unimpressed by my intervention, shoots me a scathing look before disappearing back into the shadowy tree line.

Why does all of this seem so familiar?

I cast my mind back. Dad and me and the old record player in the family room. My first introduction to not only classical music, but to Russian composers.

A songbird. A duck. A cat. A pond. That means I must be—

"Petya?" A man's voice, strangely familiar despite the Russian accent and filled with both worry and frailty, echoes off the pond's still surface. A lone bassoon plays in the distance. "Where are you, Petya?"

Before I can stop myself, I raise my voice in answer. "I am here, Dedushka."

Dedushka. The Russian word for grandfather. Another piece of information I have no business knowing.

Heavy footsteps approach from a trail that leads into the woods and before I can take a breath, a gruff man with a long flowing beard of salt and pepper appears. Dressed in a heavy wool shirt with fur about his shoulders, loose pantaloons, and knee high black boots, my father's father glares at me from beneath a tall fur cap, though his dark eyes contain more concern than irritation.

"What are you doing out here by the water all alone?"

"I'm sorry, Dedushka. I was merely taking in the morning air."

"You shouldn't be away from the cottage without letting me know where you are."

"I'm fine." I raise my arms to either side and smile. "Ten fingers and ten toes, just like the last time you saw me."

"It's not funny, Petya. You know as well as I a wild beast brought down one of the mules last week." He draws in so close I can smell the tobacco smoke on his breath. "What if a wolf came out of the forest and I was not here to protect you?"

My answer is out of my mouth before I have a chance to think. "Boys like me are not afraid of wolves."

"That's what I'm afraid of." Dedushka straightens himself up to his full height and takes me by the ear. "Now, come with me."

Dedushka drags me back to our cottage and deposits me on a chair by the front door. He locks the gate to the fence surrounding our property and grabs an axe from an old stump in the corner of the yard.

"I have one more tree to bring down and then we will have a bite to eat. You are not to get out of that chair, do you understand?"

"Yes, Dedushka."

"Do you understand?" His voice grows even gruffer with the second iteration.

"Yes, Dedushka. I understand."

"Good." He hands me a small block of wood and a whittling knife. "Now, why don't you carve another animal for our collection on the mantel? Perhaps a turtle this time?"

"Yes, Dedushka."

As he disappears around the log and stone corner of our cottage, I put blade to wood but barely have time to carve away the first sliver before a new sound fills the air. A trio of French horns blares, and I know all too well what the sound represents. I creep to the corner of the cottage and peer around into the rear corner of the yard. There, Dedushka resins up his hands in preparation to fell a beech at least as old as he is.

Good. He'll be occupied for a while. I rush for the fence, leap the gate, and race back down the trail to the clearing by the pond. There, I find a sight that terrifies as much as intrigues me. As flute, oboe, clarinet, and horns all fight for supremacy, the songbird flits from branch to branch in terror, the cat scales another tree as quickly as its clawed feet will take it, and the duck struggles through the pond's shallows, all fleeing frantically from an enormous gray wolf.

I inhale to shout, and then remember in this place I am just a boy without a gun or even a...

Knife.

I glance down and find the whittling knife Dedushka gave me still resting in my palm. There's no way such a small blade would so much as scratch such an enormous predator as the wolf, but knives can serve more than one purpose.

As the wolf continues to chase the poor duck along the pond's edge, I rush to the old swing and with a few swift strokes of the whittling knife, free the dilapidated board from the end of the dangling rope. Without wasting a breath, I shimmy to the top, drag myself out onto the gnarled branch, and pull up the full length of coiled hemp. Remembering a few tricks I learned in the year Mom had me try Boy Scouts, I tie a slipknot in the end of the rope and have just completed the loop at the end of the line when a loud squawk from below ends the oboe melody.

At the edge of the pond, the wolf crouches with a mouthful of feathers devouring the duck in bite after gnashing bite. I shudder, the image of me at the wolf's mercy rather than the poor waterfowl flitting across my mind's eye.

No time for that now.

Too far from the cottage to shout for help, I scan the surrounding trees for anyone or anything that might help. My cat, back arched and every hair on end, peers down at the wolf, terrified. The songbird, on the other hand, chirps defiantly with a piccolo flute's insistent tone at the massive gray beast as if begging the monster to face it one on one.

"Songbird," I whisper as loudly as I dare. "Hear me."

"I am the lark," it answers, its voice shrill and piercing. "For what reason do you speak to me?"

I allow a smile, realizing at some level I'm arguing with myself. "The three of us—you, me, and the cat—are all in the same precarious predicament, each trapped in a tree with a marauding wolf below us."

"You and the cat, perhaps." The lark trills a quiet laugh. "I can fly away at any time I choose."

"Today, perhaps." I shoot the songbird a knowing glance. "But next time, when it's you who are alone, you may not find an ally quite so readily."

"You are more diversion than ally, boy, and a far more appetizing snack for the wolf than my tiny body." The lark flits in my direction and lands on a branch just beyond my reach. "Still, your boldness and ingenuity intrigue me. What would you have me do?"

"Distract the wolf. Lure it beneath me." I hold up the slip-knotted loop at the end of the rope. "I'll take care of the rest."

The lark tilts its head to one side as if evaluating my sanity, and then spreads its wings wide and drops from the branch. Flitting to the ground, the bird drags one brown wing along the ground beneath me, chirping, "My wing, my wing, it is broken, woe is me, it is broken."

The wolf swallows the last bit of the unfortunate duck, turns in the direction of the struggling bird, and immediately hunches down to attack.

The trap is set, the bait is in position, and now, it's all up to me.

What else is new?

The wolf creeps close as the lark continues to squawk and drag its wing.

I'll only have one shot at this.

I lower the makeshift lariat as quickly and quietly as possible. The wolf, distracted by the flailing songbird, doesn't notice, and prepares to leap. A flick of my wrist and the slipknot encircles the wolf's tail.

"Now," I shout. "Fly."

The lark flits away and the wolf turns its head up to glare at me with hungry, haunted eyes.

For all of half a second.

A quick yank tightens the knot around the beast's tail. The wolf attempts to flee, but only makes it a few feet before the length of hemp coil hoists its rear legs up and sends the creature nose first into the ground. Again and again it attempts to escape and each time the outcome is the same. The cat and the lark, their previous conflict for the moment forgotten, sit together on a branch and laugh.

"I've heard of catching a tiger by the tail," the cat purrs, "but the Big Bad Wolf?"

The wolf smiles through its exhaustion. "I would argue the analogy is quite apt, tabby cat. Or should I call you... second course?"

"Big talk," the lark squawks, "when you can't take as much as three steps without planting your snout in the mud."

"I'll be planting my snout in something else soon enough." The wolf cranes its neck to look up at me. "As for you, boy, you have exactly five seconds to release me, or I will feast upon your entrails as you watch."

"You'll do no such thing." I pull up on the rope until the wolf hangs from the branch like a forgotten yoyo, clamber down the tree's gnarled trunk, and position myself well beyond the reach of the monster's claws. "You'll hang there and behave yourself until my dedushka arrives."

But wait. It's not the grandfather that comes. There's one more character in this piece.

The hunter.

As if on cue, a thunderous roar of tympani drums echoes through the sky and a large man in boots and a heavy jacket steps from the forest edge carrying an enormous rifle. His face wrapped in a multicolored scarf reminiscent of Tom Baker's from old school Doctor Who, he stares first at me and then the wolf from beneath a furrowed brow.

"You did this, boy?" His Russian accent is even thicker than Dedushka's. "I've been stalking this monster for days and you've captured him..."

"With the swing rope." Another one I owe Dad, though if he'd never introduced me to *Peter and the Wolf*, I wouldn't be in this mess.

Talk about irony.

"What should we do with him?" I ask.

"For starters, we finish him." The huntsman rests his rifle against the tree trunk and pulls a curved blade from his belt. "Slit his throat, gut him, take his pelt."

The wolf's comment about feasting upon my entrails notwithstanding, that seems a bit harsh.

"Hold, huntsman. Perhaps the wolf would be more use to us alive than dead."

From behind the scarf, the huntsman lets out a wheezy laugh. "You're either very brave, boy, or very stupid."

Despite the accent, there's something about the way the huntsman speaks, looks at me, carries himself that seems familiar.

"May I ask, brave huntsman, your name?"

"Certainly." He unwraps his head and flips the several feet of scarf across his shoulder before turning back to me. "Boris Godunov, at your service."

Boris Godunov. A character from Russian history and folklore, and more importantly, a piece of Mussorgsky right here in the middle of Prokofiev's masterwork for children.

Not to mention that, like so many characters I've faced in the dreamworld before, he bears the features of Dr. Thomas Archer.

Dr. Archer. Detective Sterling. Mira Tejedor. It always comes down to—

Wait.

If Godunov is Dr. Archer, then perhaps the wolf is...

"Wrong, kid." The wolf's form shifts before my eyes, becoming a touch more human. "You're thinking I might be the detective, but you couldn't be further from the mark."

Pulling himself up at his newly formed waist, the half-wolf, half-man reaches up with a clawed hand and with a single slash, frees himself from my trap.

"You lose again, *Peter*, as you did at the Lake of Swans and again at the Hall of the Sugar Plum Fairy." He draws close, his eyes gleaming as his hot breath fills my nostrils and chokes me. "Only difference is this time it's going to hurt."

"Leave the boy alone," Godunov shouts. "He's—"

The wolf slashes out with an open hand, his razor-sharp claws raking across the huntsman's neck, silencing Godunov forever.

The cat and bird flee in terror, leaving me alone to face the wolf.

"And now," he says, the fur covering his face receding as he continues his transformation from monster to man, "the moment we've all been waiting for."

The wolf slaps me with the back of a paw turned hand once, twice, three times.

The forest disappears. The sky, the trees, the earth below my feet. All gone.

My eyes open on our family room.

Dr. Archer sits unconscious across the coffee table from me, still deep within the world of dream. I pray the wounds inflicted by the wolf don't translate to this side, though with all we've seen over the last year, I haven't the first clue how to determine if he's even still alive.

Movement to my left draws my attention. Bound and gagged on the floor, Mom stares up at me, her exhausted eyes filled with a terror I've never seen before even after all we've been through over the last year.

Wait. It's not me she's staring at, but something past my shoulder.

Or someone.

I turn my head slowly, knowing all too well the face that awaits me in the near darkness.

"Hello there, Anthony." Wendell James Durgan leans in as the dreamscape wolf did in a world a million miles from here. "I've literally been dying to meet you."

XIX

PETER AND THE WOLF

Who are you?" I try to keep any hint of recognition from my eyes. "Why are you doing this?"

Durgan shakes his head, a weary smile on his lips. "You know exactly who I am, Anthony Faircloth," he whispers, the sound like chalk on a cheese grater, "and you know exactly why I'm here."

"Get away from me," I shout as he yanks me from my seat and throws me to the floor. I scream at Dr. Archer to wake up and help me but my cries don't so much as bring a flinch. My first thought is that he merely hasn't come to from our shared visit to the world of dream, but a closer look at the angle of his neck suggests he's dealing with more than just a hypnotic trance or even the wounds inflicted on Boris Godunov by the wolf.

"Dr. Archer?"

"Your shrink isn't going to be helping anyone any time soon, kid." Durgan grabs me by the collar and pulls me to my feet. Brandishing an ugly-looking club about half an inch from my nose, he adds, "And unless you want to wake up in a few hours with one hell of a headache, I suggest you keep quiet and do what you're told."

My entire body tenses, the adrenaline rushing through my veins as millions of years of evolution prepare me to either fight tooth and nail or flee for my life. A glance in Mom's direction doesn't help the situation, the dread in her eyes doubling with each passing second.

All right, Anthony. You have to play this right. If you don't, Durgan might kill all of us.

At least Jason took Rachel to the park for the day. That keeps the two of them out of this.

Except for the simple fact that I have no idea what time it is. For all I know, my brother and sister are on their way back and Jason is about to step through the door totally unprepared for yet another situation that could leave him and the rest of us dead.

"What do you want with me, anyway?" I glance in the direction of the front foyer. "Like you said, I'm just a kid."

"Oh, you're far more than that." I get one last look at Mom's fear-filled gaze, her muffled cries setting my heart racing even faster, before Durgan is dragging me toward the front door. A good foot taller than me and at least as muscular as Jason, he isn't slowed a bit by my struggles, and in fact, seems a bit amused that I'm even trying. "Save your strength, kid. You're going to need it."

Outside, the sun is high in the sky. Dr. Archer arrived a little after ten this morning so I'm guessing two or three hours have passed.

No sign of Jason or Rachel. Good. If anything happened to either of them, I don't know what I'd do.

"Hey." Durgan yanks my arm and brings me back to the present. "Quit squirming, or you're going to force me to do something neither of us wants me to do, understand?"

"Understood," I mutter as I let my entire body go limp. "Is this better?"

"Real funny." The sudden slack in my legs doesn't slow Durgan down a bit. His biceps bulge beneath the cutoff sleeves of his sweat-stained flannel shirt as he lifts me from the ground with one hand and carries me to the end of the driveway.

I don't want to think about how many hours he's spent pumping iron since the cops put him away two years ago.

Not a soul in either direction on our little suburban street. In the middle of the day, most everyone is either at work or otherwise occupied. Durgan pulls me to a nondescript blue car that appears a few years older than me and chucks me into the trunk.

"Better hold on," he says as he slams the trunk lid down. "Going to be a bumpy ride."

The trip is strangely short, taking no more than twenty minutes, and it only gets rough right at the end, the intermittently rough ride of the average

Charlotte street devolving into what feels like a dirt road.

As the car pulls to a stop, a single morbid thought pops into my head accompanied by alternating flashes of von Rothbart, the Mouse King, and Prokofiev's wolf.

Has Durgan been this close the whole time?

The light blinds me as Durgan opens the trunk lid and yanks me out and onto my feet. Despite the full July sun baking my skin, it's nothing like the oven of the car's trunk. Catching the first breath of fresh air in what must be half an hour, I pull my hand to my forehead and as my eyes readjust to the midday light, everything becomes clear.

The car sits directly behind a half-built three-story house. Durgan busies himself covering the car with a large tarp covered in paint spatter, leaving me to take in the scene.

In either direction stand empty lots, some with foundations laid and others merely overgrown with several months' worth of grass and weeds. I'm not sure exactly where we are, but from a particularly chatty friend of Mom's who works in real estate, I have a pretty good idea.

During the economic downturn a few years back, Charlotte went from a seller's market where houses were sold before the builder even broke ground to a place where entire neighborhoods stopped mid-construction when the money dried up. There are places like this all over Charlotte, some thriving after having been bought out by new owners and some that continue to lie fallow, once fertile land suffering from years of economic drought.

No reason for anyone to come looking for me out here in no man's land. I'm completely at the mercy of a madman.

Fortunately, everything points to one simple fact.

If Durgan wanted me dead, he would have killed me back at the house. Probably Dr. Archer and Mom too.

He clearly needs me for something. What that is, I haven't the first idea.

Something terrible, no doubt.

Still, as long as I keep that card in my hand, my chances of making it out of this alive go up pretty significantly.

Which leaves me with two pretty big questions.

What does Durgan want with me?

And how long can I keep him from getting it?

"Come on, kid." Durgan pushes me in the direction of the three-story house skeleton, nearly sending me to my knees. "We've got work to do."

The walls and floors inside the half-finished structure are all particleboard and bare wood and rough edges. Nails protrude from every surface, spray painted messages adorn the walls, indicating heating ducts and hot water lines, and the windows have no glass or frames. Despite the shade of the mostly completed roof, the air inside the house is stifling and still.

"Basement." Durgan points to a roughed-out staircase leading down into darkness. I hesitate for all of a second before he shoves me forward with a staccato "Now."

As I descend the steps, a sense of strange familiarity overcomes me. Much like the awareness of another presence I experience from time to time when Mira comes around, I am struck by the very real perception of someone near.

And unless I miss my guess, it's not Durgan who's pushing this particular button in my mind.

The basement is dark save a glimmer of illumination in the far corner that appears to emanate from an old-timey gas lamp. There, a girl a few years younger than me sits hunched forward in a folding metal chair. Bound at her ankles, waist, and wrists with silver duct tape, her head has been shaved bald and glistens with sweat in the flickering light.

"Wake up," Durgan grunts. "I brought you some company."

Starting awake, the girl looks up, eyes sunken with dehydration suddenly wide with fear. Despite the dim glow of the lamp, I recognize her immediately. Sarah Goode.

A couple years older than the dozens of photos of her plastered all over the internet and bereft of her distinctive golden locks, no doubt at Durgan's hand, the trembling girl before me is unmistakable. No amount of grime can hide those insightful eyes that in every picture I've seen give the impression the girl knows something the rest of the world doesn't.

"Sarah?" I step further into the light so she can see me. "Are you okay?"

She squints at me, studying my features in the poor light. "You're Anthony, aren't you?"

First Durgan, now Sarah. How does everybody seem to know who I am?

"I'm guessing you're pretty confused right now, aren't you, kid?" Durgan plants me in a chair next to Sarah. "You all figured I'd be coming for Mira, right?"

Sullen, I keep my silence as Durgan continues.

"Oh, I've been by the hospital. Seen all the police. Even seen you and your mom come and go more than once." He goes to a cooler in the corner, breaks out a bottled water, and sidles over to Sarah's bound form. "Open wide."

If I expect any defiance from Sarah, I'm sorely disappointed. She puts her head back like a baby bird waiting for a worm from its mother. Durgan pours the water down her throat and Sarah gulps down every drop.

"See, Anthony?" Durgan lets out a sarcastic chuckle. "I'm not that bad a guy."

"You kidnap little girls, leave them tied up in abandoned basements, and do the absolute minimum to keep them from dying of dehydration. I'm sure they'll put you in for a medal."

Unfazed, Durgan tosses me a bottle of water as well. "Better drink up, kid." He winks as he unscrews his own bottle. "Wouldn't want you to die of thirst."

I want to defy him, spit in his face, but my mouth is too dry.

Survive this, Anthony. You've made it through worse.

"Fine." I suck down the ice-cold liquid, toss the bottle into the corner, and then level as intimidating a gaze as I can muster in Durgan's direction. "So, you didn't kill me. I'm guessing that means there's something you need. Something only I can provide." I incline my head in Sarah's direction. "Her too, right?"

"Very perceptive." Durgan kneels by my chair and grabs the roll of duct tape from the floor. As he winds the tape around my ankles, fastening me to the chair, he allows himself an occasional glance up to study my expression. "The suspense has got to be killing you."

"It's about the dreams, Anthony." Sarah winces at Durgan's glare, as if expecting him to strike. "That's what he wants."

"Shut up, girl, or it's no dinner tonight." Durgan turns back to face me, the anger in his face shifting back toward cool contemplation. "What Sarah said is right, though. It's all about the dreams."

"The dreams?" I ask, doing my best to maintain a poker face like Jason showed me when he was teaching me to play cards. "What dreams?"

"You can stop playing dumb any time, kid," Durgan grumbles. "No matter how much you think you know about me, I'm betting I know more about you."

He finishes his job of all but super gluing me to the chair and then drags over a third seat. Sitting backward on the chair, his nose just a few inches from mine, he studies me like a watchmaker examining his work.

"Let me start with the basics. You know who I am, you know Mira Tejedor, and you clearly know exactly who the girl is. I suspect you have some inkling of what I want, but unless you're even smarter than I've been led to believe, there is no way you fully understand why I'm here or what it is I need you to do."

I keep my silence, desperate not to make the situation worse with hasty words, as Durgan continues.

"I've only actually crossed paths with Mira Tejedor twice—the first time, when she came for Sarah, and the second, the day she came to court to testify against me. Though she was all business out in the field, she showed up to courtroom dressed to the nines like some kind of goddess. A vengeful goddess. Her eyes, filled with nothing but disgust, never left me once the entire time she was in the courtroom. It wasn't till months later I figured out why."

"She felt what you did." My gaze shoots to Sarah. "To her. Through her."

Durgan smiles. "Way I see it, it was buy one, get one free." He licks the sweat from his lips. "I'm just sorry I wasn't there to take it from her in person."

"Shut up, you... monster." My voice fades as Sarah begins to sob. "Just shut up."

"Shut up? I'm just getting started." He leans in so close I can smell his breath. Coffee. A hint of alcohol. And something rotten, just on the edge of perception. "You see, that's where you come in."

"Me?"

"You and Mira and your little Exhibition." Any pretense of joviality vanishes from his features. "It may have been just the two of you and that whore Sayles walking the stage, but some of us had front row seats to the madness."

"You... saw?"

"The third time the guards had to drag me screaming from my cell." He shivers, no doubt angry he allowed himself the moment of weakness. "And not just me." He jerks a thumb in Sarah's direction. "Her too."

"Sarah?"

She refuses to meet my gaze.

I return my attention to Durgan, my heart threatening to burst out of my chest. "But how?"

"The how is not what's important. All that matters to me is that it stops." He brings his hand to my face and squeezes my cheeks so hard, I'm afraid he'll leave bruises. "That, Anthony Faircloth, is where you come in."

"You're going to kill me, aren't you?"

He shakes his head from side to side, a single sarcastic laugh passing his lips. "No, Anthony. I'm not going to kill you. At least not if you do exactly what I say."

Trembling, I narrow my eyes at Durgan in a futile attempt to see through to his soul. "What is it you want me to do?"

"Simple." He leans back in his chair and crosses his arms before his chest.

"I want you to take me with you into this world of exhibitions and gardens and fairs and help free me from this insane dreamworld you and Tejedor share."

"But..." I consider my response carefully. I've got to lead him toward the answers I need without tipping my entire hand. "I've already seen your face there. You were the sorcerer from *Swan Lake*..."

"Among others." He glares at me, his gaze just this side of manic. "It's been different lately. My connection more... direct."

Makes sense. In all the worlds of dream Mira and I have walked, I may supply the substrate, but this time Mira's mind is the battleground, and from everything I've gleaned from talking with her and Dr. Archer, the link between Mira, Durgan, and Sarah Goode is second only to mine with Mira herself.

Despite all she went through to solve every problem and defeat every enemy, her efforts have again merely led to something worse.

No wonder Mira retreated into herself after dancing *The Rite of Spring*.

"Still," he continues, "I need even more power and influence in this place you and Mira share if I am to accomplish my ultimate goal."

"And what is that?" I ask.

"Simple. I'm going to destroy her the way she destroyed Versailles." He slides off the chair and pulls a bottle of something that is decidedly not water from the cooler. "And you're going to help me."

"Like hell I will."

He takes a long slug from the bottle and rests it on a stud sticking out of the unfinished wall. "You're going to help me." He jabs a thumb across his shoulder. "Or Sarah there is going to suffer."

I scramble for a response. "I'm not even sure how we would get there. I usually do this with Mira and—"

"Don't sell yourself short, kid. You were walking the dream realm this morning with just you, your mother, and your shrink at the house." His lips part in a devious smile. "I've got faith you can make this happen."

"But why would you possibly want to go *with* me?" My eyes shoot to Sarah and then back to Durgan. "I've been doing everything in my power to stop you for days."

"And failing miserably, I might add." He takes another slug of the brown alcohol. "Still, despite losing on all three of our shared battlefields so far, Tejedor still breathes. I'm guessing your little summit with Mommy and Dr. Archer was to figure out a way to go after Mira more directly this time." He strolls over to Sarah and rests his hand atop her shorn head before yanking it back as if he were a predator exposing her neck. "I'm going straight for her jugular, Anthony Faircloth, and you're going to guide me every step of the way."

Durgan and I sit opposite each other, his hands in mine, our knees almost touching and less than an inch separating our sweat-soaked faces.

"Back to the forest of *Peter and the Wolf* we go," he whispers. "And remember, little wooden boy. In the dream, you may have me all bound up, but out here in the real world, there are no strings on me. Do anything contrary to my purposes and you won't be the only one who suffers." He glances in Sarah's direction, as if I need any further hints about exactly what will happen if I disobey. "Got it?"

"Got it." I lock gazes with Durgan. "Understand I'll give this all I've got, but I've never tried to go solo like this. It might take some…"

My eyes slide closed as I go under faster than even Dr. Archer can manage. Everything goes black and silent. Then, from the darkness, a string quartet. Then horns. Back and forth, the cacophony fades into a frantic melody of fear and courage and love and loss and then…

We're there.

Back in the form of Peter, I hold in my hand a short coil of rope that leads to a loop that encircles the wolf's thick neck and then coils around its snout, leaving both the monster's windpipe and its double row of razor sharp teeth at my command.

Or so it would appear to anyone on this side of whatever strange looking glass leads to this increasingly bizarre wonderland.

Tilting its head in my direction so it can stare at me with one yellow eye, the wolf mutters through the side of its mouth, "Lead on, boy. The day is growing short."

"Where would you have me lead?"

"I don't know. You came here before seeking answers, I can only assume. Who did you come here to speak with?"

"I came here to speak with the witch, but instead, I met a wolf. Now, I'm not sure what I'm supposed to—"

Wait. The witch and her threadbare rags.

Just like the rough excuse for a handkerchief in Peter's pocket.

"You're the one equipped with the expert sniffer." I kneel by the wolf's head, reach into my pocket, and pull out the ripped piece of sackcloth. No doubt a scrap left over from a previous trip through the dreamworld that exists between mine and Mira's mind, the torn burlap must be a link to the one entity who might possess the information I need to save Mira, stop Durgan, and finally bring this tragedy to an end.

But to find her, I'm going to have to take this monster exactly where it wants to go.

"Here." I hold the tattered cloth before the wolf's wet snout. "Follow this scent and it will take you to one who knows how you can find Mira Tejedor and be rid of her once and for all."

"And who might that be, boy?" The wolf peers at me as if attempting to divine if I am in fact telling the truth. "To whom are you leading me?"

"To the witch in the wood. She who rides the stone mortar and grinds children's bones inside with her mighty pestle. She who lives in the hut on fowl's legs." I allow the wolf one last sniff, and then return the cloth to my pocket. "If you wish to be free of this realm forever, then take us to Baba Yaga."

XX

THE HUNT

Our path winds through the forest away from Dedushka's cottage, the canopy overhead blocking out more and more of the sunlight with each passing minute. My mind rebels at the convenience of the dark wood from *The Hut on Fowl's Legs* being somehow within walking distance. Still, considering the myriad of things Mira and I have encountered in this place that exists between our minds, I push away my disbelief and focus on the matter at hand.

Our stroll through the woods starts as just that, with the wolf creeping along for a minute or two and then stopping to sniff the air for any hint of the witch with iron teeth. That all ends a couple miles in, however, when the monster on the other end of the makeshift leash finally catches the scent and nearly rips my shoulder out of its socket as it charges ahead.

The woods grow deeper and darker with each mile that passes beneath our feet. The ground uneven and rocky, I turn my ankle on more than one occasion and even the wolf loses its footing once or twice. We're both flirting with utter exhaustion when we round an enormous boulder that juts from the ground like the lone tooth in a giant's jaw and the forest takes on an eerie hue, a twilight state between day and night I remember all too well.

Flashes of another moment in this same wood ricochet across my thoughts.

Mira so brave in the face of one she thought at the time her enemy.

My sister, in her role as Trilby, crushed beneath the taloned foot of the Hut on Fowl's Legs.

My mother and father, albeit the witch and composer of the Exhibition, reunited after years spent on opposite sides of the veil of death.

Everything fading to black as, a world away, Veronica Sayles tried to suffocate me with a pillow on a couch that still sits in our home.

This is not a good place, and it holds more pain than I can possibly bear. Still, as a song I once heard repeats over and over till the final chorus, the only way out is through.

"She's here." The first words from the wolf in hours. "And close."

The wolf redoubles its efforts at pulling my arm from my torso. I bring my other hand to bear on the rope, working to keep some semblance of control over the wild beast, and scan the forest for any hint of Baba Yaga.

The sound is quiet at first, but as it gets closer, I remember Mira's description of the inexorable percussion of Baba Yaga's mortar and pestle.

Crash. Thud.

"She's coming."

"Good." The wolf stops in its tracks. "Time is wasting."

Crash. Thud. Closer this time.

"Let me do the talking." I kneel by the wolf and whisper into its ear. "At some level, I have to believe the witch knows both who I am and what she is to me. That alone should buy me at least a bit of mercy should she meet us with anything other than open arms." I look directly into the wolf's yellow eyes. "She might not, however, show similar mercy to a marauding wolf that speaks like a man."

Crash. Thud. Almost on top of us.

The wolf considers and then lowers its head. "I shall hold my tongue, boy, as long as you agree to watch yours."

"Of course."

As the next repetition of striking pestle and pounding mortar hits my ears, the witch finally comes into view. Though I know deep down the ancient crone at some level represents my mother, the knowledge does little to mollify my fears in the face of the witch's bone-chilling cackle or the heart-stopping clang of her iron teeth.

A blink and she is there, floating above us with a curious cast in her timeworn eyes.

"Who dares invade my wood?" Her voice like steel across concrete, the witch points her mighty pestle of wood at my nose, her switch broom flailing back and forth behind her like the wagging of a dog's tail. "Wait." A flash of recognition crosses her face. "I know you, boy."

"Indeed you do, though you may not recognize me in this particular incarnation."

"You're the lad from the *Tuileries* garden." Her inquisitive eyes narrow in anger. "And the face behind the mask that was Koschei the Deathless." She stills the broom but remains atop her mortar. "What business have you here? And mind your words or I'll hurl you and your dog into my mortar and grind you both into a fine paste for my stew this evening."

The old witch licks her lips, the wolf strains angrily at the rope, and my knees nearly buckle beneath me.

"Mighty Baba Yaga, I have come to your wood seeking knowledge."

"Knowledge, you say?" She throws her head back and laughs, the sound sending my pulse into overdrive. "And with what might you dream of paying me for such a boon?"

"I have in my pocket a fragment of your dress." I pull forth the scrap of ragged sackcloth and hold it before me even as I lower my head in deference. "As you said, we have met before. I felt this might buy me at least a moment's consideration."

The witch strokes a discolored mole at the tip of her chin, deposits broom and pestle in her mortar, and climbs down from her stony perch. Seizing the fragment of burlap from my hand, she studies it, pulls it to her bulbous nose for a sniff, and then unleashes her foul tongue from its iron cave to give the rough piece of cloth an intimate taste.

"This is indeed mine, but I would only have granted such a token to someone very special." Her piercing gaze wanders from me to the wolf and back. "What did you say your name was, boy?"

"Here, I am Peter. As you said, however, you have known me in many guises."

"So it would seem." She kneels before the wolf. "Take care with your dog as you travel my demesne. There are wolves that roam my forest that make your cur look like a newborn pup."

A low growl sets up in the wolf's belly, but a quick yank on the rope convinces both it and the man it represents to hold their shared tongue as agreed.

"So," I mutter, bowing my head in submission, "you'll help me?"

Baba Yaga strides over to a flat stone at the base of the enormous boulder and takes a seat, patting a large hunk of granite by her hip as an invitation to join her. "You, boy, are in luck, as I find myself in a strangely generous mood today. You may ask three questions and three questions only, and then you must leave." With a hideous grin, she adds, "Should I find your questions entertaining, I may even guarantee you safe passage."

"Thank you, Baba—"

"In exchange," she interrupts, "I will keep the fragment of my dress and you must make an oath never to return here again." Her eyes cut upward to where her pestle peeks above the top of her stone mortar. "Unless, of course, you are desirous of being my main course some cold evening."

"Three questions, then." My mind boggles. Where to begin? I've been so afraid of the witch and the wolf and of getting lost and of failure, I haven't taken the time to prepare for the most important part.

"Tick tock, boy. I agreed to answer your questions, not to sit here waiting for senility."

"All right. First question." I struggle to articulate my question in a way that I might pull water from this notoriously obstinate well. "There is a woman trapped alone somewhere in this place. She has gone by many names in her adventures: Clara Stahlbaum. Odette. The Spring Maiden. The Ballerina. Ivanovna. You, however, know her best as Scheherazade. Do you know where she is?"

"The storyteller?" Baba Yaga stares up into the dark forest canopy above our heads. "I've not seen or heard so much as a whisper of her since she danced *The Rite of Spring* and returned order to our world."

"She's here, though, or at least has visited this realm since that time. Both as Swan Princess and the love of the Nutcracker Prince. You know all, Baba Yaga. How is it possible she's visited this place twice without your knowledge?"

"Simple. In the past, I have been privy to information hidden from most, but that mainly came from keeping my fingers in many pies and my ear to the ground. Since the purging of the Exhibition, the destruction of Koschei, and Mira's sacrificial dance to end the Winter, I have mostly kept to myself. Barely left these woods have I and have taken no visitors until now." She crinkles her nose at me. "That, boy, is the answer to your second missive. You have one question remaining before you must leave and never return."

"One quest—" I stop myself before I repeat my mistake.

Dammit. The oldest trick in history and I fell right into her verbal snare. I'll have to make this last one count. Broad enough to get her talking but specific enough that she can't merely dance around the point.

Wait. I've got it.

Flattery.

"Oh, wise Baba Yaga, if even someone as all-knowing as yourself doesn't know the whereabouts of the famed Scheherazade, then what hope have I of ever finding her in this endless realm of imagination?"

The witch stares at me, incredulous and unmoving. Then, with a quiet harrumph, she runs her fingers through her stringy gray hair and hawks a wad of spittle to the ground at my feet. "The answer to your final question, boy, is twofold." She rises from the stone and hobbles over to her mortar, which in turn lowers its lip to accept her. "First, if you wish to find the storyteller, you will need the help of one who has been dispatched from this realm time and again and yet retains a tenuous hold on our world even now, her continued existence fueled in no small part by the unadulterated hatred that burns at her very core."

I know all too well of whom the witch speaks, and the thought of facing her again terrifies me. If she indeed still somehow exists here among the world of dream, we have far worse problems than Wendell James Durgan, regardless of the guise he chooses. To ask for *her* help, assuming we could even find *her*, would be tantamount to suicide.

"And the second part?"

Baba Yaga laughs. "A fourth question, but I'll allow it. The wood has been lonely these past few weeks and you and your mutt have brought a smile, however brief, to my face this day."

A smile that will give me nightmares for the rest of my days.

Another low growl escapes the wolf's muzzle, requiring another tug on the rope.

"Speak then, Baba Yaga, and let us be on our way before we overstay your more than generous welcome."

"You negotiate with wise courtesy, boy." The enormous stone mortar rights itself and soon Baba Yaga again stares down at us from atop her seat of power. "Though I stopped before for a reason."

"And what reason might that be?"

"The simplest of all. Whether you call yourself Peter or Fritz or Benno or Antoine or Tunny or even," she hesitates, "Anthony... at some level you already know the answer." At my confused stare, the witch lets out an exasperated sigh. "Very well. Allow me to answer one question with another. You came here, boy, led only by a memory left on this scrap of cloth." She holds aloft the fragment of burlap and waves it to and fro like a tiny flag. "Without this you would never have found me."

"The wolf followed your scent and that led us to your wood, but what does that have to do with finding the lady Scheherazade?"

"It has everything to do with finding her. I never dreamed you would be so obtuse." At my continued dumbfounded gaze, she groans. "Tell me, boy. Where did you get the cloth?"

"You gave it to me, oh benevolent Baba Yaga."

"Did I?" she asks. "Did I, indeed?"

And with that she spins atop her mortar and retrieves her pestle and broom. A heartbeat later, she has disappeared back into the surrounding darkness of her wood as if she were never here.

"What did she mean by that?" the wolf grumbles. "What does a scrap of cloth have to do with anything?"

"I don't know," I mutter, "but after coming all this way, it seems that's the only answer we're going to get."

The wolf stretches its back and then studies me with its yellow eyes. "And the other of whom she spoke." For the first time in either world, an edge sounds in the wolf's voice. "She can't possibly mean for us to ask *her* for assistance."

"The truth?" I bury my face in my hands. "I fear that is precisely what she means."

Sweltering heat fills my lungs as I struggle back to consciousness. My fingers tingle below the duct tape Durgan used to secure my hands and my entire body aches at having been stuck in the chair for who knows how long.

Puzzled as to why our sojourn through the world of dream has been cut short so suddenly, I peer around the dimly lit basement and find Durgan hunched over Sarah Goode's bound form. At first, it seems he's attacking her, but as my vision clears, a far more sobering reality comes to light.

Sarah hangs limp from her chair while Durgan tears the tape from her wrists and ankles with a ferocity borne of desperation.

"Oh, no you don't, girl," Durgan whispers as he pulls away the last binding from her ankle and hauls her flaccid body out of the chair. "You don't get out of this that easily."

He disappears up the rough-cut stairs to the main floor and for a while I hear nothing. No footsteps from above, no voices, not even the whistle of an ambient breeze. The utter silence is, in its own way, maddening. I struggle against my bonds for all the good it does me.

Durgan has done his work well.

Time passes. An hour? A day? My thoughts shift further into delirium with each breath. Faces and events from all the worlds and realms formed by the mingling of mine and Mira's minds flit through my thoughts like a movie montage. The common theme to each? Death.

They all end in death.

I'm sitting at the verge of unconsciousness when the sound of quick footsteps coming down the stairs brings me back to the situation at hand. In the poor illumination of the lone camping lamp, I can just make out Durgan's rushing form, though my mind twists his shape into that of the dark sorcerer from *Swan Lake*.

"Don't you try and go out on me too, boy." Durgan descends upon me like a vulture on a roadside carcass. He slides the knife from his pocket and in seconds frees me from my bonds.

"Come on," he grunts as he yanks me up from my chair. "We don't have all day."

Durgan drags me up the stairs, my numb toes catching more than once on the unfinished wood.

"Where are you taking me?" I stammer as we reach the main floor. "Where's Sarah?"

"Still breathing."

Outside, he pulls me the last few feet to his car and deposits me in the back seat. The engine running, the air conditioning is just beginning to drop the temperature inside a degree or two. Sarah lies collapsed opposite me, her skin pale and drenched with sweat.

Durgan slaps a bottle of water into my hand. "Keep her hydrated, you hear?"

"Where are we going?" I ask as he slides into the driver's seat and we pull out from behind the half-finished house. "What are you going to do with us now?"

"You sure ask a lot of questions for someone up to their eyeballs in shit." We trundle up the hill to the main road and soon leave the aborted community in our rear view mirror. "Seems you and Sarah's delicate constitutions can't take a little heat."

"Stick us in an oven," I mutter sarcastically, "do we not cook?"

"You think you're so damn clever." Durgan clears his throat and fiddles with the radio, no doubt so he can listen to anything besides me. "A word of advice, kid? Show some respect. When this is all over, you'll want to be on my good side. I assure you of that."

A thousand retorts pop into my head, each sharper than the one before. I wisely keep my mouth shut, in part to protect my own neck, but mostly so Durgan will leave me alone while I help bring Sarah around. Fortunately, she appears to be responding to the air conditioning. The color of her cheeks is returning and her pulse no longer feels like a hummingbird's.

I offer her sips of water when I'm comfortable she's awake enough not to choke. A few minutes later her eyes flutter open.

"Where are we?" she asks, her voice rough. "Did we—"

"Shhh." I bring a finger to my lips. "Quiet now." I glance up and meet Durgan's gaze in the rearview mirror. "You're safe... for the moment."

"For the moment," Durgan repeats under his breath, shaking his head. "You've got a flair for the dramatic, kid. I'll give you that."

"You have no idea," escapes my lips, and I immediately wish the words back into my mouth. My "flair for the dramatic" is the lone reason Sarah and I are in this mess in the first place. A part of me expects Durgan to pull over and show me exactly how much of an idea he might have.

Instead, he punches the accelerator and makes a sharp right turn, sending my shoulder hurtling into Sarah's chest and driving the wind from her lungs.

"Better buckle up, kid," Durgan whispers as we turn onto one of the main arteries leading into Uptown. "Ride only gets bumpier from here."

XXI

ISLE OF THE DEAD

Not exactly as private as our previous home away from home," Durgan mutters as he paces the concrete floor, "but it'll have to do for now."

The decor of this place, a restaurant or bar that appears to have been gutted for renovation, is little better than the half-finished basement where Sarah nearly suffocated in the heat earlier today, but at least it has working central air. Where we are exactly, I'm not sure, as I was busy bringing Sarah around, though it must be one of Charlotte's bigger suburbs. Maybe Matthews? Or Mint Hill? Night has fallen, as evidenced by the mercury light seeping around the sheets of plywood blocking the front window facade of the place, and therefore it's relatively quiet.

Sarah, though bound and gagged in the chair opposite me, seems to have recovered from her earlier ordeal, though she's clearly terrified out of her mind.

In that, she's not alone.

Durgan seems distracted for the first time since this afternoon when he took me from my home. I study his every move and try to get any kind of insight into what makes him tick. I'd like to think the forced change of venue would have left the man a bit shaken, but he seems to be taking all of this in stride.

I suppose a year or two in prison would do wonders for a person's adaptability.

One thing becomes clear very quickly. Durgan is nothing if not fastidious. He checks the lock of the back alley door no less than five times and surveys every possible angle that a passerby could peer through the front windows. The precision of both Sarah's bonds and mine speaks of a mind that craves order in the midst of chaos.

In a different set of circumstances, I'd almost say he was a kindred spirit.

But as I struggle to breathe past the rag stuffed in my mouth, the only emotion I can mount is hate. Hate for this man, for all he has done, for the sum total of pain he has caused, for the psychic cancer that started between him and Mira and now engulfs three families.

I grunt into the gag, louder and louder with each repetition, until Durgan finally breaks out of his self-imposed trance and drops to one knee in front of my chair.

"What?" He yanks the rag out of my mouth and leaves it hanging around my neck. When I don't answer immediately, he raises a hand as if to strike. "Don't fuck with me, kid."

"I couldn't breathe." I glance over at Sarah. "And seeing as how you already let one of us almost suffocate today..."

"Better watch your mouth." Durgan grabs the gag and starts to slide it back into place. "I need you alive, but not necessarily in one piece."

"Wait." I jerk my head to one side so he can't silence me. "You've got me, you've got Sarah, and no one has the first clue where we are."

"And?" he asks.

"I'm just wondering what you're waiting for." I turn my head back to face Durgan, locking gazes with his stony eyes. "We were finally getting somewhere before when the real world interrupted. You know. Peter. The wolf." I drop my voice to a whisper. "The witch."

Durgan allows himself half a second to process what I've said before squinting at me in the dim light. "You trying to trick me, boy?"

"To be honest, I'm just trying to make it through this alive." I suck in a deep breath, the cool air sweet on my tongue after breathing my own carbon dioxide for the last hour. "You can't break this link that's been forged between you, Mira, and Sarah without my help, and if you're not getting what you need from me, you have exactly zero reason to keep either of us breathing." An unbidden chill sends my entire body into spasm. "Do you want to do this or are you going to go check all the locks again?"

The rush of blood to Durgan's cheeks, just visible in the low light, lets me know I've really pissed him off this time. Still, he manages to keep a passably even tone as the next words pass his lips.

"Back to the forest, then."

One second, I'm lashed to a chair in Durgan's makeshift dungeon. The next, I'm standing by yet another lake at the edge of yet another wood. Beside me, the wolf sounds off with a low growl, clearly as disoriented by the sudden change in scenery as I am.

The gentle ripples coming off the mist-enshrouded lake lap at the shore in time with a quiet melody that tickles the back of my brain. Like the rhythm of waves, the strangely familiar strain begins with low strings, tympani, and harp, every note a puzzle and every beat a mystery. The tune wanders without direction, but both the volume and urgency increase with each passing measure.

A few feet down the shore, atop a tall post, hangs a brass bell roughly the size of a short barstool, the clapper peeking out from the bell's mouth like a conical metallic tongue. From the yoke extends a section of cord that falls to roughly chest level with a carefully tied loop at the end, very much like the loop I tied previously to capture the wolf.

As if the wolf has ever truly been under my power.

Driven by instinct, I give the rope a sharp tug. The bell rings once, twice, three times, and then falls silent again as its clanging tones echo from across the mist-obscured water.

"Why did you do that?" the wolf asks. "You have no idea what that bell does or who it might bring."

I set my jaw and turn to face the irate beast. "We've come here looking for someone and have no idea where to begin." I shift my attention out across the water. "Do you have a better idea?"

The wolf and I wait in silence at the water's edge for what feels like a year, and still, no one comes. No sun passes overhead to mark the minutes and hours, nor does nightfall ever bless us with its cool darkness. Instead, we remain, the wolf and I, beneath a sky of unending twilight, awaiting a fate neither of us can predict.

As my patience finally begins to ebb, I contemplate ringing the bell once more and dealing with whatever consequences that action might bring.

That's when I see it.

Breaking through the mist a hundred yards or so from shore, an old rowboat like the ones Dad would rent when we used to go camping glides across the lake's still surface. At the oars sits a cloaked figure. Though the form's face is turned from us, the rower guides the dilapidated vessel unerringly in our direction as if he or she rides atop a guided missile.

"I don't like this," the wolf growls.

"What?" I ask, holding back a smirk. "You don't like it when something happens in this weirdo dreamworld that isn't under your absolute control?" Any hint of humor leaves my voice. "Welcome to the last year of my life."

With each stroke of the oars, the pale rowboat grows closer, the music louder, the air colder. After an interminable wait, the bow of the boat crunches into the stiff grass at the water's edge with the sound of shattering icicles. Silently, the figure turns to face us, its face still hidden in the shadow of the cloak's hood. A pallid hand extends from beneath the dark folds of the cloak, the skin of the outstretched palm and fingers colorless and loose.

"What does this creature want?" the wolf whispers.

The unseen orchestra continues with the ever-building melody, a high violin interspersed with a tune reminiscent of a Gregorian chant. Though I finally recognize why the piece seems so familiar, it's another song from a completely different era that suddenly floods my imagination—one of Dad's favorites from his teen years the local 80s station plays from time to time.

"This, wolf, is the Ferryman."

The cloaked figure offers us a subtle nod.

"What does he want?" the wolf asks, assigning a gender to the nebulous specter before us.

"He wants us to pay him." As Chris de Burgh's lyrics play across my subconscious, I reach into my pocket. Inside, as suspected, I find a pair of gold coins. Each bears a Cyrillic inscription and the likeness of Pyotr Ilyich Tchaikovsky. "And I suspect he wants his payment now."

"Two coins." The wolf studies my outstretched hand as if deciding whether or not to bite it off. "The fee to take the two of us across this lake to wherever it is we're supposed to go next?"

"Precisely."

The wolf draws back its furry lips from its mouthful of razor teeth. "Then pay the man and let's get on with this."

Don't do it, comes a quiet chorus from across the water.

"No," I whisper as a gentle rain begins to fall. "Not until he gets us to the other side."

At my words, the Ferryman nods again, and motions for me to enter the boat. As I climb into the oblong vessel, my leg brushes his cloak. I break out with gooseflesh at the chill.

As I take my seat in the stern of the boat, I train my eyes on the wolf. Pacing the shore, the beast seems unsure whether to trust me or the mysterious stranger in black.

"We have enough to pay for two, wolf, and he's invited us into his boat." I motion for him to join me and the Ferryman in the tiny watercraft. "Get in before he changes his mind."

The wolf chews on what I've said for several seconds, and then, with reluctance in its yellow eyes, steps carefully into the bow of the boat.

"When you say Ferryman," the wolf asks, "you can't possibly mean *that* Ferryman."

"That is exactly what I mean." I raise an eyebrow. "Unless you have a better explanation?"

As the Ferryman pushes off from shore and turns the boat around, a low guttural sound escapes the wolf's throat, the sound somewhere between irritation and fear. "And where, may I ask, do you believe this boat will take us?"

"To a place where we hopefully will find the person of whom Baba Yaga spoke. Left to die as the Exhibition collapsed upon itself, killed by the Moor's blade, and banished as Mira danced *The Rite of Spring*, I'm guessing we've arrived at the only place where we might commune with such a person."

The invisible symphony continues its slow crescendo, building toward the piece's climax. The Ferryman rows in silence, his every stroke in time with the five-count melody that pounds at our ears.

"You speak in as many riddles as the witch," the wolf whispers. "Tell me, Peter. Where is this man taking us?"

"Ah." My lips part in a smug smile. "You don't know this piece."

The wolf shoots me its best version of a sidelong glance. "Should I?"

"It's Rachmaninoff." I peer through the swirling mists that surround us, trying to get a glimpse of our destination. "The Ferryman has come to transport us to the Isle of the Dead."

Brass and drum and woodwind and strings all take their turns as we make our way through the rain and mist toward a place none of us, save possibly the Ferryman, can see.

Then, just as the music breaks into a beautiful violin melody, the Isle comes into view.

Just as imagined by Arnold Böcklin, the creator of the painting that inspired Rachmaninoff's most famous symphonic poem, the Isle of the Dead rises out of the fog before us. Carved from white stone, the island appears an enormous grotto with a forest of ancient evergreens at its center. Carved into the interior of the stone, arched doorway after arched doorway opens on places I'd rather not consider. At the center of the opening in the marble walls, a landing for the rowboat awaits.

"Isle of the Dead, eh?" the wolf mutters as the Ferryman docks the boat. "And you're sure this is where we want to be, Peter?"

"Baba Yaga told us what we needed to do and who we needed to speak with to bring this nightmare to an end."

"To the contrary." The wolf lets out an uncharacteristic laugh as he stares up at the daunting forest of dark pine and cedar. "This nightmare is just beginning."

The wolf steps out of the boat and onto the land. I briefly contemplate seizing the oars from the Ferryman and rowing away, leaving the wolf to rot on the island with the object of our search, but if there's one thing I've learned from watching Mira navigate the murk between our minds, it's that these stories must be seen through to the end.

I climb past the Ferryman, making every effort to avoid touching him this time. Once on land, I turn and offer him a quick salute. In answer he simply holds out his pale hand a second time.

"Why pay him now?" the wolf asks. "You have only the two coins. Won't we need them to get back across when we're done here?"

My eyes dance between the wolf's and the Ferryman's, the latter's hidden beneath his voluminous hood. With a deep breath that steams the frigid air about my head, I reach into my pocket, pull out the pair of coins, and place them in the Ferryman's outstretched palm. His fingers close around the two pieces of gold and deposit them in one of his cloak's hidden pockets. Then, before pushing off from the landing, he reaches up a pale hand and pulls back his hood, revealing a face I've not seen in some time. One eye trained on me and the other on the wolf, the disconjugate gaze of the Exhibition's Janitor and the Sage from *The Rite of Spring* looks upon us in solemn silence as the boat disappears into the surrounding mist.

The music, so thunderous and brassy moments before, goes silent, the only sounds the gentle lapping of the waves on the landing, the pitter-patter of rain on stone, and the quiet rustle of wind through the trees. The damp chill in the air sets all my hair on end, though I do find some comfort in the overpowering pine scent of the island's enclosed forest.

To our right leans another post, another bell, another cord.

If this is truly the Isle of the Dead, a bell on this side of the lake seems to be superfluous at best and at worst, cruel.

Something to consider once we've found who or what we're looking for, I suppose.

"Shall we?" I ask, taking a step inland.

"No time like the present." With a decided huff, the wolf follows me.

Traveling the forest from Dedushka's cottage to the realm of Baba Yaga may have posed its difficulties, but that trip was a pleasant stroll through a backyard garden compared to navigating the alternating brambles and bogs of Rachmaninoff's famed isle. Less than a hundred steps in, the wolf gets stuck in a tangle of briars, the thorny vines at its throat threatening to choke the life from the beast. I'm tempted to let nature take its course and leave the wolf to die, but the situation necessitates its continued breathing.

At least for now.

With a few careful cuttings, I free the wolf from its prison of tendrils and together we continue through the dense underbrush.

We've barely gone another hundred yards when it's my turn to cry out in horror.

The ground beneath my feet is solid one step and like quicksand the next. Sinking faster than I can imagine, I barely have time to take a breath before the muck and mud swallow me up to my chest. I tilt my head and body back in an effort to float, but it does little to slow the sinking. The black slime rises past my collarbone, neck, and has made its way to my chin when the powerful jaws of the wolf close on my shoulder. Its razor sharp teeth as gentle as a mother's touch, the wolf drags me from the pit and deposits me again on dry land before falling down panting at my side.

"Thank you," I stammer once I've stopped hyperventilating. "That was... unexpected."

"The bog?" the wolf asks. "Or me pulling you from it?" When I don't answer, the wolf lets out a bellowing laugh and adds, "Fear not, child. Your instincts speak true."

"My instincts?"

The wolf wallows in a patch of leaves and twigs in an effort to clean the muck from its fur. "It is to each of our benefit to keep the other alive, but we are not friends and only allies out of necessity." It flips back onto its feet and stares at me hungrily. "Trust me when I tell you that if I didn't need you alive, I'd have left you to that quagmire without a second thought."

"At least we're both clear on that point." Covered head to toe in filth, I turn on one heel and head deeper into the miniature forest. "Coming?"

Ensconced as we are beneath the thick evergreen canopy, I can still appreciate the sound of precipitation pelting the trees even though I no longer feel the raindrops on my skin. The air is still, without the chirping of insects or the twitter of birds. Only the trees, vibrant and green, seem alive in this place.

The acrid smell of smoke hits my nose long before I see the cloud of billowing white up ahead. The flickering of orange flame between the trees illuminates a figure in yellow, her flaxen hair pulled up off her neck in a hairstyle that went out of fashion a century ago. As we draw close, the woman stirs and walks to the far edge of the fire to stoke the flames.

I allow the wolf to step into the tiny clearing first in case the whole thing is a trap. Far from an attack, however, the woman in yellow drops to one knee and welcomes my four-legged companion.

"I can't believe it." A familiar voice, but not the one I was expecting. "It's been so long," come the dulcet tones. "Come here, boy."

As I step out of the woods into the open air, I find the woman in yellow kneeling over the wolf and scratching its haunches as if welcoming a family pet rather than a ravening beast. The display goes on for well over a minute before she glances in my direction.

Far from the vengeful gaze I had expected to encounter upon our arrival at Rachmaninoff's famed Isle of the Dead, the eyes that stare back at me belong to none other than Julianna Wagner, or in this place, I suppose, Juliet from *The Marketplace at Limoges*.

"Antoine," she whispers. "You're here." Tears form at the corners of her eyes. "But, that means you're…"

"I'm fine, Juliet." I glance down at my muck-encrusted clothes. "And very much alive, my current state notwithstanding."

"Alive?" she asks. "Then how did you come to be here?"

"A question I would like answered as well." The words, delivered in an icy French accent, hit my ears even as a vice-like grip falls upon my shoulder and pulls me around to face the hate-filled glare of Madame Versailles. "Hello, Anthony Faircloth."

XXII

At the Fireside

Madame Versailles drags me to the fire and hurls me at the feet of the wolf.

"I'm not certain what possessed you to come here," she seethes, "but if you're so eager to visit the Isle of the Dead, I can arrange for your visit to become far more permanent."

"Leave Antoine alone," Juliet cries, hurling her body between Versailles' and mine. "He's done nothing to you."

"Done nothing..." Versailles' eyes narrow. "You haven't the first idea of what you speak, girl."

The wolf, its crafty yellow eyes taking in every nuance of the spat, maintains its silence, though I can see its wheels turning, and by proxy, Durgan's.

I stand and brush myself off, my hands trembling with a potent combination of rage and fear as I meet Versailles' glare with one of my own. "What are you doing here?" I ask, shooting Juliet a puzzled glance. "And with her, of all people?"

"It's okay, Antoine." Juliet steps to my side and drapes an arm across my shoulders. "Madame Versailles and I have become friends." She raises an eyebrow at the older woman. "At least, of a sort."

"Friends?" My brow crinkles in disbelief. "She's the reason you're here."

"I realize that, Antoine, but—"

"But nothing." I take Juliet by the upper arms and attempt to shake some sense into her. "She's the one who killed you. How can you possibly stand the sight of her, much less consider her a friend?"

"Bygones, boy." Versailles draws close. "Regardless of how we each came to be here, until the last few minutes, young Juliet and I have been the lone inhabitants of this place for longer than either of us care to remember." Her lips spread wide into a smile that could curdle milk. "Loneliness, like politics, makes for strange bedfellows."

"This is a trick." I search Juliet's features for any hint she is being coerced or is in some way under Versailles' influence, but all I find is that same innocent beauty that captured my heart even when her own belonged to my brother. "The Julianna I knew would never allow herself to associate with someone as despicable as—"

"Despicable? No." Juliet places a finger over my lips. "But desperate? Perhaps." Her head cocks to one side. "And my name, Antoine, is Juliet." She crinkles her nose. "Surely it hasn't been that long, has it?"

Confused, I glance in Versailles' direction and catch her amused grin.

"She doesn't know?" I ask.

"Alas, no." Versailles shakes her head sadly. "Not everyone confronted with the truth can see it, boy, much less believe it." She sweeps an arm in Juliet's direction. "Tell me, Juliet. Before coming to this place, where was your home?"

With a beaming smile, she answers, "Limoges, where I and the other women of the Marketplace met to discuss the comings and goings along the Exhibition."

"And before Limoges?" Versailles asks. "Where were you born? Where did you go to school? Where are your parents?"

"Just Limoges." A blank stare overtakes Juliet's face. "It's always been Limoges."

Versailles regards me with a triumphant smirk. "As you can see, boy, not everyone has been granted a peek behind the curtain."

A glance in the wolf's direction reveals a nearly identical smirk, as if the man behind the lupine facade has found a kindred spirit in the teacher from *Tuileries*.

"My apologies, Juliet." Taking a cue from Versailles, I offer the young woman a low bow. "Though if we're indeed putting everything right, then I must insist you call me Peter."

The confusion in Juliet's face quickly melts into blissful acceptance. "Very well." The bubbles in her voice tickle my ears. "Peter it is."

"So, Peter," Versailles intones, a flash of insight invading her eyes as she studies the wolf and makes the connection. "It would appear that you and your furry friend here have arrived at the Isle of the Dead a bit, shall we say, prematurely?"

Not sure what she's fishing for, I dodge the question. "We came here at the behest of an old friend of both of ours to seek your assistance in a matter of grave importance."

"And what friend might that be?" she asks.

I narrow my eyes at Versailles. "The one with the iron teeth."

Juliet gasps. "You spoke with the witch?" Her face blanches in fear. "And she sent you here?"

I raise my hands before my chest in a calming gesture. "Fear not, Juliet. We merely asked Baba Yaga where we might—"

Juliet's eyes grow wide in terror. "You spoke her name aloud." She runs to Versailles and hugs her around the waist like a frightened child. "But... such audacity was forbidden along the Exhibition."

"Things have changed, child," Versailles purrs as she strokes Juliet's hair. "Far too many things."

"And the Exhibition, as I understand it, is no more." I shove my hands into muck-filled pockets and immediately regret the decision. "Isn't that right, Madame Versailles?"

Versailles shoots me a withering stare. "The space was—shall we say—repurposed."

A sad chuckle escapes my lips. "That's one way of putting it."

"Oh really, *Peter*?" Versailles skirts the fire, her attention focused on the treetops high above. "And where exactly is it you think we are right now?"

"A place made necessary by your duplicitous cruelty." I bring myself nose to nose with the doppelganger of the woman that was once my favorite teacher, the woman who introduced me to Donaldson and Eddings and Gaiman, the woman who killed the only girl I've ever loved. "Everything that has happened, Madame Versailles, is on you. The death of the Exhibition, the suffering of Koschei's palace, the horror of the Shrove-Tide Fair." I cross my arms, defiant. "The dancing of *The Rite of Spring*."

Her eyes flicker at that last reference. A subtle tell, but a tell nonetheless.

If Versailles' omniscience and power did, in fact, end at the tip of the Moor's blade, then she doesn't know the circumstances that have led to us seeking her counsel in this strange purgatory. More importantly, she doesn't know what happened to Mira. I take heart in the fact she hasn't been sitting here gloating since the Moor ended her on the walls of the White City, though the revelation also brings a hint of despair. A part of me was counting on Versailles possessing an in-depth understanding of Mira's circumstances since dancing *The Rite of Spring*, if not her fates in the worlds of *Swan Lake* and *The Nutcracker*. Her blank stare poses a horrible quandary: if she has no knowledge whatsoever of the problem, how can she possibly know the solution?

Though a big part of me screams I'm about to tip my hand to the poker player across the table, I don't see any way around handing Versailles the best news I could possibly give her.

"To business, then." Versailles releases Juliet from her strangely maternal embrace. "You've clearly come a long way to see me and I suspect you won't go until you get the answers you seek."

"You suspect correctly," I answer, doing my best to keep the tremor from my voice. "Shall we get on with it?"

"So you and your wolf can return to the land of the living and leave young Juliet and I to our lonely fate?" She beckons me to join her on a flat stone by the fire, her every word and gesture syrupy sweet. "But of course, Peter. It would be my unmitigated pleasure."

I sit by her, half expecting the stone to open up beneath me and send me spiraling into darkness or some worse fate, another trap by the mistress of deceit. Instead, my heart flutters as Juliet sits on the other side of me, her hip brushing mine. In another time and place, such proximity was the dream of an adolescent boy, and though I know good and well that both the girl at my side along with the rest of this madness is at some level a figment of my imagination, it doesn't diminish the war of elation and sorrow raging at my core.

My lupine companion joins us as well, curling itself into a ball at my feet as if it were a lifelong family pet rather than a calculating psychopath in wolf's clothing.

"I've come here on behalf of Mira Tejedor."

Versailles' eyes sparkle with hate. "Of course you have."

"Who?" Juliet asks.

"You know her as Scheherazade." I pat her knee and immediately am overcome with self-conscious anxiety. "Though I don't believe the two of you ever met."

Versailles groans in exasperation. "And what, pray tell, could the storyteller want with me? She is, after all, responsible for my current living arrangements." Her expression sours. "So to speak."

"She's in trouble." I stare into the fire, the flickering flames as mesmerizing in their dance as any of the fantastical ballets I've borne witness to these last few days. "And according to the witch, you're the only one who knows how to help her."

"Help her?" Versailles' brow furrows in disbelief and then she throws her head back in a deep-throated laugh. "And for what possible reason do you believe I would even consider raising a finger to aid that whining shrew?"

"Redemption," I answer without hesitation. "You and Juliet, the girl who died at your hands, have somehow managed to come to an understanding. Is it impossible to believe you and the Lady Scheherazade could do the same?"

"She destroyed me." Versailles crosses her arms. "Not once, but twice."

"As you tried to destroy her, Madame Versailles." I let fly my most beatific smile. "Even you must admit that seems fair."

"Regardless," Versailles hisses, "you are a fool for thinking I would even consider coming to her aid."

"Music to my ears," the wolf whispers. "If you will not help her, then perhaps you will help me."

Versailles and Juliet both leap up from the stone by the fire.

"The wolf," Juliet stammers. "It can speak."

"Indeed," Versailles adds, her voice filled with equal parts malice and wonder. "So it can."

"I can do far more than speak." The wolf rises from the ground and circles the fire, its ruse of silent subservience over. "Madame Versailles, it would seem you and I share a common enemy." Stopping in its tracks, the feral beast locks gazes with the teacher from *Tuileries*. "Perhaps it would behoove us to combine forces."

No.

This cannot happen.

Not the both of them.

"But we came here seeking answers—"

"*You* did, Peter." The wolf stretches its back. "*I* came seeking an ally."

"Interesting." Versailles kneels before the wolf. "And what might you have to offer such a partnership?"

"To begin with, information." The wolf shoots me a warning glance and then turns his attention back to Madame Versailles. "In another world far from here, your nemesis lies catatonic, a body without a soul."

"The storyteller." Something like hunger flashes in Versailles' eyes. "Defenseless."

"Leave her alone," I cry out. "She's—"

The wolf turns on me again, this time with teeth bared. "Interrupt me again, boy, and you will have no reason to leave this place of the dead."

"Yes, Peter." Versailles strokes the wolf's fur between its ears. "Can't you see the grown-ups are talking now?"

"But—" Though it pains me, I bite my tongue and shift my focus, desperate to mentally record the conversation between teacher and wolf, though every word spoken fills my heart with dread.

"Twice already have I encountered aspects of Scheherazade in this realm," the wolf continues, "and at the conclusion of both stories, her life was forfeit."

Versailles raises an eyebrow in halfhearted admiration "Then you have fared far better against her than I, wolf. Perhaps the question at hand is not what you bring to the table but what you believe I can add to your already impressive efforts."

The wolf lets out a low growl. "I have defeated the storyteller on two different battlefields and yet am still confined to this place, cursed to wear this form or that as story after miserable story overtakes my existence. I wish to be free of this realm, yet as long as Scheherazade breathes, even a world away, I am as trapped in this world of dream as you are upon this Isle of the Dead." The wolf stares into Versailles' insane countenance. "Perhaps together, we can accomplish what neither of us has proven capable of alone and destroy the storyteller once and for all."

"Once and for all." Versailles allows herself an ebullient smile. "And then I can finally be free."

"We," the wolf corrects. "We can be free."

"Of course, dear wolf," Versailles whispers. "Freedom for both of us."

The wolf hesitates before turning from the fire and padding away in the direction of the Ferryman's dock. "Shall we, then?"

Versailles looks on, incredulous. "And how exactly do you expect to extricate yourself from this place, wolf, much less take me with you?"

"Simple." The wolf halts at the edge of the tree line and looks back. "The Ferryman comes when the bell is rung, does he not?"

"Not for me." Versailles hangs her head. "The living may be able to come and go from this place, but the dead must remain."

"Indeed," the wolf growls, "but consider this. There are two on this island who belong and two who do not. You may not know of my capabilities, but I am more than aware of yours." The wolf inclines its head in my direction. "Perhaps a different set of apparel might *facilitate* our travel."

Versailles' confused stare melts into one of glee. "An inspired plan. You are cleverer than I gave you credit." She raises her arms high and snaps her fingers, the gesture resulting in a flash of silver. Like a character from a Disney movie, a circle of stardust surrounds her head before falling about her in a curtain of blinding light. With a raised arm, I cover my eyes. When I look again, Versailles has vanished and in her place stands an entirely different sort of doppelganger.

The teacher from *Tuileries* has become... me.

A decidedly less muck-covered version, but before me, in every way that matters, stands Prokofiev's Peter and, suddenly ally rather than adversary, his wolf.

"This will do nicely." Versailles inspects her new form and then regards me with a sneer. "At least until such humble trappings are no longer necessary."

"You can't do this," I cry out to the wolf. "You have no idea what kind of evil you're unleashing."

"No, Peter," the wolf says. "You had no idea what two forces of nature you were bringing together." With that the wolf disappears into the shadows. "But you're about to find out."

"But Madame Versailles," Juliet cries out, so silent I had nearly forgotten her presence. "You can't leave me here all alone. You promised we would face the years on this island together."

"Stupid girl." Versailles grants Juliet one last withering stare. "Faced with being trapped on an island for all eternity with only one other soul to talk to, I would have befriended a cow if necessary to keep my sanity." She gives Juliet a frank up and down and adds, "A cow, indeed."

Juliet begins to cry as Versailles continues to dismantle her with nothing but words.

"In any case, you and the boy Peter or Antoine or whatever he chooses to call himself have all the time in the universe to become acquainted now." Her eyes shoot to me, a dark sparkle in her ever-malicious gaze. "Follow us, boy, at your peril."

And with that, she too vanishes into the shadows of the forest, leaving me alone with a distraught Juliet, betrayed a third time by this woman who has been to her teacher, sister, mother.

"I'm sorry, Juliet." I lead the weeping girl back to the stone by the fire and do my best to console her, all the while racking my brain for a solution to our impossible predicament.

I have no doubt two such devious minds as Durgan and Madame Versailles will have little difficulty convincing the Ferryman to transport them back to the mainland, and even less that the guardian of Rachmaninoff's famed Isle will balk at transporting the same boy back to the land of the living twice.

All of which means Juliet and I will have to find another way back.

In that moment, a solitary image brings hope to my desperate heart.

The confident gaze of the storyteller, undaunted even as the world crashed around her again and again and again.

Mira would find a way, and so will I.

XXIII

STARLIT NIGHTS

Whatever shall you do?" **Juliet leans forward to** warm her hands over the fire. "In death, this place has become a home of sorts for me. But you? You're still..."

"Alive? Don't worry. I'll be fine." I gaze up through the boughs of evergreens that block the sky in every direction apart from the stretch of darkness directly above our heads. The first star of evening twinkles down like a lone jewel on a bed of black velvet. "And I'm not ready to concede that you belong here anymore than I do." I take Juliet's hand, pull her from her seat on the stone and point up at the blackened sky. "There's an entire universe out there, Juliet. If it's somehow possible for Madame Versailles to leave this place, then it's possible for us as well."

"You would take me with you?" Juliet glows with hope for half a second, her excitement quickly fading as her mind makes the next connection. "Never mind."

"What's wrong?" I ask. "Did I say something to make you sad?"

She circles the fire, the flickering flames reflected in the tears running down her cheeks. "What place is there for me now among the living? And why would I wish to return, only to witness everyone I ever loved happily moving through their existence without me?" She flops down beside me and buries her face in her hands. "I'd rather remain here alone for the rest of eternity than see one second of pity in their eyes."

"It wouldn't be like that. I swear."

I pray I'm not telling the poor girl a lie, and then question my own sanity as I remind myself again that she is, in reality, nothing more than an afterimage.

My mind wanders through memories that are only half mine. Mira's final visit to the Exhibition. Every aspect of my fractured mind that had fallen at the hands of Madame Versailles returned to life and accepted back into the fold. Every aspect, that is, but the one that stands before me now, despondent and alone.

Why didn't Mira's triumph bring Juliet back from her grave in Hartmann's field?

Was it because Julianna Wagner's murder occurred before Mira's mind and mine ever touched, her existence relegated to the annals of a place that never truly existed?

Or was it something much simpler?

Julianna Wagner's death nearly destroyed me. Maybe seeing her alive again, even in an imaginary world of dream, was simply more than my mind could take at the time.

As if the why really matters.

Juliet is here now, as am I, the both of us stuck on an island mausoleum without so much as a paddle. No Mira Tejedor is coming to rescue me this time, no magical storyteller to whisk me away, no warrior to fight my battles for me, no sacrificial lamb upon which to cast my sins.

If either of us is going to leave this place, I no longer have the luxury of being weak.

"Peter?" Juliet's voice draws me back to the present. "Are you all right?"

"As right as I'm going to be for now." I shake off the memory and peer again into eyes that used to tie my guts into knots with every visit to our home, every trip to Dairy Queen, every wistful smile. "I was merely considering our exit strategy." An idea blossoms in my mind, and for the first time since Madame Versailles vanished into the woods with the wolf, I feel hope. "That is, if you're willing to trust me."

"You really think we can escape this place?"

I take her hand and offer her the most confident smile I can manage even as my heart leaps at her strangely warm touch. "It's a long shot, but I believe I know the way."

She squeezes my fingers, her hand trembling. "How do we begin?"

"Come with me."

I pull her away from the fire and into the darkness of the surrounding wood. With no sun visible above us, it's impossible to tell direction, but assuming the Ferryman's dock is west, then Juliet and I head east. I have no desire to cross paths with Versailles and the wolf and, more importantly, the thing I seek most likely lies in the opposite direction from the Ferryman's bell.

Or, more accurately, the place.

"Where are you taking us?" Juliet asks after an hour of avoiding bogs and pits, roots and brambles, and a myriad of other shadowy threats. "How do you even know where we're going?"

"Instinct." I don't have the heart to tell her that everything in this place, including her, is merely the first cousin to a dream occurring inside an entranced boy's mind the next universe over. "Trust me."

Our trudge through the dark forest lasts for what feels like days. Juliet, exhausted from the journey, threatens to turn back more than once but somehow I convince her to go on. Eventually the trees begin to thin and as our field of vision extends beyond a few feet, we arrive at our destination.

"We're here," I whisper.

A bell chimes in the distance, signifying that Madame Versailles and the wolf have reached the Ferryman's dock.

The race is on.

I take Juliet's hand and together we step across one final line of brush and onto an ancient path that curves off to both our left and our right. Before us gapes a massive doorway carved into the enormous wall of stone that occupies two-thirds the circumference of the island, the rectangular opening pulsing with green incandescence. Atop the door rests a solitary human skull that stares at us from empty sockets, the jaw hanging open as if surprised at our sudden appearance.

"What is this place?" Juliet asks.

A different melody, this one definitively not Rachmaninoff, echoes from the cavernous doorway. "Our ticket out of here."

She gasps. "That song. I haven't heard it since..."

"The Exhibition?" I take a deep breath and revel in the musty air emanating from the tunnel's open mouth. "That's what I was counting on."

Her lower lip trembles with fear and confusion. "I don't understand."

"This island may be a place of the dead, but it is not the first of those I've come across in my travels of this realm." I take a single step into the darkness and note the flicker of torchlight at the far end of the hall.

Jackpot.

"Now." I take Juliet's hand and borrow a line from one of my favorite movies. "Come with me if you want to live."

"Wait." She resists my pull, digging in her heels for the first time since agreeing to follow me into the unknown. "No more riddles. I trust you, Peter. I do. But you must tell me where this tunnel leads before I take another step."

I hesitate, not sure if telling her is the best plan, but in the end, opt for the truth.

"I believe this tunnel leads to the Catacombs of the Exhibition." And then, under my breath. "And the only person who can possibly get us out of this mess."

"But the Catacombs were forbidden." Juliet's eyes grow wide in terror. "The witch always said that anyone who entered *that* painting would never return."

"The witch said many things, and most of them, at least in her own mind, were for our own good. Not all of her pronouncements, however, were necessarily true." I try again to pull her into the tunnel, and again she resists.

"One last thing I must know then. Before we go on..." With a furtive gaze that dances between shame and hope, she asks, "Is Hartmann still there?"

And that's it. In my push to get things going, I lost sight of one simple fact. Both in the real world and along the Exhibition, the terrified girl trembling before me was the true center of everything that happened last year. The insecurity of Tunny the gnome, the standoffishness of Modesto, the ardor of Hartmann the Cart Man, and the unmitigated hate of Madame Versailles, all revolved around Juliet. The girl she represents may be long dead, but whatever fragment of her remains must be afraid of returning to a place that caused her so much pain.

A place where she was brutally murdered for the simple sin of falling for the wrong person.

Juliet pushed away her bitterness and somehow befriended Madame Versailles here on the Isle of the Dead, no doubt out of simple necessity, but the thought of returning to the Exhibition and facing the memories of her suffering there must be terrifying.

"I'm sorry, Juliet." I allow my eyes to drift closed and let out an empathetic sigh. "It's the only way."

"But what if he doesn't want to see me?" Her chin drops to her chest. "Or worse, what if he's forgotten about me?"

The memory of Hartmann charging Madame Versailles to take vengeance for Juliet's death flits across my imagination. The rage in his eyes as well as the sadness in all the others' gazes. The vindication that passed through us all at Versailles' final defeat.

"He remembers, Juliet, as do they all." My heart aches at her sadness. "How could they not?"

"You will protect me?"

I lower my head. "We'll protect each other."

"Very well." She stands a little taller at that and wipes a tear from the corner of her eye. "Lead on, Peter."

Juliet follows me down the darkened hallway, the flickering torch in the distance the lone source of illumination. A few steps in and the smooth stone wall of Rachmaninoff's island mausoleum tunnel shifts to skulls of every size and shape. Thousands of hollow eye sockets watch as we pass, the dead gaping in wonder at one still among the living and another long dead braving their dark home in vain hope of somehow returning to the light.

The tunnel of skulls goes on forever, the chattering of teeth and creaking of bones echoing in the space as countless empty stares follow us through the morbid maze. The few torches scattered along the walls provide scant visibility, forcing Juliet and me to feel our way along the grotesque passages of Mussorgsky's famed Catacombs.

Mussorgsky.

Yet another doppelganger of my father, like Drosselmeyer and the Charlatan, but this one the most like him—wise, calm, compassionate. To speak again with Dad, even under such strange circumstances, seems a true gift, and yet, at some level, I'm as terrified as Juliet.

What does one say to the dead?

An interesting question, considering my current company.

After what feels like a mile in near darkness, we round a corner and enter a large octagonal chamber furnished with only a small music stand and a simple wooden chair. An octet of torches, one per wall, washes the space in flickering orange light. On the stand, a lone conductor's baton rests haphazardly as if it could fall to the floor at any moment. Beneath the baton lie several pages of sheet music, the top page shivering as if alive. The gentle crosswinds responsible come from the quartet of passages leading away from what is no doubt the sanctum of the composer.

"All right," Juliet whispers. "We're here." A shiver overtakes her. "What now?"

"A good question, my dear." A deep baritone voice flavored with an unmistakably Russian accent echoes from the skull-covered walls surrounding us. "Welcome to my home."

From one of the adjoining tunnels, Mussorgsky, his thick beard and mussed hair reminiscent of my father on the Sunday mornings of my youth, steps into our presence. His tailored black suit immaculately clean and pressed despite his subterranean home, the composer strides to the center of the room, grabs up the baton, and sets to inspecting the music resting on his stand.

"Splendid." He glances up at us. "It would appear the two of you are right on time."

"On time?" Juliet whispers in my ear. "How could he have known we were coming?"

"He is the composer." I study the man before us, both clothed in and surrounded by darkness. "He just knows."

"The answer is simple, young lady." Mussorgsky traces a finger along the sheet music and hums a quiet tune I can't quite make out. "Each and every life is a symphony of moments. Yours. Mine. Peter's." The composer raises his eyes to meet my gaze. "Parents and ancestors are but prelude, and our time in the womb, an overture of the melody that is to follow. At various turns *allegro* or *largo*, *forte* or *piano*, *brillante* or *sotto*, every second of an individual's existence is part of one continuous melody, most ending far too soon."

"I'm afraid." Juliet takes my hand and squeezes it so tight I can't feel my fingers.

Mussorgsky steps from behind the conductor's stand, his baton at his side as he strides in our direction. "There is nothing to fear, my dear Juliet." His tone just above a whisper, he stops before her and strokes her hair with a father's touch. "Your death at the hands of Madame Versailles was nothing but a brief fugue and your return merely a reprise of a much loved melody."

"But to everyone among the Exhibition, I am dead." Juliet falls to her knees, her dress bunching like the petals of a yellow rose about her waist as she weeps before the composer. "Must I stay here in darkness?" Her lip trembles, soon followed by the rest of her hunched form. "I'm glad to be back among the Exhibition, but at least back on the Isle, I had the fire to keep me warm."

I scramble for an answer, for anything to say that will put her mind and soul at ease, but the composer beats me to the punch.

"Such as you cannot be kept to the darkness, my dear. Not to mention, as

Peter will no doubt attest, concepts like life and death are anything but absolute along the Exhibition." The composer claps his hands together and a hidden doorway in the wall of skulls opens, revealing a dark spiral staircase. "Shall we, therefore, return you to where you belong?" The composer beams at her, his mouth spread wide in a warm smile. "Are you ready to bask again in the light?"

"Yes." Her eyes shoot to me. "But what about Peter?"

The composer shakes his head sadly. "Make no mistake. He and I have much to discuss, but I suspect your traveling companion would agree with me that you have already languished in darkness more than long enough."

"Peter?" Juliet whispers.

"No time like the present." I raise an eyebrow in question. "Are you ready?"

At her nod, Mussorgsky turns on one heel and proceeds up the dimly lit stairs. Juliet hesitates, her hand still in mine, and then joins me on the spiral staircase leading up and away from this place of skulls and death and darkness. With each step, the fragmentary light beaming down from above grows stronger and stronger until we finally arrive at the top and find yet another of the countless doors that partition the various segments of my mind.

"And here we are." The composer peers across his shoulder at Juliet, a mischievous grin plastered across his features. "Last chance to stay in the Catacombs with me, my dear."

Juliet, the fear in her face warring with abject wonder, actually laughs at Mussorgsky's joke. "Open the door."

The composer grasps the door handle and gives it a firm tug. Blinding light pierces the surrounding gloom, forcing Juliet and me to cover our eyes. As our vision adjusts, I half expect to find the entire Exhibition gathered to welcome us home. Instead, a lone figure awaits us beyond the open door.

Dressed in his customary pine-green shirt and burgundy vest, Hartmann stands shifting foot to foot, hat in hand and head hung low. He refuses to look at Juliet, no doubt out of shame at his failure to protect her, but at some level, I understand it's more than that. Like Orpheus and Eurydice, he seems afraid to look upon his love standing just on the other side of shadow as if a single glance will doom her to an eternity in darkness.

"Go to him," the composer says, "and end this grand tragedy once and for all."

Juliet hesitates but a second before rushing to the farmer from *Bydło*.

"Hartmann," she shouts. "I'm here."

His eyes rise to meet hers. "Juliet."

Their reunion is one of tears and smiles and laughter. A part of me is still surprised to find only Hartmann here. If no one else, I thought Modesto might show up. After all, Jason loved Julianna Wagner as well. But the Exhibition, as always, speaks the truth. As hard as it may be to swallow, Hartmann is where Juliet's heart, in the end, truly lies.

As the two lovers continue their passionate reunion, Mussorgsky rests a hand on my shoulder.

"Come, Peter-Antoine-Anthony." He steps past me into the light and proceeds down the hall toward the final piece of the Exhibition. Where yet another door once stood, keeping me locked away from the pain of the world just beyond its threshold, now hangs a painting, its frame stretching from floor to ceiling.

The Bogatyr Gates, the place where Mira risked everything to save me from the dual menace of Veronica Sayles and Madame Versailles, occupies most of the great hall's far wall. The ever-changing frescoed ceiling of the Exhibition above mirrors the night sky that looked down upon Juliet and me back on the Isle of the Dead while the heavens depicted in the painting before me remain in a seemingly permanent twilight state. An ethereal light beneath the enormous triple arch beyond the canvas pulses in time with a mysterious rhythm—the heartbeat of the universe.

"The Gates." I turn to the composer. "They still exist."

The composer laughs. "During her first foray in this place of the mind, the storyteller used the Gates to travel back and forth from your realm to ours. It is only logical that you should be able to do the same."

"Doesn't matter," I grumble. "When I get back, I'm still tied to a chair and trapped with a madman. No matter what happens in here, out there I'm just a kid."

"You are far more than that." The composer stretches his arms wide and spins in place. "You found your way here, did you not? Brought young Juliet out of the darkness and returned her to the light. Persevered when many would have simply given up."

I set my jaw, angry. "I've fought and fought and yet I keep losing. Despite his ultimate defeat at *Swan Lake*, von Rothbart still succeeded in keeping Mira from us. I tried twice to help the Nutcracker Prince stop the Mouse King and in the end, he still took Clara and killed everyone."

"Killed?" Mussorgsky asks. "Everyone?"

"Finally," I continue, ignoring the question, "I figured out who I was supposed to be this time. It was all so clear. As Peter, I believed I could control the wolf. Instead, it seems the wolf was controlling me. Just like the Mouse King. Just like von Rothbart. And now, thanks to a not nearly brilliant enough plan, Durgan and Madame Versailles are together—as if either of them alone wasn't bad enough."

"Indeed." Mussorgsky steeples his fingers before his chest. "You have brought together two powerful forces and the consequences of your actions have yet to be felt. But you and the storyteller are forces to be reckoned with as well."

"That's the thing." I bring my arm before my face and lean against the cool wall by the painting's edge. "If I can just bring Mira out of this, she and I can win, but no matter how hard I try, I keep losing her."

"That is because you keep playing the hand you are dealt." He grasps my shoulder and turns me to face him. "You have yet to realize your true power here."

"My true power?"

"The Exhibition, Koschei's palace, the Shrove-Tide Fair, the Lake of the Swans, the palace of the Sugar Plum Fairy—these are all just variations on a theme." He studies me from beneath his bushy eyebrows. "Tell me, in all those places, what are the only two common elements?"

I chew on his words. "Mira?"

"And..." Mussorgsky allows the slightest of smiles to invade his features.

"And... me."

Mussorgsky nods. "You are not a visitor to this place, Anthony Faircloth. You are this place, as is Mira Tejedor in all her guises. If you wish to save her and yourself, you must learn to believe the same truth that the storyteller learned."

"And what truth is that?"

"That as long as you play your enemy's game, you will lose."

Images of *The Firebird* and *Petrushka* flash across my mind's eye. Mira, defeated time and again. And then, *The Rite of Spring*, where, regardless of the price, she finally achieved victory.

"This place," I whisper.

"Yes." Mussorgsky's smile grows wide.

"It *is* me."

He nods. "And Mira. Don't forget her."

"I'm not." I turn back to the canvas that holds *The Bogatyr Gates*.

"My house." I step into the painting. "My rules." I turn back to face

Mussorgsky, likely the last time I will ever look upon my father's face again outside of a photograph. "Thank you."

The composer gives me one solemn nod, and then returns to *The Catacombs*. Juliet and Hartmann as well wave goodbye before stepping into the alcove holding the *Bydło* painting, leaving me alone with a million thoughts swirling in my head like a raging cyclone.

"But where to go next?"

Mussorgsky. Rimsky-Korsakov. Stravinsky. Rachmaninoff. Prokofiev. And the greatest of them all, Tchaikovsky. I scour their works in my mind, seeking the answer to the composer's riddle.

When it finally comes to me, I curse myself for an idiot for not having thought of it sooner. Allowing myself a grim smile, I take my first step for the Gates in the distance.

"All right, Durgan and Madame Versailles." I break into a sprint. "Time to play a new game."

XXIV

BARCAROLLE

I awake to cool, moist air that hangs on my body like a wet shroud. Still tied to the chair in the darkness of Durgan's makeshift lair, I'm not going anywhere any time soon. At least I talked him out of gagging me before our most recent dive into madness. Didn't take much to convince him of the dangerous position he'd be in if he was inside my head and I stopped breathing.

Sarah remains asleep, her bald head pitched forward but her lungs rising and falling in a peaceful rhythm. In the chair opposite me, Durgan sits, head up but eyes closed, almost as if he were listening to a piece of music just on the edge of perception.

In any case, unless he is a far better actor than I give him credit for, he is still walking around in the La La Land between my ears.

Now, if I can just get Sarah and myself out of here before he wakes up.

I strain at the ropes that bind my wrists, for all the good it does me.

Where did all these psychopaths learn to tie knots so damn well?

"Over here." Sarah, not as asleep as I suspected, stares at me, her wide eyes piercing the dim. "I have something that might help."

"What is it?"

"Come here and get it before he wakes up."

"All right." With my hands and feet tied to the chair, it isn't easy, but I somehow manage to scoot the chair inch by inch until I'm close enough to

Sarah that our knees are touching. "What have you got?"

"Underneath my foot." She shifts her leg. Beneath the sole of her shoe rests a rusty utility knife that's seen a few years. "While you two were out, I spotted it on one of the crossbeams. One of the construction workers must have left it. Took me an hour, but I got it."

I begin to ask her why she didn't cut herself free, but the answer is obvious. She's terrified.

Just getting the knife and hiding it must have taken all she had.

"Can you get it?" she asks.

"I'll give it my best shot."

My arms tied tightly by my sides, I can't move my hand so much as an inch, much less reach for the floor.

Looks like we're bringing the mountain to Mohammed.

I rock the chair back and forth until it falls to one side with a crash. My head strikes the ground and leaves me with a pounding headache.

This is the part the Bond movies never show.

"Ow." I crane my neck around to see if I've awakened the sleeping giant. "Durgan. Is he—"

"Still out," Sarah answers. "But you better hurry."

As best I can with my shoulder and knee, I rotate my bound form until I can lay eyes on the utility knife. "Can you kick it to me?"

"I'll try." With the toe of her shoe, she pushes the knife a few inches closer to my hand. Using muscles I don't think I've ever used, I scoot myself millimeter by millimeter closer until my fingertips brush the cool metal handle.

Durgan groans, the sound barely audible.

"Hurry," Sarah whispers. "He's coming around."

Somewhere between stretching my fingers like a poor man's Mister Fantastic and willing the knife to my hand like Luke Skywalker hanging upside down in the Wampa cave, I manage to get a grip on the knife. I thumb the slider on the back and breathe a sigh of relief when a relatively fresh looking blade slides out of the paint-spattered tool. I maneuver the blade in my fingers with more desperation than dexterity and saw at the thick ropes holding my wrists.

Durgan groans again just as I get through the first rope and liberate my right hand. Fortunately, like before, he stays in his chair. Not wanting to push my luck, I make short work of my remaining bonds and for the first time in hours come to my feet. My arms and legs both tingle like they're covered in army ants, but I don't care.

I'm free.

"Hold still, Sarah," I whisper. "I'll have you out of those ropes in no time."

"The hell you will." Durgan, his voice like a fork in a garbage disposal, rises from his chair staggering. "You'll sit your ass right back in that chair if you know what's good for you."

"Run, Anthony," Sarah screams. "Run."

A thousand different scenarios play out in my mind at once, most of them ending with me right back where I started. My only hope is that Durgan is still unsteady on his feet having just emerged from the dreamworld. As the first ray of sunlight finds its way between the paper covering the windows that take up the front of whatever place this used to be, the only plan that will possibly work springs into my mind.

Without warning, I rush straight at Durgan with the knife held before me. He instinctively bats the weapon from my hand and, in doing so, opens himself up to my actual attack. Maintaining my momentum, I bury my forehead and elbows in his abdomen, sending his entire two-hundred-plus pounds to the floor. I spare Sarah a single glance and then sweep up Durgan's chair and rush at the large sheet of glass with the legs before me, the world's smallest battering ram.

I imagine myself hitting the window and crashing through like I've seen in dozens of shows over the years. Instead I bounce off the glass like a rubber ball and land flat on my back with the wind knocked out of me. My attack leaves a quartet of small starbursts in the glass but the window remains intact.

"Stupid kid." Durgan laughs as he rises from the ground and stalks in my direction. "That only works in the movies."

"Hey," comes a gruff voice from the other side of the window. "Who's in there?"

Durgan rushes to my side. "Don't you say a word, kid."

"This is security," comes a second voice, this one with a twang as if the owner hails from a couple states farther south. A pair of flashlight beams shows between the plywood sheets covering the front window. The sound of jangling keys brings Durgan's eyes down to narrow slits.

"Shit." He wraps his arm around my neck and drags me toward the exit. "Time to go."

I bite his arm so hard that warm copper fills my mouth. He flings me to the ground and clutches his wrist, blood seeping between his fingers.

"You little piece of shit." He towers over me, wounded and enraged. "You're going to pay for that."

Another rattle of keys from the door brings a contemptuous grin to my face.

"Not before those two security guards find the right key, come in here, and kick your ass."

Durgan thinks on it for all of half a second before he rushes at Sarah. Scooping her up, chair and all, he sprints for the rear exit. With one last furious glare, he forces the door open and drags her screaming into the dim first light of morning. I attempt to pull myself up from the floor and chase after them, but hours of being tied to a chair, not to mention running full tilt into a plate glass window, has left me pretty wasted.

A few seconds later, the security guards finally locate the correct key and get the door open. One rushes to my side while the other heads for the open door in the back.

"What the hell are you doing in here, kid?" the one with the gruff voice asks, his skin so dark I can barely make out his features in the dim light. "This is private property."

I roll to one side and point toward the rear of the store where his partner, a squat man with a buzz cut and about hundred pounds heavier than is healthy, is running out the door.

"Answer me, kid," McGruff says. "What are you doing in here?"

My outstretched finger trembling, I stammer three words that explain everything.

"Wendell James Durgan."

"You're sure this is where you want to go?" McGruff asks as we pull up to the main entrance of the hospital. "We really should be taking you to the police station."

"I'll be fine." Desperate to get out of the car, I spin a quick lie. "My dad's a cop and he's upstairs with my mom who's really sick."

The squint in his eyes reveals he at least half believes me.

"Please. They've got to be worried sick."

"All right." He hands me a card with his information. "If you need anything—"

"I'll give you a call." I pop the door and step out onto the sidewalk. "Promise."

"Make sure you—"

I slam shut the passenger door of his company SUV and sprint for the sliding doors at the front of the hospital. The elevator takes its own sweet time making it to the ground floor, and I nearly crawl out of my skin during the insufferable wait. The family stuck waiting with me in the hospital vestibule must think I'm either an escapee from the psych ward or a junkie looking for a fix as, when the elevator finally opens, they opt against joining me. As the twin doors close on the mother's confused face, I punch the button for Mira's floor and fall back against the elevator wall.

In a rare bit of good luck, the elevator takes me straight to Mira's floor without any stops. No sooner does light appear between the doors than I shoot out and race down the hall for her room. Mira's door still under double guard, I rack my brains for any excuse that will convince the pair of cops to let me pass. Before I can come up with anything that might work, however, Detective Sterling steps out of the room and shoots a shocked look in my direction.

"Anthony?" He moves further into the hall, his eyes narrowing in confusion. "What are you doing—"

Before I can stop myself, I nearly tackle the man, wrapping my arms around him as if I were a lost toddler who just found his dad.

"Detective Sterling." I try not to get choked up. "It was Durgan. He took me. He—"

"I know." His eyes glaze over with cold anger even as he rests a comforting hand on my shoulder. "Thank God you're all right." He whips out his phone and punches in a familiar number. A trio of rings sounds before my mother's voice comes from the other end.

"Hello?"

"Caroline? It's Sterling." Before he can say a word, Mom launches into a diatribe so loud, the detective has to pull the phone from his ear. "Hold on," he says when she lets him get a word in edgewise. "There's someone here who wants to talk to you." He presses the phone against my cheek.

"Mom?"

"Anthony?" Another breathless pause. "Oh God, Anthony. Are you all right?"

"I'm fine, Mom. I swear."

"That was Durgan, wasn't it?"

"Yes." I fight to keep the emotion from my voice. That will do nothing but pour gas on the fire. "That was Durgan."

"Dear Lord." Mom begins to blubber, the potent mix of fear and anger and relief choking out all but a few of her words. "Did he... hurt you?"

"Like I said, Mom, I'm fine. I promise." I take a breath. "But I'm not the one we should be worried about." I peer up into Detective Sterling's dark eyes. "He's got Sarah Goode, and I don't know what he's going to do to her now that I've escaped."

"So..." Mom's voice drops to a whisper. "That psychopath does have the girl."

"Yes." My head drops. "And if he doesn't get what he wants..."

"Where are you?" Mom downshifts out of frantic and into full on Mama Bear in the space of a breath. "I'm coming right now."

"Actually..." I bite my lip. "I'm at the hospital."

"The *hospital*?" The question leaves my right ear ringing. "You went there instead of coming home? I've been frantic worrying about you and—"

"I'm sorry, Mom, but we're running out of time. Mira is here, and so is Detective Sterling."

"And Thomas too," she intones, the roar of her car rumbling to life coming across the line.

"Dr. Archer?" My breath catches as I recall the odd angle of his neck as Durgan dragged me from my own house. "Is he okay?"

"Durgan clubbed him in the head just before he took you away. That left me all tied up and Thomas unconscious and bleeding from his ear till Jason got home. It was horrible."

Jason. That means... "Did Rachel see? Is she okay?"

"Jason sensed something was wrong when he found the front door standing ajar. He took Rachel next door and then came in and found us. We called 9-1-1 for Thomas after he untied me."

Every muscle in my body freezes as I prepare for the worst. "Is Dr. Archer going to be all right?"

"We don't know." Mom's quiet sob comes across the phone line loud and clear. "The paramedics took him to the ER and then he was admitted to the hospital. Last I checked, he hadn't regained consciousness."

"Doc's right down the hall," Detective Sterling adds, Mom's end of the conversation loud enough he barely has to eavesdrop. "I used whatever pull I had to keep him close to Mira."

"At least he's close." My eyes slide shut as I return my attention to the phone. "Get here as fast as you can, Mom. We've got work to do, and it's going to take all of us."

"I'm coming Anthony." Mom lays on her horn, a move I've only seen her perform when she's at her wit's end. "Don't you leave Detective Sterling's side, young man. Do you hear me?"

"Yes, ma'am."

"You swear?"

"I won't leave his sight. Promise."

"Good." An audible sigh. "I love you, Anthony."

"Love you too, Mom."

I return Detective Sterling's phone and approach the door leading to Mira's room. The guards part to allow me passage. I reach for the door handle, but pause and rest my forehead on the cool wood, taking a second to collect myself.

Beyond the doorway, one last gauntlet remains, one last adventure into the world of dream. Knowing full well the scene that awaits across this particular threshold, the answer to all of this pain and suffering suddenly seems so obvious. Yet, we had to go through all that has come before to arrive at this moment.

Pictures at an Exhibition.

Scheherazade.

The Firebird.

Petrushka.

Night on Bald Mountain.

The Rite of Spring.

Swan Lake.

The Nutcracker.

Peter and the Wolf.

Boris Godunov.

Isle of the Dead.

Not to mention every other piece of music I've ever heard. Every movie I've ever seen. Every television show. Every comic book. Every video game. And every possible combination of all of the above.

It's been a puzzle within a conundrum all wrapped around an intriguing riddle, and yet, now, at the end, it all seems so simple.

To awaken a sleeping princess, maybe this once we skip all the tangential associations and endless permutations of story and music and simply attack the problem itself.

Tchaikovsky wrote three ballets, and we've exhausted two.

Time to visit the third.

XXV

THE SLEEPING BEAUTY

Between a set of starched sheets and beneath three layers of blanket, Mira lies unconscious, her chest rising and falling in a slow rhythm in time with the mournful dirge of her monitors. Her features as placid as the mythical lake that exists in the space between our minds, she appears at peace. No worries etch her brow, no fears line her face, no anxiety spoils her rest.

The serenity is nothing but an illusion.

A war wages inside her mind, no matter how tranquil she appears.

No one knows that better than me.

Not to mention, her situation is infinitely worse than mine ever was. I was trapped inside my own mind with a cast of characters that, for the most part, existed to protect me and keep me alive. Mira, on the other hand, shares her mental prison with a pair of entities who couldn't hate her more if they tried. I can't decide which of the two terrifies me more—Durgan, who threatens us from both sides of the veil of dream, or Madame Versailles, unchained from the shackles of her shared existence with Veronica Sayles, a free agent of chaos now ricocheting around inside Mira's mind.

Still, regardless of the danger, I will not abandon her.

She came for me when I was still a stranger, and never once gave up on me.

She risked everything.

Sacrificed everything.

And that's what I owe her.

Everything.

Detective Sterling kneels by my chair at the foot of Mira's bed. "What's the play, kid?"

"Yes, Anthony." Mom takes in a sharp breath, still catching up from her sprint from the parking deck. "You've got us all gathered together. What is it you need us to do?"

"First, I need to get us all on the same sheet of music, pardon the pun." I take a breath and begin, reviewing in as gruesome detail as I can recall about the kidnapping, Durgan and Sarah, and my ultimate rescue by McGruff and his partner. Mom blanches several times as I relate the blow by blow of the last day, and that's before I even get to the important part.

As I shift into all that has happened in the world of dream since Durgan took me, my memory adopts a surreal dichotomy, my mind remembering the sequence of events both as spectator and participant.

The strange world of *Peter and the Wolf* and its repercussions both in the real world and the realm of dream.

Our visit with Baba Yaga and our subsequent sojourn to the Isle of the Dead.

My return to the Exhibition with Juliet and her fateful reunion with Hartmann.

And finally, my grand escape, both from the trap set by the wolf and from Durgan himself in the real world.

When I'm done, both Mom and Detective Sterling appear as exhausted as I feel.

"Man, kid." Detective Sterling shakes his head in disbelief. "You're tougher than you look."

My gaze drifts to Mira's unconscious form. "I learned from the best."

"And like her, I'm guessing you have a plan." Mom eyes me warily. "A dangerous one, no doubt."

"The beginnings of one." I shoot Mom a sheepish look. "As for danger, it seems we now have not only Durgan to contend with, but Madame Versailles as well."

"And yet, you're going to charge straight ahead, aren't you?" Detective Sterling looks on me with new admiration. "Into the breach. Isn't that what Mira would say?"

Mom slips behind my chair and rests a hand on my shoulder. "I'm not even going to try to talk you out of this, Anthony, but I must know how you plan to win when you now face not one monster, but two."

"The only way I can. By changing the game, just like Mira did." I cross my arms, defiant. "Tchaikovsky wrote three ballets, two of which I've experienced. The answer must lie in the third."

"But the first two times, you lost." Mom studies me, her expression curdled with worry. "What do you think will be different this time?"

"The worlds of both *Swan Lake* and *The Nutcracker* were foisted upon me. I had to make do with the characters, situations, and complications as they came. By choosing my own battlefield, as Mira did with *The Rite of Spring*, I hope to gain the home court advantage." My eyes narrow in concentration. "Not to mention, the theme of Tchaikovsky's third ballet applies far more directly to our current dilemma than any of the worlds I've been drawn into since all this started."

"This third ballet, Anthony." Detective Sterling eyes me, curious. "What is it?"

"A story we've all heard or seen a thousand times, though not quite the version I suspect we'll be facing."

Understanding blossoms on Mom's face. "You mean..."

"Yes." I take a breath. "Next stop, *Sleeping Beauty*."

The Russians call it *Spyashchaya krasavitsa*. The French, *La Belle au bois dormant*. Most Americans have never seen Tchaikovsky's ballet, or even know it exists. But the Disney film? It's as much a fixture as baseball or apple pie.

The story is simple.

A dark fairy, insulted at not being invited to the christening ceremony for the infant Princess Aurora, curses the child to die on her sixteenth birthday, her finger pricked on a spindle. The one good fairy who has yet to bless the princess amends the curse so that Aurora, along with the entire kingdom, merely enters a deep sleep, a sleep that is to last one hundred years. At the end of her century-long slumber, Aurora is awakened by the kiss of a handsome prince. The wicked fairy is defeated, and the happy couple and their kingdom live happily ever after.

Or at least that's how it's supposed to go. Neither Odette the Swan Princess nor Clara Stahlbaum got precisely the ending they were promised a century ago.

Funny thing? I've already got a pretty good idea how the three pounds of tofu between my ears is going to cast this particular drama.

"Let me guess." Detective Sterling asks, as if reading my mind. "Mira is our sleeping princess and Versailles ends up as Maleficent, right?"

"I was thinking the same thing, Detective, though in the Russian ballet, the dark fairy's name is Carabosse."

"But what about Durgan?" Mom crosses her arms. "Do you have the first idea where to look for *him* in this story?"

I rub at the bridge of my nose. "Only one villain in *Sleeping Beauty*, if you don't count the incompetent steward that forgets to invite Carabosse in the first place."

"Unbelievable." Detective Sterling shakes his head. "You're like an encyclopedia for this stuff."

Mom laughs. "You think this is impressive, just get him started on *Star Wars*."

"Anyway..." I shoot Mom an irritated glance. "I guess we'll have to wait and see how Durgan fits into all of this."

"So," Detective Sterling asks. "Your big plan is to somehow force the dreamworld to transform into the realm of *Sleeping Beauty* and then roll the dice?"

"As the storyteller, Mira could do such things." I raise my shoulders in a lopsided shrug. "As the source of those selfsame stories, I'm hoping I can do the same."

"But why *Sleeping Beauty*?" Mom's gaze shifts in Mira's direction. "Beyond the obvious, of course."

"Simple. I know the story inside and out. Every note of the music. Every character. If I'm to win this and free Mira, I'm going to need every advantage."

"You know, Anthony." Detective Sterling lets out a quiet chuckle. "As I understand it, the princess is awakened by a kiss." He raises an eyebrow. "You ready to perform such a duty if it comes to that?"

Heat rises in my cheeks. "Every story has an ending, Detective."

"I'm sorry, but I still don't understand what you need from us." Mom sits on the bed at Mira's feet. "It sounds like you're planning on flying solo."

"As you said, I'm up against not one, but two enemies this time. Even if you're not standing with me in the dreamworld, I'm hoping having your energy in the room with me will somehow help." I look to Detective Sterling. "And while we're on the subject, is it possible they could bring Dr. Archer's bed in here?"

"Is that really necessary?" Detective Sterling slides his hands into his pockets. "Whatever pull I have around here is already strained after the big hubbub the other day. Honestly, I'm not sure how the hospital staff is going to respond to such a request. Not to mention, we've got a bit of a time crunch. As soon as we notified the Goodes that we'd found Sarah, they hit the highway headed south for Charlotte. They'll be wanting to meet with me when they arrive."

I pull in a deep breath. "Having all of us together was what allowed Mira to succeed as she danced *The Rite of Spring*. I need at least as much back up if either of us plans to make it out of this thing in one piece."

"All right, then." Detective Sterling takes a breath. "I'm in."

"What else do you need, honey?" Mom shakes her head, incredulous.

"A cheeseburger." I shoot her my most confident smile. "I'm starving."

Two hours of negotiation later, Detective Sterling manages to get Mira and Dr. Archer moved from their two private rooms to a shared room down the hall. I've never heard the word "unorthodox" used more often in my life, but the end result is the same.

The five of us are again together in one space.

Mom sits by Dr. Archer's head and Detective Sterling with Mira while I've positioned my chair between the two beds within reach of both their hands in case a physical connection is needed to create the link. The nurse assigned to Mira eyes us warily as she goes about her business but otherwise leaves us alone.

The burger Mom brought up from the hospital cafeteria sits in my stomach like a brick as I steel myself for another sojourn into madness. It's rare that I can't eat, but a single nagging thought has my intestines tied in knots.

I have no idea if I can bend the dreamworld to my will the way Mira did.

If I can't, I lose. And so does everyone I take with me.

Still, I have to try. Giving up is not an option.

"So, kid." Detective Sterling looks on me with a confidence I'm not sure I'd feel if our roles were reversed. "You ready?"

"As ready as I'm going to be." I fake a smile and try to ignore the pounding headache brewing above my left eye. "How about you guys?"

"Don't worry about us, kid." Detective Sterling's grim smile appears as genuine as mine.

"We'll be right here, sweetie." Mom has somehow held back the waterworks this time. Or, perhaps she's finally cried out. Hard to tell which. "We're not going anywhere."

"And the doctors and nurses are clear on that?"

Detective Sterling glances in the direction of the door. "I've told them in no uncertain terms we are not to be disturbed."

Mom lets out a frustrated sigh. "I still say we should have someone keep an eye on us while we're... under."

"That's why I'm here." Jason saunters into the room, his usual disgruntled look present in spades.

"But, Jason." Mom shoots out of her chair and wraps her arms around my brother's neck. "You told me you wanted no part of this."

"I know." He shakes his head in frustration. "But if you're all hell-bent on going through with this, the least I can do is make sure no one screws it up on this end."

"What about Rachel?" Mom asks. "Who's going to keep her?"

"Mrs. Tejedor came through again. Mr. MacGregor and Autumn have Isabella and Mira's mom is going to stay at the house with Rachel till this is over."

I catch Jason's gaze, the cast in his eyes somewhere between worried and angry. "You're okay with this?"

"Of course not." He turns his lips up in a half smirk. "Doesn't mean I won't kick anyone's ass who walks through that door with a mind toward screwing with my family."

For the first time in hours, the pain in my stomach lets up a little. "Thank you, Jason."

"Yeah." Detective Sterling lowers his head in a respectful nod. "Thanks."

Mom retrieves a stool for Jason. "All right, then. Shall we get started?"

"How are we going to do this?" Detective Sterling asks. "We can't exactly have the good doctor here wave his penlight around and knock us out, now can we?"

"We won't be needing any of that." I take Mira's fingers in one hand and Dr. Archer's in the other. "Both of you. Complete the chain." I shoot Jason a sidelong glance. "Don't let them separate us once we're under."

"Not a chance." Jason raises a fist before his face. "Now, go and give them hell."

Darkness the color of old blood fills my vision.

I stand alone on a stage, hardwood beneath my feet and a thick curtain of deep burgundy velvet inches from my nose. Frozen to the spot, I'm unable to move anything but my eyes.

At the periphery of my vision, the ubiquitous mist swirls in miniature cyclones as one by one, other figures appear on the grand stage. Funny, as curious as I am about the identities of the forms suddenly surrounding me, I'm far more interested in two simple questions.

Have I succeeded in bending this place that was once my prison to my will?

And in this new place, whatever and wherever it is, who or what do I represent?

The invisible orchestra launches into a lively melody filled with brass and woodwinds and strings and percussion. Rolling tympani alternates with blaring trumpet, crashing cymbal plays against dulcet violin, and soothing harp fills the space left between measures of flute.

As the curtain rises, I attain control of my limbs and take a quick survey of my surroundings. Flanked by two trios of stewards carrying candelabras and dressed for royal court, I stand in the grand hall of a palace. I too am dressed for court, though my raiment seems a step up from the stewards surrounding me. In one hand, I hold a quill. In the other, a long scroll of parchment filled with names.

The music. The palace. The list.

The prologue of *Sleeping Beauty*.

It's working.

And yet, in this place, I am again neither prince nor hero, but Catalabutte, the master of ceremonies and the one responsible for bringing the wrath of the wicked fairy, Carabosse, by omitting her name from the scroll clenched in my fingers.

Sounds about right. Especially if my and Detective Sterling's guess about Carabosse's identity is proven true.

One simple fact isn't lost on me. In every scenario I've faced, not only am I never the hero, but I'm also usually in some way responsible for all the badness that ensues.

Benno is the one that convinces Siegfried to hunt by the lake by moonlight.

Fritz pulls off the Nutcracker's head and forces Drosselmeyer into action.

Peter's ill-fated attack on the wolf sets up a true "tiger by the tail" situation that only resolves when the hunters arrive on the scene.

And now... Aurora will sleep for a century because of Catalabutte's oversight.

Just like in the real world, it's all my fault.

The prologue proceeds as I've seen it a hundred times. From beneath my feathered hat and powdered wig, I review the guest list for Princess Aurora's christening, a persnickety sneer on my face, and send the various stewards to bring in the guests. A full lap of the stage takes me past a pair of nursemaids in white caring for the newborn princess in her cradle of gold.

Their faces are, of course, familiar. My sister and Mira's daughter, left under the care of others and far from the hospital room where the six of us prepare to fight for Mira's life, yet still as embroiled in this mess as the rest of us.

No sooner have I recovered from the shock of finding Rachel and Isabella in this place than the king and queen arrive to royal fanfare. Their features are similarly more than known to me.

An echo of the Stahlbaums from my trip through *The Nutcracker*, the queen wears the face of Mira's mother, Rosa, while my own father's eyes look out at me from beneath King Florestan's crown. Together, they go to Aurora's cradle where the queen places a necklace bearing a golden locket around the infant's neck. The royal couple looks lovingly into each other's eyes before turning to greet the various courtiers and maids of honor.

Soon, the entertainment begins. Dance after dance of ballerinas in palest green and gold ensues, each performance more intricate and graceful than the one before. For a moment, I almost forget where I am.

And then, the guests I've been waiting for.

One by one, five dancers rush the stage from every corner of the room, the hue of each ornate bodice and tutu as varied as the women who wear them. Each imbued with a radiance and gravitas beyond that of the rest of the court, one thing is perfectly clear.

The fairies have arrived.

In white, Candide, the Fairy of Candor, brings the gift of honesty.

In gold, Fleur de Farine, or Wheat Flour, arrives bearing the gift of grace.

In pink, Miettes qui Tombent, or Falling Breadcrumbs, offers generosity.

In yellow, Canari qui Chante, or Singing Canary, exudes the gift of eloquence and song.

And in red, Violante, the Fairy of Force, embodies passion.

Arrayed in their rainbow of matching tutus and golden crowns, the five fairies flit about the stage, at first together and then solo, each taking their turn by the infant Aurora's opulent cradle to bestow their various gifts.

Though the scene is idyllic perfection, I steel myself for what is sure to follow.

As if in answer to my silent summons, a staccato drum roll intrudes upon the previously pleasant tune and the room falls dark. Billowing white mist fills the air by Aurora's cradle, a dense fog that smells of loam and rain and electricity. Lightning flashes once, twice, three times as the unseen orchestra launches into a frantic back-and-forth of violin and woodwinds.

The moment stretches out for what seems like an hour. Then, as inevitable as the sunrise, out of the column of mist steps Carabosse, the foreordained villain of this piece. Dressed in a full-length silk gown of shimmering black and deepest purple, her skin radiates a pale blue luminescence. One hand on her hip, she holds in the other a staff fashioned from five feet of darkest ebony and capped with a silver tip that matches the crown resting atop her head.

The dark fairy surveys the room, her flitting gaze alight with violet fire, until her brazen eyes eventually fall upon me. A wicked grin spreads across her features as she saunters in my direction, her every step full of terrible grace.

As the crowd wisely parts to allow her passage and she draws close, I prepare myself for the inevitable familiarity in the dark fairy's cyanotic features. In this, I am not disappointed. Madame Versailles' cold eyes, however, are not those that stare back at me from Carabosse's mischievous gaze, but a set of eyes far more familiar.

My heart clenches in my chest as a single word falls from my/Catalabutte's lips.

"Mom?"

XXVI

CARABOSSE

Not Yaga.

Not the witch.

Not the ancient hag with iron teeth and rags for clothes.

But my mother, Caroline Faircloth, her features twisted into Carabosse's wicked sneer.

Before I can process what I'm seeing, the dark fairy taps her staff on the floor twice and a handful of creatures materialize at her feet. Covered in thick fur the color of midnight, the five monstrous newcomers cavort in time with the boisterous music, their horned heads raised high in exultation at serving their dark mistress.

Something about their strange dance triggers a flash of memory, but I can't place it.

Carabosse makes her first stop before King Florestan and his queen, lowering her head in a mocking bow, the impish grin never leaving her lips. As the queen falls into her husband's arms, the dark fairy sashays a full lap of the space, offering a scornful greeting to each of her brightly arrayed sisters before coming to a halt at the center of the room. She again taps the floor twice with her staff, pointing one pale finger at her feet as her malicious gaze finds me.

I'm halfway across the floor before I realize I'm even moving, the power of her command second to none. I kneel at the hem of her dress, my entire body trembling. She strokes my head once and then pulls my chin up to look her straight in the eyes.

To find such derisive hate in the gaze of a woman who has only ever shown me love chills me to the bone.

In a move meant to humiliate the master of ceremonies who scorned her, she rips the powdered wig from my head and then the hairpiece beneath from Catalabutte's bald scalp before hurling me aside. I scramble to my feet and hide behind a column before she can do any worse, but Carabosse has already forgotten about me.

As I know all too well, she has far more nefarious deeds on her mind this day.

Carabosse gathers her monstrous entourage around her feet as the other five fairies implore her to stay her foul plan. One by one, they silently plead on bent knee with folded hands raised, but neither Candide, Fleur, Miettes, Canari, nor Violante gets more than a mocking nod from their dark sister. Their petitions grow more and more emphatic until Carabosse finally grows impatient and sends her menagerie of monsters to intercede.

The floor clears as five pairs of fairy and fiend circle Carabosse and commence a frantic dance. The entire spectacle somewhere between art and assault, the fairies do everything in their power to free themselves while Carabosse's entourage stops at nothing to keep them in check. Faster and faster they dance, the morbid performance growing both more savage and lewd with every pass.

Images flood my mind.

The unending avarice of the children of *Tuileries*.

The chaos of *The Firebird*'s Infernal Dance.

Mira's terror as she performed *The Rite of Spring*.

The symmetry fills my heart with dread.

Her five sisters held at bay, Carabosse moves forward with her scheme. Taking an ominous position by Aurora's cradle, she holds aloft her ebony staff and points its dark tip at the baby's head. The queen's face, a mirror of Rosa Tejedor's, fills with horror, but King Florestan holds his wife fast, his wise eyes so much like my father's, betraying not a hint of emotion as the dark fairy continues her plot.

Plucking a long spindle from her elegantly coiffed hair, Carabosse mimes pricking her finger at its tip with a grand flourish and then draws the same finger across her neck in the universal sign of death. The queen faints as the curse is cast and only King Florestan's strength keeps her from hitting the floor.

The entire court, save the proud monarch who wears my father's features, kneels to plead for the royal infant's life. From queen to courtier, master of ceremonies to peasant, fairy to footman, we all fall to our knees and raise our hands in supplication.

But our efforts are for nothing.

The deed is done.

The music turns dramatic as Carabosse struts from one end of the room to the other in triumph. The fairies attempt again to intervene only to be swept into another forced dance with their dark sister's minions. Laughing, the dark fairy makes her way back to Aurora's cradle to perform even more mischief, but this time finds her way blocked by an angry Queen.

I thought Mom was the last word in mother lioness, but she's got nothing on Rosa Tejedor.

As Carabosse retreats to the opposite corner of the room, the music shifts soft, a quiet oboe announcing the arrival of one last fairy.

The most powerful fairy of all.

In a full gown of petals the rich violet of her namesake and trimmed with gold thread, la Fée des Lilas, the Lilac Fairy, strides into the room, confident in her power. If finding my mother's eyes in Carabosse's gaze chilled me, the identity of the Lilac Fairy leaves my heart a block of ice.

Veronica Sayles may be no more, but Madame Versailles, it would appear, is again free to roam as she pleases.

And if Versailles is here, can Durgan be far behind?

In pantomime, the Lilac Fairy and Carabosse first greet each other, and then negotiate the consequences of the dark fairy's actions, Yin and Yang personified. At first cordial but increasingly forceful, they argue in silence, Carabosse's gestures provoking images of death while the Lilac Fairy's suggest Aurora's sentence of death shall be only a deep slumber.

A slumber that will last a century.

Carabosse's mob of monsters gathers about her feet like a black cloud as their mistress grows angrier and angrier, all the while her lilac-clad sister maintaining a semblance of calm. As the dark fairy raises her staff above her head to attack, however, the Lilac Fairy's patience reaches its end. With one outstretched finger, she sends Carabosse and her entourage to the far end of the room where they encounter another of the fairies. Back and forth, from one corner to another, from one fairy to the next, the mass of monsters with Carabosse at its center flees the

Lilac Fairy's wrath until the dark fairy and her minions disappear in another column of mist, leaving in the same manner they arrived.

Evil ousted, however fleetingly, peace returns to the palace. The Lilac Fairy glides to the queen's side and waves her hands over Aurora, mitigating the curse as promised. The fact that she wears Versailles' face nearly has me leaping out of my skin, but for the moment, she seems to be playing her part as closely as my mother did hers.

She bows to King Florestan and the queen, and the royal pair acknowledges her in return. Soon, the rest of the court attempts to resume the celebration. In one corner, the maid wearing my sister's face retrieves her knitting and sets to work on an intricate baby blanket intended for the infant princess. Suddenly, I, in my role as Catalabutte, feel an irresistible urge to intervene.

I rush to the handmaiden's side, rip the knitting from her hands, and deliver the pair of needles to King Florestan. He studies the otherwise innocuous implements and drops them to the floor before bringing his fingers across his neck in a mirror to Carabosse's gesture from before.

His message is simple. No spindles. No needles. Nothing that will trigger the curse.

I know all too well his edict will fail, but for the time being we must all play our parts in the tragedy to come.

As the curtain falls around us and darkness returns, I pray this, the third and final Tchaikovsky ballet, will play out as written.

We could all use a happy ending right about now.

"Anthony?" Jason's voice. Stressed. "You coming around?"

My eyes flutter open. Even that small effort hurts. "Who turned out the lights?"

Jason rises from his chair and flips a switch. "Bright enough for you?"

Wishing I hadn't complained about the dim, I raise a hand and cover my eyes. My arm feels like lead. "What happened?"

"You went down first, then Mom soon after. You've both been out for an hour or so."

I peer across Dr. Archer at Mom's sleeping form before turning my attention to the empty chair by Mira's bed. "And Detective Sterling?"

"He nodded off for no more than a couple minutes. Otherwise, he just hung out in here with me and kept watch over all of you. He stepped out a few minutes ago to check on the guards and to see if there was any news on Durgan." Jason's eyes drop. "Whatever went on with the rest of you, it didn't seem to involve him."

That makes sense. I never saw Detective Sterling in the court of *Sleeping Beauty*. Or Dr. Archer for that matter.

Mom, on the other hand...

"Did Mom do okay?" I glance in her direction. "You know... while she was under?"

Jason sucks in air through his teeth. "She seemed to be resting peacefully for the first bit, but about twenty minutes ago she got pretty agitated." Jason sits by her on the bed and brushes the hair from her face. "Is she... all right?"

Carabosse's baleful sneer fills my mind. "For now."

The dark fairy's eviction from King Florestan's court notwithstanding, her part in this drama is far from over.

"What about Mira and Dr. Archer?"

"No change." Jason's lips curl into a slight smile. "Both still breathing, though. I guess that's something."

"That's setting the bar pretty low, don't you think?"

"What's that saying?" Jason raises an eyebrow. "Any landing you can walk away from?"

"I suppose." I glance at Mom again, her expression placid. It's not a look I've seen on her face all that often lately. "Should we wake her?"

"Let her rest." Jason sits by me at the edge of Mira's bed. "I want to talk to you for a minute. Brother to brother."

"All right." A bit of strength returns to my limbs and I pull myself up in the bed. "What's up?"

"This." Jason gestures around the room. "All of this. I want to save Mira as much as anyone. We all owe her so much, but... I'm worried about you." His head cocks to one side. "Can you really do this?"

"You tell me. I just survived the prologue of *Sleeping Beauty* without a scratch." A memory of Carabosse's spidery fingers stroking Catalabutte's bald scalp sends chills down my spine. "At the very least, we're on the right track."

"And how do you know that?"

"Things in the world between my mind and Mira's have a funny way of working themselves out." I take a breath. "Other than Dr. Archer and Detective Sterling, everyone was there: Mira, Mrs. Tejedor, Rachel, Isabella,

Dad..." I swallow back the fear. "And Mom."

"What about Durgan and Madame Versailles? That's who we're up against, right?"

"Versailles was there, but she wasn't exactly who we thought she was going to be." I bite my lip till it feels like I'm about to draw blood. "And neither was Mom."

"I don't..." Jason's eyes shoot open in understanding. "Wait. Mom was Maleficent?"

"Carabosse, but yes. Mom was the face of the dark fairy." I shake my head in shared disbelief. "Not the first time she's been the wicked witch of the story."

"But why?" He gestures in Mom's direction. "In a way, I get the whole Baba Yaga thing. She was there to protect you by any means possible. But now? If she's the bad guy, wouldn't that make her the one that puts the princess to sleep?"

"Actually, Carabosse's curse is supposed to kill Aurora on her sixteenth birthday. It's only the Lilac Fairy's intervention that blunts the spell's effect and leaves her asleep for a hundred years instead of dead."

"I'm afraid to ask who that was." Jason's eyes narrow as I shrink into the pillow. "No."

"Yes." I let out a sigh. "The Lilac Fairy wears the face of Madame Versailles."

"So... the most powerful force for good in this story is an entity who hates Mira with a passion, our mother is the villain, and Durgan is nowhere to be found?"

"That pretty much sums it up."

"William?" The first word out of Mom's mouth is my father's murmured name. Dead for years, he never seems far from her thoughts, and if she has any recollection of her time in the dream court of *Sleeping Beauty*, then she just came face to face with him for the first time since the funeral.

We're all going to need serious therapy when this is done.

Jason rounds Dr. Archer's bed and takes Mom's hand. "It's all right, Mom. We're here."

Her eyes flutter open and she immediately looks in my direction, her gaze frantic with worry. "Is Anthony—"

"I'm fine, Mom. Beat you awake by a few minutes." And now, the million-dollar question. "Do you remember anything?"

She focuses, her eyes drifting off to a faraway place with which I suspect we're both now intimately familiar. "There was a court. A king and a queen. And... a baby." Her eyes grow wide with fear. "Oh, God. I remember everything." She starts to hyperventilate. "Everything..."

"It's okay, Mom." Jason kneels by the chair and wraps her in his arms. "It's okay."

"But... I was the dark fairy. The villain." She peers at me, the color draining from her face. "Again."

"I'm sorry, Mom." An icy spike drives itself through my chest. "But it's not like I decide who's who in these things."

"But you do," she whispers. "At least on some level." She turns from me, unable to look me in the eye. "First I was the witch at the end of the hall, and now I'm the dark fairy who does her level best to kill the very woman we're trying to save. How is that supposed to make me feel, Anthony? What does that say about me? You? Us?" Her gaze shoots up and to the left. "Wait. The other fairy. The good one..."

"I know." I force myself from the bed onto shaky legs and round Dr. Archer's hospital bed to stand by Mom's chair. "Mom, there's something I need to tell you."

She glares up at me through her tears. "What?"

I swallow back weeks and months of lying and remorse. "You're not the only one who remembers everything."

Her eyes narrow at me. "What do you mean?"

"I didn't want to worry you before, but the truth is, I remember it all. Just like you remember being Carabosse. I remember the Exhibition. Koschei's realm. The Shrove-Tide Fair." I glance in Mira's direction. "Mira's final sacrifice."

"But you said—"

"I thought if you believed all of it had faded into the background of my mind, that you wouldn't treat me differently. That things could go back to the way they were before."

Her lip trembles. "And why are you telling me now?"

"For one reason only." I take her hand. "Baba Yaga may have been the old witch at the end of the Exhibition hall that ruled with an iron fist, but she was never the villain of that story. At her absolute worst, she had one mission and one mission only."

"And what was that?" she gets out between sobs.

"To protect me." I squeeze her hand. "Not Tunny, not Antoine, not anyone else along the Exhibition. Me." My own eyes begin to well. "At the time, we couldn't see how such a creature could be a force for good, and yet now, I can't unsee it. Maybe your role as Carabosse is the same."

"But I cursed her." Her entire body shakes with sobs. "A baby."

"It's a story, Mom." I lock eyes with Jason. "A story that has to run its course if we're ever going to get Mira back."

"You mean I have to go back?" Her voice as low as I've heard it, Mom all but whimpers. "Don't make me go back there. Please. I don't know what I might do."

"That's the thing." I let go of her hand and pace the room. "I'm pretty sure I know exactly what you're going to do." I turn to face my mother and offer the most compassionate smile I can manage. "And if we're all going to get out of this alive, we have no other choice than to let you do exactly that."

XXVII

AURORA

All color drains from Mom's face as Detective Sterling strides back into the room. Looking none the worse for wear, he notices I'm awake, steps around Jason like a professional ballplayer, and bolts to Mira's side.

"Mira?" He takes her by the shoulders and gives her a not-so-gentle shake. "Mira?"

"No such luck, Detective." Mom straightens herself in her chair. "But according to Anthony, we made some progress."

Detective Sterling pulls up to his full height and gives me a frank up and down. "What happened?"

I review for Detective Sterling all that went on during my first foray into the world of *Sleeping Beauty*. He appears just as shocked as Jason did at the revelation of Carabosse's identity as well as the Lilac Fairy's, but he takes in the rest of the story with the same cool regard hundreds of criminals have no doubt faced as they sweated it out across a table from the detective during an interrogation.

"So," he asks when I'm done. "The baby is... Mira, somehow?"

"The queen was her mother and the king, my father." I shrug, trying to keep the sarcasm from my tone. "You tell me."

"Seems pretty obvious." Jason's eyes flick in Mira's direction. "Not to mention, only one person involved in all of this qualifies as a 'sleeping beauty' as far as I can see."

"But why did it start at the beginning?" Mom peers at me, the color returning to her cheeks. "Wouldn't it make more sense for us to come in at the part where the princess is already in the midst of her hundred-year sleep?"

"Hold on a minute." Detective Sterling shakes his head, a hint of smile invading his stern expression. "You expect after all that's happened that any of this is going to make sense?" He casually musses my hair, no doubt in an attempt to show support, though the move is all too similar to Carabosse's cold touch to create any semblance of warmth. "Anthony here runs the show, and it looks like he wants us to see the whole thing."

"There's got to be a reason, though." Jason searches each of our faces for understanding. "Even if it's at a subconscious level, Anthony's mind puts these things together like jigsaw puzzles, and so far he hasn't missed piece one."

"Perhaps," comes a strained voice from the other bed, "we've started at the beginning so that we can understand the end." His eyes barely open, Dr. Archer attempts a smile.

"Thomas." Mom leaps up and rushes to Dr. Archer's side. "You're awake."

"Just long enough to catch most of Anthony's story." His eyes find mine. "And not so loud. My head feels like the entire troupe from *Riverdance* is trying to kick their way out of my skull."

"You heard it all?" I creep over to Dr. Archer's bed and sit on the edge by his knee. "Then tell me. What do you think we should do now?"

"I have no idea, Anthony." His eyes slide shut. "But if your mother is indeed the dark fairy, Mira the princess, and Versailles has somehow usurped the role of savior, that still leaves one last psychopath to ferret out before this is over."

Mom sighs. "Even if you don't know the ballet, we've all seen the movie." She buries her face in her hands. "There's only one villain in this piece."

"Perhaps." Dr. Archer pulls himself up straight in his bed. The effort appears to cost him dearly. "But if we're following the story as carefully as it appears, it would seem Mira's life will be spared, at least at first."

"Alive, but asleep for a century, and all my fault." Mom turns and strokes Mira's hair. "Not much different from where we are right now."

Dr. Archer's second attempt at smiling succeeds. "True, but look at it from a different angle. If she isn't put to sleep in the dreamworld, how can we possibly wake her?"

Mom's head cocks to one side. "I... hadn't thought of it that way."

"It's like I said, Mom." I wrap an arm around her waist and squeeze her tight. "Just like in the Exhibition, being the adversary doesn't necessarily make you the villain."

"I hope not, Anthony." She shudders despite the warm air. "I certainly hope not."

A parade of doctors and nurses cycle through to check on Dr. Archer, all of them doing their best to ignore the rest of us. After what seems like days, the six of us are again alone. Somewhere along the way, Detective Sterling ordered pizza, and as I finish gorging myself on a slice of pepperoni, Mom chimes in with the last thing anyone expects her to say.

"Well, the day's not getting any younger and Mira's counting on us." She rises from her chair and goes to the window. "Not to mention Sarah Goode."

"What are you suggesting, Caroline?" Dr. Archer sits up in bed and winces. "Didn't you all just return from our latest sojourn through Anthony's musical funhouse?"

Mom rests her forehead against the glass. "I hate to say it, but we no longer have the luxury of waiting till we're all rested and ready between trips. Not with two lives on the line." She turns and casts a conflicted gaze in my direction. "Do you think you're up for a return trip, Anthony?"

"I'm not sure that's such a great idea." Detective Sterling locks gazes with Dr. Archer. "And I suspect the only doctor in the room would agree."

Dr. Archer shakes his head. "I'm afraid I've got to go along with Detective Sterling, Caroline. I'm not sure going back so soon is a good idea for any of us, especially Anthony." He studies me, concern etched in his features. "You remember as well as any of us how wiped out Mira's mental escapades left her back when she was exploring the Exhibition."

"I'm fine." I cross my arms, defiant despite my exhaustion. "Ready to take on the world."

"You can barely keep your eyes open, kiddo." Dr. Archer shakes his head. "Now is not the time to do anything foolhardy."

"Really, Thomas?" Mom steps back over to Dr. Archer's bed. "I thought you'd be clamoring for us to get back to work waking Mira up."

"Now, everybody calm down." Detective Sterling raises his hands before him, palms out. "We all want Mira back, to save Sarah Goode, and to end this thing with Durgan once and for all, but we're not going to get anywhere if we start fighting amongst ourselves."

"I don't get it, Mom." I study her features, her proud facade about to crack. "Just a couple hours ago, you wanted nothing to do with this, and now you're all gung-ho to run back to dreamland?"

Tears well at the corners of her eyes. "I just want this to be over, whatever it takes."

"I don't know how much help I'll be," Dr. Archer all but groans, "but if Anthony says he's ready, I won't hold us back."

"Me neither," Detective Sterling adds, "though as I understand it, neither of us made an appearance last time."

I shake my head as a rueful smile spreads across my face. "That just means your part hasn't come up yet." I lock gazes with Jason. "Same as before. Don't let anyone disturb us until we're back."

"You've got it, Anthony." Though still clearly uneasy about the whole situation, my brother looks on me with pride. "I've got your back."

"Then gather round, everyone." I motion for Mom and Detective Sterling to close the circle with Mira, Dr. Archer, and me. "And watch out for any spindles."

The velvet curtain, burgundy and gold, rises on a different aspect of the previous scene. Just outside the palace, a trio of peasant women in simple shifts stands around gossiping. Before I can approach them to warn them about what is to come, they are set upon by another.

Carabosse, adorned in her ornate gown of black and violet, approaches the three women and offers each a pair of knitting needles and yarn before pulling up her dark hood and disappearing into the shadows. The women dance in celebration of their good fortune as such items haven't been seen in sixteen years, knitting all the while as the unseen orchestra fills the air with a playful melody. It isn't long, however, before the sound of marching overpowers the phantom symphony.

As the royal guard approaches, I rush the women and silently implore them to hide their knitting. King Florestan has made clear the fate of anyone possessing such items in his realm. Catalabutte's loyalty may be to the throne, but I have no desire to see these women lose their heads. At my insistence, they each hide their work behind their backs, but my efforts come too late as the approaching guards have already spotted the forbidden contraband.

Using whatever influence I possess, I order the guards to stand down, but again, my efforts are ultimately hollow as King Florestan and the queen arrive on the scene before the women can flee. The king seems quite oblivious at first, but the perceptive queen who wears the face of Rosa Tejedor sees through our deception immediately.

The three women fall to their knees at King Florestan's feet, offering up their knitting even as they beg for their lives. Unmoved by their pleas, the king orders each of them put into stockades, no doubt for a rapid triple execution. Though these women exist only in the imaginary world I share with Mira Tejedor's mind, to see such brutality imposed upon innocents is more than I can bear.

On bended knee, I beg for the lives of the three duped women, but the king's expression remains indifferent despite my efforts and the women's plaintive cries. In the end, only the queen's adamant petition of mercy melts the king's steely gaze. His impassive features flow into a forgiving smile and he motions for the women to be freed.

After their knitting is confiscated, of course.

I kiss the queen's hand in gratitude and the scene shifts into an intricate dance as the entire royal court prepares for the arrival of Princess Aurora on this, her sixteenth birthday.

My obsession with Russian ballet may have gotten us into this mess, but knowing every character, every note, and every step hopefully will help get us out of it as well.

As the entertaining performance ends with three dozen dancers paired male and female holding garlands of flowers above their heads, the music shifts yet again, signaling the moment I've been waiting for.

Time for the royal couple to greet Aurora's suitors.

One by one, they appear from the four corners of the room and present themselves to the royal couple as I, in my role as Catalabutte, do my best to facilitate.

The faces of the first pair of hopefuls for Aurora's hand are all but expected.

Prince Siegfried, the sadness at the loss of Odette to von Rothbart's evil wiped from eyes that in another place belong to Detective Sterling, strides in from my right, while the Nutcracker Prince, the face of Dr. Archer similarly devoid of the terror left by the Mouse King's assault, approaches from the opposite direction. They meet at the center of the room and study each other with something just shy of animosity. Does the part of Dr. Archer that was Petrushka still bear the Moor ill will for his death at the Arabian's scimitar?

Or am I witnessing the true rivalry between the two men bleeding through from the real world?

I have no time to wait for answers to these questions as the second pair of suitors presents themselves, again from opposite corners of the room. While the identities of the first pair were all but a foregone conclusion, the faces of these new arrivals leave me thunderstruck.

The first, who bears the features of Mira's ex-husband, Dominic, marches to the center of the room dressed in ornate raiment fashioned of red silk and gold thread and takes the measure of his two competitors. My shock at seeing Mr. MacGregor here in the space between my head and Mira's, however, pales in comparison to the identity of the fourth and final suitor.

Decked out in finery of deep purple and silver trim and his lips turned up in a demonic smile, Wendell James Durgan, or at least his proxy in this place, greets the king and queen with a strange civility, making the collection of men vying for the heart of Princess Aurora a quartet.

Durgan.

In the same place where Madame Versailles holds a position of power.

And I'm the only one who knows.

As the four suitors size up their competition in a show of masculinity I'd expect to see in a wildlife documentary, the music shifts again and the entire crowd, including King Florestan, the queen, and the various princes, all turn to face a grand door that stands ajar.

I rush to the king's side just as the violins crescendo and the lady of the hour finally makes her appearance.

Her bodice, tutu, and hosiery all a faint pink, Aurora rushes to the center of the room, a personification of grace and beauty, though the young woman before me represents far more than just a mythical princess formed by my imagination. Not as young as she appeared as Clara in *The Nutcracker*, Aurora flits before us as a youthful Mira Tejedor, her eyes and high cheekbones unmistakable. At her neck, the locket given her by her mother at her christening gleams in the light of the enormous hall.

With poise and elegance all but unattainable in the real world, Aurora performs for the court, every jump and pirouette more impressive than the one before. To see Mira like this, so happy and free, warms my heart, even as the knowledge of her impending fate weighs on my soul.

Her dance over, Aurora rushes to her parents' side where the king and queen greet their daughter with kisses before presenting her to their esteemed guests. Aurora bows deeply before the quartet of princes, and they answer by circling her, a sequence no doubt choreographed a century ago to connote the romance of the court.

With Durgan's inclusion, however, the scene reminds me more of sharks converging on wounded prey with blood in the water.

And now, one of the most famous sequences in the history of ballet.

The Rose Adagio.

One by one the suitors take turns dancing with Aurora, the illusion of civility betrayed only by the cutting glances that fly from each of the four men's eyes when the princess entertains another. Aurora, conversely, seems oblivious to the barely veiled hostility among the four men. During her turns with Siegfried and the Nutcracker Prince, she vacillates between innocent playfulness and coy passion, neither of which is evident when she dances with Mr. MacGregor's handsome doppelganger. With him, the performance appears ripped from the cover of a romance novel, the heat between them palpable, even as alternating hints of anger and hurt show in the princess's eyes.

And then, there are the times she dances with the Durgan Prince, his every movement slick and every glance lascivious. My heart turns to ice every time he comes near Aurora. And yet, in this place, as in *Swan Lake* and *The Nutcracker*, the part of Mira dancing before me seems oblivious to her plight. Not so much the Durgan Prince, however, as he takes every opportunity to fire knowing glances in my direction.

Mom worried there was only one villain in this piece.

If only she were right.

As the Rose Adagio draws to a close, the four princes gather and hold Aurora aloft, displaying her for the entire court to see. The princess lets out an ebullient laugh, and then descends from her royal perch and pirouettes around the room, eventually making her way back to her parents where she and her mother peruse her options. The suitors in turn encircle Aurora, and one by one, present her with flowers: Siegfried, an orange water lily; the Nutcracker Prince, a white amaryllis; Mr. MacGregor's clone, a bright blue aster daisy; and the Durgan Prince, a cluster of purple hyacinth. She accepts all four, and then hands the makeshift bouquet off to her mother before making a complete circuit of the room with a series of leaps and spins that would be the envy of any ballerina.

As Aurora showcases her talents for the gathered crowd, the four princes pair off with the various women of the court and perform a festive dance in an effort to win Aurora's attention. She, in turn, plays coy and pretends to ignore the entire spectacle. Then, as invisible woodwinds alternate with ethereal strings to provide a jovial melody, the four suitors approach one at a time to ask for Aurora's hand. Again, their pleas are met with dismissal after gentle dismissal. The entire spectacle would be passably amusing, were the stakes not so high.

Rebuffed, the suitors gather at one end of the hall to confer with the king and queen as Aurora continues to flit from one group of courtiers to the next like a pale pink butterfly gathering nectar.

And then, from within the crowd, a cloaked stranger appears.

Or, at least, a stranger to Aurora.

I know the face that hides beneath the hood better than I know my own.

From within the voluminous cloak, a graceful hand with fingers that terminate in scintillating violet nails produces a bouquet of blood red roses. Aurora catches sight of the beautiful flowers and rushes to accept them. Every muscle in my body tenses to run to the doomed princess, to save her from her fate, but two things hold me back: the memory of von Rothbart's invisible hands at my throat both times I attempted to warn Siegfried of the sorcerer's treachery and, more importantly, Dr. Archer's wise words from the other side of the veil of dream.

"If she isn't put to sleep in the dreamworld, how can we possibly wake her?"

Two full laps she parades around the room, playfully flaunting the beautiful bouquet to anyone who will play along. Then, without warning, she throws the flowers to the ground and clutches her hand in pain, the flash of crimson at the tip of her index finger matching the color of the bouquet's petals. Her knees wobble beneath her at the sight of her own blood and her father rushes to her side.

My father.

Joined quickly by his queen, King Florestan looks on his only daughter, sheer horror captured in his terrified gaze. A second later, Aurora appears to rally and rushes from one end of the room to the other, though she moves as if in a trance. The bizarre dance persists until the enchantment finally overtakes her and the princess falls swooning into the gathered arms of her four suitors, her closed eyes fated not to open again for a century.

Sweeping up the roses from floor, I tear into the deadly bouquet and reveal the implement of Carabosse's cruelty hiding in the tight fist of thorny stems: a bone-white spindle, long and wicked, a drop of scarlet at its tip.

The queen joins the king by their fallen daughter, the royal pair breaking down in abject sorrow as the room grows dark. In a moment reminiscent of the final scene of *The Rite of Spring*, a quartet of cloaked figures surrounds Aurora's form, descending upon her as the four witches did the Spring Maiden.

As with all things in the dreamworld, the symmetry is anything but coincidence.

A loud crack sounds from behind the king's throne and the air surrounding the royal dais fills with smoke. From within the billowing cloud, Carabosse steps and drops her cloak to the floor like a dark butterfly shedding its chrysalis. The gloating fairy disguised no longer, she struts over to King Florestan and his mourning wife and cackles in victory. Again, my heart sinks at seeing my mother cast in such a light, but I remind myself for the thousandth time that in this weird world my mind creates, everyone has their place and everything happens for a reason.

The four suitors surround Carabosse, swords drawn and eyes narrow, and I allow myself to believe they might have a chance against the dark fairy.

The truth?

She's only toying with them.

Siegfried and the Nutcracker Prince attack as one, though with a simple sweep of her staff, Carabosse sends both their swords flying and leaves them unconscious on the floor. The suitor wearing Dominic MacGregor's features charges her and is similarly dispatched, leaving only Durgan's doppelganger standing. He and Carabosse stare into each other's eyes. Then, without a word, he strides from the room, leaving the dark fairy triumphant. With a graceful spin, she claims King Florestan's throne, her absolute victory captured in her wicked grin.

Still, for all her bluster, her moment of triumph lasts just that. Before Carabosse can take another breath, a quiet fanfare steals the smile from her face, and the dark fairy disappears into the shadows as her opposite takes the floor.

Striding into our midst with the warmth of a summer breeze, the Lilac Fairy joins the king and queen by Aurora's fallen form, her kind gaze far more the Veronica Sayles I remember from more innocent times than the calculating monster that has plagued Mira and me at every turn for over a year.

Wiping away the queen's tears with one graceful finger, the Lilac Fairy smiles and with a simple gesture reminds them that Aurora is not dead, but merely sleeping. At her direction, a group of courtiers delivers Aurora's form to an ornately carved chaise at the center of the room. Then, she sweeps her arms wide and the remainder of the enchantment falls upon the court.

The lighting dims by the second as, one by one, all present fall drowsy. A yawn here, a stretch there, and within seconds, all but me and the Lilac Fairy herself have joined Aurora in deepest slumber. Even I soon succumb to the inexorable weight of my eyelids, my body aching as if I haven't slept in millennia.

My last thought: Have we come one step closer to bringing Mira back to us, or by going along with the Lilac Fairy's wishes, have we played right into Versailles' hands?

The irony of an inescapable mystical slumber in one realm forcing me back to consciousness in another isn't lost on me.

Mom, Dr. Archer, Detective Sterling, and I all awake with a start. My heart pounds in my ears as I fight to readjust to reality. Judging from the looks on their faces, the others feel the same.

After what seems an eternity, Mom is the one that breaks the silence.

"So…" she whispers, her voice a dry croak, "it's done."

"Aurora sleeps," I add, "and now it's up to us to awaken her."

"And hopefully Mira as well." Detective Sterling rubs at his brow.

"Call me crazy," Dr. Archer says, "but after everything we've seen in the last year, I had no doubt it had to be this way."

The sound of a scuffle outside grabs all our attention. A moment later, the door to our room flies open, bringing with it a voice that chills me to the core.

"I couldn't agree more." Wendell James Durgan, crimson pouring from his nose, forces his way inside. One of the police guards, a muscular man with close-cropped red hair, trails from Durgan's muscular arm while the other, a portly man with wavy brown locks, dives at the man's legs and takes him down.

"Hands where I can see them," the first guard shouts, placing his knee in the center of Durgan's back and ripping his cuffs from his belt.

"Of course, officer." Face down on the hospital tile, Durgan slides his hands out to either side, emulating Jesus on the cross. Dressed in nothing but a gray hoodie, jeans, and tennis shoes, he doesn't appear armed, but that doesn't change a thing.

I've already learned the hard way to never underestimate this man.

As the pair of officers cuffs Durgan and pulls him up to a seated position on the floor, Detective Sterling resists the fatigue that has overtaken all our limbs and forces himself from his chair. A few purposeful steps later and he stands over Durgan, staring down at the man with a mixture of baffled surprise, relief, and suspicion.

"I've got to admit," the detective mutters in an effort to hide the strain in his voice. "You've got a lot of guts showing up here." He kneels by Durgan's head, pulling in close to whisper in the man's ear. "I just don't know what the hell you hoped to accomplish."

"Same thing as all of you," Durgan grunts through clenched teeth. "To finish this thing once and for all."

"You came to kill Mira." My hands clench into fists at my sides. "Didn't you?"

"Shut your mouth, kid." Durgan tilts his head to one side and looks me in the eye, his gaze filled with undeniable hate. "After all, this is all your fault."

"Leave the boy alone." Detective Sterling takes Durgan by the shoulders. "You've already put him through enough pain."

"Pain?" Durgan lets out a bitter laugh. "He doesn't know the meaning of the word."

"Look." Detective Sterling gives Durgan a not-so-subtle shake. "I'm guessing you wouldn't have come here unless you needed something pretty badly."

"Maybe."

"Then talk."

"First things first." Durgan casts his leer around the room. "I've been watching all of you for days, especially you, Detective. One thing is clear. You're the one in charge of this shit show." His gaze trails down to the steel chain binding his wrists. "Now, call off your apes and get these fucking cuffs off me or I swear by the time you find your precious Sarah Goode, you're going to need to call the coroner."

XXVIII

CARNIVAL

Detective Sterling's entire body trembles with anger, but in the end, he steps away from Durgan and moves to the window. For over a minute, he silently stares out at the darkening sky as one of Charlotte's notorious summer squalls gathers outside the glass.

"Get him up," he eventually barks.

"But, sir." The portly guard shoots Detective Sterling a puzzled look. "We've got him subdued. Protocol states we should—"

"He's got an innocent girl somewhere, Perrault." Detective Sterling pulls his chair over to the room's far wall, yanks Durgan up from the floor, and shoves him into the seat. "You can have a chair," he grunts, "but the cuffs stay on."

"Fine." Durgan's smile actually widens. "Her funeral."

Detective Sterling's hand shoots to Durgan's throat, and I can't decide who is more surprised, the pair of guards or Durgan himself. "Yours too, if you don't start talking and fast."

Durgan's face goes scarlet, then purple, his eyes bulging as if they're about to pop from his skull.

"Detective." Dr. Archer forces himself to his feet and posts up beside Detective Sterling. "Don't."

"Let him go." Mom shoots from her chair as well, her hand on Detective Sterling's outstretched arm in a flash. "We need him."

Detective Sterling's fingers tighten before he finally releases his vice grip on Durgan's neck and storms out of the room. Durgan, in turn, launches into a fit of coughing and nearly falls to the floor. The two cops remain silent, wide-eyed at Detective Sterling's unbridled fury. Mom and Dr. Archer step back and stare at each other silently, neither sure exactly what to say.

Durgan recovers from his spate of coughing just in time for Detective Sterling's return.

"Two things," the still fuming detective says, his voice a sharp whisper. "First, understand that if you weren't an essential part of getting Mira back, you'd be on your way to the ER right now."

Durgan, his face still flushed, shoots Detective Sterling a derisive sidelong glance. "You don't say."

"And second, you piece of shit, I've got your number."

His smile from before tarnished a bit, Durgan gives Detective Sterling his full attention. "You have no idea what I—"

"Shut up." Detective Sterling silences Durgan with the whispered words. "You risked everything coming here. Capture. Return to prison. Even your life, if things didn't go your way. You wouldn't have dared show your face unless you had no other choice."

Durgan's eyes narrow. "Desperate times call for desperate measures."

"You need our help as much as we need yours. Fine. Before we go another step, though, tell me..." Detective Sterling goes nose-to-nose with Durgan. "What have you done with Sarah Goode?"

"Priorities, Detective. First, let's wake up your little girlfriend and get everything figured out on this end." Durgan raises his shoulders in an amused shrug. "Sarah will keep..." He tilts his head to one side, his calculating eyes shooting up and to the left. "At least for now."

"The dreamworld, then." Dr. Archer interrupts, studying Durgan with a diagnostician's eye. "Mira lies here comatose because of that place, it's nearly killed both her and Anthony on multiple occasions, and each of us have felt its effects." He rests a hand on the man's shoulder, the outpouring of empathy almost as shocking as Durgan's earlier charge into the room. "What has it done to you?"

Durgan bites his lip, and for half a second, I'm half convinced he's about to start crying. The hint of emotion, however, evaporates as quickly as it appeared.

"What's it to you, Doc?" His eyes resume their previous icy glare. "Don't pretend for a second you give a shit about me." He glances in the direction of

Mira's bed. "We all know there's only one person in this room you care about."

"And yet, in helping her, I suspect I'd be helping you." Dr. Archer meets Mom's apprehensive gaze. "Like it or not, as Caroline said, we're all in this together."

"Detective Sterling," the first cop asks. "What the hell is he talking about?"

"And why aren't we calling for back up?" His partner raises a puzzled eyebrow.

Detective Sterling doesn't say a word, appearing for all the world like a pot about to boil over. "Cuff him to the chair," he orders Officer Perrault. "Then I need you to keep everyone else out of here until I say otherwise."

"But, sir..."

"Just do it." He shifts his attention to the other cop. "Gibson, you stay with us and keep an eye on Durgan." He clears his throat. "Better yet, keep a *bead* on him."

"And what are you going to be doing, sir?"

"I suspect I'm going to be..." Detective Sterling peers around the room, sharing a silent moment with each of us before finishing his sentence. "Indisposed for a while."

Officer Perrault follows his orders, cuffing Durgan to the chair before stepping out into the hallway, while Officer Gibson observes the entire process, growing more baffled by the minute.

"What do you mean... indisposed?" he asks.

Before Detective Sterling can answer, Dr. Archer jumps in. "What we're about to do, officer, is a form of group hypnotism. It will likely appear very strange. At any point, any or all of us may exhibit odd behavior. Regardless, no matter what, don't try to wake us, even Mr. Durgan here. Cuffed to the chair as he is, he should be relatively harmless." Dr. Archer shoots me a quick glance and adds a muttered, "At least on this end."

Clearly puzzled, Officer Gibson pulls Durgan to the far corner of the room and positions himself a few feet away with his sidearm trained on the sulking convict. The rest of us assume our previous positions and prepare for our final assault upon the dreamworld that has ruled all our lives in one way or another for the last year.

This time, however, we go into battle with the enemy among our ranks.

God help us all.

The burgundy and gold curtain rises again, this time on a scene far different than anything I expected. The next section of Tchaikovsky's ballet typically begins with the spectacle of a party in honor of Prince Désiré, the man fated to wake Princess Aurora from her century-long slumber. Dancing and games and beautiful women in elaborate gowns fill the opening action of this scene as the unseen audience awaits Prince Désiré's inescapable encounter with the Lilac Fairy, an encounter that will change his life forever.

Instead of revelry, I bear disembodied witness to a party of four men enduring anything but a celebration. Stalking through a dark forest straight out of Tolkien, they possess the same features as those borne previously by Aurora's four suitors. The quartet before me, however, are anything but the same four men, and in the lead trudge a pair of characters I never dreamed I'd see again.

The figure wearing Dr. Archer's face is no longer the Nutcracker Prince but appears in the white top, orange-and-red checkered pants, and boots of Petrushka. Fortunately, the confidence in his every step could belong to none other than Toma, the Kalendar Prince. By his side, with Siegfried's royal tunic exchanged for the green-and-purple robes of a certain Arabian, stands the Moor. As with the last time I encountered him, the ridiculous blackface is gone, revealing Detective Sterling's strong features without a hint of the animosity I might expect given his present company.

Directly behind the pair and dressed in garb that seems more appropriate for a Dungeons & Dragons campaign than a ballet, Durgan surveys the scene. His outfit designed to proclaim the animal within, the man's cruel gaze peers out from the open maw of a dark helmet in the shape of a wolf's head. Gray fur hangs from his shoulders, cascading down the back of a shirt of chainmail to meet a pair of similar fur boots. Though somewhat out of sync with his compatriots, Durgan's attire is far from the most surprising.

Bringing up the rear, an even more handsome version of Mira's ex-husband, Dominic, strides proudly in the characteristic white tights and golden brown tunic of Aurora's Prince Désiré. Dashing from his perfectly coiffed hair to his immaculately tailored clothing, he is every bit the man destined to free Aurora from her prison of sleep.

But how can he be the one to bring true love's kiss? I'd guessed Dr. Archer, or perhaps Detective Sterling, but Dominic MacGregor? The man who broke Mira's heart?

Toma and the Moor appear to be on friendly terms, helping each other over obstacle after obstacle as they make their way through the dense underbrush. Conversely, their association with Désiré and the Wolf Knight seems at best apathetic and at worst resentful. I half expect on more than one occasion for any or all to draw the swords hanging at their sides, but somehow all keep their cool as they trudge from dismal forest to even more dismal swamp.

Assuming they are still marching inexorably toward the end of some version of *Sleeping Beauty*, a deluge of question hangs at the front of my thoughts.

What happens when these four arrive at the palace? If Dominic is in fact Désiré, what does that mean for Mira? Will Toma or the Moor even allow him to get near her?

And above all, do any of the three understand that they truly have a wolf in their midst?

In any case, there's not much I can do but watch, as I appear to be little more than a ghost in this piece.

"Oh, you are no ghost, Anthony Faircloth."

The whispered words send ice through my veins. A potent mix of venom and amusement all colored with a thick French accent, the voice could belong to only one person. It seems, however, that Mira's nemesis remains just as disembodied as me.

"Madame Versailles?" I ask, trying to keep the tremor from my disembodied voice.

"In this place, boy" the voice responds, "you will refer to me as the Lilac Fairy."

"Very well." Fearing for my very existence, I struggle to come up with any question that might prolong my life another minute. "Where are we?"

A quiet laugh fills the space. "Oh, if I were to hazard a guess, I'd say the both of us lie somewhere along the in-between. Not quite a part of the scene, and yet, still present." Her voice turns even colder. "Almost as cruel as being banished to an island mausoleum, don't you think?"

"The in-between?" I ignore her not so subtle jab. "I don't understand."

"And you think I do?" Her tinkling laugh returns. "Remember, Anthony, this is a world of your making and rules, not mine."

"But in every other scenario, I've always had a body of some kind. Here, I'm... nothing."

"That part, at least, is simple. In this particular realm, you wear the form of Catalabutte, King Florestan's master of ceremonies. He, like the others of the royal court, has lain in a deep slumber for the last hundred years. Therefore, that frame is not available to you until he awakes. Regardless, it is essential you bear witness to the events about to transpire. Your role in

Aurora's fate is crucial. A single misstep could spell disaster."

"My role?" My shouted voice echoes from nowhere and everywhere at once, and yet not one of the men so much as perks his ears. "Catalabutte's part in this drama is over." I force my voice to go quiet. "And since when do you care what happens to anyone but yourself?"

"Careful, boy," the voice whispers. "We stand at a crossroads. Do not assume that my stooping to speak to you means we are friends."

"Then why *are* you talking to me?" With silence my only answer, I shift back to my original line of questioning. "As I understand it, from here on out, Aurora's fate lies solely with you in the role of Lilac Fairy and a certain prince who is destined to kiss her awake." I cast an invisible glance at the four men in their disparate attire, all hunched beneath an enormous fallen tree to shield themselves from the light rain falling from the sky. My gaze focuses on the one wearing the face of Dominic MacGregor. "I suppose that begs the question... Is that one truly Désiré?"

"That remains to be seen, does it not, Anthony?" Far more the teacher from *Tuileries* than the most powerful fairy in King Florestan's kingdom, the quiet French voice continues to invisibly lecture me. "The name, after all, is a play on the word desire, and only one heart in all the realm knows which of these men represents Aurora's destiny."

She's right. Each of the four has a unique link to Mira Tejedor.

The psychologist who won her heart.

The cop she can't stop thinking about.

The man she once married and who will always be the father of her child.

And lastly, the maniac who stalked her to the hospital bed where she lies helpless.

I let out a quiet laugh. At least we can rule out one of the four.

"Be not so quick to jump to conclusions," she whispers. "Death comes for us all, and the ending of this story, like all you've faced both with Mira Tejedor and alone, isn't written in stone."

"But it can't end that way." If I had eyes, I'd be fighting back tears. "It just can't."

"That, Anthony Faircloth, is up to you."

And with that, the Lilac Fairy leaves my presence and materializes before the four men. Versailles hides her calculation and cunning behind the Fairy's innocent facade, but at least one among the four recognizes her for exactly who and what she is. She greets each of the men with the benevolence and grace that is the Lilac Fairy's trademark, but with Durgan's Wolf Knight, the moment lasts a bit longer.

I can't help but fret over what that might mean.

The time for greetings over, the Lilac Fairy raises her arm in a majestic sweep, and the swamp dissolves like a watercolor painting left out in the rain. One second, the four men stand in the muck of a forgotten land and the next they stand at the center of a carnival.

A very familiar carnival.

Unmistakable in its design, the Shrove-Tide Fair from *Petrushka* materializes around me. Though the streets are devoid of people, every other detail remains exactly as I remember it. The two-story theater. The tavern on the corner. The various shops and kiosks along the street. Only the Charlatan's Booth is missing from the scene.

My heart freezes as I recall my time as the evil magician, forced time and again to do the bidding of a disguised Madame Versailles. Only Mira's sacrifice freed both me and the others from the madness of this place. Now, the witch has the audacity to bring us to these streets where I was her slave, where Petrushka was forced to watch the lovely Ballerina fawn over the Moor instead of him, where the Moor was forced to strike down the pathetic clown before the entire town with the very scimitar hanging at his side.

One moment, the streets are empty—save, of course, the Lilac Fairy and the four princes—and the next, the Shrove-Tide Fair celebration of *Maslenitsa* commences. People flood the streets and a lively tune fills the air, at times with elements from the Stravinsky piece and at others with echoes of Tchaikovsky. Mere seconds pass before a mob of female dancers garbed in pale green dresses forms up at the center of the square where the Charlatan's Booth once stood. Two dozen in number, the dancers form a pair of lines that intersect on the Lilac Fairy, who in turn waves her arm, the subtle motion summoning a vision of beauty. From behind her flowing sleeve, Aurora appears from within a shower of pink rose petals, her intricately embroidered bodice and tutu accentuating her dancer's form.

The men respond as men do, jockeying for position before the lovely young woman. Each tries to draw close so that they might dance with the mysterious figure in pink, but the Lilac Fairy blocks all their efforts, the graceful deflections doing nothing but stoking the fire of their passion for what is clearly forbidden fruit. I take morbid amusement in the fact not one of them realizes the figure before them is only a representation of Aurora and the princess herself lies dormant on a chaise in a faraway castle that hasn't seen the light of day in a century.

As the four men grow more and more frustrated with the situation, I am reminded of the lengths von Rothbart went to keep Siegfried from Odile in her guise as the Black Swan, or the games Drosselmeyer initially played when teasing Clara with the Nutcracker doll.

More similarities in what seems an endless succession of parallels.

Eventually, the Lilac Fairy acquiesces and each of the men is allowed to dance with the vision of Aurora. Toma's every movement and step speaks of his unmistakable love for the princess, a truth no doubt bleeding through from the other side of the veil of dream. The Moor can't tear his eyes from Aurora's gaze, his own filled with utter admiration as they dance in time with the joyous music. The princess's time with Désiré seems a study in fiery passion, the performance so suggestive that at times I force myself to look away.

Finally, it is time for her dance with the fur-covered avatar of Wendell James Durgan, a stomach-churning spectacle at best. Graceful despite his lupine armor, the performance goes without any significant event, though I struggle with which aspect of the Wolf Knight's calculated gaze sickens me more, the loathing or the lust.

Again and again, the ethereal vision of Aurora flits from one man to the next as if she were a butterfly drawing nectar from a verdant garden of flowers. With each spin, each pirouette, each vault, the men grow more and more enamored of the princess, her beauty and poise unparalleled in this world or any other. And then, just when it seems a fight is brewing over who gets to dance with her next, the Lilac Fairy banishes the vision of Aurora with a wave of her hand and beckons the quartet to follow her down a narrow side street and away from the fair.

I move to intercept the Wolf Knight, but he passes through me as if I were so much air.

Undeterred, I follow them, observing everything and biding my time.

If what the Lilac Fairy said is true, my moment in this has yet to arrive.

She leads the quartet away from the city and toward a lake in the distance. I follow, a wraith in their company, silent and invisible. I have no doubt Madame Versailles can still sense my presence, but at no point along the path does the Lilac Fairy offer any acknowledgement or even a glance in my direction.

That leaves the big question.

Does Durgan know I'm here?

As we near the lake, a lone swan glides along at the water's edge. No crown adorns the graceful creature's head, and yet there is clearly more to the snow-white fowl than meets the eye. A look of shock crosses the Wolf Knight's features as the bird comes into his field of vision, suggesting I'm not the only one who finds this particular scene all too familiar.

Another wave of the Lilac Fairy's hand and the swan undergoes a bizarre transformation. Its neck elongates into a graceful mast, its body broadens into a hollowed out rectangle with space for half a dozen grown men, and its wings twist into enormous feathered sails. In seconds, the bird's metamorphosis into a vessel plucked from Greek mythology is complete and the Lilac Fairy steps inside. She gestures for the four men to join her and three of the four comply readily. The Wolf Knight, on the other hand, approaches the swan boat with a bit more trepidation, as if expecting a trap. Only the cajoling of the Lilac Fairy and the subtle mocking of the other men convince him to step aboard.

Strings and woodwinds vie for supremacy as the swan boat leaves the shore, carrying the party of five over the mist-covered lake to the palace of King Florestan where a sleeping Aurora awaits her long-anticipated kiss. As seems my lot, I tag along, an invisible hitchhiker on this final journey through the space between my mind and Mira's.

Minutes fade into hours and hours into days as time becomes fluid upon the magical lake. Then, just when it seems the trip will go on for all eternity, we penetrate a low bank of mist and the castle appears in the distance, overgrown and dark.

That's when a dreadful realization hits me.

The last obstacle between the quartet of armed men and the sleeping princess that has captured each of their hearts is an adversary more powerful than anything they've ever faced.

An adversary who wears my mother's face.

If Carabosse is truly all that stands between the princes and Aurora, to what lengths might they go in order to complete their quest and awaken the sleeping beauty?

Worse, what might I be forced to do to free Mira from this dungeon of our shared nightmare?

As the swan boat reaches the opposite shore, the quiet crunch of grass beneath the bow of the boat sends chills up my disembodied spine. The Lilac

Fairy disembarks and directs the men in the direction of the palace gate. Fashioned of wrought iron, the gate stands rusted and overgrown with gnarled vines as thick as my arm. With one final wave, the Fairy directs the men toward the castle as her form fades into the mist.

With the quartet of men left to fend for themselves and Madame Versailles off to do God knows what, I bide my time and wait for the other shoe to drop.

None of us are kept waiting for long.

Carabosse and her collection of horned monsters materialize before the gate in a cloud of smoke with only the plucking of a harp to mark their arrival. Terrible in her power, she raises her dark staff above her head and invites the men to attack, an invitation none of them answers.

A smart move.

The dark fairy may appear a lone woman with nothing but a stick to defend herself, but I remember all too well how easily she dispatched Aurora's four suitors when faced with identical odds. I attempt to cry out to warn the men about the danger they face and am reminded again that I have been silenced by rules of my own creation.

Not surprisingly, the Moor takes charge and divides the quartet into pairs. He and Toma draw their swords and attack from the left while Désiré and the Wolf Knight circle around to the right. Carabosse looks on, her malevolent stare taking the measure of each man as they draw close. With every inch her attackers advance, the dark fairy draws up further like a cobra about to strike. The creatures at her feet paw at the ground as if awaiting the order to kill. The clash between steel and sorcery is inevitable, and yet, when Carabosse finally attacks, all of us are taken off guard.

Two taps of her staff upon the ground and four of the five horned beasts making up her entourage spring into action.

The first knocks Toma onto his back, landing on his chest and wasting no time snapping at his throat. Toma gets his sword up just in time to block the monster's gnashing teeth, but the muscular beast outweighs him half again, and the outcome of the battle seems clear.

The second is upon Detective Sterling's doppelganger in an instant, rearing up on its hind legs and knocking the turban from the Moor's head with its first swipe. Unlike Toma, however, the Moor manages to get in a blow and brings the edge of his golden scimitar across the thing's midsection, eliciting a howl torn from one of H.P. Lovecraft's tales.

The third monster rams Désiré with its curved horns, sending the prince to the ground before landing just past him at the edge of the lake.

The fourth and final of Carabosse's creatures, unlike the others, chooses a more careful approach. This newest version of Durgan, a man who has worn the faces of prince, owl, rat, and wolf, must represent a unique encounter for the monster. The only question, I suppose, is whether the horned beast is truly wary of such an entity or merely senses a kindred spirit.

The Moor, an expert with his blade is the first to defeat his foe, ending the creature's life with a single blow to the skull. He spins to aid Toma who still wrestles with the beast atop his chest, but before the Moor can so much as raise his blade, the Kalendar Prince grasps a large stone and crushes the side of the vile monster's head.

Without a second thought, the Moor reaches down a hand—a hand Toma accepts.

Again, I'm not sure which gesture I find more surprising.

Half the battle over, Toma, the Moor, and I turn our attention on the remaining two skirmishes. The Wolf Knight and his opponent still circle each other, neither wanting to relinquish the advantage to their opponent. Désiré, on the other hand, has literally ended up between Scylla and Charybdis.

Disarmed and frightened, he backs away from the snarling monster, every awkward step taking him closer to the gate and the dark fairy awaiting him there. Toma and the Moor move to save him, but a double tap of Carabosse's staff summons another half dozen of the horned beasts. The creatures circle her feet, daring anyone to take a step closer.

Silently, Carabosse awaits her prey like a spider awaiting a particularly succulent fly to fall into its web.

If any part of the true Dominic MacGregor is in there, he must be terrified. He may not be present with us on the other side, but distance in the real world has never proven much of a problem for whatever this thing is I can do. If he is involved, I hope he survives the experience.

Step by step, inch by inch, Désiré retreats from the ferocious beast, until he is within range of Carabosse's staff. She wastes no time. With one fluid motion, she clubs him in the temple and then brings her staff around his neck in a chokehold. His arms and legs flail as he tries to escape her clutches, but like the aforementioned fly, Désiré is now trapped in a dangerous web.

Tired of their dance, the Wolf Knight dispatches his opponent with a flick of his wrist, the length of his rapier in and out of the thing's ribcage before it even knows it's been hit. The creature stalking Désiré turns to face the man in wolf's clothing and meets a similar end, which reminds me: even more so here than in the real world, never underestimate Durgan.

"Now," the Wolf Knight says, breaking the silence and shocking all present. "Allow me to pass, fairy, and you may live."

"No." As shocked as anyone at suddenly being given voice, Carabosse draws her staff tighter around the neck of her quarry. "I forbid it."

The Wolf Knight whips his blade one way, then the other. The steel whistles in the cool air. "That wasn't a request." He takes a step in the dark fairy's direction.

"Stay back." She glances down at her entourage of monsters. "I can summon as many of these as I—"

"Summon all the denizens of the night you want." The Wolf Knight slides closed the jaw of his helmet. "They know which master they serve." He mimics one of the Lilac Fairy's grand gesticulations and the remaining seven beasts leave Carabosse's side and rally at the Knight's feet. "Last chance."

Carabosse relaxes her hold on Désiré's neck a fraction even as her eyes narrow with rage. "I'll die before I allow such as you to pass this gate."

"I was hoping you'd say that."

Without another word and with a speed only possible in the world of dream, the Wolf Knight plunges his rapier straight through Désiré's chest and into Carabosse's dark heart.

XXIX

DÉSIRÉ

No!" **My silent scream goes unheeded by all. "Mom!"**
The Wolf Knight pulls his blade from between the prince's ribs and wipes his blade on the dark fairy's dress. Désiré and Carabosse slump to the ground, dark blood oozing from their matching wounds. Toma and the Moor charge the Knight as one, but come up short as the cluster of horned monsters, their allegiance shifted to a new master, bristle and bare their teeth.

The Wolf Knight pulls Désiré up from the cold earth, allowing Carabosse's limp form to fall face down into the mud. "Come on, before you bleed to death," he grunts. "We've got a princess to awake."

Gasping for breath as crimson spreads across his chest, Désiré wobbles on weakened knees as the Knight slashes at the vines holding the massive gate closed. Carabosse lies deathly still, her chest neither rising nor falling as her lifeblood spills into the muck beneath the gate. Toma and the Moor pace back and forth, blades drawn as they jockey for position to penetrate the Wolf Knight's wall of monsters.

And I continue to do nothing but watch, an impotent wraith in a world sprung from my very own mind.

The very definition of hell.

The Wolf Knight's task complete, he pulls open the palace gate and drags Désiré inside. Glaring back at Toma and the Moor, he grunts a quiet "Follow at your peril" and slams the gate closed behind him. Enforcing their master's edict, the seven creatures form a half circle perimeter around the vine-covered entrance and wait for either of their adversaries to make a move.

No sooner are the Wolf Knight and Désiré out of sight, however, then a familiar fanfare sounds. At the center of the semicircle of horned beasts, the Lilac Fairy appears, her benevolent facade betrayed only by the wicked glint in Madame Versailles' eye as she glances in my direction.

She passes her hand in the air above the seven creatures and returns them effortlessly to the darkness that spawned them. The gate cleared, she releases the latch and allows Toma and the Moor to pass before kneeling by her dark sister and pulling her head out of the muck and into her lap.

A blink, and my disembodied form is by their side, so close I can again make out the dark fairy's failing attempts at taking breath. With a gentleness that seems out of character for the woman who has on occasion tried to kill each of us, the Lilac Fairy draws close to Carabosse's ear. The whispering so quiet I can't make out a word, the one-sided conversation goes on far longer than seems proper, but, in the end, the fairy wearing my mother's face allows herself a feeble smile before both fairies disappear into the night and I am left alone.

Another blink and I'm inside the palace. Whatever light might have invaded through the numerous windows is blocked by a multitude of drawn velvet curtains, leaving the room in an eerie twilight state. Still, the silhouettes of dozens of sleeping courtiers, their forms covered in a century of dust and cobwebs, remain visible in the dim light cast by the lone candle floating impossibly above the intricately carved chaise where Aurora sleeps.

A door along the far wall crashes open, and the Wolf Knight, ferocious in his lupine helmet and cloak, pushes into the room dragging Désiré's bleeding form behind him. He makes a quick survey of the room before tromping across unconscious men and women alike to bring the hemorrhaging prince to his princess.

"There she is," the Knight growls. "Now, kiss her so we can finish this."

I ponder why Durgan is going to so much trouble to awaken Aurora/Mira when it would be so much easier just to slay her where she lies, defenseless.

And yet, he's basically done that before.

In *Swan Lake*, Odette gave her life to keep von Rothbart from winning, but even with her death, the nightmare did not end.

In *The Nutcracker*, Clara Stahlbaum similarly relinquished her freedom to the Mouse King, the ultimate sacrifice, and still the dreamworld remained.

Prokofiev's wolf forfeited every shred of dignity it had and allowed itself to be led on a leash first to Baba Yaga's wood and then to Rachmaninoff's Isle of the Dead, all in an effort to bring down this nightmare between my and Mira's minds. And still, nothing changed.

Now, this fourth version of Durgan faces a decision.

If he kills Aurora as she sleeps, history suggests the dreamworld will assume yet another form. All of this starts again. The reshuffling of identities. The madness. The pain.

No. He won't kill her in her sleep.

He's going to wait until she's wide awake, and then end her definitively.

And I'm going to have to watch.

"Stop." Toma charges through the door with the Moor close behind. "Step away from Princess Aurora."

"Or we shall strike you down where you stand." The Moor brandishes his golden scimitar, his tone somehow reserved despite his obvious rage.

"Help me," Désiré gurgles. "I can't stop him."

"Silence," the Wolf Knight barks as he pushes Désiré's face down over Aurora's. "You have but one role to play here, you worthless fop, so get to it."

Toma and the Moor leap into action, but they're too late. The Wolf Knight releases Désiré, his blood-soaked form collapsing to the floor with an echoing thud. Illuminated by the lone candle hovering above the sleeping princess, the crimson stain on Aurora's lips reveals the deed is done.

And yet, Aurora slumbers on.

Toma arrives at one end of the chaise and the Moor at the other, both their swords trained on the Wolf Knight's neck as Durgan's proxy holds the edge of his own blade to the princess's throat.

"Stay back," he shouts, "or I'll—"

"Or you'll what?" The Moor steps closer despite the Knight's threats. "If you wished the princess dead, she'd already be so." He traces the tip of his scimitar along the Knight's collarbone. "Now, whatever your schemes and plans might entail, you have failed. Leave Aurora be and allow us to tend to her or you will face the consequences."

The Wolf Knight locks gazes first with the Moor and then with Toma. A tense moment passes before he rises from the chaise, allows his blade clatter to the floor, and holds his hands before him. The Moor steps between Aurora and the Knight while Toma stoops to help Désiré.

"You are the foretold hero of this story," Toma whispers. "Why did your kiss not awaken the princess?"

"Simple." Désiré fixes his weakened gaze first upon Toma, and then, the Moor. "It would appear I am not the one Aurora loves."

Toma and the Moor catch each other's gaze as the Wolf Knight lets out a hearty laugh.

"Have at it, then, lads." He opens the lupine jaw of his helmet, revealing a sardonic grin. "Here in the end, let's finally see which of you two she truly favors."

A silent agreement passes between the two men. Toma trains his sword on the Knight as the Moor kneels by Aurora's side. He wipes away the smeared blood of Désiré's efforts and brings his mouth down upon the princess's pale lips. The kiss is long, tender, and gentle, but in the end, the outcome is the same.

"One down." The Knight laughs. "One to go." He arches an eyebrow in Toma's direction. "Think you'll fare better, clown?"

Toma's regal bearing falters as the famed Petrushka chord fills the space, reducing the Kalendar Prince to his roots as a bumbling fool.

"Don't listen to him." Clutching his wound with one hand, Désiré pulls himself up beside the chaise. "Fool or prince or puppet, it doesn't matter. Kiss her, and finish this."

The Moor stands and takes over for Toma guarding the Knight. "You're the one," he whispers. "You know it as well as I do."

Emboldened by their words, the nobility returns to the clown's stance, the confidence to his eyes, the bravery to his heart. Triumphant music builds, faster and louder with each passing second, until any vestige of Petrushka is banished and all that remains is the Kalendar Prince.

"Awaken, Aurora." Toma leans across Aurora's still form and places a single chaste kiss upon her lips. "Awaken and be with us once again."

For several breaths, nothing happens, and I fear all is lost.

Then, with the crash of a distant gong, everything changes.

Aurora opens her eyes, and my heart races, both from joy and terror.

The princess rises from her hundred-year sleep and stretches, wasting no time before racing around the room and waking the rest of the court. Soon, she is joined by her mother, her father, and every man, woman, and child present on the day the curse fell.

And yet, through it all, one thing remains clear.

Aurora may be wide awake for the first time in a century, but as with both

Odette and Clara, the part of her that is Mira Tejedor continues to slumber, unaware of who she is or what is happening to her.

Also, I can't help but notice there is one among the crowd of courtiers Aurora has yet to awaken.

There. In the corner. Left by himself.

Catalabutte.

It can't be a coincidence.

"Aurora," I shout, hoping against hope my voice might be heard. "You have one yet to awaken."

Her head turns, though I can't tell if it is merely part of her dance or whether some small part of her heard me.

"Aurora."

No. That's not right.

A simple, unacknowledged truth floods my thoughts.

Aurora isn't the one I'm here to wake up.

"Mira Tejedor." The words roll down from the ceiling and shake the walls as if the palace has been struck by an earthquake. "Hear me and hear me well."

Aurora and all present hold their hands over their ears and peer about in terror at the booming voice.

My voice.

"This is not your home. These people are not your family. This world is not your world." I focus on Catalabutte's crumpled form in the corner and a subtle golden glow fills that end of the room. "There is one Aurora has yet to awaken. One she has yet to forgive. The negligent master of ceremonies that brought this curse upon her and her home. If you would take breath again, Mira Tejedor, then allow the princess to awaken this poor man so that he might, in turn, awaken you."

A terrified cast crosses the princess's features. For a moment, I pity her.

But the time for coddling is over.

"Now."

The single word shakes the room and Aurora's body jumps as if she's brushed against a live wire. She rushes to Catalabutte's side and kneels before him. Toma and the Moor rush over to join her, and even Désiré pulls himself up onto the chaise so that he can watch. The entire room falls silent as Aurora reaches out her hand and touches Catalabutte's cheek.

Disembodied no longer, I take in a deep breath as my/Catalabutte's eyes open on Aurora's beautiful smile.

"Thank you, Your Highness." Before anyone can stop me, I bring up an open hand and slap the princess across her cheek. "Now, wake up."

Toma moves to intercede, a rare anger flaring in his eyes, but the Moor grasps his arm and holds him back, his head shaking sadly from side to side.

I strike her again across the face, this time with the back of my hand. "I said, wake up."

Tears roll down Aurora's face.

Silent tears.

Though the four men brought here by the Lilac Fairy and I have all spoken, Aurora remains mute.

"Don't make me do this. Please." I raise my hand for a third strike. "Wake—"

"Stop." Aurora's hand shoots up and catches my wrist less than an inch from her chin. Sullen and angry, the princess finally finds her voice. "You dare strike me, Catalabutte?"

I lower my hand and draw close so that she and she alone can hear my words. "No one has struck anyone. Not really. This place isn't real. I'm not real." I pull even closer, my whispered words falling directly into her ear. "And neither are you."

"Guards," she shouts. "Seize our erstwhile master of ceremonies." Her eyes fly to Toma, the Moor, Désiré. "And his friends as well."

"Mira," I whisper. "It's me, Anthony." I point to Toma. "That's Dr. Archer, your Thomas." I gesture in the Moor's direction. "That's Detective Sterling." I incline my head in Désiré's direction. "Even Dominic is here, in a fashion."

"Those names mean nothing to me." The tears continue to flow. "Nothing."

The queen chooses that moment to join us, her gentle raised hand keeping the eager guards at bay. "My daughter," comes the rolling voice that in another world belongs to Rosa Tejedor. "I know you have faced more pain in your time than any should have to bear, but it is time for you to face the truth."

"And what truth is that?" Aurora gets out between pained sobs.

"That all of this is a dream." She gestures in my direction. "Listen to Catalabutte. He is here to help."

"Listen?" Aurora glares at me, sullen and angry. "To the man responsible for our entire kingdom enduring a century-long slumber?" In a blink, her form shifts to that of Clara Stahlbaum. "To the boy who left me to face a lifetime of torture at the hands of a seven-headed rodent?" Another blink and Odette stands before me, her eyes filled with righteous anger. "To the so-called friend who could have saved both me and my love from the impossible choice between an eternity of servitude to a fiend and death at the bottom of a lake of tears?"

"Yes, my daughter." The Queen bows her head, solemn but insistent. "Yes."

"But he led me to this."

Our surroundings blur, the scene shifting to the finale of the Spring Maiden's tragic dance, the poor girl spinning faster and faster and faster until she falls dead at the center of the clearing in the woods.

"And this."

The Ballerina's heartbreak as she is forced to watch the Moor murder Petrushka the clown before a street filled with onlookers.

"And this."

Ivanovna chained to the wall of Koschei's palace as she and her daughter face death or worse at the hands of an immortal evil.

"Even... this."

Scheherazade sliding the blade of the Sultan's dagger between her own ribs in a last ditch gambit to free one she barely knows from the clutches of one so evil that she cheated death not once, but twice.

"You, Mother, want me to listen to anything this... monster has to say?"

"You must." The queen's voice drops to a low sing-song I suspect helped a much younger Mira Tejedor drift off to sleep on many a night. "For if you don't, you will never awake from this nightmare your life has become."

"And why would I ever want to wake up?" Aurora's voice grows bitter and cold. "To again face a world filled with nothing but pain and suffering?"

"My beautiful daughter," the queen intones, "there is far more waiting for you than pain if you will just let yourself remember."

"More?" she asks. "What more is there? Tell me, Mother. What more?"

Leave it to a mother to know exactly how to push her daughter's buttons.

Wait.

Daughter.

"Hear me, Mira Tejedor." I pull in a deep breath and draw Catalabutte's form up as strong and straight as I can. "If you won't wake up for any of the people who have risked everything to bring you back into the light, then perhaps you will awake for one other."

Aurora still wears at her collarbone the golden locket given her by her mother. Before she can stop me, I tear it from her neck, praying it contains what I need to finally bring Mira back to us.

"Give that back." Enraged, Aurora claws at my eyes. "It's mine."

I leap away, just out of range of her talons, and flip open the locket.

Jackpot.

On one side, a picture of Mira. On the other, one of her daughter, Isabella.

Before she can mount another attack, I hold the locket before me and force her to view the pair of portraits.

"If you won't wake up for me, perhaps you'll wake up for your daughter."

For a second time, Aurora leaps as if an electric current shot through her dancer's form. "I have no daughter."

"But you do." Again, I draw close. "It is as I said. This isn't real. None of it." I draw her attention to the pair of photographs inside the golden trinket I stole from her neck. "None of it... but this."

She squints at the picture on the right, as if a part of her recognizes her daughter even as the rest refuses to accept the truth.

"Say her name."

"What?" Aurora whispers, her eyes going out of focus. "Whose name?"

"Your daughter's." I allow my voice to sharpen. "Say it and end this charade."

"No." She buries her face in her hands. "You can't make me."

"You're right." Anger won't win this day, but perhaps kindness will. "You and you alone hold the key to this prison. Only you can free yourself. I can't, and neither can the Kalendar Prince, the Moor, nor even Désiré. However, unless you listen to me, right here and right now, then everything we've done to help you has been for nothing." I rest a hand on her shoulder, my mother's trademark move when she's trying to connect. "Mira, I'm begging you. You and a man you once loved cared so much for a tiny baby you brought into the world together that you called her the most beautiful word you could imagine. All I'm asking is for you to say that name."

"But—"

"Say it."

Aurora's hands fall to her lap, her eyes sliding closed even as tears begin to well anew.

"Isabella," she whispers.

"Say it again."

"Isabella." Stronger this time.

"Now." I hold the locket before me. "Look at her and say her name."

Aurora's eyes fly open and focus on the picture in the locket with laser precision.

"Isabella!" All strength leaves her limbs and she crumples to the stone floor.

Afraid to touch her, I take a step back. Have I done the wrong thing? Said too much?

Both Toma and the Moor draw close but I motion for them to stay back. This is the moment. Nothing must disturb or distract her.

If we are to free Mira, it's now or never.

"Mira?" I whisper. "Can you hear me?"

An instant that stretches to infinity. Then, a voice like an angel speaks words from another time.

"I hear you... Anthony." Aurora doesn't look up from the ground but her words strike my ears just the same. "I hear you."

"At last." This voice, from across my shoulder, fills my heart with ice.

Dammit. I've been so busy trying to bring Mira around, I forgot the wolf in our midst.

"Nothing I did would bring the Tejedor witch around." The Wolf Knight, perfectly silent and still for the entire conversation, sends a flying kick into the Moor's chest, sending him reeling. Laughing madly, he leaps to my side and shoves me to the floor. "I must say, though, that I find your methods most intriguing." He stands over me, his wolf helmet closed so all I can see between its iron fangs is his cruel glare. "Now, step aside so that I might end this nightmare once and for all."

"You're too late, Durgan." I drag myself up from the ground, wishing all the while that Catalabutte was armed with something more than a feather quill. "Mira is awake."

"Why do you think I've waited so patiently?" In a flash, his rapier disappears from the ground and reappears in the Knight's hand. He directs its tip at my eye. "You see, I've already rid myself of two versions of Mira Tejedor, first the Swan Princess and then the Nutcracker Prince's young love. Neither of those defeats, however, has brought me what I desire."

"And what is that?" I ask, knowing the answer even as the words leave my lips.

"Freedom, you petulant child." The Wolf Knight sweeps his arm before him. "Freedom from all of this." His gaze locks with mine. "These worlds that spring from your mind, no matter how much you protest, represent your dreams, your aspirations, everything you've ever wanted. Worlds within worlds where music and magic and story all come together for your entertainment. For me, however, the last year has been nothing but torture." He brings the hilt of his rapier before his face. "That torture ends today."

"Not if we have anything to say about it." Toma comes up on my left flank.

"Your cause is lost, foul knight." A recovered Moor appears at my right. "We have you outnumbered three to one."

"Make that four to one." Mira rises from the ground, Aurora's embroidered pink bodice and tutu shifting in a swirl of color into a familiar green sarong and golden bracelets.

"Scheherazade," Toma whispers with admiration. "You have returned."

"And not a moment too soon." She locks gazes with Durgan. "Hello, Wendell."

If I expect to find fear in the Wolf Knight's eyes, I am sorely disappointed. Instead, he offers a quiet laugh, no doubt, he must believe, at our expense.

"Ah. Such bravado. The whole thing is proceeding exactly as I imagined it." Any mirth in his voice evaporates. "But enough showboating. Let's finish this, shall we?" He redirects the tip of his blade to Mira's chest. "I've already slain the boy's mother this day. Why not his godmother as well?"

"No one has to die this day, Wendell." Mira pulls the Sultan's dagger from her belt and holds it before her. "Now, stand down before you force us to destroy you."

"You make an impassioned plea, storyteller." To his rear, the wall explodes, raining stone and soot and smoke down on us along with the remainder of the court. "But there is one aspect of the situation you've miscalculated."

A chilling howl erupts from the billowing cloud of darkness, announcing the arrival of the treacherous beast that abandoned me on the Isle of the Dead. A second later, Prokofiev's titular wolf steps from the swirling smoke, followed by von Rothbart, the Black Swan, the seven-headed Mouse King, and a legion of rodent soldiers.

"It would appear," the Wolf Knight growls, "that I am not the one who is outnumbered."

XXX

1812

The rats are upon us before the panic even fully registers in my mind.

King Florestan wastes no time evacuating the room, including the wounded Désiré, down one of the side hallways, but not before a quarter of the courtiers are slain and most of the rest wounded. Though I know all too well the forms surrounding me, both living and dead, are all basically figments of my imagination, seeing again the utter carnage an army of rodents the size of men can unleash is enough to give me nightmares for the rest of my days.

It kills me to say it, but our overconfidence is going to be the death of us. We may have briefly held the upper hand, but now we're surrounded by every aspect of Durgan we've faced, not one of which we've come remotely close to defeating.

What is it Jason's coach always says about winning and losing?

The best way to invite victory *or* defeat is to visualize that outcome.

Well, guess what.

I'm already getting RSVPs from the hundred different ways we don't win this.

Toma, the Moor, and I surround Mira to defend her from the rat onslaught, but our efforts are unneeded. The Mouse King's army seems to be avoiding the four of us—I can't believe I'm saying this—like the plague. Similarly, von Rothbart leaves us alone, the owl-faced enchanter retiring to a far corner of the room with a submissive Odile to watch the entire procession with his lone remaining eye. Even the wolf gives us a wide berth, choosing instead to toy with a terrified couple cowering behind a column along the far wall.

One thing is imminently clear.

The four of us are off limits.

Or at least Mira is.

The version of Durgan glaring at us from between the razor teeth of his dark helmet apparently wants her all to himself.

"I'm fresh back on the scene, Anthony." Mira's eyes cut in my direction. "Any thoughts on how we get out of this?"

"I know it looks hopeless," I whisper, trying to keep the tremor from my voice. "But we'll make it through this." I swallow back my fear. "We've come too far to give up now."

"As I see it," the Moor declares, "barring the legion of rodents, there are four of us and four of them." He holds aloft his scimitar, its edge gleaming despite the low light of the room. "I shall take the seven-headed rat and his foot soldiers."

The Moor takes a step in the Mouse King's direction, but Mira grabs his arm before he can break our circle.

"Don't," she whispers. "You may be the strongest of us, but even you cannot face an army of rats alone."

"What do you suggest, then?" Toma grips the hilt of his sword so tightly, the blade quivers in his grasp. "Do we wait for them to surround us, overrun us, devour us?"

"The rest of you perhaps, but the storyteller is mine." The Wolf Knight points the tip of his rapier at Mira and then whips it to his right, directing her to a bare spot on the floor. "Shall we dance, Lady Scheherazade?"

"One condition." Mira gestures to the three of us. "My friends are to be left alone."

The Knight considers her words. "I will guarantee their safety." He shoots me a knowing glance. "At least for the duration of our... discussion."

"Safe conduct from this place for the three of them, or you face us all. Understand?"

"Very well," the Knight intones. "You have my word... though I can make only so many assurances regarding their safety." His eyes shoot again to me. "After all, I'm not the one who makes the rules around here."

"Understood. Just you and me, then?" Mira scans the room as she steps between Toma and me. "The remainder of your little entourage will stay out of it?"

"I wouldn't have it any other way." The Wolf Knight stares hungrily at Mira, any pretense of civility in his expression gone. "This moment is exactly as I've imagined it."

"Mira." I grasp her wrist. "Don't. He'll kill you."

She kneels before me and allows a slight smile to peek through the grim. "Not if I can help it."

"But..." I grip her arm even tighter. "We came all this way to free you."

"And no matter what happens now, know that I am eternally grateful for all you've done." Her gaze wanders up to meet Toma's and the Moor's. "What all of you have done." She returns her attention to the Wolf Knight who waits impatiently, his rapier at the ready. "But, as always seems to be the case, this is my fight. And if I ever want to see Isabella again..."

Mira takes a step in the Knight's direction and finds my fingers still encircling her wrist.

"It's okay, Anthony." She gently pulls free from my grasp and strokes my cheek, her fingers warm against Catalabutte's cool skin. "You've already done more than anyone could ask." She turns the dagger down in her grip like an expert knife fighter. "But this is up to me."

And with that, she leaves the relative safety of our circle to face a fate worse than death.

Standing before the Wolf Knight, she offers a slight bow, though she never takes her eyes off her enemy. The Knight echoes the perfunctory measure of respect before the two of them drop into fighting stances in preparation for battle.

The other aspects of Durgan encircle us to watch the spectacle.

Von Rothbart with an apprehensive Odile at his side.

The Mouse King and his army of rats.

Prokofiev's wolf, his gaze ravenous.

The menace of their collective stare weighs heavily on my soul and the foreboding in Toma and the Moor's faces reveals they feel it too.

A second truth becomes clear.

The Wolf Knight's promise of safe passage for the three of us is a lie.

If he defeats Mira, all of us are dead.

I wish that possibility seemed a bit more improbable.

As Scheherazade, Ivanovna, the Ballerina, and even as the Spring Maiden, Mira has always found a way to win. But now, comatose in the real world and freshly delivered from a century-long slumber here in the realm of dream, not to mention facing an invincible enemy with the Sultan's dagger as her lone defense, she may finally be out of her depth.

The Knight's first move nearly proves me right. With a bold slash, he bypasses Mira's parry and opens the skin at her left shoulder. As bright crimson trickles down his opponent's arm, he offers the tip of his rapier to one of the Mouse King's minions. The mouse soldier laps at the blood, animalistic despite its military topcoat and upright posture.

The sight sends ice through my veins.

"Surrender, Tejedor," the Knight intones, "and I will make your death merciful."

"Never." Mira feints with her dagger and her adversary retreats a step.

The moment of weakness lasts exactly that. Still, a sliver of hope returns to my heart.

The Wolf Knight charges Mira, the tip of his rapier narrowly missing her neck as she dodges to one side. The Knight similarly evades Mira's blade, her counterstrike aimed at the hulking figure's cold heart. In seconds, the two of them become a blur of flesh and steel in what I pray is the only fight to the death I am ever forced to witness. Whatever veneer of civility may have existed between them falls away as knight and storyteller descend into utter savagery.

The Wolf Knight has the clear advantage in both raw strength as well as weapon reach. Mira gives as good as she gets, however, and soon both combatants are wounded beyond anything approaching survivable outside this realm of imagination. Still, both fight on, neither yielding an inch, beauty and brutality and grace and gore all mingled in an impossible struggle I fear can end only in tragedy.

I pull my attention from the fray and scan the surrounding crowd.

Every set of eyes is trained on the fight, caught up in the bloodlust.

Every set, that is, but one.

Her face still concealed behind the Black Swan's mask, Odile stares blankly in horror as the frenzied combat continues. A full head of shining blonde curls pours out from behind the dark feathers that obscure her features. As when she fled from Siegfried before, I ponder if some aspect of Madame Versailles looks out from the dark masque or if those eyes belong to another entirely.

Then, as she peers out from beneath von Rothbart's cloak, her eyes meet mine, and I finally know without a doubt who Odile represents.

How could I have been so blind?

That's when it hits me.

The answer to all of this.

In an effort to shift the odds of defeating Durgan in our favor, I forced the dreamscape between my and Mira's minds to become the world of *Sleeping Beauty*, and yet the villains of all the other places have followed us here to King Florestan's palace.

And if they can be here...

"Lady Scheherazade." Mira Tejedor may be the one fighting for her life, but it's the storyteller we need. "Blow the roof off this place."

Mira risks a glance up at the vaulted ceiling of the palace with its full crystal chandelier and frescoes that would make Michelangelo envious and nearly meets her end at the end of the Wolf Knight's blade.

"I'm a little busy, Anthony," she grunts as she parries a trio of blows.

"Trust me." I tremble with anticipation. "We need to see the sky."

"Are you sure?" She dodges beneath a slash of the Knight's rapier. "Will that even work here?"

"You're the storyteller." I peer up into the dark recesses of the palatial room. "You're going to have to make it work."

Mira lunges at the Knight, driving him back for half a second. She takes advantage of the momentary respite, casts her gaze upward, and, with a voice like rumbling thunder, makes her will known.

"Without warning, a great wind ripped the roof from the palace, allowing sunlight into the great hall for the first time in a century."

No sooner have the words left her lips than a gale force gust hits the walls of the palace, the cyclonic wind sounding for all the world like a freight train, and the top of the building is torn away with a roar L. Frank Baum only dreamed of. Sunlight bathes the space for the first time in years, the undisturbed dust and cobwebs from a century evaporating like so much morning dew. The room goes deathly quiet and even the Wolf Knight halts his assault.

"What are you up to, boy?" he asks, his voice more serpent than wolf. "Besides feeling the sun on your skin one last time before you die."

A glance down my body reveals his observation is correct. No longer do I wear the form of King Florestan's master of ceremonies, but stand upon this battlefield of the mind as myself, Anthony Faircloth of Charlotte, North Carolina.

"You brought friends, Durgan." I turn my eyes upward. "So did we."

Falling from the azure sky like a shower of feathered meteors, a deluge of swans descends upon the space and attack the Mouse King's army in earnest.

Von Rothbart flees the scene, dragging Odile with him to one of the remaining dark corners of the room. The Mouse King roars, a potent mix of rage and delight, as his army sets to defend themselves from the skyborne assault. Across the room, the wolf leaps into the air and draws first blood, dragging one of the swans from the sky and snapping its neck with a single cruel shake.

"Storyteller." I catch Mira's eye. "The walls." I pound a fist into my palm and then mime an explosion. "We stand upon a battlefield. Make it look the part."

Mira narrowly avoids a jab from the Knight's blade as he renews his attack and then shoots me a wicked smile.

At last, she understands.

"No sooner had the cyclone taken the palace's roof," comes Mira's voice, unstoppable in its fury, "than a mighty earthquake struck and reduced the walls of the palace to rubble."

Before anyone can so much as take a breath, a violent tremor hits and knocks all present to the floor. The walls crumble, the polished wooden floors splinter, and within seconds, all that remains lies in ruin.

But that isn't all that's changed.

Both forest and lake that encroached on King Florestan's palace have disappeared, all replaced by a vast plain. Fires of various sizes burn in every direction and abandoned cannons lie strewn everywhere as the sun nears the horizon in the west, yet not a single body litters what appears to be the site of a vicious battle. King Florestan's courtiers, both living and dead, along with the royal pair themselves, are nowhere to be found. In fact, other than the Mouse King's army, the bevy of attacking swans, the various aspects of Durgan, and us, the smoky plain appears empty.

Rising from the rubble, Mira and the Wolf Knight face each other anew.

"Round Two?" she asks, her lips spreading in a sarcastic smile.

"Enough." The Knight launches at her, his rapier aimed at her heart like a compass to magnetic north. "This ends now."

"Your words," Mira intones as a cannonball explodes a few feet from the Wolf Knight's feet, sending him flying. "Not mine."

The ambient music shifts from *Sleeping Beauty* to *Nutcracker* as the battlefield fills with toy soldiers. The Nutcracker Prince no longer commands this army of wood and steel, but the trio leading the charge swells my heart with hope.

At the front, the Sugar Plum Fairy strides confidently, her every step sure.

To her right, Prince Coqueluche, his golden mace shining in the failing light of the day, marches with pride and assurance. To see Dominic and Autumn racing to Mira's aid, even these romanticized versions of her ex-husband and his fiancée, is somehow gratifying.

To their left, no doubt the bravest of the three, the lone remaining Flower from the Fairy's court rushes to keep up. Her lithe form now covered in a makeshift set of armor forged from various sweets from the Sugar Plum Fairy's realm, she wields a pair of matching daggers that flash with a light all their own.

Like mother, like daughter, it would appear.

"Isabella?" Mira murmurs.

"No time for that," I shout, bringing Mira back to the present. "Time to fight." None of us can afford any distractions. Not now.

I can only pray the girl represents yet another flicker of my subconscious and that we are not suddenly fighting for the lives of two Tejedors.

"Attack," Prince Coqueluche commands, and the endless army of toy soldiers burst into a full on charge. "Death to the army of the Mouse King!"

"Destroy them," the Mouse King bellows in his guttural French accent, each of his seven faces filled with the same dismay as von Rothbart's at the swans' attack. "Destroy them all!"

His army of rats answers in kind, their number doubling, tripling, quadrupling before my eyes as man-sized rodents pour from every shadow, hole, and crevice and move en masse at the rushing soldiers of wood, leaving Mira and the rest of us, at least temporarily, alone.

The Wolf Knight rises from the rubble, clearly shaken from the explosion, but angrier than ever. "So you have brought the swans and the toy soldiers." He narrows his gaze at me. "What other tricks do you have up your sleeve, boy?"

"What have you done with Petya?" Striding across the battlefield with a sharpened axe in his hands, Peter's Dedushka appears more force of nature than man. His salt-and-pepper beard hanging to his buckle, his head covered in his distinctive fur cap, and his form wrapped in a full-length coat of gray fur, he heads for the wolf with the precision of a guided missile. "Not that the answer is going to save you, beast."

The fur along the wolf's back stands on end, and though the monster's bared teeth and low growl still send a chill up my spine, his lupine gaze radiates as much fear as fierceness.

As Peter's Dedushka and the wolf circle each other, the Wolf Knight surveys the scene and lets out a hearty chuckle. "So, the supporting cast of our many battles each gets their curtain call." He locks gazes with me. "How... final."

Von Rothbart approaches, Odile by his side. "Not that their presence will change a thing."

The Mouse King completes the circle, his seven heads all turned in our direction and speaking as one. "The outcome will remain the same."

Mira rejoins us at the center of the circle and the four of us turn outward to face our trio of foes. Neither side so much as blinks, each waiting for the other to make a move and hopefully a mistake. The unseen orchestra goes silent for the first time in recent memory, as if awaiting some sort of cue. Meanwhile, the rat army remains under aerial siege by the squadron of angry swans even as the legion of toy soldiers led by the Sugar Plum Fairy and her cavalier advances on their position.

The plan is in place. Everything and everyone I can bring to bear against Durgan has answered my call. Win or lose, it all comes down to this.

I can do no more.

Or can I?

A thought flirts with the edge of my consciousness. Something I've forgotten. The last piece of this puzzle. The key to turning this battle around.

In the distance, another cannon fires, the deafening boom bringing with it my answer.

The reason Mira stands with us as Scheherazade rather than Aurora.

Why I find characters from *Petrushka* standing to either side of me rather than figures from any of Tchaikovsky's ballets.

Why I have shed the form of Catalabutte.

And most importantly, why the music fell silent.

We left King Florestan's kingdom in the rearview mirror several exits back.

"What is happening, Anthony?" Mira whispers. "What do you have up your sleeve?"

"Funny you should ask." I cross my arms, reaching beneath the cuff covering my wrist. There, waiting for me, I find precisely what I need.

In a move reminiscent of the Charlatan and his flute, I pull Mussorgsky's baton from my sleeve and raise it high above my head.

The composer, after all, wears my father's face.

"What are you going to do with that?" the Moor asks.

I shoot him a wicked grin. "I'm going to save all our asses."

A single flick of my wrist and the invisible orchestra returns to life. A different tune this time, one everyone has heard for a change. Especially this part, all brass and bells and booms.

Yes, I skipped straight to the end.

We need the artillery.

"Wait," Toma shouts over the din. "Is this—"

"Yes." Mira takes his arm, hope radiating from her face. "The *1812 Overture.*"

"No!" the Wolf Knight screams. "Not when I'm so close."

BOOM.

The opening barrage of cannonballs decimates a third of the Mouse King's army with pinpoint precision only possible in the world of dream, leaving Prince Coqueluche, the Sugar Plum Fairy, and their battalion of toy soldiers somehow unscathed.

"You cannot do this." The Wolf Knight charges at me, the blaring trumpets in time with his every step. "Not when I'm so close."

BOOM.

The second salvo of cannon fire takes out half the remaining rats while a lone cannonball explodes mere feet from their seven-headed ruler and sends his misshapen form sprawling into the air. From the corner of my vision, I can just make out von Rothbart retreating with a terrified Odile still on his arm.

Still, if all goes according to plan, she'll make it through this.

A big if.

"Stop this, you stupid brat." The Knight raises his rapier to strike. "Or I'll stop you myself."

BOOM.

"What was that, Durgan?" I hold the baton high, and shoot him the most mocking grin I can manage. "I can't hear you over all the—"

"Anthony!" Mira screams. "Look out."

Something big slams into my back, sending the baton flying and leaving me face down in the dirt. The music stops, the silence as oppressive in its own way as the deafening cannons.

Winded, I pull my face up from the hard ground and find myself eye to eye with the wolf, its foul breath making my nose crinkle.

Guess I don't need three guesses as to what it was that knocked me to the ground.

"Hard to keep track of so many enemies at once, isn't it, Anthony Faircloth?" The Wolf Knight plants his boot in my side and flips me onto my back. "One failure is all it takes in this place. One tiny mistake."

I narrow my eyes at the Knight. "My only mistake was not doing everything in my power to leave your rabid dog a more permanent resident of the Isle of the Dead."

The wolf growls at me, but at the Knight's command, the beast circles round to heel at its master's side. Trying to ignore the wolf's hungry stare, I scan the battlefield, knowing full well what I will find.

Disaster.

Mira holds her blade before her as von Rothbart draws close, the sorcerer no doubt ready for a second chance at possessing at least a version of his much-coveted Odette.

Toma and the Moor stand back to back as the Mouse King bears down on them, all seven pairs of glowing red eyes focused on the brave pair.

The rats begin to multiply anew, doubling and tripling in number and soon surround the Sugar Plum Fairy, Prince Coqueluche, the lone Flower, and the newly outnumbered combined force of swans and toy soldiers.

And there, where Peter's grandfather and the wolf circled each other moments ago, lies Dedushka's body. Peter's grandfather wore the face of my father's father, features now maimed beyond the point of recognizability. I have no doubt this small piece of me fought bravely against the wolf, but Durgan was clearly too strong.

Dedushka's day as a part of all this is over.

The Wolf Knight rests the tip of his rapier just to the left of my windpipe. A warm rivulet of blood runs down my neck and pools above my collarbone as I spare one last thought for Grandpa Faircloth, praying he has been spared his doppelganger's fate.

"Do you believe in God, Anthony Faircloth?" the Knight asks, as if reading my mind.

"I suppose." I struggle to think of anything I can say to stay his hand for even another second. "If the last year has taught me anything, it's that nothing is impossible."

"A pleasant sentiment, boy," the Knight intones. "Soon, you will get to test that belief." He plants a soiled boot on my chest and raises his blade above his head. "Whatever deity would be so cruel as to allow you to die on a battlefield within your own mind, send him my regards."

XXXI

PICTURES AT AN EXHIBITION

The Wolf Knight's eyes draw down to slits behind the iron canines of his helmet.

"No!" Mira ducks beneath von Rothbart's grasping hands and runs at my adversary. "You can't."

"But I can." The Knight's muscles bulge as he swings his blade at my neck. My eyes instinctively squint shut in preparation for one final moment of agony.

Instead, an air-splitting clang sounds by my ear.

"Get the hell away from my brother."

My eyes open on Modesto the troubadour, clad in blue and white, standing over me. His silver saxophone crushed by the Wolf Knight's blow, a single wink from my brother's eye returns hope to my heart.

The Knight steps back and directs his rapier at Modesto's heart. "You dare attempt to deny me my moment of triumph, troubadour?"

"No." Modesto allows his horn to drop to the ground and draws his own blade from the scabbard at his hip. "*We* dare."

The thirteen notes of the "Promenade" trumpet fanfare blare down from the darkening sky, the volume—as they say in one of Jason's favorite movies—turned up to eleven. The Mouse King and his army, von Rothbart, and even the Wolf Knight and his cur all look about with more than a hint of confusion in their collective gaze. I have no idea if any of them recognize the tune, but it's clear they all know one fact beyond a shadow of a doubt.

The battle is joined.

Modesto goes on the offensive, narrowly avoiding the wolf's snapping teeth as he leaps at the Wolf Knight. The Knight parries Modesto's thrust and answers in kind, his blade blocked just as expertly.

Its master now focused on Modesto, the wolf turns its full attention on me, licking its lips as it flexes its haunches to leap at my neck. Before either of us can make a move, however, the ground by my hip begins to stir as if Bugs Bunny is about to pop up and bemoan taking a wrong turn at Albuquerque. A moment later, a most welcome addition rises from the earth in the form of a squat wooden body clothed in worn leather and bronze buckles.

"Hello, Antoine." Tunny the gnome smiles at me with oaken teeth from beneath the forked leather hat sitting askew atop his head. His stubby fingers clench the handle of his well-used mace. "Looks like you could use assistance."

"It's just Anthony these days." Both our gazes shift to the perplexed wolf. "Now, whatever shall we do about our mutual friend?"

Tunny doesn't say another word, but spins on one heel and swings his mace. The head of the impressive cudgel impacts the wolf just below its eye, the crunch of wood on bone nauseating. Enraged, the beast leaps upon the gnome and the two tumble to the ground, my presence forgotten.

At least by the wolf.

Half a dozen of the Mouse King's army break off from the main force and surge at me. Still flat on my back, I kick away from the rushing rodents, sliding backward across the rough terrain.

"Ow," I grunt as my head impacts what feels like a small tree. I tear my gaze from my attackers and find it's actually someone's leg. A leg clothed in carefully creased black tuxedo pants and terminating on a black leather shoe shined to a high gloss. A glance up reveals the kind but unamused gaze of my father looking down at me.

Mussorgsky, it would appear, has left the Exhibition.

"Hello, Anthony." The composer's expression remains inscrutable behind a beard thicker than my father ever attempted.

"Dad." I scramble to my feet. "I mean... Mr. Mussorgsky. You're here."

"I am." He spares me only the briefest of glances before returning his attention to the approaching rats. "Now, would you be so kind as to retrieve my baton?"

I scan the uneven ground, but the conductor's baton is nowhere to be found. "What if I can't find it?"

Before the composer can answer, one of the mouse soldiers leaps at him. Mussorgsky ducks beneath his attacker's claws, catches the rat beneath its furry chin, and hurls the monstrous rodent to the ground in a single fluid motion. The snap of the rat's neck echoes across the battlefield, giving even the Wolf Knight a moment of pause.

"My baton, Anthony." The composer drops into a low martial stance as the remaining five mouse soldiers move to flank him. "Now."

I drop to all fours and scour the ground for the one item that can save us all. From the corners of my vision, I catch snippets of the battle. The deadly duel between Modesto and the Wolf Knight continues with both sides having drawn blood. Tunny and the wolf circle each other, both waiting for the other to so much as flinch. Scant feet away, Mira wrestles with von Rothbart, the one-eyed sorcerer slowly gaining the upper hand. Toma and the Moor attempt to fend off the Mouse King's vicious assault, but even their coordinated defense proves insufficient against an enemy with seven mouths filled with razor sharp teeth.

Despite everything we've been through, we're not going to win this.

They were all depending on me.

Detective Sterling. Dr. Archer. Mira.

Mom.

And I've let them all down.

"It's not fair." I pound the ground with my fist and my knuckles impact something that sends a charge straight up my arm.

"Ow." I pull up my hand. There, among the splintered wood, rests the object of my search.

Mussorgsky's baton, the ebony knob just visible amid the rubble.

Is it chance? Or did I will it to be there?

The truth is it doesn't really matter.

"Mr. Mussorgsky." I scoop up the baton and hurl it at the composer. "Catch."

I was never into sports growing up like my dad was, and I can likely count the number of times we played catch on one hand. We were more likely to be found playing chess or listening to classical music through matching headphones, oblivious to the rest of the world.

On this day, however, none of that matters.

Mussorgsky seizes the hurtling baton from the air and the music begins anew.

A brief bit of "Gnomus" energizes Tunny in his fight with the wolf.

A strain of "The Old Castle" similarly puts new wind in Modesto's sails.

The rats continue to move on the composer and I fear he has forgotten himself in his efforts to help the others.

I needn't have worried.

As the quintet of mouse soldiers all crouch as one to pounce, the composer slows the meter of his baton and the plodding melody of "Bydło" fills the space. A blink and yet another of the residents of the Exhibition that once held my mind hostage makes an appearance.

A pair of oxen drawing an enormous cart materializes and bears down on the five rats, crushing them beneath their mighty hooves. Atop the wheeled box, Hartmann the Cart Man holds the reins while at his side, resplendent in a dress of yellow silk and lace, Juliet shoots me a wink.

"Go, Hartmann," Mussorgsky shouts to the Cart Man. "Help the others."

With a jaunty salute, Hartmann turns the cart and directs the oxen at the main body of mouse soldiers, the dirge accompanying their movements growing in volume as their inexorable plodding moves them into position for their next attack. In turn, the multitude of rats surrounding the last survivors of the Sugar Plum Fairy's court parts like the Red Sea allowing me to see the fairy and her beleaguered cavalier. They fight bravely, though sorrow is now etched in their features, the despair no doubt in response the twisted body resting at their feet.

The last Flower of *The Nutcracker* cut, she now lies discarded on this battlefield of the mind.

Mira has yet to notice.

God help Durgan when she does.

With every death, I can't help but wonder if a piece of my mind dies as well.

But I don't have the luxury of worrying about that right now.

"Mr. Mussorgsky." I direct his attention to Mira's struggle with von Rothbart. The sorcerer has forced a fold of his feathered cloak past her teeth to keep the storyteller from accessing her most powerful weapon. "I'm begging you. Help Mira."

"Alas," he lowers his head, "the Lady Scheherazade isn't one of my creations and I cannot aid her as I can the others." He casts a worried gaze in Mira's direction. "Her fate is her own."

"No." Odile appears behind von Rothbart. "It isn't." She rips the Black Swan mask from her face, making plain a simple fact I've known since we locked gazes earlier.

She was never a false face of Madame Versailles.

Instead, the brave eyes that stare back at us belong to none other than Sarah Goode.

"I'm sorry, Anthony," she says, wringing her hands. "I'm sorry it's taken me this long."

Von Rothbart looks up from the ground where his fingers encircle Mira's neck. "Put the damn mask back on, girl. You belong to me."

"Not anymore." A graceful pirouette and the young woman before me is the Black Swan no longer, her bodice and tutu shifting with a silver flash to gleaming white. "Odile is dead. Long live Odette."

"What?" Von Rothbart leaps up from the ground, his remaining owl eye somehow even wider than normal. "You cannot do this."

"I can." She raises an arm and then points a lone finger at the suddenly terrified sorcerer. "And I have."

Over the alternating sounds of battle and music, a new sound hits my ears. The flapping of dozens of wings.

From every corner of the battlefield, the entirety of the remaining swans fly at von Rothbart, a flock of feathered guided missiles. Soon the owl-headed figure disappears in a mass of white. The attack lasts but seconds, but when the swans separate and land around Odette like a platoon of well-trained soldiers, von Rothbart is no more.

"What would you have us do now, Anthony Faircloth," the newly christened Odette asks.

"Help the others," I whisper, "but first, there's something I need to know."

She leans in, knowing full well what I intend to ask, and whispers into my ear.

"I'm sorry." My entire body trembles. "I couldn't make out what you said."

"Don't worry. You just don't have time to think about it right now." She smiles. "Trust that when you need to know, you will remember."

And with that she and her bevy of swans rejoin the battle.

With von Rothbart defeated, I turn my attention to the fight against the Mouse King. Poor Toma lies wounded at the seven-headed rodent's feet, a large gouge in his forearm leaking crimson and the injured Moor all that stands between him and anything but a painless death. Mira, Scheherazade's green sarong in rags, rushes to the aid of the two men who would do anything for her though little chance remains she'll arrive in time to save either of them.

I'm not, however, the only one who has noticed the losing battle. The composer again switches up the cadence of his baton and the music changes, the slow dirge of "Bydło" shifting to the quick flitting woodwinds of "Ballet of the Unhatched Chicks."

A new figure drops from the sky and lands atop the cluster of heads that crowns the Mouse King's rotund form. Attired in the ruby red bodice and black tutu she sported along the Exhibition, Trilby the ballerina somersaults down from her precarious perch and lands beside Toma's wounded form. Shooting me a sidelong wink that is my sister Rachel's trademark, she launches into a display of martial arts straight out of *The Matrix*. Their battle quickly becomes a stalemate, as the Mouse King remains far too powerful for her to stop and Trilby far too nimble for him to catch. Still, the distraction gives the Moor an opportunity to drag Toma to safety.

As if anywhere on this battlefield is safe.

"Mr. Mussorgsky." I rush to the composer's side, dodging the Mouse King and the wolf who are fortunately occupied fighting Trilby and Tunny. "The tide has turned. Do you think we can actually win this?"

"Anthony." Mussorgsky rests a hand on my shoulder. "I would love nothing more than to reassure you here in this moment of despair, but at some level, both of us know that you talking to me is tantamount to you talking to yourself. Therefore, I suppose I must turn the question back on you." A grim smile spreads across his face. "Do *you* think we can win?"

"Now that you've brought the majority of the Exhibition..." I take a deep breath, the tang of cannon smoke flavoring the air. "I believe we can."

"Your optimism serves you well, young man, but it wasn't me who brought them." His gaze shoots to the horizon. "We're all here on *her* behalf."

At the composer's direction, the music shifts again, the bombastic "The Hut on Fowl's Legs" filling the air and drowning out every other sound.

Can it be? Can she have survived the Wolf Knight's wound?

Has my mother, so recently slain at the tip of the Wolf Knight's blade, come to save me?

The back-and-forth crash and thud of Baba Yaga's mortar and pestle hits my eardrums long before it appears. Then, out of the corona of the setting sun in the west, I see it: an enormous stone bowl driven by a madwoman bearing a long wooden club and an ever-swishing broom that whisks away any evidence of her passing.

But the woman atop the mortar isn't the iron-toothed witch, but Madame

Versailles, the rough implements belonging to Baba Yaga gripped in her unblemished hands.

Has it really come to this? With Carabosse dead at the hands of the Wolf Knight, has Versailles finally achieved her goal, to be the most powerful among the Exhibition? And what does that mean for the rest of us?

In less time than seems possible, the teacher from *Tuileries* arrives in our midst, cold and imperious atop her stony perch. The various skirmishes along the battlefield halt, as if the battle were a living being holding its breath. Shock fills every face on both sides of the fight as the mortar tips forward and allows Madame Versailles to step down into our circle, such as it is. Without a word, she reaches into the darkness of the enormous bowl and drags Carabosse's limp form into the light, allowing it to flop to the ground at our feet.

"Ding dong," she intones. "The Witch is dead."

"You shut your mouth." I tense to rush her, but the composer's firm grip on my shoulder convinces me to hold my ground. "This is all your fault."

"Is it, Anthony Faircloth?" Her smile barely hides the venom behind her eyes. "Am I the one who truly set all of this in motion?" Her eyes shoot to Hartmann and Juliet atop the oxen-pulled cart. "I would suggest you think before you answer."

"Enough toying with the boy, Versailles." The Wolf Knight steps forward. "You have brought the Exhibition as agreed and therefore your part of the bargain is complete."

Tunny, Modesto, and even the composer stare blankly at Madame Versailles.

"Traitor." Hartmann and his oxen charge the teacher from *Tuileries*. "I knew you were not to be trusted."

I'm not sure which strikes me harder, Hartmann's proclamation or the hurt betrayal in Juliet's gaze.

Regardless, neither can make a move before a shouted command from the Mouse King sends his army of rats rushing at the cart. In seconds, Hartmann's singular mode of transportation lies on its side, its wheels crushed beneath the cart's weight. The oxen disappear beneath the swarm of man-sized rodents as Hartmann pulls Juliet up from the ground and onto the cart's wooden side. In seconds, the mouse soldiers surround them five deep. One larger than the rest looks to the Mouse King who in turn levels one of his seven sets of eyes at Madame Versailles.

"Shall I allow my soldiers to feast?" he asks, the guttural French accent a perfect counterpoint to Versailles' own speech. His remaining six mouths drip with thin drool.

"Leave them to me." Versailles draws herself up straight and narrows her gaze at the pair. "I've waited a long time for this moment, and I would like to savor it, if you please."

"So," Mussorgsky whispers, "you've brought us all here not to help, but to betray."

"Bringing the Exhibition to this place was a necessary evil." Versailles' gaze dances between me and Mira. "As both the boy and the storyteller are painfully aware, matters such as these always require a sacrifice."

"Matters such as these…" I cast my thoughts back to the final moments of *The Firebird* and in an instant, everything becomes clear.

What Versailles wants.

And what is about to happen.

I step in front of Mira. "You still want her body, don't you, you vampire?"

Versailles tilts her head to one side. "Anywhere you can hang your hat, isn't that the saying?"

Toma and the Moor pull up on either side of me.

"You'll have to kill us." Toma directs the tip of his blade at Versailles' heart.

The Moor brandishes his golden scimitar. "If we don't end you first."

"Sir Knight," she breathes. "I believe these three mean me harm." She casts her gaze upon the wolf resting at the Knight's knee. "Perhaps a little help from your companion?"

"But of course." The Knight nudges the wolf with his knee and the beast leaves his side to heel by Versailles' leg. "Anything for you, my dear."

"Much better." Versailles returns her attention to the three men standing between her and the woman she came to kill. "Not so brave now, are we?"

Mira steps between me and Toma, dagger drawn. "Stop this madness, Versailles. This is between you and me." She glances back at me and then returns her attention to Versailles. "Let's end this, once and for all."

"My intentions exactly." With one fluid movement, the teacher from *Tuileries* drops to one knee, takes the wolf's head in her hands, and snaps its neck with a strength unimaginable outside the world of dream.

"No!" The Wolf Knight charges her. "What are you doing?"

"As I said, matters such as these require a sacrifice." She hurls the wolf's carcass into the shadows of the great stone bowl behind her. "And out of respect for the fallen, I chose your cur." Her eyes fall upon Carabosse's still form. "I didn't think *she* would appreciate me dirtying up her mortar with rat's blood."

"King of Mice," the Wolf Knight commands, his voice desperate. "Kill them." He points a finger directly at me. "All of them."

The Mouse King issues another barked order and the rats flow from around Hartmann's overturned cart to run at us.

"We have to retreat." I pull Toma and the Moor away from the onrushing mob of rats, my legs tensing to launch into a full on sprint, when my eyes meet those of the teacher from *Tuileries* and I find an emotion in her face I never dreamed possible.

Kindness.

"Madame Versailles," I ask, my voice choking. "Why are you doing this?"

"I merely seek to set things right," she murmurs. "And fear not, Anthony. The Wolf Knight may have brought an army, but he is not the only one who's been planning for this day." She turns her head in the direction of the mortar. "Children, come forth."

From behind the witch's mortar, the children of *Tuileries* swarm, pouring around Mira, Toma, the Moor, and I like a river of flesh. The wave of boys and girls crashes into the oncoming tide of rats, stopping the Mouse King's attack cold.

"Ladies?" Versailles' voice echoes in that strange way Mira's does when Scheherazade the storyteller gives a command. "Your turn."

On the heels of the mob of children, the three women of the Marketplace step from behind the upended mortar, though in their trio of gazes, I find far more evidence of the witches from the Bald Mountain than the aristocratic ladies who spent their days with Juliet in Limoges.

"Brigitte." Versailles offers the woman a polite curtsy, a gesture that is reciprocated.

"Sophie." Another greeting. Another response.

As Versailles turns to welcome the third, her eyes flick from the woman to me and back again. Subtle, but telling.

"Antoinette."

"Madame Versailles."

Versailles pushes the witch's pestle into Antoinette's hand and turns to join the children of *Tuileries* in the battle against the Mouse King and his rodent minions.

Without hesitation, Antoinette rests the pestle across her shoulder and steps inside the mortar's lip. "Sophie? If you please?"

Sophie sweeps up the broom and joins Antoinette inside the mortar's mouth. The two then turn as one to the remaining woman of the Marketplace and together whisper, "Bring her, Brigitte."

If I'm expecting the usual caustic sarcasm that is Brigitte's trademark, I'm sorely disappointed as she hauls Carabosse's flaccid form up from the ground and joins the others.

Then, all together, their three gazes converge on Mira.

Or, I suppose, Scheherazade the storyteller.

"One last time," Sophie murmurs.

"Into the breach," Brigitte adds.

Antoinette smiles. "You know what to do, storyteller."

"I do?" The confusion in Mira's face melts into understanding. "Mortar," she commands, "right yourself."

No sooner have the words left her lips than the enormous stone bowl rises from the ground and sets itself upright with the three women standing atop its open mouth. With inhuman strength, Brigitte cradles Carabosse's still form in her arms as Sophie dances with the crooked broomstick and Antoinette sets to grinding the wolf's carcass into pulp with the witch's pestle.

The horrible crunching sends a wave of nausea through me, even in this place.

"What are you doing?" the Wolf Knight screams. "What do you hope to accomplish?"

Antoinette ignores him, and instead stares down into the witch's bowl. "Double, double."

Sophie whisks inside the mortar with the witch's broom. "Toil and trouble."

Brigitte hurls Carabosse's limp body into the makeshift cauldron. "Fire burn."

Beneath the mortar, an inferno erupts, scorching the earth as the three women focus their collective gazes on me.

"And caldron bubble." These words from another time fall from my lips and in answer, the massive mortar rocks as if a bomb went off inside its granite walls. For the second time since all this began, the battlefield falls silent as child and rat, toy soldier and swan, friend and foe all look to the top of the enormous stone bowl, knowing full well what they are about to see.

And, more importantly, *whom* they are about to see.

A single orchestral hit followed by a deafening couplet leaves no doubt.

With a double clang of her iron teeth, Baba Yaga crawls from the confines of her mortar and joins the women of the Marketplace along its rim.

To horribly misquote Sir Elton John, the witch is back.

"So," Yaga hisses. "It's come to this, has it?"

The Mouse King points a clawed paw at Baba Yaga. "Forget the rest," he commands in his harsh French accent. "Kill the witch."

"Oh, there will be killing, King of Mice." Yaga holds out her hand and Antoinette places the pestle in her rough palm. "But it is not me who will die this day."

"No," the Wolf Knight whispers.

"Yes." In a move reminiscent of Jack Kirby's vision of the Norse god of thunder, Yaga hurls the pestle at the Mouse King, the length of ancient wood striking the enormous rodent center chest and sending his seven heads flying like a bunch of grapes hit by a grenade. As the seven-times-decapitated body of *The Nutcracker* villain crumples to the ground, his subjects scatter into the shadows. In the space of a breath, the Wolf Knight stands alone on the battlefield.

Baba Yaga climbs down from atop her mortar, the pestle returning to her like a well-trained dog. With her weapon held gently in her gnarled hand, she strides in the Wolf Knight's direction, fearless despite the apparent disparity between his armor and weaponry and her ramshackle dress.

Two lessons among many I've learned over the last year.

The first? In this place, appearances are deceiving.

And the second? Exactly who sits at the top of the food chain in this world I've created.

"Lay down your weapon, Knight, and face me." Baba Yaga's lips part, her iron smile sending a chill through me despite the fact she represents a woman who has loved me since before I was born. "You're not facing a fairy this time. Still, perhaps a witch shall show you mercy." Her ancient eyes flick in my direction. "Perhaps."

"I'd rather go down fighting than give any of you the satisfaction of my surrender."

"That can be arranged." The Moor steps forward, but Mira's hand on his shoulder convinces him to stand down.

At least for the moment.

"Enough blood has been shed this day." Mira steps from our small circle and approaches the Wolf Knight. "You have lost. Von Rothbart, the Mouse

King, your wolf, your army of rats... they're all gone. Surrender, Wendell. Surrender, and we can sort all this out." She meets my gaze and raises a curious eyebrow. "Perhaps even in slightly more normal surroundings?"

"You want to sort this out." The Wolf Knight seethes. "In another place, I spent the last year in not one, but two prisons." His eyes narrow at Mira. "One of walls." Then, his angry glare shifts to me. "And one of the mind." He raises his sword. "I won't go back."

As the impasse between Mira and Durgan continues, we all draw close to listen. Tunny and Modesto shepherd together the children of *Tuileries* and bring them to Madame Versailles. Juliet and Hartmann, conversely, keep a careful distance from the teacher despite her apparent change of heart. The Sugar Plum Fairy and Prince Coqueluche, the latter carrying the body of the last Flower across his shoulder with her face mercifully hidden from view, join Toma, the Moor, and I behind Mira. All around, the mixed forces of toy soldiers and swans maintain a perimeter, whether to fend off another assault or to keep the Wolf Knight from escaping, I have no idea. The women of the Marketplace look down from above as Trilby flits over to the mortar and kneels in its shadow. The final scene set, the dwindling light from the setting sun finally fails, sending the world into twilight.

"Night has fallen, Wendell." Mira spreads her arms wide. "Regardless of your decision, all of this is coming to an end."

"Is it?" The Wolf Knight directs the tip of his rapier at Mira's heart. "Did it end when you sent that dagger in your hand through your own heart? When you danced *The Rite of Spring*? When Odette drowned or the Mouse King took Clara Stahlbaum? No. This hell just keeps recreating itself." He peers across her shoulder, his eyes narrowing in hate. "And each time, it's more hellish than the time before."

"You speak like you're the only one who has suffered." Mira's voice goes ice cold. "As if you're the only one left with scars."

"What you and the boy have done is not natural." The Knight peers all around, his eyes attempting to pierce the gathering darkness. "This place... is not natural."

"Then leave." The clang of the witch's iron teeth makes me wince. "Leave and do not return."

"As if that were an option." With inhuman speed, the Wolf Knight rushes at Mira. Despite his wounds, Toma leaps in front of her only to fall from a brutal blow to the temple from the Knight's gauntleted fist.

"Thomas," Mira cries.

"He should be the least of your concerns, storyteller." Before any of us can make a move, he has her, his hand snaking around her waist to hold her dagger in its sheath. He brings his own blade to her throat and glares out at us from his fanged helmet. "This woman is the tether that binds me to all of this insanity. If she has to die to set me free, so be it."

XXXII

APOTHEOSIS

Don't," **Versailles shrieks. "If you kill her..."**

"You reneged on our deal, Madame Versailles." The Wolf Knight pulls away from us with Mira clutched tightly to his body. "Tejedor's flesh was yours for the taking, but you decided to take the noble path. Now, you can die along with her."

"You don't get it, do you?" I take one cautious step in the Knight's direction, leaving the relative safety of the Moor's seething anger. "That's not what she's afraid of at all."

"What, then?" The Knight casts his gaze over the entire assemblage. "What is it that has all of you trembling like leaves in a hurricane?"

"This place." I take another step forward, careful not to trip over Toma's fallen form. "It's not just a part of me. All of us—you, me, them— stand on a common ground that exists between my mind and Mira's. If you kill her..."

"Then we all die," Madame Versailles and Baba Yaga speak as one.

"Perhaps even you, Wendell." Despite the blade at her throat, Mira's voice doesn't waver. "Is that what you want?"

"What I want is for the madness to stop." His eyes flash with desperation. "No more gnomes. No more witches. No more fairy tales."

"That's what all of us want." A sigh that has been building for more than a year escapes my lips. "But not like this."

"Then how?" The Knight pulls the blade tight to Mira's neck, the resulting rivulet of blood letting us know he means business. "What is the answer, boy?"

"Think about it." Another cautious step. "You're privy to all that's happened in this place from the beginning. The events along the Exhibition. The dancing of *The Rite of Spring*. The fight at the Lake of Swans. The battle between the Nutcracker Prince and the Mouse King. Time and time again, Mira in her various incarnations sacrificed herself on the altar of the greater good, and yet here we are, all of us, on yet another battlefield in yet another impossible situation."

"What are you suggesting, then?"

"Simply that the answer doesn't lie with Mira." I sweep my arm before me, indicating the endless battlefield upon which we all stand. "This place may exist as a juxtaposition of our two minds, but no one would argue whose mind it is that provides the stage."

Mira's eyes grow wide. "What are you doing, Anthony?"

"Following your example, Mira." One last step and I stand before the Knight. "If this is going to work, I'm going to need the Sultan's dagger."

"No." Baba Yaga rushes forward. "I won't allow you to do this."

"I'm sorry, Mother." I allow my gaze to flick in her direction and find tears coursing down the ancient hag's face. "But it's the only way." I turn my gaze back on the Wolf Knight. "The dagger, if you please."

"You would sacrifice yourself for me?" Incredulous, he stares, his eyes barely visible within the confines of his helmet. "What kind of fool do you take me for?"

"You want this to end, don't you? You've already defeated Mira twice, first as Odette and then as Clara Stahlbaum." I gaze around the desolate battlefield. "Where have your so-called victories led you?"

"Hm." The Knight's eyes draw down to slits. "Perhaps it *is* you that must die," he whispers, "but not before I take my revenge on this cow." He pulls his blade across Mira's throat and hurls her lifeless form to the ground.

"No!" I scream. "Not her."

"Don't worry, boy." The Knight charges me. "You won't be far behind."

I duck beneath a sweep of his rapier and dodge the follow up thrust, but it's clear I won't last long against the Wolf Knight's onslaught. Weaponless, and alone, it's only a matter of time before he kills me.

"But you're not alone." Tunny appears at my side, the tip of his hat no higher than my waist.

"You are never alone." Modesto comes forward, his blade drawn and eyes keen.

"We are here." Hartmann and Juliet speak as one as they join the gathering throng.

"And we will never abandon you." Trilby pirouettes in from the side, her usual smile replaced with grim resolve.

"Even if you can't see us." The women of the Marketplace float down from atop the mortar and land in our midst.

"We are there." Madame Versailles joins the trio of ladies and, surprisingly, is accepted into their ranks.

"No matter if we are a brief visitor along your life's journey." The Moor brandishes his scimitar, his words starting in Samuel Goldenberg's deep baritone and ending in Schmuÿle's screeching tenor as he looks down on Toma's fallen form. "Or a trusted advisor for years."

"Or even present from the very first day." Baba Yaga raises the pestle above her head.

"No matter what, my son." Mussorgsky raises his baton, and at his direction, the entire Exhibition sings as one.

"We will be with you always." Their voices form a rising chorus, their words sung to the opening strain of "Promenade." "Until the end of time."

"Surrender, Wendell." Still covered in the remains of Scheherazade's sarong, Mira rises from the ground, whole and uninjured. "I will not ask again."

"But how?" The Wolf Knight draws back as if he's seen a ghost. "I ended you."

"We exist in a world of dream, Wendell. This place has dealt me far more fatal blows than yours, I assure you." Her gaze flicks to me. "Not to mention, as you so recently reminded us, you aren't the one who makes the rules around here."

"The boy," the Wolf Knight snarls. "It's always the boy." Like the animal he wears as his totem, he leaps at me, rapier held high above his head.

"Anthony!" Mira shouts.

End over end, the Sultan's dagger flips through the air, all but invisible in the dim light. A silent prayer falls from my lips as I throw my hand up and snatch the bejeweled blade from the top of its arc. Instinct takes over as I bring the dagger before my chest and drop one foot back to brace for impact. Unable to halt his momentum, the Wolf Knight impales himself upon the curved blade, his dead weight sending us both tumbling to the ground. Crushed beneath Durgan's doppelganger, my mind flirts with unconsciousness until a familiar voice returns hope to my heart.

"Anthony?" Mira kneels and peers beneath the Knight's hulking mass. "Are you all right?"

"I think so." Together, we push the Knight's body off mine. As Mira helps me to my feet, I breathlessly ask, "Is he..."

"Dead?" She runs a cursory glance across the crumpled pile of iron, fur, and flesh. "Here, it would appear so, but back in the real world? I guess we'll find out."

I raise an eyebrow. "This place, though. It's free of him, isn't it?"

"God only knows, Anthony." Mira shakes her head. "God only knows."

She kneels by Toma's crumpled form, her hand going to his chest. "It's different this time." Her lip trembling, she looks up into the eyes of Baba Yaga and the Moor who each offer a solemn nod. "You found a way to bring everyone with you, didn't you, Anthony?"

"Everyone. Dr. Archer. Detective Sterling. Mom." I catch Modesto's raised eyebrow and grim smile. "Even Jason, I think."

Her outstretched fingers upon the Kalendar Prince's broad chest balling into a fist, she stands, her face resolute despite the moisture gathering at the corners of her eyes.

"Nothing to do now but finish this, then." Mira's gaze drifts across us all, her voice taking on the timbre of the storyteller. "And then, in a moment that would go down in legend, the Exhibition gathered together one last time and banished the Wolf Knight from their realm forever."

As if by instinct, the Exhibition converges on the Wolf Knight's body. After seeing von Rothbart, the wolf, and the Mouse King each meet their respective ends, I steel myself for the inevitable brutality to come, but, as always seems to be the case in this world of dream, the truth is far stranger.

The various characters of the Exhibition work silently, stripping the Wolf Knight of his armor, his furs, his helmet—all the things that give him identity. Not one manifests any emotion other than the solemn respect due the dead. Most striking of all, Madame Versailles and Juliet work shoulder to shoulder, all the while exchanging words and even smiles. Does the kindness of Juliet's heart truly know no bounds? Or was the venom Versailles spouted on the Isle of the Dead simply an act, a ruse to bend the wolf to her will? Have these polar opposites that live within my mind truly reconciled?

I will likely never know the answer to any of these questions.

Regardless, all that eventually remains is Durgan's dead body, naked as the day he was born. At that point, the gathered Exhibition pulls into a tight phalanx, raises his still form high above their heads, and marches toward the horizon.

With a look of sad resignation, the Moor lifts Toma from the ground and throws his limp form across his shoulder.

"I will bring him back to you, Mira. You have my word."

"Thank you." Mira murmurs as the Moor turns and joins the procession.

Next, surrounded by the remaining swans and toy soldiers, the Sugar Plum Fairy guides Sarah/Odette away from the battlefield. Behind them, Prince Coqueluche carries the fallen Flower. As pale as the petals she represents, Isabella Tejedor's head bobs in the crook of his arm. Prince Coqueluche, his eyes those of Dominic MacGregor, looks back at Mira and offers a solemn nod before turning to join the Exhibition as they follow the recently set sun into the west.

Please, God. Don't let us have gone through all of this pain to save Mira only to lose both her love and her only daughter in the process.

Bringing up the rear, Baba Yaga follows atop her stone mortar. She pounds the ground once more with her pestle and, in answer, the Bogatyr Gates materialize before the strange procession, the bright glimmer beneath the arch hypnotic in its radiance. Mussorgsky's triumphant fanfare blares one last time as the morbid march passes through the Gates' gleaming surface, every step in time with the composer's baton. As the various puzzle pieces of my soul, some of whom I've come to count as friends, disappear one by one beneath the massive arch, the sadness at my core doubles and redoubles. I suddenly feel more alone than I've ever felt in my life.

I brush away the tears to clear my vision and find one last figure remaining, her silhouette dark against the scintillating light of the Bogatyr Gates.

Beneath the massive arch, Yaga stands as straight as her hunched shoulders will allow and studies me with a mother's concern. "Don't tarry too long in this place, boy." Her iron teeth clang together, the sound harsh on my ears. "You've spent quite enough time here already."

Her words send the hair on my neck standing on end. "And why would I stay here a moment longer than I had to?" The witch bristles at the lack of respect in my tone. "Oh wise and powerful mistress of the Exhibition."

"I know you all too well, young man." Her cackle sends shards of ice through my chest. Still, the revulsion that usually accompanies a grin from the witch doesn't come this time. Her smile is—dare I say it?—warm. "Despite the terror, the danger, the abject horror, a part of you loves this place. The music. The adventure." She glances at Mira. "The romance."

"Perhaps." I flush at the witch's comment, a reaction no doubt mirrored in the cheeks of a boy lying in a hospital bed a million miles from here. "Don't worry. I'll be right along."

"I am glad to hear it." Her voice shifts from Yaga's to my mother's. "See you soon... Anthony." And with that she steps through the shimmering gate and is gone, leaving Mira and me alone on the otherwise empty plain.

Together, we stare at the Bogatyr Gates, the pulsating light that fills their expanse beckoning us to follow the witch into the unknown. Neither of us speaks for a long while, but for once, it's me that eventually breaks the silence.

"So... this is it, isn't it?"

Mira laughs sadly. "I believe so, kiddo."

"I know we've done this before—more than once, in fact—but this time feels different."

"This time *is* different." She looks on me with a mother's kindness. "Every time before, and through no fault of your own, you've always been forced to leave me behind to face whatever happened next." She takes my hand. "This time, however, we're walking out together."

"Together." I take a step toward the shimmering exit from this shared dream. "I like that."

"One last thing," she whispers, "while it's still just you and me." We stand before the Gates, both of us trembling with the emotion of the moment. "I want you to know I'll never forget what you risked for me, coming back to this place time and again, despite the danger."

"Come on, Mira." I bite my lip, trying to keep my voice from choking. "It's nothing more than what you did for me."

"Still..." She draws close and kisses my forehead. "You are truly a brave young man, Anthony Faircloth, even braver than I thought." She raises an eyebrow and smiles. "Someone special is going to appreciate that quality someday."

"Making predictions, now, are we?" My lips turn up in a sarcastic grin. "I didn't think you were that kind of psychic."

"Just call it a woman's intuition." She turns and steps toward the Gates. "Shall we?"

I give her hand a confident squeeze and follow in her footsteps. "Let's go home."

Sarah Goode.

My first thought as I awaken from the realm of dream.

I sit up straight in my chair and survey the room. My eyes open already adjusted to the dim light and I find everyone exactly where I left them. Dr. Archer lies in the bed to my right with Mom seated by his head, neither awake as yet. Mira rests in the bed to my left, hand in hand with Detective Sterling, both breathing quietly as if in deep slumber. Jason sits asleep by the door, his chin resting on his chest.

And there, still cuffed to a chair and under guard, Durgan sits. His head lolls to one side, but, from what I can tell, he's still breathing.

Good. We're going to need him if we want to find Sarah.

"Officer... Gibson, is it?"

The man nearly jumps out of his skin. Makes sense, I guess. Who knows how long it's been since anyone in the room has said a word?

"What's up, kid?" he gets out with a slight stutter.

"How's Durgan? Is he... still with us?"

"He's fine." The cop shoots me a strange look, as if unsure how to respond to a fourteen-year-old asking such adult questions. "Hasn't moved since you all went down."

"And how long *have* we been out?"

"A couple of hours." He holsters his gun and comes over to me. "Hey, kid. Let me in on the joke. What is all this, really?"

"A group hypnosis session." A rousing Detective Sterling pulls himself up from his chair. "That's what your report will reflect, Officer Gibson. A group hypnosis session authorized by me and led by Dr. Archer in an effort to bring important facts of the case to light. Is that understood?"

"Yes, sir." Officer Gibson disengages, returning his attention to Durgan.

Detective Sterling studies Mira's placid features, shakes his head, and then rounds the bed to talk with me. "What now? Do we just wait for everyone to wake up?"

"I have no idea." I peer around the room. "I'm just making this stuff up as I go along."

"What if Mira doesn't come out of her coma? What do we do then?"

Before I can answer, Officer Gibson chimes in. "Umm... sir? What's happening?"

I'm not sure which sends my heart racing faster, the fear in Officer Gibson's voice, or the sudden rhythmic clanking of metal on metal.

Detective Sterling spins around and out of my direct field of vision, revealing Durgan in the midst of a grand mal seizure, the cuffs the only thing holding him in the chair.

"Shit," Officer Gibson blurts out as thick foam builds at the corners of Durgan's mouth. "I'll get a nurse."

He's out the door in a flash, leaving Detective Sterling and me to deal with the fall out.

"What's happening?" Mom starts awake and goggles at Durgan's jerking form.

"He's seizing." Detective Sterling rushes to Durgan's side. "I'm supposed to get a belt between his teeth, right?"

"Just keep him breathing." Jason, who is coming to, forces himself upright to help Detective Sterling. "From what I remember from health class, these things normally take care of themselves in a couple minutes."

Detective Sterling lets out a bitter chuckle. "As if anything about this is normal."

He's no more than rested a hand on Durgan's shoulder when a team of doctors and nurses flood the room with Officer Gibson hot on their heels.

"Who is this man?" shouts an Indian woman wearing a long white coat. "And why in God's name is he handcuffed to a chair?" Clearly in charge, she scans the room, her angry gaze settling on Detective Sterling. "We gave CMPD a little latitude, Detective, and this is what you pull?"

"Just fix the creep." Detective Sterling jerks a set of keys out of his pocket and works with Jason to get the cuffs off Durgan. "We need him."

"What did you do to him?" the doctor asks. "Why is he like this?"

"He was just sitting in the chair," Officer Gibson announces from his post by the door. "We didn't touch him."

"Right." She eyes Detective Sterling with an exhausted glare. "And I'm guessing his nose just broke itself."

Detective Sterling shoots the other cop a stern look and inclines his head in the direction of the door. "Hey, Gibson. Why don't you go check on Perrault? Get him up to speed."

"Yes, sir." Officer Gibson excuses himself as Detective Sterling frees Durgan from the chair.

"Thank you." As he and Jason lower him to the ground, the doctor kneels by his head and checks his pulse. "Now, you two get out of the way."

The team of doctors and nurses descends upon Durgan. In seconds, they have an IV in his arm and push syringe after syringe of medicine into his veins, for all the good it does.

"Dammit," the doctor says. "He's not responding."

And then, a voice I haven't heard in weeks. At least not on this side of the veil of dream.

"Let me try."

"Mira." Detective's Sterling races to Mira's bedside. "You're awake."

"As perceptive as ever, Detective." Mira rises from the bed, her legs unsteady beneath her, and forces herself across the room. After a long look in Dr. Archer's direction, she and the doctor lock gazes. "May I?" Mira asks.

The doctor furrows her brow in puzzlement. "What are you going to do?"

"I'm going to help this man." Jason and Detective Sterling aid her as she kneels by Durgan's head. "Whether he deserves it or not." She rests her fingertips at his temples as she did mine at our first meeting. Her eyes slide closed and her voice adopts a motherly singsong quality.

"It's okay, Wendell," she whispers. "It's over." She takes a deep cleansing breath. "Do you hear me? It's over."

Like a bonfire beneath a deluge of rain, the seizure stops and Durgan's body relaxes.

Seeing him like this, so helpless, I almost feel sorry for him.

Almost.

The gurney arrives and the team scoops Durgan up from the floor and continues to work with him. Still, at least for the moment, the crisis has passed.

"I don't know what you did, Ms. Tejedor," the doctor says, shaking her head in disbelief, "but thank you."

"Just closing a loop." Mira's face fills with distaste as she stares down at Durgan's strangely serene features. "Hopefully forever."

"How long till he wakes up, doc?" Detective Sterling asks.

"Why?" the doctor asks, her voice like a razor. "You planning on 'interrogating' him some more?"

"This is no joke." Detective Sterling's voice drops an octave. "This man knows the location of a missing girl who we believe to be in serious danger."

The doctor's face pales a shade. "I'm sorry, Detective, but he's likely going to be in a postictal state for the next while. It could be half an hour or more before he regains consciousness and likely longer before he's ready to answer questions reliably."

"Understood." Detective Sterling steps into the hallway briefly as they take Durgan away.

No sooner does he leave the room than Mira stumbles to Dr. Archer's bed and sits by his hip. She pulls his hand to her chest, her entire body jerking with sobs. "Oh, Thomas…"

"Fantastic." Detective Sterling steps back into the room, his hands balled into fists at his sides, and goes to Mira's side. "Now, what the hell are we supposed to do?"

"I may have the answer." I drag myself out of my chair and join Detective Sterling by Dr. Archer's bed.

"Do you know something?" he asks. "Do you know where Sarah is?"

"Not exactly." I clear my throat. "On the other side—"

"Sarah?" Mira's gaze dances between mine and Detective Sterling's. "Wait. Sarah Goode. She was the Black Swan. Is that why we saw her there? Does Durgan have her?"

"He's stashed her God knows where." Detective Sterling rests a hand on Mira's shoulder. "He said we had to wake you first or he wasn't talking."

"And you listened to that psychopath?"

"Mira?" I ask, my voice quiet.

"Do you have any idea what he did to her? What he did to me?"

"Mira?" Despite my insistence, they both continue to ignore me.

"We had to get you back, Mira." Detective Sterling raises his hands before him in mock surrender. "I'm sorry, but—"

"You can't trust a damn thing the bastard says. He's a liar and a rapist and a—"

"Mira!"

"What, Anthony?" Mira turns on me, her eyes flashing with exasperation that quickly melts into regret. "I'm sorry. What is it?"

"I think I know how to find Sarah…" I look away, feeling sheepish in the face of what looks for all the world like a lover's quarrel. "But I'm going to need your help, Mira."

"Okay." She grasps my hand in her own trembling fingers. "What have you got?"

"After the swans obliterated von Rothbart and Odile shifted into Odette, Sarah's doppelganger whispered something into my ear. I couldn't hear it at the time, but she said when I needed the information, I'd remember. The thing is, I've been racking my brain since I woke up, and whatever she told me just won't come."

"And you want me to see if I can... take a peek?"

"Do we dare?" My heart does a flip-flop. "What if we try and we get sent back to the other side? I'm not sure we'd survive another run."

"If that happens, we'll make it through." Mira's eyes cut to Mom. "And God help anything that gets in our way."

"I trust you, Mira." Still exhausted, Mom stumbles over and wraps her arms around me. "Just find the girl."

"What do you need?" Detective Sterling asks. "Anything."

"Just watch over us." Mira pulls me between the two hospital beds where we sit knee to knee. "If all goes well, this won't take but a few seconds."

Mira brings her fingertips to my temples. Both of us hold our breath in preparation for whatever might come. We're not kept waiting long.

No music this time. No fantastic landscapes. No dashing heroes or dastardly villains. Just utter darkness, suffocating heat, and a repeating pull to one side as if I'm stuck on the world's most repetitive rollercoaster. My body damp with sweat, my wrists and ankles are each tied together and my aching jaw won't close. I try to breathe, and find my airway blocked by a saliva-soaked cloth. Then, the squall of tires on concrete and a crashing sound like thunder hit my ears as my body rolls across a knobby surface of steel and rubber.

A spare tire.

Mira and I both start from the trance, both of our eyes shooting to Detective Sterling.

"She's tied up in the trunk of a car," Mira whispers.

"In one of the parking decks," I add.

As best I can, I give Detective Sterling a description of Durgan's car. I can't help but notice the frequent tense glances between him and Mira, but whatever the two of them have to work out is clearly back burner at the moment.

They've got work to do.

Detective Sterling rushes from the room to coordinate the search, leaving me alone with Mira, Jason, Mom, and the still unconscious Dr. Archer.

"Why hasn't Thomas come to with the rest of us?" Mom brushes the hair from Dr. Archer's face. "Is he going to be all right?"

Mira circles the bed. "He took a pretty significant blow to the head trying to defend me from the Wolf Knight." She looks to me. "What do you think, Anthony? How do we wake him?"

"I don't know, Mira." I consider for a moment, and then my lips break into a hopeful smile. "Call me crazy, but a kiss seemed to work pretty well on the other side."

Mira's cheeks flush.

"What can it hurt, Mira?" Caroline circles the bed and drapes an arm across Mira's shoulders. "This whole thing has been like one long crazy tale out of the Brothers Grimm." She gazes down at Dr. Archer's serene features. "Maybe, just this once, you actually get *your* fairy tale ending."

"Worth a shot, Mira." Jason comes up behind me and musses my hair.

"All right." She sits on the bed next to Dr. Archer and leans in, the moment strangely intimate. "Here goes nothing."

As Mira's lips touch his, my cheeks burn at the passion that fills the room.

And yet, when she pulls away, nothing changes. Dr. Archer remains as still as the dead.

"What now, Anthony?" Mira asks as frustrated tears form at the corners of her eyes. "What now?"

A single tear falls from Mira's cheek and lands at the corner of Dr. Archer's mouth.

"Salty." The single whispered word brings with it a collective sigh of relief from everyone in the room.

"Thomas." Mira pulls Dr. Archer up from his pillow and envelops him in her arms. "You're okay."

"Mira..." Dr. Archer croaks. "Thank God."

A moment later, the door swings open and in strides Rosa Tejedor with Isabella at her side.

"Mami!" Isabella rushes to her mother's side. "You're awake."

"Isabella." Mira whips out an arm and brings her daughter into the embrace with Dr. Archer. "I've missed you so much."

"I made Nana bring me to see you, Mami." Isabella trembles, her expression oscillating between excitement and fear. "I was taking a nap and had the most terrible dream. There were monsters and they were trying to hurt you and—" She breaks down into sobs as her mother pulls her in even tighter.

"It's okay now, sweetie. Everything's okay." Mira's eyes find mine and her gaze fills with gratitude. "The nightmare is over."

EPILOGUE

HARVEST

Fall semester. As always, a time of new beginnings. New challenges. New opportunities.

The biggest question at the moment, though? Which is going to kick my ass more, finishing this stupid thesis or teaching yet another semester of Abnormal Psych?

If history serves, a few eager first-year grad students will show up ready to cut their teeth on some serious stuff. The remainder, however, will be a random collection of undergrads eager to discuss their deepest thoughts about *Psycho* and *Silence of the Lambs*.

Honestly? One more joke about fava beans and Chianti and *I* might be the one who loses it.

Now, Anthony. The composer's voice echoes from somewhere within. *Some perspective, if you please. You've been through far worse than this.*

Easy for him to say.

He's right, though. He's always right.

Ten years have passed since the death of Julianna Wagner sent my life spiraling out of control. Ten years since my own mind swallowed me up and left me a zombie wandering through my own imagination.

Ten years since Mira Tejedor came into my life and set things right.

Mira. I really should give her a call. That is, if she and Thomas are back from their big trip to New Zealand. Won't get to see them and little Benjamin outside of social media till I head home for Christmas. Unless, of course, I can convince them to come up to Boston with Mom and Robert when they bring Rachel over fall break...

Okay. Back to reality. Fifteen minutes till show time. Game face... on.

I'm still getting everything organized when the new crop of students begins to file in. Each one a new name to learn. A new face.

All, that is, except one.

I sense her presence long before I see her, a nagging at the back of my mind like the aroma of a food you loved as a child or a snippet of a favorite song you forgot existed.

What is *she* doing here?

What, indeed? The amused words, punctuated by the clang of iron teeth, well up from my very soul. *Pay attention, young man.*

A pair of lanky male undergrads at the door parts to reveal her stepping into the lecture hall.

Eight years have passed since we last saw each other, but I've never forgotten those eyes.

Eyes that stared at me terrified in the scorching basement of an abandoned house as our lives hung in the balance.

Eyes that peered out from behind the mask of the Black Swan during my final sojourn through the world of dream, a glimmer of hope in a moment of despair.

Eyes of a girl who saw far too much far too early.

Still, for someone who considers himself relatively perceptive, one aspect of those hazel eyes apparently escaped the notice of my oblivious fourteen-year-old self.

Their utter beauty.

"Anthony Faircloth." She pulls up in front of my desk, hands crossed before her waist and lips turned up in a nervous smile. "It's been a long time."

"Indeed it has."

A quick scan of the roster of grad students in the class reveals a name I somehow overlooked as I prepared today's lesson.

Sarah Goode.

"It's... great to see you." I stand and offer her my hand, the enormous desk between us providing an awkward yet necessary barrier. "So, you're taking my class?"

"I am."

"I didn't even know you were enrolled here."

"I graduated from UVA in the spring." Her cheeks go pink. "I thought a change of scenery would be nice."

"And you're pursuing a degree in psychology?"

"I'm actually working on my masters in social work." She bites her lip. "I just wanted to check out your class. It sounded... interesting."

My own cheeks grow a degree or so warmer. Neither of us says a word for a few seconds, though a name from a decade ago floats between us like a ghost.

"Durgan." Her lip trembles at the name. "I'm guessing you heard."

"Yeah." My eyes drop. "Can't say I'm all that sorry."

Wendell James Durgan was ten years into the first of two consecutive life sentences when he died peacefully in his sleep a month or so back. No fanfare accompanied his death. No major news coverage. Just a quiet phone call to my mother from a western Virginia area code.

"I don't wish suffering on anyone." I pull in a deep breath through my nose. "But I guess I always thought when he finally went, it would be a lot more bang and a lot less whimper."

"I know what you mean." Her eyes close briefly and a shudder passes through her body. "I'm just glad it's finally over."

"Agreed." I give her my best smile. "Time to move on with life."

"Truer words were never spoken." She answers my undoubtedly goofy grin in kind. "You're looking well."

"Thanks." The fluorescent light reflecting off her golden hair reminds me of my trip with Jason to see Niagara Falls last year. "You look pretty fantastic yourself."

"Damn." The color in her cheeks steps up another shade as her entire face melts into thoughtful acceptance. "And there it is."

"What do you mean?" I furrow my brow. "What's wrong?"

"I'm sorry, Anthony." She raises one shoulder in an apologetic half shrug. "I'm afraid I'm going to have to drop your class."

"Why?" My intestines tie themselves in knots. "Was it something I said?"

"No, nothing like that." One corner of her mouth turns up in a mischievous smile. "It's just that... it seems I have a conflict of interest."

"A conflict of interest?" I take a step back. "I'm sorry, but I don't understand."

"You will." She raises an eyebrow. "The symphony is playing Dvořák's *New World Symphony* this weekend. You busy?"

My heart does a somersault in my chest. "I'll check my calendar, but I'm pretty sure I'm free Saturday night."

"Good." She grabs a Post-it from my desk and scribbles down her number. "Call me."

And with that, she turns on one heel and heads for the door.

The majority of the class has taken their seats and several among the first few rows understand, maybe better than I do, exactly what has just occurred. A few of them snicker under their breath, but for once in my life I really don't care what the rest of the world thinks. Instead, I find myself captivated by the enigmatic woman striding for the hallway, her curly blonde locks bouncing with every confident step. I half expect another of the many voices that resonate inside my head to make a statement about the encounter, but for once, not one offers a word of advice or even a snide comment.

My mind, at least for the moment, is at peace.

As Sarah Goode steps through the doorway, she shoots one last furtive glance back before vanishing into the mob of students outside. Forcing down the urge to rush after her, I turn to face my class, the usual rank and file of my thoughts in total disarray.

In that moment, for the first time in years, the invisible orchestra in my mind springs forth and drowns my thoughts in music.

This time, however, the composer isn't Russian, but German.

And the significance of my psyche's choice of song isn't lost on me.

It's the song to which my mother walked down the aisle.

Beethoven's Piano Sonata No. 14.

Moonlight.

ACKNOWLEDGMENTS

All stories have a beginning, a middle, and an end. *The Mussorgsky Riddle* was supposed to be all three of these: one complete story, one book, no sequels, the tale of Mira Tejedor and Anthony Faircloth and their adventures on a mindscape based on two pieces of Russian classical music finished in one fell swoop.

But then Stravinsky spoke to me. And Prokofiev. And Rachmaninoff. And Tchaikovsky.

And now, at long last, Anthony and Mira's story is finally and truly complete. I already miss writing about this intrepid pair and their many friends and foes, but new adventures with new characters and new dangers await. I will be getting to those shortly.

Before I move on, though, I want to again thank all the people that have supported me as I wandered the halls of an imaginary boy's mind and reinterpreted some of the most beautiful music ever written.

To my critique group of J. Matthew Saunders and Caryn Sutorus, thank you again for the hours spent shining necessary spotlight on the many speedbumps along this manuscript's winding road. The ride is much smoother now, and for that, I am grateful.

To all my friends and fellow purveyors of the written word in Charlotte Writers, thank you, as always, for your constant support.

To Mom, Dad, and Jilly, thank you as always for being my biggest fans. This series, and this book in particular, is all about family, and I couldn't have asked for a better one.

To Stratton, Katelyn, and Olivia, keep following your dreams. Believe it or not, some of them actually come true.

To Stacey Donaghy, thank you for taking a chance on a burgeoning writer and helping me to achieve the first steps of a dream.

To Lisa Gus and Eugene Teplitsky, thank you again for all you've done to help me bring this story and series into existence.

To Olivia Swenson, thank you for your exceptional and expedient editing and for finding all the speedbumps left along what is now a much smoother road.

To Mike Robinson, thank you for your excellent proofreading and helping me to stick the landing on this one.

To Brice Chaplet, thank you for another spectacular cover. I didn't think you could top the cover for *The Stravinsky Intrigue*. I was wrong.

To Clare Dugmore, Tanya Yakimenko, Nina Post, and the rest of the team at Curiosity Quills, thanks again for all the hard work behind the scenes to make this book and series a reality.

As always, to all my teachers and professors over the years, thank you for all the time and energy you put into making me a better writer and, more importantly, a better person.

To Micki Knop, thank you for your suggestion at the 2016 ConCarolinas of including Prokofiev's *Peter and the Wolf* in this story. I was halfway through this book and needed an interesting place to go before stepping into the realm of *Sleeping Beauty*. Our brief detour through Prokofiev led to Anthony's trip to Rachmaninoff's famed *Isle of the Dead* and even to our brief return to Mussorgsky's Exhibition. Without your excellent suggestion that day, this book might have gone in a completely different direction.

A special thank you to Mercedes Lackey for taking me under her wing for a couple of hours at the Bookmarks event in Winston-Salem a couple years back and teaching me all I needed to know about *Swan Lake*. Your insights led to Anthony becoming Benno, and, therefore, Fritz and Peter. Without your insights into the source material, this would have ended up an entirely different story. Also, I incorporated your idea about including Tchaikovsky's *The Seasons*. I think you will find all twelve safely tucked away in the Libretto at the beginning of the book.

And now, allow me to visit the Catacombs one last time and thank an individual long dead for inspiration, for beautiful melodies, and for being the fuel that ran this engine. The works of Pyotr Ilyich Tchaikovsky, more so than any of the other composers I've incorporated into this story, are familiar to the world at large. We've all seen *The Nutcracker* at Christmas with our families. We've all heard the *1812 Overture* played as fireworks lit up the sky. Disney borrowed much of the soundtrack for the *Sleeping Beauty* movie from the very ballet chronicled in this book. And who hasn't heard of *Swan Lake*? (Though to be honest, I was not as familiar with that piece as I was some of the others included here and now believe the main theme may be one of the most beautiful and versatile melodies ever crafted.) If you have a chance to see these works performed by your local ballet company or symphony, just do it. You can thank me later.

This third book explored new territory while touching back upon all the worlds chronicled in the first two volumes of the story. I did my best to tie up every loose end and close every loop. Now, it's up to you, the reader, to decide if this study in composition, fugues, and ternary form lived up to its potential. I certainly enjoyed composing this symphony of words and hope that it has left you wanting more. The well from which this story is drawn is bottomless and may you all find the same inspiration in whatever you love as I found in the music captured in these pages.

ABOUT THE AUTHOR

Darin Kennedy, born and raised in Winston-Salem, North Carolina, is a graduate of Wake Forest University and Bowman Gray School of Medicine. After completing family medicine residency in the mountains of Virginia, he served eight years as a United States Army physician and wrote his first novel in the sands of northern Iraq.

His Fugue and Fable trilogy was born from a fusion of two of his lifelong loves: classical music and world mythology. *The Mussorgsky Riddle, The Stravinsky Intrigue*, and *The Tchaikovsky Finale*, are the beginning, middle, and end of the closest he will likely ever come to writing his own symphony. The first novel in his The Pawn Stratagem contemporary fantasy series, *Pawn's Gambit*, is available from Falstaff Books. His short stories can be found in numerous anthologies and magazines, and the best, particularly those about a certain Necromancer for Hire, are collected for your reading pleasure under Darin's imprint, 64Square Publishing.

Doctor by day and novelist by night, he writes and practices medicine in Charlotte, NC. When not engaged in either of the above activities, he has been known to strum the guitar, enjoy a bite of sushi, and, rumor has it, he even sleeps on occasion. Find him online at darinkennedy.com.

THANK YOU
FOR READING

Please visit http://curiosityquills.com/reader-survey to share your
reading experience with the author of this book!

Archaeopteryx, by Dan Darling

While investigating a mass bird death in New Mexico, John Stick, zookeeper and giant, discovers a conspiracy to create chupacabra monsters and use them to hunt down undocumented migrants. His journey unravels a web of collusion between a white supremacist militia, a biogenic research lab, and a private immigrant prison. At the center of it all is a madman who believes that he is a god born on earth. In order to solve the crisis facing himself and his homeland, Stick must face his family's secret history, bare the scars on his own heart, and make tough choices about his identity.

The Curse Merchant, by J.P. Sloan

Baltimore socialite Dorian Lake makes his living crafting hexes and charms, manipulating karma for those the system has failed. His business has been poached lately by corrupt soul monger Neil Osterhaus, who wouldn't be such a problem were it not for Carmen, Dorian's captivating ex-lover. She has sold her soul to Osterhaus, and needs Dorian's help to find a new soul to take her place. Hoping to win back her affections, Dorian must navigate Baltimore's occult underworld and decide how low he is willing to stoop in order to save Carmen from eternal damnation.

CPSIA information can be obtained
at www.ICGtesting.com
Printed in the USA
FFOW03n0743100218
44934944-45176FF